"What are you looking at, my lord?"

"A'm looking at ye, lass. Yer looking tae."

"I haven't the foggiest idea what you have just said."

"Thin A'll be showing ye." His hand came up and around her cheek, warm and strong. Kitty's breath petered to a wisp. His fingertips slipped into her hair at the base of her head, his palm shaping to her skin. Slowly, so slowly, the pad of his thumb caressed her lower lip.

She sighed. Nothing could halt it, nor the catch in her throat as he bent his head.

"I shall find this quite easy to resist." She had repulsed men in similar circumstances before. Many times. She knew how to do this, even so far removed from civilization in the wild abandonment of a country snowstorm. The wild abandonment of her scruples proved another sort of challenge.

"Will ye?" He spoke just over her mouth, his breath warm like his touch . . .

Romances by **Katharine Ashe**

When a Scot Loves a Lady
In the Arms of a Marquess
Captured by a Rogue Lord
Swept Away by a Kiss
A Lady's Wish

KATHARINE ASHE

WHEN A SCOT LOVES A LADY

AVON
An Imprint of HarperCollinsPublishers

AVON BOOKS
An Imprint of HarperCollins*Publishers*
10 East 53rd Street
New York, New York 10022-5299

Copyright © 2012 by Katharine Brophy Dubois
Excerpt from *How to Be a Proper Lady* copyright © 2012 by Katharine Brophy Dubois
ISBN 978-0-06-203166-2
www.avonromance.com

First Avon Books mass market printing: March 2012

Avon Trademark Reg. U.S. Pat. Off. and in Other Countries, Marca Registrada, Hecho en U.S.A.
HarperCollins® is a registered trademark of HarperCollins Publishers.

Printed in the U.S.A.

10 9 8 7 6 5 4 3 2 1

To Lucia Macro and Kimberly Whalen.

In the words of Scotland's favorite son,

May still your life from day to day
Nae "lente largo" in the play,
But "allegretto forte" gay
Harmonious flow,
A sweeping, kindling, bauld strathspey—
Encore! Bravo!

With my utmost gratitude.

WHEN A SCOT LOVES A LADY

Prologue

London, 1813

A lady endowed with grace of person and elevation of mind ought not to stare. At two-and-twenty and already an exquisite in taste and refinement, she ought not to feel the pressing need to crane her neck so that she might see past a corpulent Louis XIV flirting with a buxom Cleopatra.

But a lady like Katherine Savege—with a tarnished reputation and a noble family inured to society's barbed censure—might on occasion indulge in such minor indiscretions.

The Queen of the Nile shifted, and Kitty caught another glimpse of the masculine figure at the ballroom's threshold.

"Mama, who is that gentleman?" Her smooth voice, only a whisper, held no crude note of puerile curiosity. Like satin she spoke, like waves upon a gentle shore she moved, and like a nightingale she sang. Or so her suitors flattered.

Actually, no longer did she sing like a nightingale. Or any

other bird, for that matter. Not since she had lost her virtue to a Bad Man and subsequently set her course upon revenge. Vengeance and sweet song did not mesh well within the soul.

As for the suitors, now she was obliged to endure more gropes and propositions than declarations of sincere devotion. And for that she had none to blame but herself—and her ruiner, of course.

"The tall gentleman," she specified. "With the dog."

"*Dog?* At a ball?" The Dowager Countess of Savege tilted her head, her silver-shot hair and coronet of gem-encrusted gold glimmering in the light of a hundred chandelier candles. An Elizabethan ruff hugged her severe cheeks, inhibiting movement. But her soft, shrewd brown eyes followed her daughter's gaze across the crowd. "Who would dare?"

"Precisely." Kitty suppressed the urge to peer once again toward the door. Of necessity. If she leaned too far to the side she might lose her gown, an immodest slip of a confection resembling a Grecian goddess's garb that her mother ought never have permitted her to don, let alone go out in. But after thirty years of marriage to a man who publicly flaunted his mistress, and with an eldest son who'd long been an unrepentant libertine, the dowager countess was no slave to propriety. Thus Kitty's attendance at a masquerade ball teetering perilously upon the edge of scandalous. Truly she should not be here; it only confirmed gossip.

Still, she had begged to come, though she spared her mother the reason: the guest list included Lambert Poole.

"Aha." The dowager's penciled brows lifted in surprise. "It is Blackwood."

To Kitty's left a nymph whispered to a musketeer, their attention likewise directed toward the tall gentleman in the doorway. Behind her Maid Marian tittered to a swarthy Blackbeard. Snippets of whispers came to Kitty's sharp ears.

"—returned from the East Indies—"

"—two years abroad—"

"—could not bear to remain in England after his bride's tragic drowning—"

"—infant son left motherless—"

"—a veritable beauty—"

"—those Scots are tremendously loyal—"

"—vowed to never again marry—"

Louis XIV kissed Cleopatra's hand and sauntered off, leaving Kitty with an unimpeded view of the gentleman. Garbed in homespun, a limp kerchief tied about his neck, a crooked staff in hand, and a beard that looked as though it were actually growing from his cheeks rather than pasted on, he clearly meant to pass himself off as a shepherd. At his side stood an enormous dog, shaggy quite like its master, and gray.

The ladies that surrounded him, however, paid no heed to the beast. Hanging upon his arm, Queen Isabella of Spain batted her eyelids and Little Miss Muffet appeared right at home dimpling up at the man who, beneath his whiskers, was not unattractive.

Quite the opposite.

Kitty dragged her attention away. "Are you acquainted with him, then?"

"He and your brother Alexander hunted together at Beaufort years ago. Why, my dear? Would you like an introduction?" The dowager purloined a glass of champagne from a passing footman with all elegance, but her eyes narrowed.

"And risk covering my gown in dog hair? Good heavens, no."

"Kitty, I am your mother. I have seen you sing at the top of your lungs while dancing through puddles. This hauteur you have lately adopted does not impress me."

"Forgive me, Mama." Kitty lowered her lashes. The hauteur had, however, saved Kitty from a great deal of pain.

Pretending hauteur, she allowed herself to nearly believe she did not care about the ever-decreasing invitations and calls, the cuts direct, the occasional slip on the shoulder. "Naturally I meant to say, 'Please do make me an introduction, for I am hanging out for an unkempt gentleman with whiskers the length of Piccadilly to sit at my feet and recite poetry about his sheep.'"

"Don't be vulgar, dear. The poor man is in costume, as we all are."

As they all were. Kitty most especially. A costume that had nothing to do with her Athenian dress. Music cavorted about the overheated chamber, twining into Kitty's senses like the two glasses of wine she had already taken—foolishly. She was not here to imbibe, or even to enjoy, and certainly not to indecorously ogle a barbaric Scottish lord.

She had a project to see to.

As at every society event, she sought out Lambert in the crowd. He lounged against a pilaster, an open box of snuff on his palm, his wrist draped with frothy lace suitable to his Shakespearean persona.

"Mama, will you go to the card room tonight?" She could never bear fawning over Lambert with her mother nearby.

"No introduction to Lord Blackwood, then?"

"*Mama.*"

"Katherine, you are an unrepentant snob." She touched Kitty's chin with two fingertips and smiled gently. "But you are still my dear girl."

Her *dear girl.* At moments like this, Kitty could almost believe her mother did not know the truth of her lost virtue. At moments like this, she longed quite desperately to throw herself into her mother's arms and wish that it all go back to the way it was before, when her heart was still hopeful and not already weary from the wicked game she now played.

The dowager released her. "Now I shall be off. Chance

and Drake each took a hundred guineas from me last week and I intend to win it back. Kiss my cheek for luck."

"I will join you shortly." Kitty watched her mother go in a cascade of skirts, then turned to her quarry.

Lambert met her gaze. His high, aristocratic brow and burnished bronze hair caught the candlelight dramatically. But two years had passed since the sight of him afforded her any emotion except determination—since he had taken her innocence and not offered his name in return—since he had broken her heart and roused her eternal ire.

She went toward him.

"Quite a lot of skin showing tonight, my dear." His voice was a thin drawl. "You must be chilled. Come to have a bit of warming up, have you?" He sniffed tobacco dust from the back of his hand.

"You are ever so droll, my lord." Her unfaltering smile masked bile behind it. She had once admired this display of aristocratic ignobility, a naïve girl seeking love from the first gentleman who paid attention to her. Now she only sought information, the sort that a vain, proud man in his cups occasionally let slip when she cajoled him sufficiently, pretending continued adoration in the face of his teasing.

That pretense, however, had excellent effect. Through months of careful observation, Kitty had discovered that Lord Lambert Poole practiced politics quite outside the bounds of legal government. Once she'd found papers in his waistcoat with names of ministry officials and figures, numbers with pound markings. She required little more information to make his life in society quite uncomfortable were she to reveal him.

But heat gathered between her exposed shoulders, and a prickly discomfort. Where plotting revenge had once seemed so sweet, now it chafed. And within her, the spirit of the girl who had sung at the top of her lungs while dashing through puddles wished to sing again instead of weep. To-night she did not care for hanging on his sleeve and playing her secret game, not even to further her goal.

"Come on, Kit." His gaze slipped along her bodice. "There's bound to be a dark corner somewhere no one's using yet."

She suppressed a shudder. "Of course I deserve that."

"Precedent, my dear."

She forced herself to step closer. "I have told you before, I—"

Something swished against her hip, a mass of gray fur, and she jolted aside. A steadying hand came around her bare arm.

"Thare nou, lass. 'Tis anely a dug." A warm voice, and deep. Wonderfully warm and deep like his skin against hers, which made her insides tickle.

But tickling insides notwithstanding, Kitty's tastes tended decidedly toward men who combed their hair. A thin white streak ran through Lord Blackwood's, from his temple tangled amid the overly long, dark auburn locks. And beneath the careless thatch across his brow, he had very beautiful eyes.

"Lady Katherine." Lambert's drawl interrupted her bemusement. "I present to you the Earl of Blackwood, lately returned from the East Indies. Blackwood, this is Savege's sister."

"Ma'am." He nodded by way of bowing, she supposed.

Drawing her arm from his hold, she curtsied. "I do not mind the dog, my lord. But"—she gestured toward his costume—"isn't it rather large for chasing sheep about? I daresay wolves would suit it better."

"Aye, maleddy. But things be no always whit thay seem."

Now she could not help but stare. Behind the beautifully dark, hooded eyes, something glinted. A hint of steel.

Then, like a thorough barbarian, without another word he moved away.

But she must be a little drunk after all; she followed him with her gaze.

In the shadows at the edge of the ballroom, a satyr with a matted chest of hair and a hand wrapped around a half-filled goblet leered over a maid—not a costumed guest but an actual maid. A tray of glasses weighed down her narrow shoulders. The satyr pawed. The girl backed into the wall, using her dish as a shield.

Lord Blackwood stepped casually between the two.

"Weel nou, sir," he said in a rough voice that carried above the music and conversation. "Did yer mither nae teach ye better as tae bother a lass when she's haurd at wirk?" His brow furrowed. "Be aff wi' ye, man, or A'll be giving ye a lesson in manners nou."

The satyr seemed to size him up, but the earl's measure was clear. Shepherd's garb could not disguise a man in the prime of his life.

"She's going to waste working on her feet," the satyr snarled, but he stumbled away.

"Ah," Lambert murmured at Kitty's shoulder. "A champion of the laboring class. How affecting." The touch of his breath upon her cheek made her skin crawl.

Lord Blackwood spoke quietly to the maid now, and Kitty could not hear him. The girl's eyes widened and she nodded, her face filled with trust. As though she expected it, she allowed him to relieve her of the tray of glasses. Then she dipped her head and disappeared into the crowd.

Lambert's hand came around Kitty's elbow.

"Don't bother, Kit." His blue eyes glittered. "Since his wife died, Blackwood's not the marrying type either." His grin was cruel.

He enjoyed imagining she was unhappy because he

would not marry her. Years ago, ruining her had been entirely about insulting her brothers, whom he despised. But now Kitty knew he simply liked to think she pined for him. Indeed she had pretended gorgeously, allowing him liberties to keep him close, because she believed she needed to see him suffer as she had—first when he refused her marriage, then when he proved to her that she was barren.

She looked back toward the man who had lost his young wife years earlier yet who still remained faithful to her, a rough-hewn man who in the middle of a society crush rescued a serving girl from abuse.

From the shadows the Earl of Blackwood met her regard. A flicker of hardness once more lit the dark warmth of his eyes.

Things were not always what they seemed.

But Kitty already knew that better than anybody.

Chapter 1

London, 1816

Fellow Subjects of Britain,

How delinquent is Government if it distributes the sorely depleted Treasury of our Noble Kingdom hither and yon without recourse to prudence, justice, or reason?

Gravely so.

Irresponsibly so.

Villainously so!

As you know, I have made it my crusade to make public all such spendthrift waste. This month I offer yet another example: 14½ Dover Street.

What use has Society of an exclusive gentlemen's club if no gentlemen are ever seen to pass through its door?—that white-painted panel graced with an intimidating knocker, a Bird of Prey. But the door never opens. Do the exalted members of this club ever use their fashionable clubhouse?

It appears not.

Information has recently come to me through peril-ous channels I swim for your benefit, Fellow Subjects. It appears that without proper debate Lords has ap-proved by Secret Ballot an allotment to the Home Office designated for this so-called club. And yet for what purpose does the club exist but to pamper the indolent rich for whom such establishments are already Legion? There can be no good in this Rash Expenditure.

I vow to uncover this concealed squandering of our kingdom's Wealth. I will discover the names of each member of this club, and what business or play passes behind its imposing knocker. Then, dear readers, I will reveal it to you.

—*Lady Justice*

Sir,

I regretfully notify you that agents Eagle, Sea Hawk, Raven, and Sparrow have withdrawn from service, termination effective immediately. The Falcon Club, it appears, is disbanded. I of course shall remain until all outstanding cases are settled.

Additionally, I draw your attention to the pam-phlet of 10 December 1816, produced by Brittle & Sons, Printers, enclosed. Poor old girl is doomed to disappointment.

Yours, &c.,
Peregrine

* * *

"Thank you, sir." The lady pressed her trembling finger-tips into Leam Blackwood's palm. *"Thank you."*

In the iron mist of the moonless December night, he lifted her hand and placed the softest kiss upon her knuckles.

"God be wi' ye, lass."

Twin fountains of gratitude sparkled on her cheeks.

"You are too good." She pressed his kerchief to her quivering lips. *"Too* good, my lord." Her lashes fluttered. "If only . . ."

With a gentle shake of his head and a regretful smile, he handed her into the carriage and closed the door. The vehicle started off, clattering wheels and hooves shrouded by the hush of fog enveloping London's wee hours.

For a moment, Leam stared after. He released a long breath.

'Twas a night like every other night.

'Twas a night like no other night.

'Twas a bushel of bad poetry, quite like the bad poetry of his life for the past five years. But tonight it would come to an end.

Straightening his shoulders, he buttoned his coat and raked his fingers through the itchy beard. By God, even his dogs didn't go about so scruffy. It was a sorry day when a man wanted a razor more than a brandy.

"Well, that's that." His voice held no trace of Scots, the thick burr of his homeland he'd trained his tongue to suppress as a youth. And yet five years earlier, in service to the crown, he had reclaimed that Scots. Five numb years ago. Quite willingly.

But no more.

"Bella. Hermes." He snapped his fingers. Two giant shadows emerged from the park opposite. He'd brought the dogs along tonight to sniff out the woman from a scrap of her clothing provided by her husband. Sight hounds by breeding, they were helpful enough in a pinch. The manager of the seedy hotel in which they had run the woman to ground hadn't minded the animals, and the agents of the Falcon Club had once again found their quarry. Yet another lost soul.

Of course the pup, Hermes, had stirred up trouble in the hotel kitchen. But Bella hadn't bothered anyone. She was a good old girl, *maistly wonderfu' contented*.

That made one of them.

"Quite sure you wish to give this up, old chap?" The gentleman on the sidewalk behind Leam murmured into the damp cold. From the tone of Wyn Yale's voice, Leam guessed his expression: a slight smile, narrowed silver eyes. "Must be satisfying to wrap lovely matrons so easily around your little finger."

"Ladies admire tragic heroes." Beside Yale, Constance Read's soft voice lilted with northern music. "And my cousin is very charming, as well as handsome, of course. Just like you, Wyn."

"You are all kindness, my lady," Yale replied. "But alas, a Welshman can never best a Scot. History proves it."

"Ladies don't give a fig about history. Especially the young ladies, who like *you* quite well enough." She laughed, a ripple of silk that relieved the tension corded about Leam's lungs.

"The hotel manager's wife called him a ruffian," Yale added.

"She was flirting. They all flirt with him. She also called him a tease."

"They haven't any idea." The Welshman's voice was sly.

No idea whatsoever.

Leam passed a hand over his face again. Four years at Cambridge. Three after that at Edinburgh. He spoke seven languages, read two more, had traveled three continents, owned a vast Lowlands estate, and was heir to a dukedom possessed of a fortune built on East Indian silks and tea. Yet society imagined him a ruffian and a tease. Because that was the man he showed to the world.

By God, he'd had enough of this. Five years' worth of enough. And yet *in his heart there was a kind of fighting that would not let him sleep.*

Good Lord. Shakespearean thoughts in the wake of silly females and bad poetry. Brandy seemed an excellent idea after all.

Leam swiveled on his heels.

"If you two are quite finished, perhaps we might go inside. The night advances and I have elsewhere to be." He gestured toward the door to the modest town house before which they stood. Like the falcon-shaped knocker, the bronze numbers 14½ above the lintel glistened in the glow of a nearby gas lamplight.

"Where elsewhere?" His cousin Constance, a sparkling beauty who at twenty had already sent a hundred men to their knees in London drawing rooms, lifted azure eyes full of keen curiosity.

"Anywhere but here." He drew her up the steps.

"Don't set your hopes on that too securely, old chap. Colin has plans." Yale pressed the door open and winked at Constance as she passed through.

"Colin can go hang," Leam muttered.

"I would rather not." At the parlor threshold, the head agent of the Falcon Club, Viscount Colin Gray, stood as he had any number of nights, calmly awaiting their return from yet another assignment. The edge of his mouth ticked up ever so slightly. Gray rarely smiled. His was a grave sort of English rectitude, one Leam had admired since their school days. He met Leam's gaze, his indigo eyes sober. "But if you wait long enough, my friend, you might get lucky."

"More likely to be a guillotine than a noose, though. Hm,

Colin?" Yale moved directly to the sideboard. The young
Welshman's speech never slurred nor did his gait falter. But
Leam had watched the lad drink an entire bottle of brandy
since noon.

A brace of candles illumined crystal decanters. Glass in
hand, Yale settled into a chair as easily as a boy. But nothing
ever looked as it seemed. Leam had learned that years ago.

The dogs padded in, Bella settling on the rug by the fire,
her pup greeting Gray, then following him to the hearth.

"How did matters proceed tonight at the hotel?" The viscount leaned against the mantel. "Mr. Grimm has gone off
in the carriage and you are all here, so I must assume you
found the princess and that she is now on her way home."

"To the loving bosom of her anxiously awaiting husband."
Yale smiled slightly.

"Leam flirted with everything in a skirt." Constance
paused at a window, drawing open a drapery to peer out into
the darkness.

"Always does. Sets the ladies' breasts aflutter in sympathy
so that they utter every word they ever heard." Yale sipped
his brandy. "Or, always did, rather."

"He is quite good at it." In the glow of firelight, Gray's
face was like chiseled marble.

Leam remained on the threshold, eyes half lidded as was
his wont even now and here. The habit of years died hard,
and he had not yet shaved away the vestiges of his false persona. His costume still clung.

But not for long.

Constance glanced over her shoulder. A sumptuous gold
lock dangled along her neck in studied artifice so unlike her
actual character. She played a part too. They all did.

As members of the Falcon Club, for five years Leam,
Wyn Yale, Colin Gray and their fourth, Jinan Seton, had
used their skills to seek out and find missing persons whose

retrieval merited a measure of secrecy. For the king. For England. But Leam's cousin Constance had only entered the game two years ago, when he invited her.

"It is so odd every time," she said, "seeing them go off like that with Mr. Grimm in the carriage, returning home." She peered at the viscount. "Colin, how on earth do people find out about us? It's not as though we advertise in the papers. Do they all know our secret director personally? But then, of course, if that were the case he wouldn't be very secret, would he? And we might know him too." Her lips curved sweetly.

"Perhaps if you remain in the Club you might someday," the viscount replied.

"Oh, you know I could not. Not when Leam, Wyn, and Jinan are all calling it quits."

Leam studied her. "You needn't as well, Constance."

"I shall do as I wish, Leam."

"Come now, cousins." Yale waved a hand, brandy swirling in his crystal goblet. "Don't let's quarrel. Haven't yet had enough to drink."

"They aren't your cousins, Yale," came the rejoinder from across the chamber.

The Welshman tilted a black brow and allowed his opinion of the issue to be known to Lord Gray with the barest glitter of silvery eyes.

"I should never have dragged her into this in the first place." Leam crossed the chamber to his cousin, lowering his voice as he neared. "But at the time I believed you required diversion." He lifted her hand and gently squeezed her gloved knuckles.

"Oh, don't." Constance withdrew her fingers. "You will make me weep with your poet's eyes. I am quite as susceptible as all those other ladies, you know."

"Cad," Lord Gray muttered.

Constance shot him a laughing look. "Weep with affection, Colin. Only slightly greater than the affection I hold for you."

Lord Gray tilted his head in recognition of the beauty's gracious condescension.

"You see, Leam? Colin will have your neck now if you cause me to cry." Her blue eyes twinkled.

"Second that, Blackwood. Never like to see a lady in tears," mumbled Yale with a sleepy air.

"The lady would not be morose if you weren't dragging her into retirement with you so abruptly," Gray commented.

"Tut-tut, old man. Mustn't scold during our good-bye party." Yale's eyes were barely creased open, but that signified little. After working with the Welshman for five years, even Leam did not always know when his friend was truly foxed or merely pretending it.

It mattered nothing—Yale's acting, Constance's reluctance, or Gray's insistence. Leam was through with secrecy and living like a Gypsy. He'd never much cared for it in the first place and now, at thirty-one, he was far too old to be in this game.

"I take it we shan't see Seton tonight." Gray's voice remained even. "Shoddy of him bowing out like this without even appearing to do it in person."

"Jinan has never been fully the Club's man," Leam said. "You are fortunate he sent word even to me."

"Wyn, what did you mean with that comment about the guillotine?" Constance tilted her head.

Yale's slitted gaze went to Gray. "Perhaps our august viscount will explain. Have news of French doings, do you, Colin?"

"How you know that I shan't ask." The viscount reached to a box on the mantel and drew forth a folded paper. "The director wishes a last task from the pair of you."

"No." Leam's voice fell like an anvil.

Gray lifted a brow. "Allow me to apprise you of the task first, if you will."

"No." Leam's jaw tightened. "I am through with it, Colin. I've told you so any number of times. I am going home. Full stop."

"But French spies, old man . . ." Yale murmured. "'S what got us into this in the first place, haring off to Calcutta to save England from informers and all that."

French spies had not sent Leam to India five years ago. His desperation to escape England had. And they all knew it.

Yale flashed the viscount a glance. "*Is* it spies this time, Colin?"

Lord Gray passed him the paper. "The director and several members of the Board of the Admiralty believe so. Informants to the Home Office have identified Scots—Highlanders—whom they believe to be potential threats for leaking information to the French."

Constance's clear brow furrowed. "But the war is over."

"The concern is not French aggression, particularly, but Scottish rebels."

"Ah." Yale sipped his drink thoughtfully.

"Indeed." Gray's face remained grim. "Scottish insurrectionists may be currying favor with certain French parties to gain support for a rebellion."

"What could Scottish rebels have that the French would be interested in?"

"Not much, if they were merely northern rabble. But our director and several members the Board of the Admiralty have reason to think the rebels are being fed sensitive information directly from a member of Parliament."

Yale whistled through his teeth.

"Unless you believe I am one of those insurrectionists," Leam said, "then I haven't any idea what it has to do with me. Leave it to the Home Office where it belongs, or to the fellows in Foreign, like you should have five years ago. It's none of my business and never should have been."

"You didn't mind it at the time."

Leam met Gray's knowing gaze stonily.

"It is honorable work, Leam."

"Believe you're saving the world all you wish, my noble friend. But since the war ended we are no more than glorified carrier pigeons and I've no taste for it."

The snapping of a log in the fire seemed to punctuate his statement.

"Symbolic nonsense," Yale mumbled. Without a breath of sound, he stood, brushed out the creases in his trousers, and moved toward the door. "I'm off to the races, then. Evening, all," he said as though it were any evening and not the last. But the spy clung to him, in his every movement and in the perspicacity of his quick gaze. He had been wasted on the Falcon Club.

"If men like you, Leam, do not continue this work, there may be war again much sooner than we like," the viscount said soberly.

Yale paused, propping a shoulder against the doorjamb. But Leam felt no responsibility. No need to see matters settled.

"During the war at least we retrieved persons of some importance to England's welfare." He shook his head. "Now . . ."

"Your quarry tonight was a princess."

"I don't care if she was the goddamned queen. It was never my fondest wish to go chasing after other men's runaway wives."

Silence descended upon the room again, this time heavy and fraught with memory. Yale finally broke it, his voice lightly pensive. "They aren't all runaway wives."

Leam stared into the fire, feeling his friends' gazes upon

him. The rest of the world imagined poor Uilleam Black-wood a tragic widower. Only these three and Jin Seton knew the truth.

"Remember that little Italian girl we found in 'thirteen? The archbishop's niece?"

"Just after you returned from Bengal," Constance added. "You told me about her, Wyn. You and Leam found her working as a maid at a masquerade ball, though I still cannot imagine you dressing in costume." She smiled.

"I didn't. But Blackwood did, of course. Recall that one, old chap?"

Leam had never forgotten it. Not in the three years since then. It had been their first assignment in London after India. But that was not the reason that ball had never slipped from his memory.

"He intends to shut himself away this time, Colin." Constance said quietly. "He thought he was doing so when he joined the Club and went to India upon your behest. But he has found out his mistake finally."

"One final task, Leam."

Leam's gaze met Gray's. "And after that?"

"I shall never ask again."

Yale folded his arms. "What does our shadowy director wish this time?"

"He wants the two of you to meet with Seton. Two months ago our sailor friend sent word he had news that could not be imparted to a courier or by post. We haven't heard from him since then, however, and suspect that at least you know where he is. Do you?"

Leam nodded. Men cut from entirely different cloth, Jinan Seton and Colin Gray had never gotten on particularly well. But the sailor kept Leam apprised of his ship's location roughly every month. He knew where to find him.

"Is that all?"

"The director would also like confirmation of Seton's resignation from the Club, from his own hand."

"Then, no Scottish rebels or French spies after all?" Yale's gaze shifted between Leam and Gray.

"Not at this time."

"Then why did you mention them?" They'd known each other for years, but Leam did not entirely trust his old friend. Colin Gray possessed one purpose in life: to keep England safe. Leam did not fault him for it, but neither did he understand it. He felt no such staunch loyalty to anything. He only pretended it.

"I hoped you would bite at the bait. But clearly that is not to be." Gray's regard remained sober. "Will you do this last favor?"

Jin's ship was berthed in Bristol. Leam could make it there on horseback and still arrive at Alvamoor in time for Christmas. He would like to see the sailor once more before retreating to Scotland. And he owed it to Gray, the man who had come to his rescue when he'd needed it five years earlier.

He nodded.

"Good." Gray strode toward the door. He paused there. "Keep yourself out of trouble, Yale."

"Not a breath of scandal shall be linked to my name."

The viscount looked as though he wished to smile. "I daresay." He bowed to Constance. "My lady." He departed.

Upon the hearth rug, Hermes shifted onto his side with a lazy sigh.

"What do you say, Con," Yale quipped, assessing her from brow to toe. "Join me for a midnight stroll? With you on my arm I shall be in heaven."

"Oh, Wyn. Go."

Silvery eyes alight, the young man grinned, bowed, and followed Gray from the house.

Constance chuckled. "He is incorrigible."

"He holds you in very high esteem."

"He likes to pretend he does, but I have yet to encounter the girl who could—" Abruptly she turned from her contemplation of the door to Leam. "Are you truly going to Scotland? Permanently this time?"

"Aye."

She tilted her golden head. "Can you be happy at Alvamoor?"

"It is my home, Constance."

"Won't she always be there, in a manner?"

"Better in the ground than in the house."

She flinched, a delicate withdrawal of tapered shoulders. "Those words are not you."

"They are as much me as aught else." More so. Nothing remained of the foolish lad he had been six years ago.

"You have not forgiven her in all this time?"

"The righteous make far too much of forgiveness."

She remained silent a moment. Then, "I am to dine with Papa this evening. He will no doubt read the paper while we eat and leave to me all the conversation."

Leam smiled for her sake. She sought to divert him. Even as a mere slip of a girl she had. But she had been too late. "Give my best to His Grace."

She lifted her cloak from a chair. "Why don't you join us? Papa asked after his favorite nephew only this morning."

"Thank you. I am otherwise engaged." If he were to make it to Alvamoor by Christmas, he must move swiftly to meet Jinan on the coast. Yale, of course, would accompany him.

Her carriage stood at the curb, an elegant vehicle with the ducal crest covered. He handed her in.

She squeezed his fingers. "After the season I will come up to Alvamoor for the summer."

"Fiona and Jamie will be in alt. As will I. Until then." He

reached to shut the door. Constance's hand on his sleeve arrested him.

"Leam, have you considered marriage? Again?"

"No." Never again.

She held his gaze. "Have a pleasant trip, darling," she said softly. "Happy Christmas." She drew her cloak close about her and sat back on the squabs.

The rumble of the carriage receded down the street. He pivoted about and for a long moment stared at the door to 14½ Dover Street. For five years he had given his life to the king's pleasure, behind that door with the raptor-shaped knocker, and in ballrooms, drawing rooms, and squalid alleyways throughout London. Throughout all of Britain. Commenced in desperation on an eastern-sailing ship, his tenure as a member of the Falcon Club had distracted him. Aye, for a time, it had distracted.

He turned away and started up the street. Gas lamps and the tread of his boots marked his passage through the midnight gloom. He needed the scent of the north in his senses. The Lothians at midwinter called, vibrant skies crystal clear unless they were fraught with clouds or pouring buckets of rain or barrels of snow upon a man's lands.

Christmas at Alvamoor. This year, the first in five, he would remain past Twelfth Night. He would remain indefinitely.

As he walked, the back of his neck prickled, and he knew he was watched. As with so much of late, he cared little.

Chapter 2

A fortnight later
Somewhere along the road, Shropshire

Kitty, I do beg your pardon." Lady Emily Vale dragged up the hood of her cloak to cover pale, short-cropped locks and a finely tapered jaw. "My parents' home is not three miles distant, yet I am certain Pen cannot drive the carriage another yard in this blizzard."

"Come now, Athena, it cannot be helped."

"I meant to tell you, I have changed it to Marie Antoine." Emily buttoned the throat of her cloak and pursed her lips. "Those ninnies in the Ladies Regiment ruined Athena for me. They hadn't any interest whatsoever in literature or politics. All they knew of ancient Greece were gowns and headdresses."

Kitty smiled. Through the carriage window and a curtain of snow she surveyed the excessively modest inn in the failing light of evening. A squat two stories, the structure boasted a peeling marquee, rough-hewn door, and four wretchedly small front windows. The yard stretched less than forty feet in either direction, blanketed in snowy furls and cords.

Beyond, along a string of unprepossessing stone and timber buildings, the village's main street, thickly white and swirling with wind, simply fell away into the river. Save for smoking chimneys, the only other visible movement was at the door of a pub teetering over the edge of a dock as a patron passed into it, escaping the storm.

The inn's stable, however, seemed sturdy enough for the carriage and team. A donkey brayed. The stable, it seemed, was already inhabited.

The accommodations could not be helped. But it mattered little where Kitty lost herself in England as long as it was far from London.

"This will do," she murmured. "This will do quite well."

"I suppose it has the advantage of being as far from your mother and her beau as my parents' home," Emily offered.

"I daresay." Kitty's grin widened. Douglas Westcott, Lord Chamberlayne, adored her mother as much as her mother adored him. But the dowager would not even go to the shops without her spinster daughter. For years they had been inseparable, as close as mother and daughter could be. In Kitty's estimation this did not leave sufficient space for proper lovemaking, or for a widowed gentleman to address his suit to a widowed lady with any measure of success. And so four days earlier, at shockingly short notice to the woman with whom she had spent every day for the past decade, and with only a kiss on the cheek, Kitty had set off to Shropshire for Christmas.

She pressed open the carriage door. "This storm will help with your little problem too, Marie."

"Do you think so?"

"It could not have been more fortuitously arranged."

A boy emerged from the stable, clomping through the white up to his knees. The coach leaned as Mr. Pen jumped off the box, snow descending from his coat in chunks.

"Poor man." Kitty pulled her hood over her hair arranged into elegant plaits that morning by her superior maid. At some point during the day of increasingly slow travel, Emily's first coachman had outstripped the servants' carriage on the road, declaring his determination to achieve his master's estate before the storm set in.

Alas, no such luck. They were here, in the middle of nowhere apparently, and now the servants' carriage was also nowhere, but a rather different nowhere.

"Do you think this will persist?" Emily shouted into the wind, linking arms with her to press through the snowfall toward the door.

"The night through, to be sure, mum!" The stable boy, all teeth and elbows, tugged at his cap. "Settled in right snug."

In a flurry of ice and powder they entered the inn.

"Good eve, ladies!" A man approached, of middling age, whiskered salt-and-pepper, garbed in a simple coat and abundant red neck cloth. "Welcome to the Cock and Pitcher."

"Mr. Milch," Emily said in the forthright manner Kitty admired, "I came through here with my mother and father, Lord and Lady Vale, a year ago. Your wife served us an excellent roast and pudding. Will you have the same for me and Lady Katherine tonight, and bedchambers?"

"Of course, miss." He smiled amiably and reached for their cloaks. "My missus will send your girls right up to prepare the chambers."

"Our maids are behind, still on the road," as well as Emily's companion, the formidable Madame Roche. London gossips had made Kitty's unwed state a happy topic for five years now; she *deserved* spinsterhood after flaunting her love affair with Lambert Poole, they tittered. But as yet those gossips had little for which to criticize Emily, except of course her friendship with Kitty. Not that Emily would give a fig for it. Content in her books, she didn't even care that the highest sticklers considered Kitty unfit company for a maiden.

But Kitty cared for Emily's spotless reputation on her friend's behalf. It seemed, however, that an unchaperoned night on the road could not be helped.

Mr. Milch clucked his tongue. "Well, then make yourselves comfortable." He gestured them from the foyer. "I'll fetch my Gert to see after you while Ned and I arrange matters with your coachman. I hope he'll be all right sleeping at the pub a'ways. We're all filled up here."

Emily nodded. "I don't suppose Pen shall mind over much if he has good woolens." Good woolens, good books, and good conversation—Emily Vale's only needs. A practical girl, she was unconcerned with a person's wayward past. It made her a lovely friend, one of Kitty's few and cherished.

The ground floor of the inn was a modest chamber divided into two parts by the stair to the upper story. Two square tables flanked by benches and laid with plain lace coverings adorned the right side, and on the left a sofa and a pair of threadbare chairs crouched before a hearth. On the walls hung quilted samplers and an impressive rack of antlers, the windows draped with unadorned wool. The place smelled of onions and mutton stew and coffee.

"Kitty," Emily said flatly, looking about the chamber, "I suspect you've never been in such a place in your life. You will never forgive me."

"Don't be absurd. It is delightful." Rustic and shockingly simple.

The rug before the hearth shifted. Kitty leaped back. A gray shaggy head lifted from the floor and stared at her with great, deep eyes. Smiling, she removed her muffler and hat, and stepped to the fireplace, taking care not to tread on the dog's tail and holding her palms out for warmth.

"I suppose it cannot be helped, as you say." Emily dropped her slight form into a chair without any grace whatsoever, threw her damp bonnet onto her lap, and ran her fingers through her short locks in a manly gesture. For eighteen, she lacked every female grace and was a thorough relief from the rigidly cool femininity Kitty had perfected over the past five years.

She chuckled. "Really, you needn't fret. But where exactly are we?"

"I daresay quite near Shrewsbury. Pen said we came to the Severn hours ago. But Kitty, I cannot help being concerned." Her fingertips scratched at the bonnet's brim.

"Emily—"

Emily's bow-shaped lips pursed.

"*Marie*," Kitty corrected. "You mustn't worry. Even if the snow does not persist long enough to hold us from Willows Hall while Mr. Worthmore remains there, I will devise a plan to dissuade your parents from this unsuitable match. I promise."

Emily's fine features set in earnest lines. "That is why I asked you to come, Kitty, because you are terribly clever with this sort of thing. This situation my parents have devised entirely befuddles me, but I know it shan't pose any problem for you. After all, if you could rout a lord from Britain so successfully last summer, you can surely chase a mere mister from my parents' house."

Kitty's throat caught.

Emily's green eyes went wide. "Oh, I am terribly sorry, Kitty," she rushed. "Madame Roche told me I should not mention it, but I am horrid at remembering such things, you know."

None of her acquaintances had yet spoken of it aloud. Leave it to Emily.

Three years earlier, after a masquerade ball at which she had told Lambert Poole she no longer cared enough to even hate him, she had locked away all the sensitive information she'd collected on him. For two and a half years that file sat untouched in a drawer. But six months ago, as the season was drawing to a close, Lambert had threatened her brother Alex, accusing him of criminal activities to disguise his own. And Kitty finally unlocked her files. Along with information provided to the Board of Admiralty by another source, her knowledge of Lambert's untoward activities had damned him.

Of course, no one was supposed to know the part she'd played in his banishment. But the information leaked out, and for months now gossips had made a feast of the spinster Lady Katherine Savege's astounding involvement in bringing to justice a criminal lord, those same gossips who even now still snubbed her because she had given her virtue to that very man.

"You mustn't allow it to concern you, Marie. I am quite—"

Boots scuffed on the stairs. In sticky relief, Kitty looked up. Her stomach turned over.

On the landing above stood a gentleman of considerable height, broad-shouldered and loose-limbed, yet without particular merit to those estimable masculine qualities unless one were enamored of natural beauty of form wholly lacking in companion beauty of mind. Or character. Or education. Or taste.

Good heavens. She had wanted to escape London, but not to eschew civilization altogether.

No. This was not the entire truth. Yet only now, as her hands went damp, did she realize it. She wanted to escape a great deal more than London. She wanted to escape the gossips, the association of her name with Lambert's in drawing rooms across town, her misguided past that clung no matter how she wished to escape it.

The presence of *this* man in the middle of nowhere abruptly made all of that impossible.

Lord Blackwood smiled, a lazy curve of his mouth amid a veritable forest of whiskers, his gaze fixed on her. She curtsied.

The smiled broadened. It was, in point of fact, quite a dashing smile. Despite the outrageously barbaric beard, she had noticed this once before. The streak of white running through his dark hair lent him a comfortably roguish air as well. Then he opened his mouth, and out stumbled that which ought to have remained on the battlefield with Robert the Bruce six hundred years earlier.

"Maleddy, 'tis a bonnie surpreese tae meet wi' ye here." The rough words lumbered across his tongue like a flock of black-faced sheep running from wolves. A massive blur of gray streaked around his long legs and leaped down the stairs. Kitty braced herself.

"Hermes, *aff*."

The beast flattened itself to the floor at her feet, its tail wagging frantically.

"Sir!" Emily sprang up.

"He winna harm ye, miss."

"How do you do, my lord?" Kitty drew in a steadying breath. "Marie, allow me to present to you the Earl of Blackwood. My lord, this is my traveling companion, Lady Emily Vale, who at present goes by the name Marie Antoine."

"Ma'am." He slanted Emily a grin and started down the stairs. Kitty rooted her feet to the floor. She would not retreat. But this sort of man nearly required retreat.

He stopped on the other side of his dog and bowed, perfectly at ease. "Maleddy."

Not retreat. That was foolish. Because there was no *this sort of man*. There was only this man, a man she had only spoken with once before, three years earlier, barely to exchange greetings. Yet he had changed her life.

He had remarkably high cheekbones, a rawboned borderlands hollowness from the plane of his cheek to his whisker-covered jaw, and his eyes were indolently hooded. Kitty knew better than to trust in that indolence. At least she'd once imagined so, on that night when that dark gaze had seemed to look right through her. *Into* her.

"What brings you to Shropshire, my lord?"

"The fishing, lass." A rumble of easy pleasure sounded from his chest behind a coat of excellent quality and no elegance whatsoever. "Catching up frae the summer. Raising mair dails than ye can lig, than, I wis."

"I see." She had no idea what he'd said. There was no rationally conversing with a barbarian, even a very handsome one. "Are you lodging here as well?"

"Aye. Storm's a beast."

The innkeeper appeared. "My ladies, here's Mrs. Milch to see you to your chambers. I'll have dinner laid when you prefer."

"We've only the mutton sausage, and the gentlemen ate half already." His wife glowered, swathed from skinny neck to knee in dull cambric. "Nothing else came today but them and the eggs, and I'll be saving those for breakfast."

"Mutton sausage will do splendidly." Kitty moved toward the woman, away from the fire and the large man.

"Didn't expect the Quality to be taking up with us tonight," Mrs. Milch muttered in a damp voice. "Don't have anything on hand."

Kitty followed her and Emily up the stairs. But at the top she could not help glancing back. Lord Blackwood watched her. No grin lit his face now, only a glint behind the indolence of something cold and sharp.

That night three years ago his warm, dark eyes had glimmered with that steel. Across a dimly lit ballroom he had looked at her as he did now, and that was all she had needed to redirect the course of her life.

For three years Kitty had wondered if her imagination had invented that hard gleam to serve her own need at the time. Now she knew.

Chapter 3

Katherine Savege is here." Leam scraped the razor along his chin. "And Lady Emily Vale."

"Lady Katherine, the unwed exquisite?" Yale lounged in the chamber's single wooden chair, playing a guinea between his fingers. Back and forth, gold flickered in the thin morning light filtering through the window. Nothing wasted. The game improved agility.

"The very one. *Haut société*. Political. She frequents the Countess of March's salon," and through friends at that salon six months earlier, she had sealed a treasonous lord's fate.

"Beauty and intelligence." Yale's gaze remained on the coin. "But the latter would not interest the cretin Earl of Blackwood."

"Her mother plays cards."

"Ah. More to the point."

"Lady Katherine has a number of close acquaintances on the Board of Admiralty in particular."

With a flick of his wrist, the Welshman pocketed the coin. "Not our business, then."

"Not any longer." Cold metal swished along Leam's skin. Soap dropped to the cloth below, laden with the past. "Deuced inconvenient, though."

"Then why are you shaving?"

Leam drew the linen from about his neck and swiped it across his clean cheeks and chin. He ran his hand along the smooth skin. By God, it felt good to be civilized again.

"It was on the schedule," unlike this detour that kept him from Alvamoor where he should be by now. Damn Jin for changing their rendezvous from Bristol to Liverpool. If it weren't for the snow, Leam would have left it to Yale and washed his hands of the Falcon Club's business once and for all.

"Who is Lady Emily?"

Leam knotted his cravat. "Less than a fortnight off the job and already losing your edge? You were introduced to her at Pembroke's ball last spring."

Yale's face sobered. "Athena?"

"She goes by Marie Antoine now, apparently."

The Welshman stood and headed for the door. "Well, I shall be off and away before *les belles* bestir themselves for breakfast."

"Two feet of snow on the ground." If Leam could bear to abuse his animals so, he would saddle his horse and take Bella and Hermes to the road without delay. But he could not. He was well trapped hundreds of miles from where he ought to be two days hence. "Where do you expect to go?"

"I shall dig a trench to the dock, purloin a punt, and once at the river's mouth cast mine eyes to the sea in search of a tardy privateer."

"Wyn."

"Leam?"

"Behave yourself."

The younger man bowed with a flourish. Save for snowy

linens, he wore all black, his single honest affectation. "As ever, my lord."

Leam tugged his coat over his shoulders, leaving it unbuttoned. Trapped in an inn with a pair of ladies who moved in the highest circles, he could not yet fully divest himself of the court jester; his public persona was too well-known. At home there would be fewer encounters with the existence he had led for half a decade. There he could dress and behave as he pleased. He would not go to Edinburgh. He had no reason to see others, and sufficient work on his estate to keep him there. He had neglected it for too long already, and not only the estate.

He slipped a knife into the slit sewn into his sleeve at the wrist. Company had followed on the road the previous day. But each time they stopped to water the horses, the path had been empty and no one caught them up. Someone was following at a discreet distance.

The inn's ground floor was no more than a rustic ale room, set now for breakfast. Sounds stirred in the kitchen behind a door, the clinking of dishes and the continuous limp scold of the innkeeper's wife to her lord and master. The aroma of coffee tinted the fire-warmed air.

Lady Emily sat in a chair before the hearth, a book between her hands and a pair of spectacles perched atop the bridge of her nose. She glanced up with an abstracted squint.

"Good morning, my lord."

"Guid morning, ma'am."

"Breakfast is to be served shortly. Eggs and little else, I believe." Brow furrowed, she returned her attention to her page.

Leam went around beneath the stair to the rear foyer. On hooks hung two ladies' cloaks, his own overcoat, and several others of lesser quality. The exit let onto the yard behind the inn, and Leam had not yet investigated it in the light of day. But danger rarely entered through the front door.

The heavy wooden panel, bloated with damp, stuck. He nudged it with his boot and it jerked open. Lady Katherine Savege, standing on the tiny covered porch, swung about, slipped, and tumbled forward.

Leam grabbed her up. Her hands clutched his coat sleeves. Her breath hiccupped, sending a cloud of frosty air between them. He scanned her face, a swift perusal of fine features—pert nose, wide mouth, eyes shrouded with thick lashes. She wore neither bonnet nor cap. Her satiny hair, dark like crushed walnut shells and carefully plaited with bejeweled combs, enhanced the perfect cream of her skin.

"Weel, nou, maleddy," he said slowly. "Mind the ice."

"I beg your pardon, my lord." She did not lift her gaze. To his surprise.

Leam did not care for surprises.

Her breaths came rapidly against his chest. Her grip on him slackened and her arms dropped.

"I lost my balance when the door opened. The step is slick, yet I came out only in slippers. I wished to see the depth of the snow."

"Did ye?"

"I shall be quite careful not be so careless again." Her voice grew cooler with each utterance. Here was the sort of female with whom Leam had little commerce. Ladies like Katherine Savege held their own counsel and had done him little good in his former labors. But he was no longer an agent of the crown constantly seeking information. He could now do as he pleased, and he held a beautiful woman in his arms.

And despite her unwed state, Lady Katherine was no innocent. Of this he was certain.

"But yer a pretty bundle, lass."

She stiffened, the effect of which was to flatten her thighs quite nicely to his.

"I am not a bundle. You should have already released me. You do know that, don't you? Or is what they generally say of you actually true?"

"Aye, yer a bundle, an than some, wi' that tongue."

"My tongue is none of your concern. And I am not a lass. I am six-and-twenty. Rather, nearly so, on February twelfth."

"Nearly? Who woud hae thought it?"

Her lips were a stony line Leam might soften; laughter would sit well upon them. Her remarkably large gray eyes, the color of wistful fall thunderclouds, slowly drew upward beneath a veil of sooty lashes.

"Will I truly be obliged to order you to unhand me, or were you planning on doing so shortly?"

By God, she felt good in his arms, her full breasts pressed against his chest, hips nestled comfortably along his thigh. Remarkably good. Would that the rumors spread about him were true. Alas, it was largely smoke and mirrors to start the ladies talking. Informing. After that first job in the East Indies, three quarters of the work had been encouraging gossip.

"Eventually," he said.

"Ah. Finally a word I recognize. Unfortunately, the wrong word."

Leam couldn't help chuckling. Her lashes flickered.

"My lord, you are a renowned flirt. But perhaps you are not aware that I am not likewise. Unhand me now."

He should. He had no desire to. Warm feminine beauty pressing to his body, a cool clever tongue soothing his ear, and a lovely face shaped with intelligence could not be abandoned so abruptly.

"Whit threats will ye level if I dinna, I wonder?"

She tilted up her nose, releasing upon him the full force of her glorious eyes.

"I would not demean myself by leveling threats at a gentleman. But are you one?" Her voice was frosty. But those eyes . . . they *questioned*, far beyond her words. And within the thunderclouds, Leam fancied, a song wept.

His chest hollowed.

He released her.

She smoothed her palms over her skirt. Without again looking at him, and without a word, she went into the building.

Leam stood on the porch, boots sunk in snow, heartbeat quick and uneven. His stomach sickened at that sensation in his chest, for so long so alien to him. Clearly, that bit of flirtation had been a mistake. He would not repeat it.

Kitty willed her racing pulse to slow. She'd never imagined that the removal of facial hair could transform a merely handsome man into . . .

She pressed cold palms to hot cheeks as she hurried from the rear corridor. He was not following. She had insulted him. She'd *had* to. At the moment she would have said anything to encourage him to unwrap those strong arms from around her waist. Inside, she had been melting. It lingered now, liquid heat mingled with twining nerves.

She had not been so close to a man in years. Three years. She had, in point of fact, largely convinced herself that that state had come about because of this very man.

Could such coincidences occur? She must be mad to think it.

She hurried into the taproom. Emily perched on a bench at a table, wrestling butter onto a slice of bread.

"The bread is not fresh," she announced. "Mrs. Milch says

the village baker has taken to her bed today due to the snow, and her serving girl will not come to help in the kitchen as she lives in Shrewsbury three miles distant. I told her we might assist in baking if we are to be here long, which it seems we shall. Have you seen the snow? It is extraordinarily deep."

"Yes. Deep," Kitty finally managed, dragging herself from reverie. "For how long is Mr. Worthmore to remain at your parents' home?"

"At least until Twelfth Night. You do not think it will hold off melting until after then, do you? I might avoid meeting him altogether." The glimmer in Emily's eyes suggested she was banking on wishes.

Kitty shook her head. "I haven't the foggiest idea how to bake bread."

"Neither do I. But I shall learn." Emily bared her teeth and bit into the stale slice.

Heavy steps sounded on the floorboards behind Kitty. She was to have no reprieve of even minutes in which to compose herself. But the man must want breakfast too, the man with a jaw carved of stone that a woman could wish to run her fingertips over, then her lips and tongue, as though he were a salt lick and she a deer.

She was very foolish.

He halted behind her and the lapping heat deep inside her resumed with astounding vigor. She pressed it away even as something heedless inside her *enjoyed* it.

"There is bacon, my lord," Emily said. "The stable boy, Ned, found some in the shed. One would imagine salted fish could be had as well, but apparently not."

Lord Blackwood moved around Kitty and took up the coffeepot.

"'Twas a lean season for the herring."

Emily studied him curiously. "How do you come to know that?"

" 'Twas in the papers, lass." He smiled.

Kitty could not prevent it: a breath of pleasure stole from her lips. He glanced at her, but briefly.

"Will ye be regretting the lack o fish too, maleddy?" He passed her a cup of coffee as though he were a footman, this man of great wealth who stood to inherit a dukedom. He dressed with careless ease, not slovenly although without the slightest hint of fashion. He had large hands, strong and ridiculously underused by the delicate cup he proffered. Hands more suited to chopping wood. Or shearing sheep. Or holding a woman indecently close upon an icy stoop.

Her cheeks warmed.

She accepted the cup. "Not at all, my lord." She tempered her tone with great care. "I prefer caviar."

His gaze met hers, lazily hooded on the surface yet perfectly aware, as though he of all persons knew she donned her hauteur like a cloak.

Kitty held her breath.

His mouth lifted at the edge.

A breeze of cold air came with the sound of a door opening and the thunking patter of large paws in the front foyer. Then the dogs themselves appeared, a gentleman of about Kitty's age following. Drawing off his greatcoat and hat, he surveyed the chamber with a quick, light glance. He bowed to Kitty with youthful elegance, all correctness, and entirely unlike the large man standing on the other side of the chamber whose enormous dogs jostled his legs.

"Good day, ma'am."

Kitty curtsied.

"Maister Yale," Lord Blackwood supplied apparently by way of introduction as he leaned back against the sideboard. "Leddy Kath'rine and Leddy Marie Antoine."

"How do you do, Lady Katherine?" Mr. Yale bowed, then turned to Emily. "Ma'am."

"Sir, I see you have been outside already," Emily said without looking up from carving a sausage into bits. "How did you find the snow?"

"Cold and wet." He returned his attention to Kitty. "I regret that your journey has been stymied, my lady."

"Thank you, sir. In fact we are mere miles from Willows Hall, Lady Marie's home."

"And do you travel alone, ma'am?" He looked about curiously.

"My governess was lost on the road behind," Emily said.

"I am crushed to hear it. I daresay she is quite cold and wet now as well."

Emily peered at him over the rim of her spectacles. "What an odd thing to say."

"And yet an odder state for her to be in." He quirked a brow. "At first opportunity Blackwood and I shall take our horses out in search of her carriage."

"Thank you, sir," Kitty said. "Are you also close to your destination? Lord Blackwood would have us believe you are on a fishing trip, but I fear he esteems teasing more than truth."

Mr. Yale smiled. "Your fears are well founded, my lady. My friend enjoys laughing."

"I hope not at the expense of others." She felt the earl's gaze upon her.

"Never. But he is an odd fellow, s'truth. It is often difficult to understand him." Mr. Yale glanced at the coffee and bread. "Will you break your fast?"

In knots, her stomach protested at the mere idea. "I shall await the promised eggs." She gestured for him to sit.

He did so, across from Emily. "Lady *Marie Antoine*, what text has so engrossed you that you bring it to the table?"

"Shakespeare. *Richard III*."

"Ah."

Finally she looked up. "Are you an admirer of the Bard's history plays, sir?"

"Only the comedies."

Emily's brow creased. He grinned, and it sat very well on his face. A scruffy gray head bumped beneath his arm. He fed the dog his bread. "Your hounds, Blackwood, will eat us out of the house before the snow is melted. On the stoop just now I watched this one tear through two pound of sausage as though it were a thimbleful."

"He's a pup," came the quiet response. "He haesna yet learnt his manners."

Mr. Yale twisted his shoulders to regard the earl, a sliver of a smile on his lips. Lord Blackwood tilted his head, but he did not grin. Something shimmered through Kitty's insides—not the delicious liquid heat now, but more insistent and uncomfortable. She moved to the window and pressed the draperies open. Without, all was blinding white and the heavens still heavy with clouds.

"Mr. Yale, have you studied the road? Is it passable?" She had gone out to glimpse the rear yard, directed to that view by Mr. Milch. The stable boy, Ned, had shoveled that stoop before tackling the front, to make a path to the chicken coop. Thus, because of laying fowl, Kitty now knew that the Earl of Blackwood's eyes were of the darkest brown, like coffee, and that the flicker of steel behind those rich depths was not in fact a product of her imagination.

Something cold resided within him. It made her shiver, even as his gaze on her now turned her warm. She did not have to look at him to know he watched her.

But perhaps she imagined it.

She glanced at him. He met her gaze, then his slipped away, and with it her breath.

"We shan't have use of even a saddle horse for two or three days, I suspect." Mr. Yale skewered a sausage and fed it to the dog drooling at his knee.

"Days?" Emily looked hopeful. "Past Christmas, do you imagine?"

"Unless a vast melt comes of a sudden." He drawled this.

"The sky is still quite gray," Kitty murmured. "We shall miss church."

"I don't know about that, Lady Katherine. It is but Monday. In six days the road should again be passable. The mail coach will come through and dredge a path."

"Wednesday is Christmas Day." She had not ever passed a Christmas without attending church with her mother at the cathedral in town or the chapel at Savege Park. But perhaps this year Mama would attend on the arm of Lord Chamberlayne. "Will you miss not going to church for Christmas, Marie Antoine?"

Emily shook her head. "Not really."

Lord Blackwood reached to the table, took up a piece of bread, and moved toward the rear foyer. He returned in a moment with his greatcoat and, chewing, slung the coat around his broad shoulders. "Come." The dogs followed him out the front door.

The innkeeper entered the room. "Eggs for my lords and ladies!" He had an affable air and a platter of steaming food.

"Only one lord, and he has gone out." Emily accepted a dish with a sidelong glance at her table companion. Mr. Yale tucked into his meal.

"If you're needing aught else, don't hesitate to ask it of Mrs. Milch or myself."

"Mr. Milch," Kitty said, "is there a church near the village?"

"In it, my lady." He departed.

Kitty sat down gingerly on a bench, her spine erect, hands

not entirely steady. She stared at the doorway to the front entrance. She was being a fool. In mere minutes a Scottish lord who barely spoke a word she understood and did not bother to excuse himself from the presence of ladies had made her blush, tremble, and lose her tongue. Renowned in society for a cool façade that masked a heart filled with vengeance, she was now behaving like a thorough ninnyhammer.

"Kitty, have you brought any books?"

She swallowed her distraction. "Yes."

"With our journey so slow, I have nearly gone through all of mine already, and Mr. Milch says he keeps none here but Scripture. I shan't have a thing to read when I am finished with *Richard*."

"I have only a few novels, and that tract on trade to the East Indies that Lady March suggested, but you told me yesterday that does not interest you."

"Blackwood will have something a lady would like." Mr. Yale pulled the slender volume of Shakespeare toward him and took another forkful of eggs. Scanning the open page, he swallowed. "He always does. Poetry and such."

Poetry?

Emily tugged her book from his grip and returned it beneath her elbow. "I enjoy most books, Mr. Yale. Not only those ladies prefer."

He gave her a slight, provoking smile, much like Kitty's elder twin brothers used to cast her when they taunted. Emily's brow creased anew, her lips uncustomarily tight.

Kitty looked from one to the other. "Oh, dear."

Mr. Yale's grin broadened. "I daresay."

"The two of you have previously made each other's acquaintance."

"Once," Emily said without looking up from her book. "I trod upon his toes and he does not like me above half for it. He is very shallow. Just look at his waistcoat." She gestured.

Mr. Yale placed a palm on his chest. "My lady dances with the grace of a swan."

Kitty frowned. "His waistcoat is black, Emily— *Marie*."

"Do you know how many pounds he spent on that scrap of brocaded silk, Kitty?"

"Twelve," the gentleman promptly supplied.

"Thank you, sir, that is very helpful." Kitty glanced at the offending garment. "*Twelve* pounds?"

He quirked a jaunty smile. The cost of the waistcoat meant nothing to him, the rancor in Emily's stare all, apparently.

"Good heavens." Kitty stood. "This is not propitious given our circumstances."

"Coincidences so often are not," he offered.

Coincidences.

The tension in her middle twisted. "Is civilization lost to us here, then?"

"There is no such thing as civilization," Emily stated, "only vanity and greed cloaked in imperial arrogance."

Kitty deposited her napkin upon the table and made her way up the stairs to her bedchamber, to lock herself in and not come out until the thaw. It seemed the safest course of action.

Chapter 4

Far from the comforts of Mayfair, a diminutive brown creature scurried across the boards of Kitty's bedchamber in the full light of midday. She closed her book, stepped gingerly, and shut the door behind her, the inch-high crack beneath it notwithstanding.

Lord Blackwood and Mr. Yale lounged in worn chairs before the hearth. The earl's long legs stretched out before him, coat scrunched up around his shoulders, hands clasped atop his waist. His eyes were closed as though he dozed. Mr. Yale dandled a pack of cards on his knee. The stable boy sat bowlegged on the floor, a dog's head filling his lap.

She descended the steps. "You appear a contented lot."

Lord Blackwood opened his eyes, and touched by that lazy regard, Kitty simply foundered.

She must find occupation as soon as possible, away from him. But the inn was odiously small. The kitchen must do. He would not enter there and she would not find her insides turning to jelly. She would learn to bake, perhaps a Christmas pudding into which she might sink her head and not come out until Easter, or at the very least when he departed.

Mr. Yale stood and bowed. "Care for a game, Lady Katherine?" He gestured with the deck.

"Thank you, no. I have had my surfeit of cards." For three years now since she had given up her dogged pursuit of Lambert's ruination, games of deceit had not interested her. She played only when her mother wished.

"Ah, then, the rustic amusements of the country must suffice, whatever they may be. But I understand you have an excellent hand."

"How is that, sir?"

"Blackwood told me."

He did? "And do you trust him on this?"

"On anything. With my life," the young man said lightly, swiftly.

"That is quite a tribute." She chanced a glance at the Scot. "Have you earned it, my lord?"

"Cubs weel speak sic nonsense whan aff their feed." Now he did not look at her, and Kitty could not ignore her fluttering pulse. Lord Blackwood played cards almost as often as her mother, but Kitty had never played against him. She socialized with politicians and literary people, men and women more interested in conversation of substance than gossip—a rather different set than the Scottish earl enjoyed. She'd never seen him since that night at the masquerade three years ago. But when she arrived yesterday, he remembered her.

"The gov'nor let me run his bitch, mum." The boy flashed a jaw full of prominent square teeth.

Kitty welcomed the intervention. "How far did she run in such weather, I wonder?"

"To the river and back. Capital race. She's a right quick goer."

"I have no doubt. Ned, where is your mistress?"

"I'll fetch her for you, mum." He leaped up and went into

the kitchen. The dog sighed and laid its muzzle on the floor. Kitty moved to the window. From her bedchamber, she had watched the snow begin falling again and met the sight with both hope and unease. The longer she remained away from London, the more opportunities Lord Chamberlayne would have to press his suit. And Emily's absence from home might serve to frustrate her suitor. But Kitty could not like the situation entirely.

"We shall be trapped here for days, and our servants stranded on the road who-knows-where," she murmured.

"They'll hae found a farmer's cot, lass. Nae tae worry."

How could her skin *feel* him looking at her?

She glanced over her shoulder, purposefully arching a brow. "Perhaps I am merely concerned for my luggage. I have but this one gown."

His gaze slipped along her body, from the high neckline of her modest carriage dress to its hem.

Mr. Yale bowed gracefully. "It is all charm on you, my lady."

"Thank you. Are your servants likewise separated from you?"

"We haven't any. We travel light this journey, on horse-back."

Kitty could not help it. She must look at the earl again. She was drawn like a cat to milk.

Not milk.

No cat.

Moth to flame.

This could not continue. At five-and-twenty she had danced and dined and driven with men of rank and power. In society since her nineteenth year, unmarried all that time, she had rarely flirted, maintaining instead a cool, distant mode. A few persisted with sincere attentions, despite all, but she put them off smoothly. In the intimacy of familiarity lay danger, a lesson Kitty had learned at a tender age. She'd now had her moments of giddy curiosity, but they must cease. She would nip this in the bud.

Dark eyes partially lowered, he was staring at her without any attempt at concealment.

"Lord Blackwood, can you not manage to keep your eyes to yourself?"

Like a big dog, he shook his head slowly, his gaze scanning her from brow to toe once more, this time lingering about her waist. Kitty's breaths shortened. His brow creased, as though he were perplexed.

She knew she oughtn't to ask. "What is it? Have I a smudge on my gown? Why do you look at me in that manner?"

His eyes shifted upward and a hint of a grin played about his lips.

"Be there ony manner in which A might look at ye that ye woud approve, lass?"

Mr. Yale chuckled.

The earl's gaze slipped downward again. "'Tis the dress."

"My gown?" The finest, thinnest woolen carriage dress she'd ever owned, sewn with tiny beads and embroidered about the collar and wrists, all in the loveliest shade of green imaginable. "What do you mean to say is wrong with this gown?"

A single dark brow rose. "'Tis a wee bit snug, nae then?"

Kitty's cheeks went hot, her palms damp.

"It fits remarkably well, in fact." She should turn and walk away. She should not encourage this impertinence. She could not stop looking at his eyes. "What do you know of ladies' gowns, my lord?"

He shrugged, a rough, careless gesture.

"Nothing," she supplied, "of course."

"Maun be the girl in it, than."

Kitty got warm—deep and central. He called her a girl.

No one had called her a girl in years. She was Katherine Savege, redoubtable spinster, and gossips remarked on it regularly, in parlors and in the columns. They wondered why her brother, the Earl of Savege, had not wed her to one of the few suitors who dared pursue her despite her stained character, no doubt for the dowry attached to her marriage. They questioned why her mother had not insisted on it. And endlessly they speculated: she flouted convention merely to fortify her vanity; she preferred salons and political meetings to the joys of the nursery; she was secret mistress to a great man.

Only some accusations bit. A nursery was never to be her joy, not according to the doctor Lambert had taken her to see after so many months when she did not conceive, just before he pointed out to her in the park the daughter he had fathered upon a former lover.

And no married man would ever call her mistress. Watching her mother suffer the indignity of taking second place in her husband's life after his mistress had assured that.

She peered at the earl, apparently lazy yet not in fact when one looked carefully. Instead, unnervingly still. Far too still for a man of his supposed habits and character.

He was wrong. She was not a girl. A woman who had sent a man into exile could not be so called. A woman who had used her body for revenge and who had lied—over and over again—to effect that revenge had nothing left of innocence in her.

"Here she is, mum," Ned chirped.

Mrs. Milch set a tray of food on the table. "I found some cheese." The gray pouches beneath her eyes seemed to lengthen her narrow face when she spoke. "And we've got a keg of ale and turnip soup. It's not what the Quality expects."

"I am certain it will suit. Mrs. Milch, an uninvited guest has visited my bedchamber. A very small one."

"It's them mice again." Ned shook his head, snags of hair sticking out at angles. "The cat's fixing to drop a litter. She's run off and the snow's kept her gone. Probably snug and warm at the smithy's cuddling with half a dozen tiny mites this minute."

"Fetch the broom, boy."

"Yes, mum."

"Gi' the lad a rest." Lord Blackwood came to his feet. "He's dane a loud o' wirk already the day. The dugs'll rout the vermin." He gestured and the wolfhounds unfolded themselves from the floor and followed him to the stair.

"I shoveled a path to the road, mum, and another to the stable," Ned said. "The gov'nor helped." He looked wistfully at the dogs padding behind Lord Blackwood up the stairs.

On the landing the earl paused and gestured to Kitty, much as he had to his pets. She had no choice but to follow.

Four doors let off the corridor, and another smaller door to the attic. She went to hers.

"Did you really help Ned shovel snow this morning, my lord?"

"Aye." He was right behind her, closer than he ought to be. "A man's got tae busy his hauns whan there's naught else tae dae." He was very tall, and were she to allow it he could trap her between him and the door with little effort. Then he might busy his hands quite usefully.

Good heavens. Errant thoughts run amok.

"You could have played cards with Mr. Yale."

"Nae wi' a brassic whelp, I wadna."

"Brassic?"

"Pockets tae let."

"Ah. I shall remember that if I succumb to his entreaties to play." Her fingers around the doorknob were slippery. She imagined she could feel the heat of his body along her back.

"Weel ye open the door, lass," he said quietly at her shoulder, "or dae ye prefer tae wait on the wee one tae come frae beneath it?"

She sucked in breath and pushed the panel wide. "I suspect the mouse is long gone now."

The dogs entered around his legs. The larger one, as high as Kitty's waist, moved to the hearth, sniffed about in the ashes, and sneezed. The other padded toward the window and set its nose to the ground. Lord Blackwood folded his arms across his chest and leaned against the doorjamb.

Subtly wiping her damp hands on her skirt, Kitty forced herself to look at him. His attention was fixed on the floor before her feet, his jaw oddly tight.

He lifted his gaze.

"I am not afraid of mice." Her words came too quickly.

A lengthy silence ensued during which they stared at each other as though gentlemen and ladies who were barely acquainted frequently stared at one another without note.

"Whit be ye afeared o than, maleddy?"

"Very little." Rather, the staccato rhythm of her heart, a condition caused by the proximity of a large, handsome man to her bed. A titled gentleman who spoke like a barbarian and helped little boys shovel snow. A man of such staunch Scottish loyalty that all of society knew him to be still mourning the horrible loss of his beloved bride years ago, engaging in flirtations for brief amusement only, never sincerely.

But his tragic story had no relevance to Kitty.

Except one night three years ago, it had. That night when he had looked into her as though he could see her soul and, without a word, seemed to tell her that weakness must no longer rule her, that she was worthy of better. On that night she had finally left her anger at Lambert Poole behind. She had broken free from wicked games.

She tore her gaze away. "Your dog seems to have found

something." The animal snuffled at the rear of an old wooden chest.

The earl crossed the chamber and crouched, setting his hand on the beast's neck. The other dog pressed its head into the space between him and the box. Gently he nudged it aside. His back was wide, shoulder blades pronounced. Pale light slanted over his thighs revealing fine muscle starkly defined by his breeches. Kitty's breaths shortened. She felt hot. *Hot.*

She should flee. This could not be happening to her, this foolishness. This preoccupation. It was irrational when directed at such a man, for every conceivable reason. But his body, his sheer masculine presence . . .

As though drawn by a pulley, she moved forward. His coat tugged across his shoulders as he pushed the heavy box at an angle away from the wall. She leaned in closer.

"Aye. Thar's the hole." He stood abruptly, coming toe-to-toe with her. He looked down at her. "Best tae shore it up," he added as though her brow weren't two inches from his chin.

She swallowed against the hard pulse in her throat. "I shall ask Mr. Milch for appropriate stuffing. Thank you, my lord." She backed toward the door.

He moved to her in two strides, took the door in his hand, and pulled it to. Retreat cut off, she backed up against the post. He loomed over her, broad and dark-eyed and staring quite intently. But he said nothing.

"What are you looking at, my lord?"

"A'm looking at ye, lass." His chest was so close that her breasts prickled as though they were aware of the nearness of solid man.

"Well, you must look from farther away."

"Ye told me A may nae."

Her throat felt like a desert, her belly quite as fevered but not in the least bit dry. She was honey inside.

Could this be happening?

"Clearly you have not taken that to heart."

His gaze dipped to her mouth. "Yer looking tae, lass."

"I am not."

"That's a wheen o blethers."

"I haven't the foggiest idea what you have just said."

"Thin A'll be showing ye." His hand came up and around her cheek, warm and strong. Kitty's breath petered to a wisp. His fingertips slipped into her hair at the base of her head, his palm shaping to her skin. Slowly, so slowly, the pad of his thumb caressed her lower lip.

She sighed. Nothing could halt it, nor the catch in her throat as he bent his head. She tilted hers back.

"I shall find this quite easy to resist." Her voice was nearly even despite the careening of her heart and the liquid state of her knees. She had repulsed men in similar circumstances before. Many times. She knew how to do this, even so far removed from civilization in the wild abandonment of a country snowstorm. The wild abandonment of her scruples proved another sort of challenge.

"Will ye?" He spoke just over her mouth, his breath warm like his touch. She sensed no expensive cologne of a gentleman but snow and fresh pine and leather.

"I daresay." Her lashes fluttered, every nerve in her body focused on the sweet, slow stroking of his thumb. She fought not to turn her mouth into his palm, to feel his skin fully across her lips. "But I suppose you are not accustomed to that—ladies resisting your rustic charms?"

His mouth curved. "Nae aften." His rich eyes were alight. "Ye were looking."

"You—" The word came forth as a rasp. She cleared her throat. "You would like to believe that, wouldn't you?"

His gaze scanned her face, then her neck and hair. She felt the caress of that perusal and the touch of his hand to the soles of her feet. He looked into her eyes again. His grin faded.

"Aye." His voice was low. "A woud."

"Then I beg your pardon for the disappointment." She must not allow her words to tremble as her insides did. She would not betray her foolishness. She was Lady Katherine Savege, coolheaded spinster and ruiner of titled men. She could not be moved, although quite obviously that was a wheen o blethers. "Now, my lord, your task here is finished and you may go away."

His hand slipped from her face and he backed off and Kitty found herself draped against a doorframe, loose-jointed and breathless, like a woman aching to be kissed.

He swung the door open. Emily stood in the aperture.

"I have come to borrow that tract on eastern trade, Kitty. Ned told me about the mouse. Have you found it?" She looked between them at the wolfhounds.

Kitty untangled her tongue with some difficulty. "Lord Blackwood's dog discovered a hole in the floor, which shall be mended shortly." She smoothed her palms over her skirt. "Thank you for your assistance, my lord."

"Maleddy." He nodded and moved into the corridor toward the stair. The two great beasts lumbered after.

"Kitty?" Emily looked after the earl. "What were you and Lord Blackwood doing in here with the door nearly closed?"

"Nothing at all." And yet not one iota of her pounding blood and quivering insides believed that.

Leam scrubbed a palm over his face, considering the snow and the great good it might do him poured into his breeches. Her skin was soft as silk, her eyes lustrous, her generous mouth a pure fantasy. A man need only catch a glimpse of her pink tongue to imagine a great deal he oughtn't to be imagining about a woman of her caliber. Imagining what her tongue could do to him and precisely where.

He hefted the shovel, an unhandy tool intended for manure, but it must do.

The moment he had touched her skin, and her eyes shaded with longing, he realized his mistake again. *Je reconnus Vénus et ses feux redoutables.* He recognized Venus and her dangerous fire. Very well indeed.

He had gone to her chamber to touch her. For no other reason than that.

She was not afraid of mice. *Not afraid of mice.* Not afraid of anything, Lady Katherine Savage. *Very little*, she had said.

Then fear the madman who must ply the shovel through thigh-high snow to drive the sensation of a woman's skin from his hands.

On the other side of the stable Hermes let out a yowl, echoed by the donkey inside. The snow fell lightly now and Bella's shadowy shape came into view around the corner of the building. Haunches bunched, head high, she barked.

Setting the shovel aside, Leam moved toward her. The drifts grabbed at his legs but he trudged the distance swiftly. He needed activity and Bella never alerted him lightly. She waited for him, then flanked him around the corner of the building. Her pup, already larger by a stone, leaped about a depression in the snow.

Leam slipped the knife from his sleeve.

The trough was roughly the size of a man's prone body, half-filled and covered by several inches of new snow, with foot holes moving from it and a hoofmarks as well. He cast a glance at the scrubby trees flanking the Tern, sparse, gray with white sleeves, shifting forlornly in the wind. Nowhere to hide in there, but the tracks were lost in any case.

He slid the knife back into place. Bella nudged his arm. In thanks he ran his hand around her ears, but she bumped her long muzzle against his chin.

"What is it?"

She pawed at the edge of the depression. Leam pushed the snow aside, his breath frosting in damp clouds. Buried beneath was a brown clump of fabric. He shook it out. A man's muffler made of fine cashmere.

Cashmere did not come cheap. If this was the man who pursued Leam he was not, it seemed, a hired sniper, unless he was exceptionally good at his trade and demanded much for his services. But the fellow had had plenty of opportunities to attack, if not in London, then on the road from Bristol and even this morning.

Beneath the muffler, tucked in the snow, were a handful of coins and a broken chain of thick gold links. The man had dropped them, apparently when he'd fallen, perhaps off his horse, or perhaps simply due to the driving wind and blinding snow. But he hadn't come to the inn only a few yards away.

He plucked the objects out of the packed ice and pocketed them, then straightened and pushed through the snow to the stable door. Inside all was crisply cool and scented of straw and horse. Hermes went straight to the Welshman lying on his back across a bench, a bottle propped in one hand.

Passing the somnolent carriage horses and squat ass, Leam moved toward his horse's stall. "Knitting the ravelled sleeve of care?"

"I've no care. However, I do have whiskey." Yale's voice was heavy. "Care for a drop?"

"I am being followed."

Yale squeezed his eyes shut and pinched the bridge of his nose. "How do you know it isn't I who is followed?"

"If one of your enemies determined to murder you, he

would not be hesitating." Leam dropped the muffler beside the bottle.

"S'truth." Yale struggled to sit, setting the whiskey on the bench and taking up the garment. "But murder? Perhaps he is merely seeking information, like we were wont to do." He lifted a black brow over a preternaturally clear eye. "Or p'raps it's Lady Justice, chased us all the way from Dover Street to ferret out our purpose."

"In a Shropshire snowstorm?"

"In a Bengalese monsoon?" He dropped the muffler. "That fellow we sought in Calcutta tracked you all the way through the jungle, if you recall."

Leam shook his head, moving to his horse's stall. "I've no idea why this one hasn't come closer. He's within spitting distance yet he balks."

Yale leaned back against the cold stable wall and swung the bottle once more to his lips. "Much as the lovely Lady Katherine?"

Leam would not oblige him with a reply. But it was a damned nuisance sometimes that the lad had the instincts of a real spy. Always watching.

"He is closer than I like given the circumstances."

"P'raps you ought to simply wait for him behind a wall and shoot him when he appears. Works like a charm, you know."

The big roan bumped its head into Leam's chest. He ran his hand along its smooth face.

"Is that how it happened, Wyn? When you shot that girl?" Leam didn't know the whole story of it; Yale had never shared it. But he knew well enough that his friend had not always drunk the way he did now. It had started after one assignment went terribly wrong.

The Welshman pushed up from the bench and hefted a saddle into his arms. On steady legs he moved to his horse's stall. But this time Leam could see the drink in his eyes and the set of his mouth. The soberer the lad grew, the more he laughed. For years they had gotten along famously together: Mr. Wyn Yale, the drunk, and Lord Uilleam Blackwood, the man with a hole where his heart should be.

Yale unfixed the latch on a stall door and heaved the saddle and blanket to his black's back. It was an elegant creature, beauty and strength in its Thoroughbred lines.

"Going for a ride, Wyn?" Leam spoke mildly. "It is unwise in this weather, of course."

"When you call me by my Christian name, Leam, you intend to lecture me. I will save you the trouble. Ta-ta." He tightened his mount's girth and reached for the bridle.

"I could knock you down. You would sleep this one off."

"You couldn't, old man."

"I haven't bothered to in years, it is true. But I am tempted now."

Yale slid the bit into the black's mouth and dropped the reins over its neck. He drew the horse from the stall, its hooves clomping across straw-strewn wood.

"Are you trying to kill yourself, or the horse?"

The Welshman pushed the stable door open and mounted amid lazy swirls of snow blowing off the roof.

Leam followed. "Don't be a fool, lad."

"Save your lectures for your son, Blackwood. He's still young enough to find some use in them." He spurred the horse into the snow. It stepped high, wary of the drifts, but the Welshman pushed it forward.

His *son*.

"You will ruin that animal's legs, you idiot!" The wind grabbed Leam's voice. Heedless, the black-clad man and black-coated horse disappeared around the corner of the stable.

He cursed and headed for the inn. He shook his coat and

pushed through the entrance. Bella and Hermes came in behind and he shut the door—too forcefully. He tugged off his gloves and threw his coat onto a hook, bending to swipe his boots with a cloth, his head a wretched mash of anger.

Anger, he could feel in spades. Only anger, still after so long. His tenure with the Falcon Club had done nothing for that, nothing at all, although that had been the reason he'd joined five years earlier. To cast off grief and guilt, and most of all fury, with purpose. To release his anger by keeping himself occupied.

All idiocy. He'd run away, accomplishing nothing but alienating himself for far too long from his home, the house in which his son lived.

His son.

He went into the parlor.

Lady Katherine stood by a window. The pane was open and the cold air blowing in rippled the delicate fabric of her skirt. But she did not seem to note it. Her wide gaze rested on him, strangely questioning once more.

His anger slid away, heat of an entirely different kind replacing it, low and insistent again. By God, those thunder-cloud eyes could bewitch a man.

"An ye wish, lass, A'll saddle ma horse an search the road behind," he heard himself say.

"For our servants?"

"Aye."

"You would do that when you have just told Mr. Yale he oughtn't to ride?"

"Aye." That, and quite a bit more he began to fear with a sick twist in his stomach. He wanted to please her and see those thunderclouds glimmer with desire as they had in her bedchamber. "An ye wish."

She remained silent a moment, slender and poised like a portrait, but shimmering with muted life in the gown that caressed her curves as his hands might. There was every newness about her, yet every familiarity, as there had been for the briefest moment that night three years ago. His heart beat a frantic pace.

A tiny crease appeared between her brows. "I would not have you put yourself at risk."

He nodded. "Nae tae worry, lass. Thay'll hae found shelter."

"I hope so."

"A ken ye dae."

Her frown deepened. "*Do* you know?" Then the corner of her lips twitched, her winged brows quirking. "That is what you said, isn't it?"

She was ice and fire at once, diamonds and feather down, soft heat bubbling forth through a cool veneer.

"Aye." Leam backed toward the door. Distance was safest. Imagining she would shy from his blatant barbarity, he had redoubled his incivility earlier, boorishly commenting on her gown. The ploy had rewarded him only with the sensation of her skin marked upon his hand and the sweet, humid heat of her breath upon his lips.

But this honest conversation was going no better.

Distance. Sanity. Alvamoor, where his son awaited him to celebrate Christmas. His son. Nearly six now, his appearance no doubt altered since the previous year, as always with the swiftly growing young. But Leam knew the boy's face well. Better than his own.

Without bidding the lady adieu, he grabbed his coat and gloves and retreated once more into the wild out-of-doors. The cold without could not touch a man with a soul of bleak barbarism like his.

Chapter 5

Kitty folded linens. She had not performed such a domestic task in an age. Permanently residing with her mother in her brother's town house, she left the housekeeping to Alex's capable London staff. But Mrs. Milch had complained again of the lack of the serving girl, and Kitty's brain was good for nothing more taxing this afternoon.

By the stable Lord Blackwood had spoken perfect English to Mr. Yale. Nary a hint of brogue or tumbling roll had marred the cadence of his deep voice speaking clearly and smoothly the king's own English. *Better* than the king's.

She'd heard it by accident. She had opened the window to release from the parlor a cloud of smoke a hard wind had sent down the chimney. But she had tarried there in the frigid air to spy on him. She would deny it to herself if she could, but she had no wits to now.

Perhaps he had been putting on airs to tease Mr. Yale, like an actor employing a false voice to mimic another. But he'd sounded like a gentleman. Quite nicely. So nicely that Kitty was barely able to find words when he had stormed through the door.

But why would he feign otherwise? And what sort of renowned flirt backed away from a woman so obviously wishing to be kissed, on such slight discouragement?

An honorable one. An honorable one who teased a lady about the suitability of her gown?

Kitty released a tight breath.

"Two horsemen have come into the yard, Mr. Yale and a stranger with a portmanteau." Book in one hand, Emily peered out the window. "Mrs. Milch, I believe you are to have another lodger."

"It'll be mutton sausage for him too." Mrs. Milch stacked Kitty's linens and headed toward the kitchen.

The innkeeper met the gentlemen at the door.

"Welcome back, sir," he said to Mr. Yale. "I see you've found another lost traveler."

"Yes, indeed!" The newcomer gave the room an open smile that creased his attractive face into an attitude suggesting sheer pleasure at being stranded. His gaze met Kitty's and his blue eyes brightened. He drew off his hat, revealing close-cropped gold curls and fashionably long sideburns.

"Ma'am." He bowed, then to Emily. "What good fortune to find such company upon such a road. I should not have dreamed this luck."

"Where have you come from, sir?" Emily asked.

He offered another charming smile. "Cheshire, ma'am."

"I meant just now." She turned to his companion, who was removing his coat and hat. "Mr. Yale, where did you find him?"

"At the pub." He moved toward the hearth and held forward his palms.

"I'm afraid I had a nasty time of it last night," the gentleman said with a light air of regret. "Stuck upon the road, the most frightful winds howling, my horse terrified. I found this village when I was nearly dead with cold, but I'd no idea of an inn until this good gentleman informed me of it minutes ago." His regard shifted to the stair, and his brows lifted. "Ah, your party grows augustly." He bowed. "My lord, it is an honor."

"An who might ye be?" The deep voice shivered through Kitty. She had to look. She could not in point of fact prevent herself from doing so. He was far too handsome, far too unnerving, and far too confusing. She wanted to look without ceasing.

"Cox, sir. David Cox." The newcomer affected a martial snap of his heels. "A Lloyd's man. Shipping insurance of late, but before that Wellesley's army. Fact, I am already acquainted with you of a sort, if I may be so bold. I knew your brother, James, back in the dragoons. He was a bruising rider, a favorite amongst his men. You have quite the look of him, and he always carried a cameo portrait of each of his siblings, just as I do of my . . . dear sister." His brow lowered handsomely. "My condolences, sir. I understand you were quite close."

Lord Blackwood nodded, his gaze hooded.

"Well now, sir," Mr. Milch said cheerfully, "I've got all my chambers spoken for upstairs. But that pub is no place for a fine gentleman such as yourself. If you don't mind it, there's the garret. It's got a grate, so you'll find it suitable warm, and my Gert has made up the mattress with a good woolen quilt. Can I tempt you to remain?"

Mr. Cox's smile flashed once more. "You could not tempt me *away* from such company." His appreciative gaze returned to Kitty.

She curtsied. "Mr. Cox, did you by chance encounter a carriage and four on the road yesterday or today?"

"Fact, I did, ma'am." He moved to her. "Last night near Atcham I spotted a very fine carriage, pulled up before a farmhouse not far from the road. It seemed out of place, but any port in a storm will do. Quite literally." He chuckled, deep enough to be pleasingly masculine. "Are you lacking members of your party?"

"Our servants, sir."

Lord Blackwood came to her side. He extended his hand to the newcomer. Mr. Cox passed his gloves into his other palm and shook hands.

"It is excellent to finally meet you, my lord. It must be six years since I had the pleasure of your brother's companionship in arms."

"Seiven." The earl released him. "Take a dram of whiskey afore denner, Cox?"

"Thank you. Don't mind if I do."

"Whiskey?" Emily furrowed her brow. "May I have a dram as well, Lord Blackwood?"

The Scot's mouth curved upward. "Aye, miss. If ye wish."

If you wish.

He was too close now. Memory of the sensation of his hand on her face, his caress on her lips, weakened Kitty, and it felt at once thrilling and horrid. He welcomed this tradesman as though he were an equal. He acted like a ruffian and occasionally spoke words that rendered her perfectly breathless. He was the most peculiar nobleman she had ever been acquainted with, and he made her heart race merely standing beside her.

"Lady Katherine, will you take a glass as well? Join us in celebrating Christmas early?" Mr. Yale handed Emily and Mr. Cox glasses. Kitty welcomed the opportunity to cross the chamber, away from the earl's unnerving presence.

"Capital idea." Mr. Cox lifted his glass in salute. "We shall be in this village until the snow melts, I suspect. In Shropshire for the holiday!"

"Some of us were intended in Shropshire for the holiday already," Mr. Yale said, offering a half-filled glass to Kitty.

She sipped. It burned, then invaded the place behind her breasts with heat. She drank again, deeper.

"Then you are not of a single party?" Mr. Cox glanced with interest about the group. "I had imagined these elegant ladies in your company, my lord."

"'Tis a sorry disappointment." Lord Blackwood raised the glass to his mouth and looked directly at Kitty.

"Lord Blackwood and Mr. Yale are on their way to no admitted destination, Mr. Cox," she said in impressively measured tones given her quivering insides. His hand around the glass was beautiful, strong, and long-fingered. She could still feel it upon her. "Lady Marie Antoine and I are intended at her parents' home not many miles distant."

"Ah, then I am sorry you have not reached your family, Lady Marie Antoine." He looked truly contrite. "But, I say, we shall make a party of it here instead."

"What do you have in mind, sir?" Mr. Yale lounged on the sofa, his glass full to the brim.

"Lady Katherine and I were to bake bread tomorrow," Emily said. "Perhaps we could find the ingredients for a pudding and make one of those instead."

"Have you any idea how?" the Welshman drawled.

"Have *you*?"

He offered her that slight smile Kitty now recognized, and took a long quaff of whiskey.

"No doubt Mrs. Milch will know a recipe," Emily said.

"Then pudding it shall be." Mr. Cox appeared all contentment. He turned to Kitty with a glimmer in his very blue eyes. "What else shall we have, my lady?"

"Ned plays the fiddle. We'll have music." Mr. Milch set plates atop the lace covering. "Gert! Where's the boy? He must play for these good folk before dinner."

"The boy?" Mr. Cox lifted a brow. "Why, he is seeing to my horse, of course. I gave him a penny for it."

Lord Blackwood met Kitty's gaze. His mouth curved into the barest hint of a smile. A private smile, meant for her it seemed. Her breath faltered.

"We canna lack a bonfire." He spoke as though to her directly.

"A bonfire?" she said. His gaze seemed to caress her lips as his thumb had in her bedchamber. "Whatever for, my lord?"

"Scots believe evil elves hasten down the chimney on Christmas to spirit away little children," Mr. Yale supplied, staring into the flames now. "We must build the hearth fires high lest we be invaded by sprites."

The earl's grin tilted up at one side, and his gaze upon her mouth did not falter. Kitty swallowed. She felt dizzy and feverish again. From the whiskey, certainly. Or from the heated regard of the rough-hewn, superstitious Scot across the chamber.

"I have read that Scots like to drink quite a bit at Christmastime." Emily spoke in a singsong voice. She looked into her empty glass, then handed it to Mr. Yale. He stood and refilled it. "Is that true, Lord Blackwood?"

"Scots drink all the time," Mr. Yale threw over his shoulder.

"We're nae alone in that."

"Scholars and great drinkers," Kitty murmured, and before she could school her tongue, "Which are you, Lord Blackwood?"

The larger dog pressed to his master's side. The earl's long fingers stroked the beast's shaggy brow. "A'll be letting ye guess that on yer own, lass."

"Lord Blackwood." Emily's voice slurred slightly now. "I am ever so grateful for the volume of poetry you lent me this morning. It is difficult to be without one's books, is it not?" She sighed uncharacteristically. Mr. Yale laughed. Kitty blinked.

Poetry.

"Why, how long have you been waylaid here already, my lady?" Mr. Cox inquired in surprise.

"A day," Kitty said in the hazy grip of the effects of very little drink and a great deal of perplexing, enthralling man. "A single day."

Leam smiled. Lady Katherine Savege was apparently unaccustomed to whiskey. So too her young friend. Yale was already disguised, although hiding it well as always. On the other side of the chamber, the inn's proprietor whistled a jig, several fingers of the Welshman's brew under his belt as well.

That left Cox, the man with gloves lined in brown cashmere who had shown up to join their little party in the midst of a snowstorm. Cox was drinking too; his eyes were bright. Far too often they rested on Kitty Savege.

He dressed like an agent in shipping insurance might, in a nattily tailored coat and waistcoat, expensive and flattering to his athletic build. He enjoyed the advantages of charming address and winning good looks, the sort of pleasing fellow an untried girl like Leam's young sister Fiona would admire.

Cox turned to Lady Emily and offered her light flattery as though she gave a damn for that sort of thing, a smile of sheer earnestness on his face. Yale mumbled a comment and Cox chuckled, no doubt gratified to imagine himself privy to the joke. But every few moments he cast Lady Katherine another admiring glance. She returned his smiles, but her attention was scattered, occasionally on the others, occasionally on the glass in her hand, but most often on Leam.

He was having the devil of a time looking away.

Curse Yale. Drink had not been wise tonight, at least not for him.

He set his glass on a table.

"My lord, it is a great man who shares poetry with others," Cox said with unexceptionable deference. "Tell me, who do you admire more greatly, Byron or Burns?"

And there it was again, the slightest hint of *ey*, the barely discernable *ow*. As a man who had struggled his entire youth to banish the rough borderlands from his speech, Leam could recognize a countryman within a phrase. Cox was a lowland Scot.

"Aeschylus."

The fellow's clear brow beetled. "That name is unknown to me. But I've been traveling in the Americas until quite recently. Those colonials never learn of the latest great writers until they are far out of date." He chuckled.

Lady Emily blinked like a fish. "Aeschylus, the ancient Greek tragedian?"

Yale glanced up, a glimmer in his silver eyes.

Leam felt like a fool, showing off his erudition. A jealous fool who had absolutely no reason to feel jealous.

He didn't like the fellow. And he didn't like the way he was casting calf's eyes at a lady far above his station. But now Leam was both feeling like a fool and thinking like a jackass. If he did not take care, the evening would proceed apace.

Dinner was served and enjoyed in good cheer and a measure of general hilarity. Leam participated when required. He took a glass of wine, leaving the whiskey untouched, and watched the tradesman. Cox made himself agreeable to all, showing no sign of discomfort among his new acquaintances yet a suitable modesty. When Yale searched for a taper to light a cheroot, Cox produced a flame. When Lady Emily begged to be excused on account of the tobacco smoke making her ill, Cox opened a window and held a steady arm beneath hers while she inhaled fresh air and Yale doused his cigar. When Lady Katherine applauded young Ned for his fine fiddling, Cox requested an encore.

After some time, Leam had seen enough. No man was that pleasing to everyone and all without good reason. He knew this from personal experience.

Throwing on his greatcoat, he announced that he would go outside for a smoke. Yale followed, leaving the ladies to Ned, Mr. Milch, and the coxcomb.

"Had enough of Tommy Tradesman, have you?" Yale brandished his cheroot and cupped his hand to encourage the spark. He took a long pull and puffed contentedly, staring out at the snow and the narrow river lit with indigo moonlight. The street was empty, a murmur of voices emanating from within the pub several doors away, echoing between the double row of modest buildings as sound always did upon snow.

As so often after such a storm, the sky had finally cleared. Ten thousand diamonds sparkled in the midnight canopy, an eternity of unfulfilled wishes. At one time, an infinitely foolish university student reading poetry had wished upon them all.

Leam moved along the path flanking the inn that he had shoveled earlier that afternoon while endeavoring to avoid the company of a female with wide, storm-tossed eyes.

"To where dost thou hasten, oh noble lord?" Yale called after him. "To thine balcony from which thou might cast forth petals of rose and lily for thy elusive lady's dainty toes to tread upon?" Yale was fully in his cups now. Only then did he ever make such foolish mistakes.

Leam retraced his steps, pulled his arm back, and planted his fist on his friend's jaw.

The lad hit the packed snow with a thud.

"Damn it, Blackwood, you villain," he snuffled, cupping his cheek with one hand and casting about with the other in the snow. "You've made me lose my cigar."

"I have discovered a stair at the rear of the house." Leam glowered down at him. "If you weren't so soaked in drink I would tell you to go up and investigate his belongings. As is, I suggest you step back inside and do your best to keep him entertained for as long as you are able." He pivoted about and nearly lost his footing on the ice. "By *God*, would that I were in Scotland already."

"Ah, but then you would not have made the acquaintance of the lovely Lady Katherine." Yale had found his cigar and was wiping it free of snow on the lapel of his coat.

But Leam hadn't made her acquaintance here. Three years ago he'd met her in a ballroom, and even then he hadn't been able to take his eyes off her. But she had been with another man. A man who did not deserve her.

"I would hit you again, Wyn, but you're still on the ground."

"More than welcome to come down here and further impress me with your pugilistic talents, old man." He smirked and bit the cheroot, his jaw red with the pattern of Leam's knuckles. Yale wanted the beating, and much more. He wanted oblivion, and Leam didn't blame him.

He turned on his heel and stormed away.

From within the kitchen door that let onto the alley not far from the rear foyer entrance, another staircase ascended. The inn's proprietress had long since gone to bed; the kitchen was piled with clean dishes, occupied only by a pair of mice content with a minuscule floor scrap.

Leam passed through a remarkably well-stocked pantry to the narrow staircase behind. He was halfway to the first landing when a door creaked above. He halted, making himself invisible in the dark. The small panel to the floor above opened, and into the stairwell, candle in hand, came Kitty Savege.

Leam held his breath, a metallic taste filling his mouth. He stood in shadow. She might not see him if she were climbing up to the coxcomb's attic chamber. Foolishly, Leam had imagined her above this. But he knew better of beautiful women. He had known better of this particular beautiful woman for three years.

She turned down the stair.

Air once more filled his lungs. There was nothing for it but to announce his presence; within a few steps she would collide with him. He ascended, making his boots heard.

With a soft yelp of surprise she halted and peered into the darkness beyond her candle. In the gold light of the flame her fine wide eyes glowed, her cheeks cast in a rosy hue, lashes like fans.

Leam moved two steps beneath her.

"My lord?"

"Maleddy."

"I thought you out in the yard smoking with Mr. Yale." Alcohol had rounded the edges of her voice, softening the hauteur. "What are you doing here?"

"A coud ask ye the same, lass."

"I am going to the kitchen to find a basin of water. I have not bathed in—" She swayed toward him slightly. "Good heavens, here we are in a remarkably dark stairwell, and I upon the verge of informing you all about my bath. Whiskey is most remarkable at loosening one's tongue."

"Aye, 'tis." That loose tongue was delectably pink, her lips dusky in the dim light. He should now turn and go back to the yard and pummel Yale. Any moment Cox would enter and see him here, on his way up in secret.

The image of Kitty Savege at her bath rooted him to the step.

"And now you must return the favor," she said. "I have informed you of my program, so you must tell me where you are going. This sneaking up the back stairs makes you look like a spy." Her generous lips curved into an impish grin, sparkling like her eyes and so entirely at odds with the crystalline town lady, Leam stared. "Are you a spy, Lord Blackwood?" Her smooth cheek dimpled like a girl's.

"Nae ony mair." His voice came forth hoarse. He stared at her mouth as her smile faded, as his groin pulsed with heat, as the candlelight wavered and she fumbled for the nonexistent rail, and as he began to wish that he had drunk more whiskey after all. Then at least in the morning he, like his friend, would have an excuse for the unwise behavior in which he was now about to engage.

Chapter 6

The earl reached to Kitty's hand and drew from it her teetering candle.

"Hae a care, lass. Ye'll drop it."

Excellent. She hadn't really needed it anyway. She hadn't really needed a bath either; that could wait until morning. She probably most needed sleep, but her blood seemed to whoosh through her veins. No doubt this had something to do with the whiskey, and the fantasy replaying itself in her mind of the Earl of Blackwood kissing her. A fantasy she had been nursing for hours, just like the glass Mr. Yale continually refilled.

As he had been doing all evening, Lord Blackwood stared at her mouth now, but this time from a very short distance away.

"If you are so bent on kissing me," she heard herself say in a remarkably throaty voice, "you may as well do it and cease this foolishness. I am no schoolroom miss and can, I suspect, withstand the insult."

He smiled a provoking smile, his rich eyes laughing. "Oh, can ye, lass?"

"Of course. I have lived in London nearly my entire life, you know."

He didn't seem to like that. But after that night three years ago, this did not surprise her. His eyes at exactly the level of hers now looked somewhat disapproving and quite intense. Kitty had never particularly liked men of great intensity.

But she liked the Earl of Blackwood. She liked the way he stared at her lips and the hot lapping pool it generated in her. She liked it that he built up the fire when the innkeeper was otherwise occupied, that Mr. Yale seemed to listen to him even when he pretended not to, and that his brother had carried his portrait into battle. She liked his hooded gaze, never mind that he was a barbarian, except in the yard earlier when he had spoken so beautifully.

Gentleman or barbarian? Spy or fantasy?

She giggled. It was preposterous. Years of cool, collected, directed precision, now all subsumed in intoxication over a highly unsuitable man. She wanted him to kiss her, it seemed, more than she had wanted anything else in her life.

He stepped up to the riser beneath her, filling the space with his broad shoulders and sheer size, filling every corner of her senses. She leaned forward. The hint of leather and pine still curled about him, not at all as a gentleman should smell and thoroughly delicious. She inhaled, filling her nostrils, then her head. He remained perfectly still, watching her.

She tilted forward and pressed her mouth to his.

She sighed, right there on the step in the near dark with her lips pressed to a man's, a stranger's for all intents and purposes.

He felt *so good*.

Her palm found the front of his coat. She could not seem to prevent her fingers from spreading and discovering hard muscle beneath fine wool. Ever so gently his mouth moved against hers, cupping her lower lip, and heat shot through her body like a sizzle of lightening. He kissed her back and she allowed it, the fitting of shape and texture, and the delectable heat curled into her belly—then swiftly, thickly, between her legs. A tiny gasp escaped her. He seemed to take it into his mouth. In sheer relief, upon a soft utterance of pleasure, Kitty opened hers.

A large, strong hand wrapped about her shoulder. In complete control, Lord Blackwood put her away from him.

Stomach twisting, Kitty opened her eyes.

She did not see on his face that which she expected. Instead his dark eyes seemed to shimmer with surprise and a hint of confusion, echoing the shock slipping through her body. He had not expected it either, the jolt of real desire, and something more. The awareness of it in his gaze weakened Kitty. Her shaking hand sought a stair rail, but none could be found. His attention followed her action, then abruptly returned to her face.

With one deliberate movement he drew her against his chest and covered her mouth with his.

This time the kiss was not a mere brushing of lips. This time his hand wrapped around her jaw to hold her close. He tilted his head and crossed her lips with his, and a rumble of pleasure came from his chest. She gripped his shoulders, a thrill of pure, sweet pleasure coursing through her. He was all hard male beneath her touch and she felt it to her toes. His tongue stroked her lips, coaxing to enter. She let him in, feeling him at the sensitive soft insides of her lips, then against her tongue. She gasped in breath and he caught her tongue with his and she *wanted* him.

Good heavens, *no*.

But resistance was futile. She might tell her hands to press at his arms now to push him away, but they would not obey. She might command her lips to seal themselves, but they adored the sensation of his tongue, masterly and damp, entering her. He wanted his tongue in her and she allowed him full liberty.

His palm slipped away from her face to spread on her back, trapping her to his chest and it was like heaven to be so trapped, to be wanted by a man. *This* man. And Kitty's muzzled head told her that perhaps these three years she had been lying to herself. Perhaps she had broken free of Lambert Poole's hold on her that night not because of the particular message she had read in Lord Blackwood's fathomless eyes but simply because she had wanted *him* to hold her instead—quite literally.

Madness. She was not a wanton. She was a coolheaded, rational being. This man was a flirt, a cretin, and she had nothing whatsoever in common with him except that they clearly seemed to enjoy kissing each other. She ran her hands along his arms, drunk on him now, the caress of his mouth carrying her along the insanity. She touched his face and everything inside her softened. The plane of his high cheekbone and hard jaw was perfection, taut and barely rough from the day's whisker growth.

"I wanted you to kiss me." She heard herself utter the words, breathless and trembling, unable to control anything. It was the whiskey, the dark stair, the man holding her to him. His eyes were so dark in the wavering shadows of candlelight and heavy with desire. He took her mouth anew and she gave herself up to the strokes of lips and tongue now turning her liquid. There was hot breath and more heat where his palm splayed upon her back, and her breasts and belly pressed against the hard wall of his chest, her fingertips gripping his arms. She wanted to feel even more, to make this secret indiscretion a moment to remember every night as she lay on her spinster's couch.

She shifted her hips.

Abruptly he released her.

Kitty's breaths came in little jagged bursts. She could do nothing but stare at the mouth that possessed such skill and the eyes that seemed none too pleased.

"Weel, nou ye've had yer kiss." His voice was rough. Rather, rougher than usual. He grasped her shoulder and put her away from him entirely. Peeling her hand from around his arm, he brought the candle between them and wrapped her fingers around the holder, then released both. The flame flickered too hot, but neither moved to widen the space between them.

Kitty's mouth would not close.

"If you did not wish to kiss me"—her voice sounded foreign—"you needn't have."

"Oh, A wished tae." He drew a thick breath, turned his head away and rubbed a palm across his face.

He pivoted and clattered down the stair. The kitchen door smacked shut behind him. Hand shaking about the candle-holder, Kitty sank back against the wall. She closed her eyes.

She would not regret it. Not until the morning. With the morning would come sobriety and a return to rationality. For now whiskey reigned, and the sensation of his lips on hers lingered, and the desire pulsing inside her was wonderfully welcome.

Tomorrow would be soon enough for regret.

Chapter 7

The following morning Kitty's head ached, her stomach hung like a sack of sour milk below her ribs, and her cheeks burned incessantly. But this paled in comparison to the news Emily announced on waking her.

"A portion of the stable roof collapsed beneath the weight of the snow and nearly injured Lord Blackwood's horse. It got off with a minor scratch, however."

"Good heavens!" Kitty sat up in bed. "Was anyone hurt?"

Emily peered at her. "What a peculiar question to ask, when I have said a horse escaped harm."

Kitty drew the covers off and turned away from her friend to climb from the bed. Emily was an odd duck, but no slow top.

"I only wondered how it came to be discovered. Ned, I must suppose."

"Lord Blackwood. He went out to feed the animals and the roof fell while he was within."

The peer who kissed like a god tended to his own cattle like a stable hand and was nearly injured doing so. Kitty rubbed the sleep from her eyes, her hands unsteady.

"We must be happy, then, that he and the horses are safe." She drew off the nightshift Mrs. Milch had lent her and shivered in the cold. She reached for her own fine linen garment and pulled on her stockings. Emily came to her to tie the stays about her ribs.

"The gentlemen and some men from the pub are seeing to the repairs now."

"I hope they are not under the influence of strong drink." Had he been the previous evening in the stairwell? She had been far too inebriated to judge. He said he'd wanted to kiss her, but he certainly hadn't looked it after he actually did so.

But, before . . . She must have imagined that look in his eyes. They hardly knew each other. Yet for a moment an uncanny awareness of something shared had glistened between them.

It was certainly all in her imagination. After all, her imagination had once convinced her that Lambert Poole loved her. Her imagination had made him into a man worthy of being loved.

"Mr. Yale, it seems, can hold his liquor well enough," Emily commented.

Kitty darted a glance over her shoulder. "I am sorry you must be trapped here with a gentleman you so dislike."

Emily secured the laces and reached for Kitty's petticoat and gown. "I do wish we had a button hook." She began fastening the wool. "I don't dislike him, Kitty. I disrespect him. The two are far different."

"Are they?" Kitty saw nothing in Lord Blackwood that she typically admired in gentlemen, no elevation of mind or character. Except something about him was not right. The pieces did not fit together. The steely glint in the backs of his eyes that had been there even as he'd said he wanted to kiss her did not suit the man he otherwise appeared. And how strange his expression when he had come in from the stable earlier and told her he would go out after the servants if she wished.

But perhaps that coldness was only a remnant of his tragedy. And perhaps Kitty was refining upon it far too much and making herself a complete ninny.

"Of course they are different, Kitty," Emily said soberly. "Liking has everything to do with character and disposition. Respect has to do with a gentleman's mode of life. But I shall get along well enough until we leave. Lord Blackwood has lent me another book," she finished as though that was all in the world a woman needed to be happy.

"More poetry?"

"A play in verse. Racine's *Phaedra*." Emily made quick work of fastening Kitty's gown and then Kitty went to the pitcher of water on the stand. She broke the thin crust of ice and washed her face.

The handsome barbarian with big shaggy dogs liked to read French theater. Her insides felt somewhat trembly too now.

"Has Mrs. Milch prepared breakfast yet?"

"Eggs again. We must make the bread for dinner tonight."

"You are determined to do so?"

"Of course."

"How is the road this morning? Has anyone seen the mail coach?"

"Mr. Yale reports that no one has passed yet."

No escape then from her foolish nerves and this unwise preoccupation, made considerably worse since she now knew far too much about him—his scent, the caress of his tongue, the hard contoured man-shape beneath coat sleeves and waistcoat. She could not think, could not organize her thoughts at all, it seemed, a thoroughly unprecedented state.

Being infatuated with a man at five-and-twenty felt absolutely idiotic. But perhaps it was not so singular. Her mother occasionally showed moderate giddiness over Lord Chamberlayne. Of course, Lord Chamberlayne was intelligent, a consummate gentleman, and a successful politician. While Lord Blackwood . . . had very large dogs.

She must be mad.

And so bread baking it would be.

Kitty stood before a wooden block in Mrs. Milch's kitchen, bent over a lump of dough as the inn mistress offered instruction on kneading. In a matter of days she would be sweeping floors and plucking chicken carcasses. Possibly feeding slop to the pigs if there were any pigs to be fed.

"One must press it like this, Mrs. Milch?" Emily queried, brow creased.

"No, miss. Like this. But the Quality shouldn't be making bread, I still say," she added damply. "As like, milady agrees with me."

"Oh, I haven't any feeling about it one way or the other." Kitty didn't care how she busied herself. At this point she would do anything to escape her confusion. The snowbound inn was closing in on her with merciless vigor, much as Emily's knuckles now dug into the dough.

She felt ill, betrayed by the spinsterish longings suddenly burst upon her. For over five years, since Lambert took her innocence and she began to hate him, she knew she would never marry. She was ruined to be a bride to a respectable gentleman, and as she could not provide children even if a man were to offer for her, she could not in good conscience accept. She'd told herself she did not want a husband. Men were not to be trusted. She would be perfectly happy living out her days with her mother as her closest companion, Lord Chamberlayne or no.

But Kitty could pretend no longer. In truth she had known that the night she determined to follow Emily into Shropshire. She'd left her mother and Lord Chamberlayne to settle matters between themselves because she did not wish to live with her mother her entire life. She wanted something else of life.

Her hands stilled, then slipped from the dough. She had not been honest with herself. Her infatuation with a man of the Earl of Blackwood's cut proved it.

She was tired of justifying her childhood mistake through sophistication and pretending to the world that she was glad to be spurned by so many among polite society. She was tired of the lonesome future she had envisioned for herself. Her heart ached for something else, something sweeter and finer. She *longed* to fall. Image shattered. Innocence regained in simple, unpremeditated happiness.

But a woman like her was not allowed to fall. A woman who had given away her most precious possession without benefit of marriage was, rather, propositioned and groped. She was kissed in dark stairwells, and the gentlemen who did the propositioning, groping, and kissing did not feel obligated to offer anything more. Anything respectable. Anything permanent. Anything that might fill the loneliness.

"Milady, you mustn't muss your skirts." Mrs. Milch lifted Kitty's hands and wiped them with a clean cloth with the delicacy of a lady's maid. "I never mind a bit of flour on me, but don't you be getting it on your fine silks and what have you's when there's Quality gentlemen about."

Kitty looked into the woman's droopy eyes and saw understanding. But that was impossible. Everything about this dreamlike sojourn in snowy Shropshire was impossible.

She cast her gaze to the kitchen doorway as though it were a portal for escape, like the open door of Emily's traveling carriage had seemed to her in London.

The earl appeared there.

Her entire body flushed with heat. She had always before

admired the unmarred visages of gentlemen who spent most of their time in town. Lord Blackwood's cheeks glowed with cold and exertion, and she revised her position. He was wonderfully tall and as thoroughly gorgeous as the night before by firelight during dinner and in the dark stairwell during her own private dessert. She *felt* like the girl he had called her, idiotically infatuated and wanting him to kiss her again more than she could bear.

"Guid day, leddies." He took them all in with a glance, then looked to the inn mistress. "Ma'am, yer husband begs ye set a kettle o tar on the fire for sealing the boards."

"Now the man's sending the Quality on his errands instead of Ned. Where's that boy got to?" Mrs. Milch released Kitty's hands.

"Gane tae the smithy tae retour the saw."

Emily looked up. "Have you finished the stable roof already?"

"Aye, miss. Moony haunds, as ye be at weeman's work here." He glanced at the dough-covered table and smiled.

Kitty had to look away. *Women's work*. He approved of ladies baking bread, she understood possibly three out of four words he spoke, yet his smile took her breath.

Oh, God, *what* was going on inside her? How could she swing from one extreme to the other?

"I am astounded at the difficulty of this task," Emily commented. "But Mrs. Milch is a very competent teacher after so many years laboring at it."

Kitty swallowed over her lumpy throat. "My lord, is y—"

His gaze shifted to her.

"—y-your—" Her tongue failed.

An exceedingly uncomfortable silence filled the kitchen.

His mouth quirked slightly to the side. Kitty could not spare a thought to care that Emily stared at her now, or that she had never stuttered before in her life. If only he would *talk* more and *look* less she might make it through this without embarrassing herself completely.

"Is your horse all right?" she managed beneath his dark regard.

"Aye, lass. Ma thanks." His expression remained pleasant as he broadened his attention again to include them all. He was a casual flirt. One might believe he had not in fact kissed her thoroughly on a stair the night before. But she knew his reputation, and he had no doubt kissed her because he imagined he knew hers. "Leddies, ye dae us all a fine service far the holidays."

"There'll be no goose," Mrs. Milch muttered.

"Who needs goose when fine ladies are about such noble work?" Mr. Cox announced at the earl's shoulder, casting a pleased glance about the chamber.

"There is nothing noble in baking bread, Mr. Cox," Emily stated. "The poor labor at such work and they are barely compensated for it."

"I have labored my whole life, Lady Marie Antoine," he said brightly, moving to Emily's side. "Yet I have never had the pleasure of baking bread with a lady. I beg to assist."

"Have you baked bread at all, sir?" She seemed truly curious.

"Why, no." He laughed.

"Then you'd best put on an apron as well." Mrs. Milch shook her head sorrowfully.

"You must remove your coat first," Emily instructed.

"Certainly not in the presence of ladies." Mr. Cox cast Kitty a playful grin and tied the cloth around his elegant coattails. "My lord, will you join me with our fair companions in this charming domestic task?"

Lord Blackwood shifted his booted feet at the threshold.

"A'll best be leaving that tae those mair fitted." He bowed, cast Kitty the swiftest and most enigmatic glance, and disappeared.

Kitty pulled in steadying breaths, every iota of her tingling nerves drawn to follow him.

"Mr. Cox," she spoke to fix her feet in place, "is Mr. Yale still in the stable?" She couldn't care less. She only wanted to know where the earl was going now. It was impossible. Grown women did not feel this way. But perhaps this was her punishment for the dishonest program she had pursued for so many years, no matter that the man she had helped bring to justice was in fact very bad.

"He has gone to the pub with the carpenter who helped us patch up that roof. Nasty business. Nearly caught Blackwood on the shoulder."

"He only said his horse was in the way of it," Emily said.

"He was grooming it." Mr. Cox set his fingertips to the dough. "Odd for a gentleman of his distinction to care for his own cattle, I say. But the nobility will have its eccentrics," he added with a confiding smile.

Emily pointed at the round of dough. "You must put the heels of your hands into it, Mr. Cox. Like that."

Kitty's heart pattered. She wiped her palms on a cloth.

"Will you excuse me?" she muttered. Mrs. Milch was sufficient chaperone for Emily, a chaperone like the one Kitty ought to have had in the stairwell the night before. Emily dug into the dough anew and Mr. Cox studied her actions. Mrs. Milch did not look away from the pot of sealant. Kitty fled.

She must escape the inn, if only for a few moments. She needed cold air in her lungs to clear her clouded head. It was vastly unwise to fixate on the Earl of Blackwood, his breathtaking jaw, his skillful caress.

In the parlor Ned stood with one of the dogs. The boy's head came up and something gold glimmered in his palm.

He grinned. "Sky's fair clear today, milady."

She could barely think to put together words. "It seems so." She went toward him. Distraction of this sort was exactly what she required.

The dog snuffled his hand.

"Are you feeding treats to the animals, Ned?" She tried to smile, but her lips felt wobbly like the rest of her.

"No, ma'am. It's only a trinket I found a fortnight since on the road down a'ways at Shrewsbury." His brows perched high under jutting hair. He turned his hand upward. A painted cameo covered his palm, a portrait set in a gold frame of a young woman with gold ringlets and a pleasingly dimpled cheek.

"How pretty she is, and how sad her beau must be to have lost it." Kitty smiled, nerves jittering recklessly. Distraction, it seemed, was not helping matters.

"Reckon." Ned tucked the cameo in his pocket, tugged his cap, and went with the dog out into the yard, where the earl had presumably gone returning to the stable. She could go out there and . . . *No.*

She would brave the icy rear stoop where she might press her fiery cheeks into a handful of snow to calm her heated nerves. Then perhaps she could throw herself into the snow entirely to cool the rest of her. She hurried toward the rear foyer for her pattens and cloak.

Lord Blackwood stood in the nook behind the stair, shoulders against the wall, one large hand covering his face. He dropped his arm, met her gaze, and a hard breath left him.

"My lord, what are you doing here?" An atrociously inelegant greeting. Now she had lost all propriety *and* civility. Falling, it seemed, would not be pretty.

"Catching ma breath, A think."

Low light slanted into the foyer; she could not clearly make out his expression. But she could sense him well enough. His entire person seemed to breathe of the outdoors, of rugged, untamed northern wilderness, which was profoundly silly since his estate was quite close to Edinburgh and anyway he mostly lived in London.

She stepped toward him; indeed, she could not prevent herself from doing so. He seemed to flatten his shoulders to the wall.

"It must have been dreadfully unpleasant work." She had nothing to say to him really. "Terribly cold. Did you go up on that roof?"

"Aye." His jaw looked tight. Kitty imagined tasting it. She should have done so last night. Foolish oversight. Her breaths shortened.

"I understand that you were in the stable when the accident occurred."

"Aye."

"You were tending to your horse?" How could she get closer without appearing ridiculously obvious? Her very skin tingled to touch his.

He nodded. "The lot of 'em."

"You were feeding the carriage horses as well? And the gentlemen's mounts too, I daresay." She could not do it subtly. But subtlety was often overrated. "Mightn't you have left that to Ned, rather?" She took another step forward, tilting her head back to look into his face, perfection of masculine form and shape.

"Aye." He was not smiling.

"But you did not."

"Nae." Beneath hooded lids, he was staring at her mouth again. Kitty could not halt herself; her hand moved seemingly of its own accord to his chest, as though she were allowed to do such a thing, as though ladies touched gentlemen in rear foyers beneath staircases every other day.

It felt right to do so. Frighteningly right.

As the night before when she had been about to kiss him, he remained perfectly still. She spread her fingers and sank her palm against his ribs. His heartbeat thumped quick and hard. A coil of anticipation shimmied up from her core to her very fingertips. She released a little breath.

"You are a man of few words, aren't you?" Her voice was crackly.

"Aye." His was deeper than she had heard it yet. His breaths were uneven beneath her hand.

"I—" She whispered over the lump of constricted anticipation in her throat. "I—I—"

"Ye whit, lass?" He barely spoke aloud.

She shifted her hand, sliding her fingertips beneath his waistcoat. With a sharp exhalation he grasped her shoulders and pulled her to him.

Kitty sighed. She'd wondered whether her drunken imagination invented the sensations she'd felt pressed to the firm wall of his body. Now she was sober and heady with them. She could barely form the words she'd been thinking since he had released her on the stair ten hours earlier.

"I—I wish to ask you a question."

She was slender and delicate in his hands, all curved lusciousness against his chest. Leam hadn't held a woman in too long, except the night before, when he'd held this woman far too long for his own good. Her eyes were feverishly bright now, spots of crimson high on her cheeks, so far from the pristinely elegant Londonite she was to society. In this inn, over the course of mere hours, she was coming apart, piece by piece, before his eyes. *In his hands.* The exquisite shell was breaking into tiny shards.

By God, he wanted no part of it.

Release her.

He bent his head. Her fragrance tangled in his senses. "Whit's that, lass?"

Release her, fool.

"Will you kiss me again?" She hadn't even the presence of mind to look into his eyes. "I want you . . . to." Her hot gaze upon his mouth nearly unmanned him. Nearly.

Nearly . . .

Entirely.

His hand slid over her shoulder, up the silken curve of her throat to cup her head.

"Dae ye nou?" His voice was husky. No surprise there. After that kiss last night he'd stood outside in the snow for an hour to relieve the tension in his body. It had not sufficed. Now she pressed herself up against him and as a woman of experience she must know perfectly well how he wanted considerably more than her kiss.

She nodded, her breasts rising heavily against his chest. "Quite dreadfully a lot."

There was still time to release her.

She did not look like a woman of experience. She looked like a girl, trembling and wide-eyed and not truly knowing what she asked. For years now Leam believed such a face of innocent desire could not be real. He had discovered at great cost to himself and a man he loved dearly that it was not real.

It seemed real upon this woman. She lifted her storm-cloud gaze to his and he got caught in its brilliant candor. He lowered his head, her mouth beckoning, full and shapely and all feminine beauty. The scents of wood smoke and cherries breathed through her parted lips, straight to his foolish poet's head and rigid man's groin. God, but she was perfection—as perfect as in the stairwell when it had taken every ounce of his considerable self-control to put her off—as perfect as that night three years ago when he first heard her speak, silken-smooth and quick-witted, and saw the cur's possessive hand at her elbow, Poole's proprietary eye.

"Just do it." Her voice was a mere utterance. "Just kiss me again. Please. Once."

A beautiful woman, begging for his kiss.

He brushed her soft lips. She sighed into him. He slipped his thumb along the delicate curve of her jaw.

Her hand shot up, gripped his neck, and pulled him against her.

He wrapped his arms around her and dragged her to him, as she wanted, as he had wanted since she'd walked into this damned inn. She kissed like a courtesan and a virgin at once, openmouthed and seeking, hungry yet oddly hesitant, and with little finesse. He had done this to her—robbed the exquisite of decorum. He was staggered by it, and by her lovely hands moving all over him, first his neck and shoulders, then his arms, chest, and beneath his coat. He sought the inside of her hot mouth with his tongue, tasting, sampling the softness he wanted to dive into. So soft, so hot. Dear God, she couldn't know what this did to a man.

He slipped the tip of his tongue into her, aroused beyond endurance, struggling to hold back. He could make her want what he wanted. But she was not for him, not this beauty whose rain-cool surface masked heated thundercloud eyes. Not that cyclone of confusion and mixed messages. Not for Leam ever again.

But by God she was flawless. He spread his hand around her porcelain cheek and jaw and with his thumb and forefinger urged her lips wider. She responded like clay to a master's touch, and he delved deep within. He stroked, encompassed in wet heat, and a gentle moan escaped the back of her throat. Her hands clutched his shirt.

He kissed her, drawing her lower lip between his teeth and caressing it with his tongue, then thrusting soft and deep again, and his palm slipped down the silken column of her neck, seeking, his blood running fast and hot. He had to touch her. Just once. Feel the beauty of her breasts wrapped in fine, snug wool he'd been struggling not to stare at for a day that seemed like an eternity. This was a mistake. He should peel her off him and tell her in no uncertain terms that they must not do this again.

He could not. But perhaps if he went too far, she would.

He covered her breast with his hand. She sucked in breath, stiffening. Then she sank into his touch, filling his palm with voluptuous beauty and his head with blaring trumpets warning that this was a grave error in judgment and he should run while he could.

"Lass—"

She attached her mouth to his, a sweet perfection of eager feminine heat. With his hand he gently urged her face away while his other fully cupped her sublime womanly body, her exquisite breast. By God, he simply could not take his hand off her.

Her lashes lifted, sooty layers of demure temptation revealing sky-gray pools swimming with need. Lips ripe and glittering parted, her breaths staggered. Leam swallowed with difficulty, his throat constricted, and gazed into heaven and hell at once. He knew that place of matched ecstasy and misery well. Too well in his memory, as though it were yesterday.

She reached up, spread her hand over his, and, securing his hold on her breast, moaned softly as her lashes dipped.

To the devil with memories.

He pressed her to the wall amid cloaks and coats and kissed her hard. Harder until memory fled with her submission to everything—to his hands on her breasts, his tongue along the sweet curve of her throat and in her mouth, his knee pushing hers apart. If Kitty Savege wanted him, who was the fool Scot to deny such a woman?

Chapter 8

Kitty wanted to crawl up him, to climb right inside him. By the way he was kissing her it seemed as though he wanted that too. His hands, large and strong, scooped up her back, his fingertips pressing in, shaping around her shoulder blades to hold her high and tight to his chest. But she wanted them back on her breasts. It made her weak to be held so, weak with an aching so intense she could barely breathe.

She could not seem to control herself. Control had been her weapon, her costume, her masquerade for years. Now his touch was dissolving her into sheer helplessness. His mouth, his hands—she could not get enough. The more he kissed her, touched her so intimately, the more she ached for him.

It began to alarm her.

She gripped her hands in his hair and tore her lips from beneath his.

"I—"

"*Goddamn*, wumman. Dae ye wish tae strip ma skull?" But his deep voice laughed and his gaze covered her face, a look of ravenous wonder upon it. He was beyond handsome, the hollow plane of cheek and the dark eyes that seemed to hold unspoken words.

"Not your skull."

Good heavens, she'd said it aloud.

He breathed hard, his hands trapping her to his chest, forcing her to feel him so completely with every bit of her body, most especially and thrillingly that part of him against her belly. His mouth hovered above hers, a temptation to do wicked deeds now and thoroughly. She had never felt this way, so desperate and so needy. Never.

He bent and captured her lips somewhat roughly and she clung to him. His kissed the corners of her mouth, then her jaw.

She struggled for speech, her voice barely audible. "This is happening too fast."

"Aye."

He did not ask her what she meant. He knew. She knew. She stretched her neck to give him leave to continue touching her for as long as he wished. *Forever, please dear God.* She was trembling and aching and she *craved* him.

Perhaps if she argued, he would end it as he had the night before, despite her repeated advances. Her body did not know her mind, but her words might still be of some use.

"This is because you held me yesterday morning on the stoop after I slipped. You should not have."

His mouth was open and hungry on her throat, casting perfect shivers into her breasts and lower.

"It wadna cut ony ice."

She gripped his neck, struggling to drag him closer, desperate for more of this touching, kissing, total insanity. "What does that *mean*?"

"A near well kissed ye than."

"Yesterday *morning*? But—"

He cut off her words with his mouth. They could not be closer, her body flattened between his and the wall, her fingers in his thick, silky hair. He caressed her everywhere, as though he must touch every part of her. Her gown rose to her neck, practical for winter travel and wretchedly impractical for being embraced by a man in this manner. But no man had ever before kissed her like this and she hadn't known she would encounter Leam Blackwood in a Shropshire inn during a snowstorm, thus she had planned her wardrobe poorly.

"You near well kissed me," she repeated upon a sigh.

"A near well called oot that blast cur Poole three years aby for treating ye like a doxy." His voice came thickly against her neck, his hands on her breasts.

Kitty choked. "*Oh, my God.*" She groaned, feeling him with her hands, the tight peaks of her breasts he caressed, her thighs around his. She did not believe it. "Don't say it. It is not true."

"Ye ken 'tis true."

"*No,*" she whispered, because it could not be true. Such things did not happen. She had imagined it. He had. Men and women did not speak to each other without words. Not such momentous things. Certainly not a man and a woman so unalike in all matters of import. Except this. *This was madness* and every part of her wanted him to keep touching her and making her need with glorious abandon.

He cinched his hands beneath her arms and pressed the hard muscle of his thigh upward between her legs. She moaned softly, delirium skimming through her body.

He spoke above her lips. "Ye shoudna been wi' him."

"I should not have." But to find sufficient evidence to damn Lambert, she had remained in his company. Until that night when this man had silently given her courage to break free. *The night he remembered as she did?*

Her throat thickened. "With whom should I have been instead?"

His big hands slipped down her waist to surround her hips, and he shifted her fully onto his thigh.

"Dear heaven." She scrabbled for air, sensation sweet and forbidden drawing tightly through her. Her skirts tangled about his legs, her fingers gripping his shoulders as he pleasured her so easily. He smoothed a palm upward to cup her breast. With thumb and fingers he teased the taut peak through layers of clothing, his breathing unsteady. Kitty wanted his hands beneath the fabric. She rocked against him, the ache building in her unendurable, and she had never felt so close to ecstasy. She had never felt like this at all, so encouraged, so *touched*.

A footfall sounded nearby. Somehow in the haze of pleasure she heard it. So too did the earl, apparently. He released her and without a moment's pause grabbed a cloak, then grasped her shoulder and pivoted her to face the door. She nearly toppled over. The cloak came over her back, his hands steadying around her arms, and he spoke quick and quiet at her ear.

"Begging yer pardon, lass. A've nae answer for ye."

"My lord," the innkeeper said jovially behind her. "And my lady too. Stepping out for a breath of air? It's a fine day after such a storm."

Kitty felt as though she'd been dashed with ice water. She fumbled with the clasp.

"Yes, Mr. Milch. But I don't suppose I shall get very far, shall I?" Just as with the Earl of Blackwood. Her cheeks burned.

"Watch your step, ma'am. And thanks to you, my lord, for repairing the boards on that roof. Sorry I was that you nearly saw much worse there."

"'Twas but a wee fix." He had moved away. Kitty was

afraid to look. She hated being afraid, and she hated this lack of control. Most of all she hated not understanding what was happening to her. Good Lord, she had embraced him quite scandalously in full view of anyone who might walk by. She wasn't thinking.

She *never* did not think. More importantly, if she had kissed him in a more private location he might still be kissing her now.

She yanked her hood up to hide her face, swung around, and brushed past the innkeeper and the earl. She could not return to the kitchen. Perhaps the outdoors would offer her sanity she could not find within.

Leam pulled his coat off the hook and shoved his arms into it. With a quick nod to the innkeeper he pushed through the rear door. He would slog through the snow to the pub, find Yale, and dig a path all the way to Liverpool if need be.

The cold hit his face like a woman's slap. The Welshman and the carpenter had made an inelegant trail through the snow. Leam followed, slipping and stumbling and barely noticing his progress.

She'd said it was happening too fast, and Leam couldn't agree more. Nothing good could come of putting his hands all over Kitty Savage, only an aching cock and a hard slap when he went too far, which he was bound to do if she kept pressing herself up against him. By God, he wasn't made of ice, although stone seemed appropriate enough right about now.

But perhaps she would not slap him. Perhaps she would . . .

It didn't matter what she would do. She was not for him. Not a woman of ice on the surface and fire within. Not any woman who made his heart slam inside his ribs, his mouth go dry, and his head start rhyming couplets.

Dear God, how much of a fool could one man be?

He entered the pub, demanded a pint, and drank it in a

swallow. Pushing the glass back toward the tavern keep, he gestured with a jerk of his chin for another, and finally looked about.

Low-ceilinged, with narrow windows and plenty of dark nooks, it was the sort of place well suited to knavery. He might hang his head in shame if he cared any longer about Colin Gray and the damned Club. Everything he'd learned as an agent, every lesson in studying his surroundings swiftly and efficiently, he had forgotten already. Kitty Savege held his entire attention now.

He pressed his eyes shut and blindly took up the glass again.

Dear God, he really wanted her. And the more she touched him with eager innocence, the more difficult it became for him to believe she had been Poole's mistress.

He scrubbed his hand across his face. He knew better. He knew much better. In London, rumor had raged through the summer and into fall that she had brought criminal evidence against her former lover to the Board of the Admiralty because he had once scorned her. Listening to the gossips and knowing what he'd already known, Leam hadn't had any reason to disbelieve that rumor.

Taking a heavy breath, he opened his eyes. Yale lounged in a rickety wooden chair, watching him. Leam straightened and the young Welshman stood and sauntered over, set his tankard on a table, and gestured him from the bar.

"I prefer to stand," Leam said gruffly.

"Can you for much longer?"

"Can you ever?" He pushed away from the bar and took a seat. The table was tacky, the place smelled of stale ale and sawdust, and something nasty crunched beneath his feet.

"After the scolding you gave me last night, I've had but this one glass."

"You remember the scolding?"

"I've the jaw to remind me." He did, a bluish-black mark coloring his chin. He lifted his half-empty pint, silver eyes narrowed. "Happy Christmas, old chap."

Leam scanned the pub's patrons, a half-dozen men in caps and rough trousers, farmers and shopkeepers who looked like they'd spent half their lives on these benches.

"It's Cox."

Yale's expression did not alter. "Your interested party?"

"I believe so. And I think he's behind that faulty stable roof. But I still haven't the foggiest why, or why he's made himself plain to us."

"P'raps he hoped to hide here and I routed him out. Or perhaps he simply admires your high fashion and is mad with jealousy. Quite a natty fellow, isn't he?"

"Goddamn, Wyn." Leam shoved back his chair and stood.

"Huffing off again? And so swiftly this time."

"I huffed off swiftly last night as well, which you would recall if you hadn't been immersed in a barrel of whiskey."

Yale smiled. "And where is the fair Lady Katherine now?"

"Far and away from me as she may be, I pray."

"I *prithee*."

Leam ground his molars.

Yale crossed his arms over his chest. "Well, you might as well get it right if you're going to go off spouting verse."

"That was not verse. It was an actual prayer." He passed his hand across his face again. He still tasted her on his tongue. It was hopeless, the need rising within him as swift and sure as the panic.

Physical exertion might do it. He would shovel more snow. Perhaps if he exhausted himself he wouldn't have sufficient energy to lust after her. Or if he continued to lust—a more likely scenario—he wouldn't be able to lift his arms to do anything about it. She was curved and hot and he wanted to tear that damned green gown off her and pin her beneath him, to a mattress, the floor, any surface would do.

More shoveling it must be.

Yale hummed something under his breath, clicking a blunt fingernail against his glass.

"Blackwood, old man."

"What?" he snapped.

"The tavern keep says there's a very pretty farm girl who works the place every few nights." He sounded far too casual. "He assures me she is expected this afternoon, despite the snow. Quite punctual when fine gentlemen pass through town, don't you know." Now he grinned.

"Wyn."

"Leam?"

"Go to hell."

"I'll save you a seat."

Leam set his palms down and leaned into the table. "What do you know of Lambert Poole?"

"Only common knowledge, that in July he was stripped of his estates and exiled for supplying arms to insurgents and attempting to bribe Admiralty officials into treason." Yale met his gaze squarely. "And that three years ago you looked into him rather assiduously."

Leam drew back slowly. What he did not know about his closest companion of the past five years occasionally astounded him.

"If your interest in Poole now concerns Katherine Savege, Leam, it's your own business, of course. But if you think it has got something to do with Cox you will tell me, won't you?"

"Why wouldn't I?"

"Because you've quit the Club." His eyes looked flinty in the dim light. "But the mantle is difficult to cast off, is it not?"

"For some, no doubt." Leam gestured toward him.

The Welshman laughed, loosening the tension corded between them. "Well, I haven't anything better to be doing, after all." He leaned back in his chair, abruptly a study of elegant ease.

Leam had no further use for the spy. He left the pub. The dogs bounded to him across the thick expanse of white street, young Ned in their wake. He wasn't more than three or four years older than Jamie, but the lad with his toothy smile looked nothing like the sober-mouthed child Leam would meet at Alvamoor if he ever left this village.

"I run them to the butcher's, gov'nor. Got us a nice young goose for Christmas Eve dinner." He lifted a wrapped parcel, his reddened cheeks shining with pride. Leam hadn't any idea if Jamie ever smiled like that when he wasn't around. Leam's youngest sister, Fiona, said he was a happy boy. Leam had never wanted to hear. He'd never wanted to remember. But now he was going home for good and he would be obliged to remember every hour of every day.

At this moment he was trapped. Not only in a snowbound village. Trapped between the life he cared nothing about and the life he had avoided for half a decade, the place where his wife's and his brother's bodies rested not six feet from each other in a massive marble mausoleum.

He did not wish to ponder it deeply. Never again deep ponderings, he had vowed. It would be easier to let himself think ceaselessly about Kitty Savege, to caress and seduce her—or perhaps more accurately to allow her to seduce him as she seemed intent upon doing—and spend his holiday in a limbo of hedonistic captivity.

"Ned, I've two questions for you."

"Yessir, gov'nor." He fluffed the shaggy fur atop Hermes's head, and the big dog leaned into him, setting the boy to teetering on the icy path.

"What can you play on that fiddle of yours?"

"Anything you like, milord." He smiled wide.

"Good. My second question: Is there a man in this town who might know something about smithing gold or silver?" He had returned the cashmere muffler and coins to Cox earlier in the day, watching his reaction. Cox had thanked him affably but said nothing of the broken gold chain still in Leam's pocket. It could prove useful to know what might have hung on such a chain, information Cox clearly did not wish to share.

"Sure is, gov'nor. Old Freddie Jones. Used to be a watchmaker in Shrewsbury till he lost three fingers to an angry cow." His grin never wavered. Leam could not help returning it.

"Can you take me to him?"

"Yessir. Now?"

Anything to avoid a beautiful woman with amorous intent. At least until he cooled off a bit.

"Now is perfect."

They set off along the street through drifts up to the boy's thighs, Ned chattering the entire way about his master and mistress, Lady Emily's coachman and the carpenter who had both helped mend the roof, Freddie Jones, and any number of other villagers. Leam listened carefully, for the moment content to be doing what he'd done for five years. And if his boots were ruined because of his need to prepare himself for his next encounter with Kitty Savage, that would be what he best deserved.

Lord Blackwood did not return to the inn. Mrs. Milch planned dinner for five o'clock, remaining with Emily in the kitchen all day, leaving Kitty to wallow in confusion and frustrated intent. As she was a woman of action, those emotions had never been her fond companions.

She set about decorating the place for Christmas. Clipping bits of low-hanging branches from an old pine at the edge of the yard, she tied them with green and white ribbons. A basket of cones arranged around a thick candle with a gold cord purloined from her reticule made a lovely centerpiece. She was considering what might be done to rearrange the furniture in the sitting room for greater comfort when hushed voices came to her from the rear foyer.

"It's quite precious, Milch." Mr. Cox's tone seemed abnormally tight. "I shan't be happy to discover that one of your people here has taken it."

The innkeeper made a coughing sound. "Well now, sir, you needn't be worrying. If you dropped it about here Mrs. Milch is bound to find it while she's cleaning and it'll be restored to you right and tight."

"It had better be, or I'll make things very uncomfortable for you, Milch."

"Now, now. That won't be necessary. Could be you lost it before you arrived?"

"I did not." But the gentleman didn't seem quite as adamant, rather more anxious now. Footsteps sounded in the corridor. Kitty busied herself arranging cushions. Mr. Cox emerged into the chamber.

"How convenient for you to come along, sir, for I am contemplating shifting these chairs about but they are too heavy for me to move."

Kitty had never before witnessed a man so obviously shake off anxiety and don an amiable façade.

"I would be happy to assist you, my lady."

They accomplished the remainder of her project easily enough. She thanked him and went to her bedchamber to straighten her hair and don the single accessory she possessed, a pair of ear bobs she carried in her traveling purse. Her mother had given her the pearls set in antique gold during her first season in town. Kitty's father apparently had chosen them three years earlier, on her sixteenth birthday, not understanding that they were too mature for a girl.

Now she understood better why her mother had not allowed the gift. Her father's mistress had chosen them, the woman Kitty never once met but who shared his life for thirty years.

Kitty fiddled with the ear bobs between her fingertips. Lord Blackwood said she should not have been with Lambert. He assumed she had been Lambert's mistress, as everyone did. They were not wrong, to a degree. She had given herself to Lambert Poole when she was foolishly young and in love, and then again when she sought information that would ruin him. She had made her spinster's bed; she could be no respectable gentleman's bride now. But her behavior with a barbaric Scot made it perfectly clear that she needed a man in her life.

No. She needed that man. A man wholly unsuitable for her in every manner except one in which he suited her better than she had ever imagined possible. Hurried and unsatisfying, her experiences with Lambert had not prepared her for Leam Blackwood. Beneath the Scot's heated gaze and strong hands she felt as helpless as the bird Ned had brought home for dinner, and just as easily consumed.

Innocent . . . as she had been when she first met Lambert—not during her first season in society, but years before that, at the age of fifteen, in Barbados. At that time her father's mistress had taken precedence in his life. Kitty's mother sought to win him back and she had not wanted her daughter to witness the struggle. Conveniently, the earl was rusticating his eldest son for yet another occasion of unfilial behavior. Aaron went along with his twin as always, and Kitty and her governess were sent too.

Lambert, managing his father's neighboring plantation, came to Kitty in secret, encouraging her to sneak away from her governess to be with him. Aaron soon discovered it and brought it to an end, and Kitty was sent home to England heartbroken, not believing what Aaron told her—that Lambert hated Alex and only wished to use her dishonorably. Four years later, after their family emerged from mourning the earl's death, Kitty finally made her bows to society and met Lambert again in London. He pretended to still love her. She believed his promises and she finally gave her innocence to him.

But in all of that, in the tumult of girlish infatuation, she had never felt the heady confusion and sheer, unrelenting desire she did now.

She set the pearl earrings in place, smoothed her tired skirts, and for the hundredth time that day tried not to think of the earl's words, that he did not know who she should have been with, that he had nearly called out Lambert three years earlier at that ball. Upon what grounds she could not guess, and it made her stomach flip over. He had adored his wife and remained faithful to her in refusing to again marry. Society accounted him an incorrigible flirt, but not a philanderer; he did not engage in indiscriminate affairs. He would not take full advantage of her.

In the corridor Mr. Yale appeared, trailed by a wolfhound.

"My lady." He bowed. "I understand you are to thank for the holiday aspect of our surroundings below. You are all graciousness."

"Sir, we stand upon the most brief acquaintance, I realize—"

"And yet one feels as though we have all known one another an age," he finished with his slight smile.

"I suppose there is a sense of familiarity due to our remarkable circumstances." A familiarity that had encouraged her to wrap her arms and mouth around a stranger in the alcove beneath where she now stood.

"No doubt."

"Will you cease teasing Lady Emily?"

His brow lifted. "Ah, a champion arises for Marie Antoine."

"Do not imagine you can flummox me, Mr. Yale. I have two brothers and both are masters at plaguing me."

"I know that you can hold your own in company a great deal more exalted than mine."

Kitty's tongue felt dry. Everyone knew of her involvement in Lord Poole's exile. It would never be forgotten.

"Will you treat her civilly, please, sir? She is young and bookish and hasn't the knack for the regular concourse of ladies and gentlemen."

He studied her a moment, in his face intelligence and thought. Kitty could not but wonder again how he and the earl had come to be such close companions.

He took her hand and bowed over it, this time deeply.

"It will be my pleasure to abide by your wishes, my lady." But his eyes twinkled, mischief just beneath the surface.

She smiled. "Really, sir. You could at least—"

Boots tread upon the stair and the dog's tail set up a racket slapping against the wall. Lord Blackwood entered the corridor.

"Back so late, Blackwood? Your animals returned hours ago."

"Flirting wi' the leddy, Yale?" He looked perfectly at ease and not at all like he had kissed her out of her senses that morning.

"I wouldn't dream of it." Mr. Yale released her hand and moved toward the stair. "Leaving that to a better man than I, old chap." He descended.

The earl set his hooded gaze on Kitty and she could not

bear the lazy caress, not after seeing something so different in his eyes when he had held her. But she must pass by him to go downstairs.

Silence stretched. She fidgeted.

"This is extraordinarily awkward and not at all pleasant," she muttered, entirely bereft of every social grace and attitude of comportment.

The corner of his very talented mouth twitched. "Than A'm tae take it ye winna be casting yerself at me again?"

"Oh, good heavens." Her face flamed. "You haven't any civility at all, have you?"

He laughed outright. Amid her complete consternation, and no little shame over her thorough hypocrisy, Kitty had the urge to laugh as well.

"Well, you needn't be so plain speaking," she insisted, hiding her smile. "I am exceedingly mortified." And still exceedingly in need of his hands on her. Simply looking at him made her hot and a little hungry.

"Scots be a practical folk, lass."

"I've heard that. But I had never seen it in action before and frankly wish I hadn't still."

"Forgie a puir fellow, than." He bowed, never releasing her gaze.

"For precisely what? No! Don't answer that." She covered her face with a hand, an action she had never, ever once affected. But her palm seemed stuck to her nose. She was falling apart. "Good Lord, I haven't any idea what to do or say now."

Through her fingers she caught a glimpse of his eyes glimmering with pleasure.

"Mrs. Milch has called dinner early," she mumbled. "Country hours for the holiday, I daresay." She moved forward, entirely tongue-tied and perfectly, gloriously alive beneath her skin. It felt so good to laugh inside, like a girl again, the girl she had put behind her at far too young an age.

She passed him. He grasped her arm, barely a touch that ground her to the spot like a Chinese candle planted in earth, bursting with fire.

"Lass." His voice was unmistakably husky. "A winna take it amiss if ye chuise tae cast yersel at me again."

Delicious weakness spilled through her. She tilted her gaze up.

"You will stare at my mouth quite distractingly often, won't you?" she said breathlessly.

"A canna seem tae nae."

She was trembling in his touch. She could do nothing for it. He bent his head, his mouth mere inches from hers.

She whispered, "You are not being consistent, my lord."

"Naither be ye, lass."

Kitty swallowed around the lump of courage in her throat. "What do we do now?"

He paused, then: "Whitiver ye wish."

She gulped in air, drew away, and hurried down the steps. She did not know exactly what she wished, only that for the first time in an age she looked forward to the next minute, the next hour. She felt like a girl awaiting her first Christmas. Like a gift, wrapped up, waiting to be opened by the Earl of Blackwood.

Chapter 9

Nothing had happened between Kitty and the Earl of Blackwood at that masquerade ball three years earlier. Nothing of any rational substance. Yet he remembered it as something significant. And it had changed Kitty's life, a life set on a single, wretched track until that moment.

Five years earlier, after Lambert took her innocence, then told her she must be content to have him as a lover but not a husband, Kitty had taught herself to spy. For the sake of revenge. To satisfy her angry soul.

In society she did not hang upon his sleeve. Rather, she made it a habit to remain at a slight distance from him in company, straining her ear to hear his conversation, especially hushed conversation with gentlemen. When he moved through a ballroom or parlor, she followed discreetly. She believed herself infinitely clever; she was collecting information. A man such as he—who used an innocent girl the way he had used her—must have other secrets at least as dishonorable.

His secrets were in fact considerably more dishonorable.

She redoubled her efforts.

When he noticed her doggedness, she allowed him to believe she still harbored hopes of marriage. He mocked her. On occasion he even bragged, revealing more than he should and making her despise herself that she had once admired such vanity and arrogance. Occasionally he propositioned her, finding her in private, making certain they would not be disturbed. She bore his embraces so that she could gain access to his pockets, his billfold, even once his private apartments.

Endeavoring to appear sincere, she suggested to him that perhaps she would find herself in an interesting condition, then he must wed her, to which he replied that were that to occur it already would have, that she was deficient, and that he certainly would not continue to meet her privately otherwise. She submitted to a secret examination by a physician to prove her determination to him; what she learned there hurt nearly more than she could bear. But the hope of revenge masked the pain. All for the cause of revenge.

She had been very clever. Very proud. And very cold.

Then, in her twenty-third year, it came to an end. The night she made the acquaintance of a cretin of a Scottish lord. A very handsome cretin. A cretin with dark, fathomless eyes. In a ballroom filled with costumed revelers, the earl's gaze seemed to say to her what her heart had told her for years already—that she was better than vengeance, that she must release the past and allow herself to live again.

Moments later, beneath her breath and with perfect poise, she told Lambert she was finished with hating him or caring about anything he did. And since then she had been free, until six months ago when he tried to hurt Alex and she finally ruined him.

Now, settled into a soft chair in the parlor of the Cock and Pitcher, she studied the Earl of Blackwood as she had once studied Lambert. The draperies were drawn against the cold night without, candles glimmering and firelight filled the chamber with a warm glow, the aromas of cinnamon and wine tangling in the warm air. She spoke with the others, even the earl on occasion. But, using her old skills, she listened to him almost exclusively, and watched.

She noticed interesting things.

As the evening progressed and dinner became tea, then more whiskey for the gentlemen, his gaze upon Mr. Yale altered. At first it grew watchful. Then concerned. Mr. Yale exhibited no change except perhaps a more relaxed air as he sipped his spirits.

Emily and Mr. Milch produced a dish of brandy with raisins floating in it. The concoction was set aflame and a game of snapdragon ensued during which Kitty burned two fingertips and the earl did not take part but seemed unusually pensive, if such a man could be said to think deeply.

Kitty felt like a spy, or what she imagined a spy might feel like. But this time no sticky discomfort accompanied her covert attentiveness, no niggling sense that this activity did not respect her, that she pursued her basest urges in such an endeavor.

It seemed remarkable that lust did not now rouse the guilt that vengeance once had.

Or perhaps not merely lust.

As he had three years ago, now he shifted his regard to her through the fire-lit chamber, his eyes dark with a mystery that should not be there, but still she saw it. She feared lust did not suffice to explain her feelings, which did not make any sense at all; she knew nothing of him.

From his spot on the floor between the dogs, a grinning Ned set bow to strings, fiddle trapped between chin and shoulder. With a glass of wine and the earl's gaze warming her blood, Kitty smiled. Sunk in a soft chair, she felt like a pampered cat curled up before the fire being watched by a dog. A dog with unclear intentions and a gorgeously firm jaw.

"Aha!" Mr. Cox exclaimed. "We shall have music to celebrate the birth of Our Lord and Savior tonight. And singing. We must have singing." His bright blue eyes smiled, but with an odd glitter that seemed unnatural as they darted back and forth between her and the earl.

"Will ye sing for us, Lady Kath'rine?" the Scot said.

"She never sings." Emily had eschewed spirits tonight, and now seemed intent upon her book but happy enough in company.

"She did at one time, lass. Like a lark."

Kitty could say nothing. That night at the masquerade ball after turning off Lambert, she had sung. He stood beside her turning pages as she played, whispering that she would regret her decision and come back to him eventually. After that night, she had not been able to sing again.

Emily poked her nose up. "Why don't you sing now, then?"

"I haven't the feeling for it any longer."

"It does not require feeling, Kitty, only the proper vocal apparatus and a suitable chest cavity."

"I am continually astounded at the accomplishments of ladies," Mr. Cox put in, but again an odd note tinted his voice. "They sing, dance, paint with watercolors, speak French and Italian, embroider, and perform all number of domestic tasks. Why, if I had a wife I would give her roses and chocolates every day in thanks for such bounteous talent and effort."

"Rather expensive habit that would become," Mr. Yale said, unwrapping a pack of cards.

Cox chuckled, peculiarly brittle. "Ah, but she would deserve it." His gaze darted to the earl, then away.

"Why don't you have a wife, Mr. Cox?" Emily asked. "You must be thirty. Don't tradesmen like yourself seek early in their careers to marry daughters of impoverished nobles and assure a connection within society that can be useful to their business interests?"

Mr. Yale smiled with undisguised pleasure.

Kitty sat forward. "What my friend means to say—"

"It's quite all right, Lady Katherine. I don't mind it at all, and I suspect she has the right of it." Mr. Cox darted another glance across the parlor. "I've been traveling in the Americas for several years now and haven't had the opportunity to look about me for a suitable life's partner."

Emily's brow beetled. "Lord Blackwood, you were married, were you not? You even have a son."

Kitty's heart tripped.

"Aye."

"What was marriage like?"

In the silence the cards cracked as Mr. Yale's fingers split them, and the fire snapped.

"I mean to say, my father wishes me to marry shortly and I haven't the taste for it at all." Emily's pretty face seemed so sincere. Kitty could not rescue her, or the earl. She wanted too much to hear his response. "I think it might be unexceptionable to be married to a person one liked. But I wonder what it would be like to be wed to a person one does not care for."

"A wretched stew, I should say." Mr. Yale stacked the cards.

Emily set her book down. "I should too."

Kitty could not bear it that her friend's pretty green eyes had dimmed.

"I believe that is the first time I have heard the two of you agree on anything." She forced a smile. "How lovely. Just in time for Christmas."

Mr. Yale bowed. "Your servant, ma'am."

Emily did not reply. Kitty wrapped her fingers around her hand.

"Who wants a game?" Mr. Yale brandished the deck.

"It is Christmas, sir," Emily said in a rather dull voice. "Kitty, you will mind it, won't you, gambling tonight?"

"Not at all. I shall play happily." Not happily. But Emily needed distraction from her worries. "Would you like me to go retrieve your purse so that you can join us?"

"No. I shall do so, and yours as well." She stood and went up the stairs.

"Cox, will you make our fourth?" Mr. Yale stood.

"Afraid I'm done in for the night, sir. What of my lord? I suspect he plays well." Again that strangely anxious glint directed at the earl.

Mr. Yale scoffed, moving into the dining area. "Too well. I'd rather have a groat in my pocket at the end of the evening." He arranged the chairs about the table. "But if it must be."

"Grand." Mr. Cox bowed. "My lady, gentlemen, I bid you a fine Christmas."

He went to the steps quite swiftly and up, as though in a hurry.

Kitty frowned—Emily was still above, and alone. She moved to follow him. The earl lifted a hand to stay her and set his foot to the stair. Emily appeared on the landing just as Mr. Cox reached it. He smiled, this time appreciatively.

"Good night, Lady Marie Antoine."

She nodded and they passed each other. Lord Blackwood came off the step and Kitty released a breath.

Emily went to the playing table and set their purses on it. "I would like Lord Blackwood as my partner."

"A surprise, to be sure," Mr. Yale murmured.

"I shall refuse to play if the two of you continue in this manner."

"Kitty," Emily said, "Lord Blackwood is widely accounted an extraordinarily fine card player. Even I know that. Yet I have never heard a word said about Mr. Yale's playing abilities. It would be foolish not to wish to partner the earl."

"Ma thanks, maleddy," he said with a grin, but his gaze flickered again to the stair.

Kitty sank into the chair beside her friend, her knees like water. She mustn't think it meant anything. A true gentleman would protect ladies even if they were not his to protect by any right other than sheer mishap upon the snowy road. But she had not known he was a true gentleman, certainly not by the way he kissed her.

"Well there's a sight I like." Mr. Milch entered from the kitchen, eyes bleary. "Ned, your mother's wanting you home." The boy popped up and the innkeeper lifted a thick hand. "Happy Christmas, milords and ladies. My Gert sends her wishes as well." He retreated through the door.

"See you in the morning, then, gov'nor?" The boy's toothy grin flashed up at the earl.

The nobleman laid his hand on Ned's shoulder. "A'm coonting oan it, lad. Nou be aff wi' ye."

Ned scurried into the kitchen and the door swung shut.

Mr. Yale proffered the deck to Emily. "Will you take the first deal, ma'am?"

She distributed the cards. Warmth from the huge fire curled through the chamber, doors and shades closed tight to the cold without, and through a crack in the draperies the sparkling night shone dark. Lord Blackwood took a seat beside Kitty and she allowed herself to look at his hands as he took up his cards. Large hands, and beautifully capable of all sorts of things.

He wanted her to cast herself at him again. She was not a woman of loose morals, no matter what the gossips said. Naïvely she had given herself to Lambert in love—in what she had thought to be love. But Lambert Poole had never made her heart race by simply sitting beside her. She had never watched his hands and imagined them on her. She had never watched his hands at all.

They played cards. All went well for some time, except for Kitty's nerves strung end-to-end. Points were counted and Emily laid down the final trick.

"My lord," she said, "did your brother fall in battle?"

The earl did not look up from his hand. "Nae, miss."

Slowly Mr. Yale slewed his gaze across the chamber to the foyer. Kitty followed. No one stood there, but a cool filter of air seemed to twine about her now. She did not believe in ghosts, but Emily would persist in speaking of one.

"That is a pity," Emily said. "I understand many soldiers succumbed to disease, especially in Spain."

"He wisna in Spain when he passed, maleddy."

Mr. Yale laid down a card. The earl placed his on the table. Kitty followed.

"Our hand, my lord." Emily's brows lifted. "Then where did he perish?"

"In Lunnon, miss. 'Twas a duel that teuk him."

She blinked behind gold-rimmed spectacles. "I do hope his opponent was duly punished."

He regarded her for a moment, then his mouth crept up at one edge. But there was no pleasure in the smile.

"He wis."

Mr. Yale leaned back in his chair and seemed to contemplate the empty glass at his elbow.

"Blackwood, old chap," he said in an oddly slow voice, "you have emptied my pockets."

"Wadna be the first time."

Mr. Yale stood. "I'm wrapped up for the evening, then." He bowed. "Ladies, I bid you adieu on this holiest of nights." He went upstairs.

Emily counted coins. "We did quite well for ourselves, my lord. How gratifying, although I suppose game is like that, of course, or otherwise sensible people would not be so taken with it. My father and mother certainly are, but they are not sensible and I believe they do it mostly to appear fashionable." Her brow furrowed more deeply than usual. She stood. "Kitty, Mr. Yale's departure has effectively ended our play. Will you go to bed now?"

Kitty's stomach leaped with jitters.

"I will be up shortly, Marie." The reply of a Jezebel, but an hour sitting beside him had made its mark on her senses. Emily peered at the contents of her purse with apparent displeasure and went up.

Lord Blackwood seemed to study the empty stair while Kitty's insides did pirouettes. Slowly his gaze came to her.

"Whit are ye doing wi' that bairn, lass?"

So much said in so few words. He was master at it. Kitty now understood that. Fools did not speak succinctly, wise men did. Kitty had few unwed friends in society. Most mothers did not allow their daughters her company.

"I realize it must seem that Lady Emily and I have little in common. But she is not a child, only young and disinterested in niceties. And she is concerned about her visit with her parents. They intend to betroth her to a most unsuitable gentleman."

"Dae they?"

"One of their cronies. Not an appropriate match for a girl like Emily. So you see that distresses her. But she is quite lovely under normal circumstances." Kitty paused, during which time his gaze remained level on the surface but the glint within it moved her inside. "And coming here with her offered me opportunity," she said rather more quickly than she liked.

He lifted a brow.

"For running away," she whispered.

His eyes seemed to still.

"Nou, frae whit woud a wumman the likes of ye be needing tae rin awa?"

Kitty's mouth opened, then closed. Could he understand, as he had seemed to understand that night three years earlier? That she did not want to have her existence linked with Lambert Poole's any longer?

For an eternal stretch of moments, he said nothing. Then:

"Care for anither game, maleddy?"

Kitty drew a long breath. Sat back in her chair. Adjusted her skirt.

"I haven't any money left. You are a sharp, my lord. But that is to be expected." She could not entirely meet his eye.

"Niver cheated a day in ma life. But tae be fair, lass, A'll give ye the chance tae win it back."

"I said I haven't the funds for it. Weren't you listening?"

"Ta'every word." He had listened when she begged him to kiss her when he did not wish to. Twice. On the surface his eyes looked lazy. Within, that hint of steel flickered. It did not seem cold now, but molten as it had been beneath the stair. "Wi' or wi'out money, ye've still got something A'd care tae win."

She waited.

He rumbled, "Those fine garments ye've got on."

Kitty stared, mouth agape, a wild flutter of nerves tangling about her middle.

"My *clothing*?" She sounded like a perfect nincompoop. But she had not expected this. She had expected . . .

More.

Apparently she was, as ever, quite a pathetically naïve fool.

"Ye lose a hand, A tak a piece. Ye win a hand . . ." A grin curved the corner of his gorgeous mouth.

"Is this what I have brought upon myself then?" Her tone sounded diffident without any effort, her breaths shallow, and someplace in her chest wretchedly flat. "A game played by rogues in hells?"

"The idea intrigues ye."

"You are actually serious." He was not a gentleman. She had imagined all the rest, his silent understanding and his honor. It was almost a relief to know it. It mattered nothing at all what he had said beneath the stair about Poole. He simply wanted her to remove her clothes before him and perhaps more. That was all.

That was all.

It surprised Kitty how horrid that realization felt, in the very pit of her stomach, and how much she wanted to play his scandalous game, even so. Perhaps the gossips knew her better than she knew herself. Perhaps she was a wanton. Perhaps she always had been.

"Ye look warm."

"What?"

"Yer cheeks are pink." Deliciously pink. And her eyes glimmered with muted thrill beneath the mask of sophistication.

"They are not." But she slipped her slender hands over her cheeks and her lips parted. Leam could taste those lips, sweet cherries and wood smoke, and glimpse the pink flash of temptation within. He wanted that tongue wrapped around his again and at present he did not care what he must do to ensure it. *He cared for nothing.* His creed for five years could serve him well tonight.

"Well, I suppose they are," she conceded. "But it isn't to be wondered at."

"For a wumman like ye, lass, it isna."

She regarded him warily. And well she might. He should not have spoken so. That libertine arse Poole be damned, Kitty Savege was a lady, and she deserved to be treated as one, which he had not been doing since she set foot in this inn. Of course she hadn't helped matters any.

But it was far too late for regrets. He was already damned, and she with him. Folly's fool knew no solitude.

"That is not what I meant," she said, voice cool but eyes bright.

"A ken whit ye meant."

"I do not—" She halted. Her gaze fixed on his mouth, lingering until Leam's cravat tightened. Then it slid slowly down his neck and chest, oddly searching. By God, she looked like a girl at times, vulnerable and uncertain beneath the façade of the ice princess she tried to appear, poised and tantalizingly aloof.

Her gaze returned to his, direct.

"What game are we playing, my lord?"

Leam did not wish to consider the consequences any longer. Not tonight. The frustration from her earlier kisses proved too much. He wanted one thing now.

"Piquet."

Slowly her lips curved up, first at one edge, then the other. His chest ached.

"I accept your offer. It sounds like a splendid idea. I don't know why I didn't think of it first," adding beneath her breath as she moved to the opposite seat, "except that I am not a roguish barbarian, of course."

"O coorse."

"I thought you didn't like this gown." Her fine eyes danced, releasing the pressure behind his ribs. She would play. He must remember what he knew of her and disregard what the poet in him would believe, would he but give the poet rein.

"'Tis the reason for the game, lass," he said smoothly.

"You will not win it. Mr. Yale plays well, but I am not Lady Emily. I know my way around a card table." She paused. "But were you to win it . . ." Her cheeks flamed. "You cannot burn it or some such nonsense. I must have it back, at least until my luggage arrives. I cannot very well go about in my petticoat, can I?"

Leam sucked in a breath. He passed her the deck and she dealt.

"How shall we do this, my lord, by declaration and tricks or by hand? I daresay the former, as it is quite late already."

Leam smiled but he wished to laugh. At this moment, he lived a fantasy. She was intelligent, beautiful, brazen, and could indeed laugh with him, albeit quietly. He should cut out his tongue. He should run and bolt himself into his bedchamber—alone. He should never have done this, for more reasons than he could count.

"Declaration an trick."

Her lashes flickered.

They played, and she played extraordinarily well, considerably better than she had earlier.

"Four queens." She did not look up from her cards. Leam had nothing to match them. He untied his neck cloth and removed it.

An unexpected trick went to the table beneath her fingertips. Leam's signet ring followed it.

"Ye withheld yer skill afore," he murmured.

"I had no particular desire to win then." Her gaze came up, shining, and shifted to his neck. Leam had never before felt less dressed wearing so many clothes.

She took another trick. "Now what, my lord?"

He removed his shoes. It seemed safest. This had not been wise. But he could not halt it now. He wanted to see her undressed more than he wanted to breathe.

Cards shifted from table to hands, hands to table. His stockings came off, then his kerchief came from his pocket, followed by his watch.

She studied the timepiece on the table.

"You are not playing fairly, my lord. What shall it be next, a snuffbox?"

"A dinna tak snuff." Perhaps she only wished to make a fool of him, but her eyes remained lit, her beautiful lips irrepressibly twitching. "Yer fixing to have me in ma drawers and ye still laced up tight, aren't ye?"

"I am not *fixing* anything. I am simply playing cards and you are losing."

"A've been letting ye win, lass."

"I doubt it."

"Deal the cards."

He won the jewels in her ears. Watching her remove them was like watching art at its creation, the tilt of her fine jaw, the ivory curve of her throat, the deft movement of her graceful fingers. She laid the ear bobs on the table.

"You have had your impressive sequence, my lord. But no more." She spoke with only a hint of unevenness in her voice, but she did not now meet his gaze.

Her shoes and shawl went next. He could see no more of her than before, but as she discarded each item her cheeks grew pinker, her hands less steady.

"My trick," he murmured, setting down a king to stop her run of hearts.

"Hm. I should ask you to look away, but that seems absurdly prim given the circumstances."

Leam averted his gaze.

A minute later she said, "All right."

On the pile of shoes and shawl rested a pair of stockings. Of fine woven wool and modest hue, they seemed suitable for traveling. Leam had seen silk stockings thin as water; he had removed them from feminine legs they had barely covered. But these practical scraps of fabric did to him what no stockings on or off a woman had before.

Beneath Kitty Savege's skirts, her legs were now bared.

He must have those skirts.

He set to his strategy afresh.

She won his coat. As he pulled it off and laid it aside, she took a quick, deep breath.

"I told you I would win." Her sweet voice had lost all smoothness. "You mustn't play against opponents you do not know, Lord Blackwood. Hasn't anyone ever told you that before?"

"Whit if A want ye tae win, lass?"

"You don't."

He didn't. And he did. He could see the same in her eyes, reluctance yet eagerness. The day had felt like an eternity, the evening endless waiting. But her slightly hesitant surrender now was undoing him like nothing ever had. The mix of innocence and confidence intoxicated. Entranced. Watching her was to witness the most elegant of carriages slowly, surely crash of its own will, as though crashing were to be desired.

"Nine," she said. "You cannot have better. Your waistcoat, my lord?"

He removed it. She stared. Leam locked his grip around the chair arm, holding himself in his seat.

How she finally won the hand with her gaze glued to his shirtfront he hadn't any idea, unless it was that he wasn't looking at his cards at all any longer. Her thundercloud eyes widened yet further as he unbuttoned the linen and tugged it off.

Her face snapped away. Her knuckles and fingertips showed white about the cards. His heart beat so hard he suspected she might see the flinching of flesh. But since she now seemed to be studying the waning fire across the chamber with great interest, he did nothing to hide. The cool air slipped over his shoulders. He leaned back in the chair and took up the cards to shuffle.

"I daresay this is not a very wise idea." Her words were breathless. "What with Lady Emily and the gentlemen just upstairs, and Mr. and Mrs. Milch only on the other side of the kitchen."

It was not wise for many more reasons than that. It hadn't been since they'd started this.

"They're all abed, lass. But if ye've had eneuch o cards . . ."

Finally she turned to him, and her eyes were clouds of confusion. Her gaze slipped across his chest and he felt it as though she touched him. He wanted to feel her hands on him. He *must* feel her hands on him.

"My lord," she whispered, "I believe it is your deal."

Chapter 10

He dealt, his hands not entirely steady, but her gaze was as skittish as a filly's. Idiot that he was, when the set presented itself, Leam could not lay it down.

"My lord, you hold an ace."

"Be ye shuir, lass?"

"Fairly. But—" She blinked rapidly several times.

"But?"

"But if you lead the trick as I imagine you will now, I shall be at something of a loss."

"Aye."

"I don't mean the gown, which I have already told you I intend to recover." Her cheeks were afire. "I mean that I cannot remove it by myself. A number of the buttons are beyond my reach."

Leam laid down an ace, followed by a king, queen, jack, and ten. She had nothing to suffice.

"My concentration is somewhat off," she mumbled. She stood and turned her back to him.

Leam was glued to the chair.

She glanced over her shoulder, slender brows arched. "I

will not renege. I haven't the courage for it." The words seemed to slip from her lips like water and her shoulders dipped as though she released a sigh. She smiled, a smile of girlish delight and simple pleasure.

Great God in heaven, *what was he doing*?

He stood and moved to her.

Her hair, pinned into a thick satin twist, draped just above the gown's neckline. Leam set his fingertips to the tantalizing arc of pale skin at the base of her head, a silken pulse resonating beneath, and allowed the thick tresses to lean heavy upon his palm.

"What are you doing?" she whispered.

"First things first." He released one gem-studded comb, then another. Her shining hair fell like a wave over his hand.

She sucked in a breath. "I had not intended—"

"Whit did ye intend, lass?" Her fragrance tangled in his senses, wood smoke and ripe, dark cherries, and he leaned closer. Closer to divinity. Closer to the damnation of a soul already once damned. He breathed her in.

"I— Honestly I don't know." She spoke quickly. "But I think you should unhook my gown while you are here. Then you may go back to your seat."

Leam grinned. This woman beguiled with her very breath.

"Ye think A'll win the next trick?"

"Of course."

"Whaur be the confidence in yer game nou?"

"In my shoes on that chair, I daresay. Unbutton me, please."

He spread his hand across her back, then his other around her shoulder, and drew her to him, brushing his cheek against her satin hair.

"Or we coud say ye've already lost the trick."

She seemed to hold her breath. "That would not be playing fairly. Again."

He set his fingers to the top button and pried it loose. Then the next and the next. The gown gaped beneath her fall of hair. With all his might Leam resisted sweeping the tresses aside to touch her.

"That should be sufficient." She spoke very quietly, standing still as a statue. "I can unfasten the remainder should I have need."

He backed away from the woman with her gown hanging open and her hair tumbling in glorious abandon over her shoulders. He nearly fell over his chair.

He lowered himself gingerly. She sat down and took up her hand again. He produced another unbeatable card.

Watching her silently unfasten the remaining buttons, he dared not speak, or move, or breathe. She stood and peeled the sleeves down her arms without any attempt at seduction, seducing him beyond his imaginings. She pushed the gown over her sweetly curved hips, stepped out of it, and laid it on the chair.

"I am thoroughly weary of it anyway."

His throat was tight. "'Tis a fine dress, lass."

"I thought you didn't like it."

She was beyond exquisite, from her blushing cheeks to the delicately ruffled hem of the petticoat that revealed a hint of slender ankle.

"A'm a lout tae hae suggested it."

She grinned and finally lifted her gaze to him.

Would that she had not.

Excitement animated her eyes, and hunger he had only dreamed. He dealt. She reached for her hand, but a glance at his cards told him he'd already won. He deposited them face up, stood, and moved around the table. Wrapping his hands around her shoulders he drew her against him. She sighed, her lashes fluttering.

"I can remove it myself." The words barely sounded from

her parted lips, lips that Leam could write ten odes to and another dozen sonnets. If she would but open her eyes again he could compose an epic in verse to their raincloud depths alone. She was hot against him, the soft touch of her silk undergarment on his skin like fire.

"As ye wish." He brushed the backs of his fingers across the laces binding the thin silk across her breasts. Through the fabric the deep cleft between showed like an invitation to heaven. She inhaled, tightening the fabric.

"Or perhaps you can," she whispered.

The laces came undone beneath his hands, the fabric gathered, the garment discarded. He held her arms above her head and brushed his body up hers, hearing her pull in breaths and feeling her fullness with his skin. Her head fell back.

"Tell me this is not real," she whispered. "Tell me this is my imagination."

He drew her arms down to her sides and buried his face in her hair.

"Aye. An mine." He set his hands on her waist and the stiff barrier of stays between him and perfect woman. He squeezed. "Except for the whalebone."

"You haven't won it yet."

"A will." His fingers worked at the corset's lacing up her back.

"You don't know that."

He drew back and something made him speak, something unwise and impetuous as youth.

"Ye dae."

Her mouth worked, but no sound came forth. Then finally, "This is not typical, is it? I mean to say, this—this between us, so swift and—and unsuitable."

He touched her chin, lifting her face so that she must meet his gaze.

"Yer nae a typical lass."

"That is not an answer to my question." She looked so direct once more, sincere amid her quivering. "I haven't done this, you know. You might imagine I had because of—"

He captured her exquisite mouth beneath his and she ceased speaking, as he wished because he wanted to know nothing of what she had or had not done. He wanted only to feel her wanting him.

But the kiss was merely the slightest caress, the borrowing of her lips for a moment. He deepened it, urging her lips apart, and she gave him what she had earlier in the day, her sweet tongue and the hot, damp insides of her beauty. He kissed her until she clung to him with both hands on his shoulders, fingertips pressing into his skin, until he was weak with need and very hard. Then he slid his hand up and cupped a perfect breast.

She moaned, a soft utterance of pleasure and invitation. His fingertips smoothed upward, brushing her skin and she was like cream, silken and smooth and beautifully full. He swept his thumb beneath corset and shift.

She gasped, then: "Yes." The barest whisper.

Gently he stroked, teasing. She was beauty in his hands, tight as he could wish and swollen with pleasure. Her breaths came stuttered, her body responding with sublime feminine eagerness to his touch, little movements revealing her need, and Leam could not catch his breath. Beneath her hands his muscles hardened, his entire body. Good God, it hadn't been that long since he'd been with a woman that he should feel this burn, this blinding urge to drag her shift to her waist and her to the floor and get inside her without delay. He was finally the barbarian he'd pretended to society for years, ravenous for a woman and intent upon making her his.

She slipped her hands down his chest, moaning softly, and he plunged into her mouth. She was a lady yet he was treating her like a whore. It mattered little what rumor claimed. Kitty Savege was nothing of the sort. Her touch of eager hesitation and sighs of sweet innocence gone astray told him so.

He mustn't do this.

He broke the kiss. She allowed it, not seizing him as she had earlier in the day, not pulling him close again. Instead she trembled and looked up at him through thick lashes.

His hands gripped her shoulders, his brow pressed to hers. He forced out words.

"Kitty, lass, we'd best be saying guid nicht."

Her breaths came in soft, jagged pants, tickling his chin.

"I daresay we had best." The tip of her tongue passed along her lower lip. Leam sucked back a groan. By God, he wanted to taste her unto eternity. To lick every inch of her mouth and throat, her beautiful breasts, the palms of her hands, and her hot womanhood.

"But— *No.*" She said upon a little choke. "What I mean to say is— What are you doing?" Her voice quivered. "Are you merely teasing me?"

"A'm slowing it down for ye, lass." *What was he saying?* There was no *it*, and he didn't want any slowing down. He wanted to haul her up to his bed and do to her everything he'd been imagining. And more. Plenty more. Then he wanted to leave her in this little village and return to Scotland and sanity.

Her hands dropped. She backed away.

"Well, then. Good night, my lord." She gathered up her garments, held them to her middle as though they were a fur muff and she was strolling through the park, and hurried up the stair in nothing but her shift and loosened stays.

Leam swallowed a full five times, hard, like the rock in his trousers. He took a step forward.

He halted.

A few sessions of groping might pass. But anything more

would not suit him. His heart had never beat so furiously, swift with sheer warning. He had been down this mistaken path once before, thrown himself headlong into peril that remained unmatched in the following five years he'd spent working for the crown. Peril he had spent those years trying to forget.

He did not want that.

But he wanted *her*.

He swiped a hand across his face. He was no celibate, by God. He could enjoy a tumble with a beautiful woman without fear. She wanted it, and he would give it to her. He wasn't the foolish youth who had lost himself so thoroughly to a woman that he became blinded to everything around him, including her. And Kitty Savage might not be a doxy, but she was no virgin to be misled.

Yet he stood, paralyzed, no shoes, no shirt, and staring at nothing, unable to move a single muscle.

Kitty barely made it to her bed. She sank onto it, strewing her garments at her feet and covering her face with her hands.

What horrid, nasty, taunting divinity had provided her with a man who looked and kissed like a god yet seemed to possess an astounding ability to detach himself from an unclothed woman throwing herself at him? Despite her remaining scruples she wanted his touch, his kiss, the sensation of his hot skin and hard muscle beneath her palms. She had tried to win at cards although she ought never to have played. But when he removed his shirt she'd nearly *died*.

Good heavens, were all men so beautiful beneath their clothing, so perfectly proportioned like Greek statues? It couldn't be. She felt certain at least ten gentlemen of her acquaintance wore stays and another half dozen purchased buckram padding by the bushel.

Leam Blackwood did not do either, obviously. Everything in his coat was defiantly real man, broadly structured and muscular yet slightly underfleshed, an athletic man who ate perhaps not quite enough.

She had touched that. She had touched him.

It made her weak inside. It made her feel insane.

Why didn't he want her? Or did he, and he was too decent to take full advantage of her? They called him a flirt. Was this flirting, teasing with kisses and touches until she could think of nothing but him? He said he was slowing it down for her. Why would he do that for a woman of her besmirched reputation? Did it mean he wanted more from her—eventually? As she did. Oh, Lord, *as she did.* How could that possibly be?

She yanked off her wretchedly confining stays that he had begun to remove yet had not, turned onto her side, and wrapped her arms about her middle.

Why must he be decent? Why must he be even a little bit gentlemanly? She wanted him to be a barbarian, the lout he'd said he was. She wished he had not followed after Emily on the stair to protect her from possible danger. Kitty wished instead that he'd made quick, careless love to her in the parlor, on the sofa, the floor even, wherever rogues had their way with loose women, so that she could revel in being known by a man who could not touch her profoundly. So she could revel in running away from the cold, controlled woman she had come to be.

But if she did, if she took him as her lover, she would be precisely what the gossips of society believed her already.

The door creaked. Her hands jerked away from her face. The panel opened a crack and he came into her bedchamber.

She leaped up.

He was absolutely beautiful, his eyes dark, his jaw firm and hair tousled. A triangle of male flesh was revealed by his shirt, recalling her palms to the taut smoothness of his skin, the texture of dark hair descending in a line to his trousers, the strong beat of his heart.

She shook her head. "But you said—"

"Kitty—"

"I cannot." The words slipped through her lips.

His chest rose and fell hard. He tilted his head.

"That moment when you—" She gulped in thick breaths. "You said you would slow it down for me, which I believe is an excellent idea. And—and—" She stuttered. "And when Mr. Cox went to follow Emily upstairs, and you were ready to . . ." Would he understand? She hadn't really until now. "Don't you see? You are no longer a stranger and it changes everything. I know that must make me the greatest wanton this side of—"

He moved to her swiftly and covered her mouth with his palm, warm and encompassing and sending her heartbeat flying. He bent his head and spoke above her brow.

"An A'd hae kent this afore." His voice was low. "A woudae gladly left the bairn tae her fate wi' him."

Kitty laughed, muffled against his skin. He released her.

Her tongue stole along the edge of her lips, tasting him there. "You would not have."

His gaze dipped to her mouth. "Aye, A might have." It turned quite sober. "Lass, ye dinna know me frae Adam."

"But I—"

"Than pretend ye dinna." A note of haste colored his words now, or perhaps desperation, like hers. His dark eyes shone. "Pretend for the nicht."

"Oh, God. No," Kitty groaned, feeling him without even touching him. Knowing everything was changing now.

He knew it as she did. He had tried to put her off before, but he had succumbed below stairs, and again now. He had come to make love to her although it could not be wise. They were not for each other despite this *thing* that drew them together, the hot familiarity that should not be there between them.

But perhaps he was merely a man, unknown to her as he said, who would say anything to gain entrance to a woman's bed. She would depend upon it. She would pretend there was nothing else, nothing she could feel each time he looked at her.

It felt like a lie to even consider it! And she wanted no more lies. No more secrets. She wanted life and laughter, and this man made her feel those with barely a word. And he made her want him as she had never wanted anything simply by standing before her in gorgeous disarray.

"This is a very bad idea," she whispered. "You must go."

He took several deep breaths.

Silently she prayed.

He turned and went to the door. Kitty's knees gave way. She collapsed to the bed, dropping her face into her palms again. The door clicked shut. The bolt knocked into place. Her eyes flew open.

He moved right to her, with a firm hand on her shoulder pushed her onto her back and climbed over her, sinking the mattress with his knees. He looked down at her, both their breaths audible.

"Tell me nae."

She could not.

Holding her gaze, he nudged her thighs apart and lowered his body onto hers.

Kitty trembled, every muscle paralyzed. This was too much. Too fast. It was not her life, her rigid existence of purpose and poise. This was a man's body brushing hers from chest to knee. A breathtaking man with raw desire in his hooded eyes.

She whispered, "Yes," barely a breath.

He shifted his hips into hers. Her body erupted in sensation. His need was hot and hard against hers. Her eyelids fluttered and she moaned softly, her knees coming up to clasp his hips, hands seeking his waist. The desperate ache spread as she pressed to his erection. He moved against her again, pushing her into the mattress, and she nearly came apart. She groaned in pleasure and lifted, rocking herself against him.

"Yer wanting mair than this," he said above her lips, each thrust through the friction of their clothing like sin, making her feel everything. His hand circled her calf, moving beneath her shift, along her thigh. "*I* am." His voice was rough, as hot with need as her body.

"Yes," she uttered, and on a breath, "If you would oblige."

He pushed her shift up, past her hips and breasts. She would have kept it; he yanked it over her head. He shoved his shirt under his arms and brought his chest against her naked breasts and his mouth down upon hers.

She drowned. Feeling him, skin against skin, his taut muscle against her nipples, was utterly bewildering and spectacular. His tongue delved into her, demanding, his hands sweeping down the sides of her breasts, curving along her waist and hips. He dragged her against him, releasing a cascade of pleasure in her and coiling the ache tighter. She drank him, ravenous for his tongue sliding in and out of her mouth, nibbling at his lips, wanting more.

He broke away from the kiss and pulled off his shirt. His hungry gaze swept her from brow to toe. Kitty sucked in breath and turned her face away. She knew what he would say. She had been here before.

"Pray, do not—"

"Your body is art, Kitty Savege." His chest rose on hard breaths. He caressed her hip, his strong hand possessing. "Perfection."

Kitty couldn't breathe. The man who spoke was not the man she had taken into her bed. His words were beautiful, deep, and smooth, the Scots burr entirely gone, like that moment in the yard.

Her lips parted. "Per-perfect—" she stuttered. "But—"

"No," he ordered.

She gripped his shoulders to push him off. "But, *yes*." She scrambled out from under him, her arm a brace holding him away, her other hand grabbing up a corner of bed linen before her as a hasty covering.

"Kitty—"

"What you said," she panted, feeling his hard breaths through her palm with every nerve in her body. "Why did you speak that way?"

His eyes were so dark, liquid with desire.

"Kitty, luve," he said somewhat raggedly, "A dinna ken whit A'm saying nou A need tae be inside ye."

A sound escaped her, a surprised whimper that was nothing like her.

"All right," she heard herself whisper. "That will do for now." She threw herself at him.

He grabbed her up and bore her down beneath him, and cupped the sides of her breasts, the pads of his thumbs seeking the peaks, and she moaned. Then he caressed her into silence, and submission. Her hands sought the waistband of his trousers and clutched around his tight buttocks. His hand slipped between her legs. He held her a moment, neither of them breathing, then he delved into her.

"Kitty," he groaned, sinking his finger deep, and she clutched the bedclothes. He caressed, and she trembled as he touched her so perfectly—*sublimely*. He drew out, but she was breathless for more. Then he entered her again. Her body shook, his fingers driving her, slowly in and out, teasing. She arched into him, begging for more with her body.

He kissed her mouth, her throat, the valley between her breasts, then her tight nipple until she moaned, wanting him.

"I must have you now." Deep, husky, perfect, a fantasy of words and cadence.

"But I— *Now*," tore from her. "Do it now."

He pulled off his trousers and moved between her legs, spreading her thighs with his hands. His shaft pressed into her, opening her, and it was a hard invasion, welcome, at first almost unbearably so; it grabbed her breath.

Then delicious. *Perfect*.

He groaned; she echoed him. His arms and jaw were taut with restraint. With each gentle thrust he gave her more, and it was an agony of tortured pleasure. Push in, retreat. Again farther in. And again, each thrust better than that before. She quivered, strung. She hooked a leg around him and tried to pull him close.

But he would not give it all to her. She struggled beneath him, sliding against the bed linens, pushing herself up to meet him. His big hand curved around her face, a fingertip tracing her lashes.

"*Please*," she whispered.

"*Vainement je m'éprouve.*"

Kitty's eyes flew open.

His eyes were nearly black. He kissed her hard, then whispered above her lips, "Is this whit ye be wanting, lass?" He braced his hands to either side of her and drove up into her. Their moans mingled. He filled her completely. She did not want him to withdraw. She did not want it to end.

He knew her mind.

"'Tis anely the beginning."

"Make it last," she uttered as she shifted her hips to feel him thoroughly. Her fingertips sank into the muscle of his buttocks, holding him tight to her.

"For ye an me both, luve." His voice was as strained as

hers. Breaking her hold, he pulled out, she gasped and he thrust in again. Again, harder with each thrust, and a little bit deeper each time, caressing her so deep within. He met her center. She bucked, dragging herself onto him, and he went deeper still, giving it to her over and over until she whimpered. She bit her lips to withhold her shouts, breaking the skin. He covered her mouth, sucked on her lip. His voice came rough and deep.

"Contre vous, contre moi."

"Leam." He forced her down into the mattress. "Now—*oh!*" But he kept coming until her breaths shallowed and dizziness gripped her. Then rapture, rolling, sudden. Her sounds of pleasure tangled with his, his hands holding her hips down as he rose high in her. His body strained. She met him, taking his fast thrusts amid her shudders and feeling him thick and powerful. His hips pressed hard into her a final time, and with a great breath he went perfectly still.

She sighed a stuttering exhalation. He fell upon his forearms. She pressed her cheek to the mattress. Their breaths came heavy, her breasts flattened beneath his chest. She ought to unwind her arms from around his waist. His skin was damp beneath her palms, his heartbeats thunderous like hers.

Finally he pulled away and rolled onto his back, taking a tress of her hair with him, between his fingers. His eyes were closed and as his breathing slowed his thumb stroked the lock across his palm.

Kitty shifted onto her side, curling her knees up to hug, and the strands slipped from his hold.

For long minutes they lay like that, his fingertips by her shoulder but not touching. The chill air tingled over her cooling skin.

"What was that you said?" she finally said. "The English part."

His breaths seemed to pause. "A dinna ken, lass," he finally replied.

"I don't believe you." But she was, after all, well suited to games. She would demand an explanation, but tomorrow. Not now. Not filled up and trembling as she was at this moment. "What do we do now?" she said, repeating her question from earlier, the confusion welling within her ever stronger now. She had never given this to a man, not this abandon.

He turned his head, and his eyes were all gentleness. Somehow it did not surprise her, this warmth.

"Ye weel ask that quaisten, winna ye?"

"It is a good question."

Silently his gaze traveled the line of her hair, across her features.

"And?" She must try to understand at least this. She was accustomed to having a plan. "What now?"

"Whitiver ye wish, lass." The words came upon a hard breath, as though brought forth reluctantly this time. He curved his hand around the side of her face and passed the pad of his thumb across her lips, the same caress that had made her want him so swiftly. It was at once tender and demanding.

She did not know exactly what she wished, so she did not speak.

" 'Tis best an A go nou," he said quietly.

Her throat was dry. "Of course." She had never considered an alternative. Lonely wanton, her imagination did not extend further.

He pushed onto his elbow and surrounded her face with his hands. His eyes, like pitch cast in the sheer silver of night without, sparkled. He placed a warm, astoundingly gentle kiss upon her lips.

"Happy Yule, Leddy Kath'rine."

She could not reply to wish him the same. Her throat was closed finally, somewhat belatedly. She had not actually known that she could moan in such a manner. No one had ever warned her it was even likely. No one had told her anything, of course. And she had most certainly never discovered it on her own.

She had been kissed so very differently before, by a man who told her she was imperfect, her body inside and out something to be ashamed of, even as he used her, telling her that she was not desirable. She had not known a man could kiss a woman with such tenderness. She had not known *this*.

Leam sat on the edge of the bed, drew his trousers on, and shrugged his shoulders into his shirt, then stood. For a moment he remained so, his broad back to her, looking out the window. Then he turned, touched two fingertips to her cheek, gave her another smile, and left.

Kitty stared at the closed door.

Nothing could have been worse than Lambert Poole's cruelty, how he had used her, then laughed at her, telling her he had ruined her out of spite to her brothers whom he despised. Kitty believed for years that she had experienced the worst a man could do to a woman. She had told Lambert that herself.

Clearly, she had been wrong. Somehow, astoundingly, a sweet, simple good night from this man after everything was worse.

Chapter 11

Church bells woke Kitty. Uneven, inharmonious church bells rung by an inexpert hand, which seemed unlikely, so she dragged herself from the bed in which a near stranger had made love to her hours earlier, and peeked out the window. Glare from the snow pricked her eyes.

Rapid knocking came at the door. Not a man's knock. Of course not. Kitty had little doubt that in company the Earl of Blackwood would appear today as he had after each previous encounter, the same mildly flirtatious, lazy-eyed semi-barbarian she still could not quite believe she had invited into her bed. Although in point of fact she had not really invited him. He had climbed in.

Her entire body got hot, most especially where she was tender and slightly sore.

Ignoring Emily's knocking, she crawled back to the bed and curled up in the mussed linens, twisting them about her fingers and toes and imagining everything over again. No detail was too small to recall thoroughly. She must revel while reveling could be done, before she must see him among the others and be cool, self-possessed Lady Katherine again. And before she must fully confront the fact that Uilleam Blackwood was not all he appeared to be in public.

The door opened. Emily marched in.

"Happy Christmas, Kitty! Good gracious, what a mess." She picked up garments. "You must rise. It is half past ten already and we will be late for church."

"Church?" Kitty pushed herself up to sit and the hair out of her eyes—the hair he had stroked so gently after making love to her. She still could not entirely believe it had not been a dream.

"It seems there will be church after all. So come now. Up."

She allowed Emily to dress her. She herself was good for little useful employment. If any of her sophisticated political and literary friends in London could see her now, hazy-eyed and flush-faced, they would not recognize her. She peered into the glass and blinked. She did not even recognize herself.

"How would you like your hair arranged?"

Kitty frowned and set down the glass. She took a steadying breath. "Very tight and secure."

"I haven't any talent for it, you know, but since it is Christmas I will do my best."

"Thank you, dear."

It looked a fright. But Lord Blackwood didn't seem to mind it. Contrary to Kitty's expectations, he met her at the base of the stair with a lovely smile, warm eyes, and a neat bow, his dogs hanging about his legs. She managed to curtsy without falling over, which was an accomplishment of sorts as her joints had turned to jelly and her insides to warm caramel.

Making love with him had only worsened matters. She was thoroughly infatuated. But of course she was. What an immensely pathetic fool she had turned out to be after all these years of endeavoring not to be precisely that.

Mr. Yale offered her cloak and then his arm. A good thing indeed, since touching the earl would surely result in her becoming a puddle on the foyer floor.

"How on earth will we get to the church through all the snow?" Emily said, grasping Lord Blackwood's arm as they stepped over the threshold into the yard.

"Via the path, one imagines." Mr. Yale gestured, leading Kitty toward a neat, flat corridor cut in the snow from the edge of the yard a considerable distance down the street. "It is somewhat slippery, Lady Katherine. Do take care."

"Should I fall I will endeavor not to drag you down with me."

"That's all right. The other night Blackwood's fist sent me to the snow already, so I am accustomed to it." Indeed, a bruise colored his chin.

"Good heavens, sir."

"All in an evening's amusements." He winked.

The dogs ran ahead, leaping through drifts.

"Well, isn't this the most pleasant journey to Christmas services I've ever taken?" Mr. Cox said, smiling for all as he came behind them. "I haven't been in such grand company for church in years, I daresay."

"Don't you go to church, Mr. Cox?" Emily asked from behind Kitty where she thankfully could not see the handsome man with whom she had spent the wicked portion of her night.

"I suspect he meant the 'grand company' part, rather than the 'church' part," Mr. Yale said, and Emily's brows went up.

"All right, then. With whom do *you* usually go to church?"

"No one you would know, I'll merit," Kitty's escort murmured.

Kitty pressed her fingertips into Mr. Yale's arm and he slanted her an apologetic glance, then a grin.

"I suspect you are correct," Emily said, apparently not minding his teasing today, "although my companion, Madame Roche, always seems to know everybody and introduces me to the most remarkable people whenever we are about. Two weeks ago I met a dozen chimney sweeps at the market."

By the time they ascended the church steps, swept clean and the remaining film of white already melting in the sparkling sunlight, Kitty was breathing hard from the exertion and possibly because the earl was right behind her. He had yet to speak, but in company he was taciturn at best. In the company of more than one, that was. Alone with one person he spoke French verse and, in perfect English, said delectable things she had not dreamed any man would ever say to her.

The tiny church was nearly full, villagers crowding the pews despite the snow. But the building was tidy, white-washed inside and out, with modest decorations and a minister standing behind the pulpit dressed in an oversized black jacket.

Kitty screwed up her brow. "Marie, isn't that your coachman?"

"By George, it is. What are you doing up there, Pen?"

The coachman came out from behind the pulpit. Kitty recognized the coat of casual cut yet fine wool. Lord Blackwood had removed it for a trio of jacks the previous night.

Mr. Pen reached up as though to tip his cap and tugged on his bushy gray hair instead.

"Happy Christmas to you, miss. Milady. Milord. Sirs."

"Pen, what on earth is going on?"

"Well, don't you know, milady, the vicar ain't been seen since the snow hereabouts." His clear baritone filled the little church. He shook his head sorrowfully. "When His Lordship were looking about for someones to preach services this morning on behalf of it being the birthday of Our Lord and Savior, well, I don't mind telling you, I was happy to step up to the job."

"Are you an Evangelical, Pen?"

"Methodist, miss." He tugged again at his nonexistent brim.

Mr. Yale chuckled. "Let the man get on with it," he said. "It's cold as a desert night in here."

"Ye've niver been tae the desert," Lord Blackwood murmured, defraying Kitty's own chill by sending little eddies of warmth through her entire body.

"Well, I couldn't very well say it's as cold as a Bengal summer, could I?"

"Yer forgitting the muntain."

"Perhaps intentionally."

"Lord Blackwood," Emily said, "did you really ask my coachman to say the service today?"

Mr. Yale chuckled. "Someone had to."

"Now ladies and gents, if I'm to get to our lesson today, I'd best be starting." Mr. Pen retook his place at the pulpit.

Kitty could not say what the coachman's sermon was about, although she heard the word *virgin* a number of times, perhaps because she was primed to hear it through mingled ecstasy and shame.

He had lived in Bengal and had traveled in the mountains, presumably the Himalayas. He could recite French poetry. He had arranged for someone to provide a Christmas sermon, albeit a creative alternative.

When the bright notes of a violin echoed throughout the high-ceilinged building, matched by Mr. Pen's baritone and Mrs. Milch's thin alto, Kitty dragged herself from her study. Emily and Mr. Yale sang, and Mr. Cox at the end of the row, his cheeks bright.

She looked over Emily's bonnet. The earl stood with his

head slightly bowed, his beautiful mouth a straight line. As though he sensed her regard, his eyes flickered up, and he met her gaze. He smiled. But the steely glint was back, and Kitty's nascent pleasure wavered.

They walked back to the inn in pleasant company, Mr. Cox and Mr. Pen providing most of the conversation in spirited form. The others came along the narrow path behind and before, the innkeepers, Ned, and the villagers invited to take a mug of ale at the inn and a slice of Christmas pudding.

"Pen, did you shovel this path to the church as well?" Emily asked.

"No, milady." Ned's piping voice came cleanly across the snowy street as he plodded along, wolfhounds at his heels. "Me and milord did it yesterday. Finished it up this morning just in time, didn't we, gov'nor?"

"Aye, lad. An yer playing was verra fine at the kirk."

The stable boy winked at the lord of the realm.

Within the inn, Kitty stripped off cloak, bonnet, pattens, and gloves and took a chair by the fire, warming her toes. Emily settled beside her, then Mr. Cox. The inn filled with people, villagers arriving to stomp the snow from boots and hems, throw off coats, and take up a pint.

"Why, it seems to be a regular party," Mr. Cox said with lifted brows. "Isn't it, Lady Katherine?"

"Madame Roche would like to see this, farmers and artisans talking so freely with gentlemen of rank," Emily said. "She is a Republican."

"His Lordship condescends with such a natural air, almost as though he enjoys it." The gentleman's eyes seemed intent on the earl and not particularly kind. A prickle of discomfort slipped up the back of Kitty's neck.

"I believe it is his disposition." Like fixing broken roofs and shoveling snow, which certainly explained his physique.

She was dying to simply look at him, but she must immediately thereafter drag her gaze away for fear that she would linger too long.

He met her regard. She lingered. When he finally looked away she might have sighed like the perfect ninny she was, if not for her pique. She was after all quite weary, having not slept perfectly well or really at all. He'd left her with many questions. And now she had more.

Her need for answers was to be eternally frustrated. Toasts were made—many, many toasts; pudding was consumed, despite its rather leathery texture and flat flavor (no nutmeg had been found); and revelers only began departing well into the afternoon.

Contrary to her earlier warnings, Mrs. Milch set a roast goose on the table, as well as basted turnips, apples braised in brandy, and a loaf of fresh bread. The party roundly congratulated Emily for her contribution and they dined in relative splendor. Mr. Yale and Mr. Cox entertained with stories from their travels abroad. Kitty might have been vastly diverted if she weren't so preoccupied with endeavoring not to glance at a handsome Scot. Every time she did, he seemed to already be looking at her, and they could not very well stare continually at one another throughout dinner.

Outside, the sun shone at long angles on the snow as the innkeepers cleared away the remains of dinner. Mr. Yale settled into a chair by the fire, glass in hand and a week-old journal atop his knee. Emily and Mr. Cox set about mapping out Shropshire topography with raisins and nuts on the table. It all had the happy, peaceful aura of home and holiday about it, and Kitty wished she could enjoy it. But she must content herself that her friend seemed distracted from worries of that which awaited her at her real home as soon as the road was passable.

Lord Blackwood came to Kitty's side, bearing her cloak.

"Maleddy, care for a daunder?"

She could not look at him, but she allowed him to place her cloak around her shoulders. She drew her hood up. "Daunder?" It must be unremarkable; about him now hung no air of roguery.

"A stroll," Mr. Yale explained. "Bit cold out, isn't it, Blackwood?"

"Care tae come alang, Yale?"

"Thank you, but do go on without me." He lifted his glass in salute. Kitty felt as transparent as crystal. She could refuse the earl. She could once again embrace propriety. Emily and Mr. Cox did not raise their heads from their game.

Kitty went.

"Where to, my lord?" She glanced about at the snow-laden street, pale in the late afternoon sun. "Back to the church?"

He shut the inn door behind them.

"The stable." His voice was husky.

So, perhaps roguish intent after all. She did not take his proffered arm, heading straight for the outbuilding and her continued ruination without anyone assisting her to it.

Inside, he pulled the door shut, came to her, surrounded her face with his hands, and covered her mouth with his. Her hood tumbled off and she sank into him, reaching for him beneath layers of wool. He kissed her slowly at first, as though he were savoring her, then with increasing intensity like he was starving, pushing her back against the wall and bringing their bodies together as he used her mouth to excellent purpose. She wanted every second of it.

She wanted it too much, given the circumstances.

She tore her lips free.

"Wait! *Wait*." She pushed him to arm's length, but her fingers betrayed her, clutching at his waistcoat to prevent him from going farther away. "What do you think you are doing?"

"Whit A been wishing tae dae all day. An it wis an awfu lang day, lass."

"You recited poetry to me last night. In French." Then he'd left. And it took her hours to fall asleep. And now, exhausted and strung tight from the day endeavoring not to stare at him, she was excessively peevish. But mostly because he now stood arm's-length away, only his big warm hands wrapped about her waist, and she wanted instead every bit of him pressing up against her again.

"*Contre vous, contre moi, vainement je m'éprouve*," she whispered, "I struggle vainly to be free, from you and from myself. It is from Racine's play, *Phaedra*. You lent it to Lady Emily."

Beneath his waistcoat she felt his heartbeat and taut breaths. He did not speak.

"But it is a tragic story," she added.

He smiled. "An it's bonnie varse ye be wishing, rather, A'll be fain tae oblige." He grasped her hands and moved close again. Warily, she let him. Bending his head, he nuzzled the wonderfully sensitive spot beneath her ear. Kitty sighed. He murmured with only the gentlest lilt of Scots, "'Around me scowls a wintry sky, that blasts each bud of hope and joy; and shelter, shade, nor home have I, save in these arms of thine.'"

"Your countryman, Burns, I think." A new sort of trembling overtook her, deep as where he had been inside her the night before. "What happened to the French?"

"A'm warming up tae it. *Blanditias molles auremque iuvantia verba adfer, ut adventu laeta sit illa tuo.*" He kissed her neck, her throat at her speeding pulse, and she tucked her hands beneath the capes of his greatcoat, holding on to his shoulders.

"I don't know Latin," she quavered. "I shall require a translation."

" 'Bring soft blandishments and words that soothe the ear, that your coming may make her glad.' "

Kitty's breaths thinned, her knees weak. He must simply be mimicking, and a master at it. What man would disguise such a voice of rich, masculine power if it were natural to him?

"And who wrote that bit of advice, my lord?"

"Ovid."

"Ovid?" *Ovid.*

"Dae ye prefer the modern poets tae the ancients, than?"

He knew no respect for her sensibilities. "I waver between. Perhaps medieval would do." Laughter welled inside her alongside desire, even as the slice of disquiet expanded.

"*Y así mi suerte ignoro en la contienda, y no querer decirlo y que lo diga: vagando voy en amorosa erranza.*"

She circled her palm around his collar into his hair, feeling him as she had not given herself allowance to do the night before. "And that?"

"Dante."

"That explains why I did not perfectly understand it."

" 'And thus' "—his hands shifted down her back, his mouth teasing hers with light nibbles—" 'being all unsure which path to take, wishing to speak I know not what to say, and lose myself in amorous wanderings.' "

This was nearly too much to bear. "Wandering speech," she breathed, "or hands?"

"Baith."

"I s-see." He pulled her tight to him, his palm spread across her behind nesting her snug against his hips. Kitty's blood turned to warm syrup, but even as her breaths shortened from his words and caresses, unease overruled her pleasure. What game was he playing with her? And why, given the liberties she allowed him, wasn't she privy to it yet?

With the backs of his fingers he stroked tenderly along her cheek.

"'So beautiful with her delicate limbs, fair waist, and long eyes,'" he murmured, "'that she put the splendor of the moon to shame with her radiance.'"

Kitty could not draw air. "Wh-what was that?"

"Hindustani. Verra auld."

"I daresay." She steeled her voice and said at her most proper, "I am still waiting for the French."

A marvelous smile split across his lips, a glimmer of sheer admiration in his eyes. Then something changed. The glimmer grew warm, warmer.

"*Je reconnus Vénus et ses feux redoutables*," he said, his voice beautiful and deep and not in the least bit teasing, "*d'un sang qu'elle poursuit tourments inévitables.*"

Kitty trembled. "Venus's torment," she whispered. She felt that fire in her blood too. For two days it had sought to consume her and now she wanted nothing more than to submit to it fully again. Everywhere they touched he heated her, his thighs and hips pressed to hers, his hands on her back. But she would be a fool to think that was all of Venus's torment.

And finally she understood perhaps too well how her pretense with Lambert had been wrong. He had done very badly by her, but she should never have pretended anything with him, no matter her reason, as this man was clearly pretending. If she allowed herself to be with the earl now when he was denying her the truth so obviously, she would suffer. When she had been young and impressionable, a man claimed to care for her but had only been using her. More than even her ruined reputation, her heart still bore the scars of that falsity. She could not allow herself to be with a man who would not tell her the entire truth now.

"You are wonderfully well versed in verse, my lord," she said, gathering her courage. "Do they teach all of that at Edinburgh University?"

"The Athens o the North, they call it."

"I thought Scotland produced mostly engineers and doctors. Poets too?"

"Aye, poets. Philosophers an churchmen. Cads an thieves." A grin slipped across his lips. Kitty could not manage to look away.

"You must have studied prodigiously hard."

"Must hae."

"Now tell me the truth."

He stilled.

"About why you spoke the way you did last night," she added, more certain now.

A single brow rose beneath a tangled strand of dark and white hair. She wanted to run her fingers through the streak and to ask him how he had come by it or if he had always had it, to know something of him real and tangible. But another lazy grin slipped across his lips.

"A man's bund tae say any nummer o things at sic a maument, lass."

"It was not what you said." *Your body is art. I must have you now.* "It was the manner in which you said it that caught my attention." And the devastating play of his fingers.

He held her gaze, and the place where those fingers had dallied hours earlier ached.

"I heard you speak to Mr. Yale in that manner too."

"In whit manner's that, maleddy?" His gaze revealed nothing now.

"What game are you playing, my lord? Why the deception? Or is the deception the poetry-reciting London beau? A fine tool of seduction, I suspect, for the unwary."

"Nou, ma girl, why woud A hae been needing tae seduce ye at precisely that maument?"

But she would not be sidestepped.

"My lord, are you a rogue, a gentleman, or a barbarian? I must know."

"A wee bit o ilk, lass."

"A bit of each? Which is *sincere*?" With enormous effort of will, she pushed him off and ducked out of the reach of his arms. "Perhaps—perhaps you should hold to tragedy after all. Allow me to play your game now as well, won't you? You mentioned Aeschylus the other night, so I suppose you know Greek."

"Some." His brow was drawn.

Kitty crossed her arms. "Well?"

He did not reply immediately. Finally, "In the Greek?"

"English translation, if you please."

He regarded her steadily. " 'He burneth to enjoy a mortal maid, and then torments her. A sorry suitor for thy love, poor girl, a bitter wooing.' "

Kitty squeezed her eyes shut. *This could not be happening to her again.* She had left torment behind years ago.

His voice, so beautiful, so deep and smooth, came again through the cold. " 'I have but now ceased mourning for my griefs.' "

Her eye snapped open.

He looked . . . *uncertain.*

"Another play by Aeschylus, my lord?"

"*Prometheus Bound.*"

"Ah, no wonder it seemed familiar. I have seen it performed. It is the scene in which Prometheus, chained to a cliff face for eternity, speaks those words before the eagle sets upon him to devour his liver. *Daily.* Am I correct?"

He shrugged. " 'Tis tragedy, lass."

She pivoted about, putting her back to him and a hand across her mouth, and Leam's heart beat so hard he could hear it. He had brought her to this state, again rendering the exquisite undone.

He was a complete ass revealing himself in this manner. He knew it and he couldn't care. This clever woman—this beautiful woman—this woman whose rare and precious laughter stole beneath his ribs—she had given herself to him and he wanted more. Fool that he was, he wanted much more. He wanted to let himself feel what he knew he could feel with her if he allowed it.

He simply could not.

So he spoke now without disguise, disguising himself in the language of his youth's passion, the poetry that his once reckless heart had adored. For the first time in his life, his tongue would not behave.

"I have played the fool before, my lord." Her voice held steady, unlike her body that trembled when he held her, that had trembled the night before as he lost himself so completely in her. "But that was some time ago and I do not intend to repeat the experience now." She moved toward the door.

"A dinna wish ye tae play the fool, lass." The Scots clung. Leam willed it away, but it would not go. He suspected why. He knew their names. Their son awaited him at Alvamoor for the holiday. Their son who called him Father.

He must maintain this charade with her until he could leave. It was his only protection against the danger he wanted to dive into with her. He could not allow his heart to become engaged. He could not trust in his self-control, the self-control that had deserted him entirely when he had met his wife and became blind to all else. When he discovered her infidelity and his jealousy knew no limits.

A man who had sought his own brother's death because of his jealousy over a faithless woman must not allow himself to love again.

Kitty turned partially toward him, her hand on the latch.

"Oh, you needn't worry." She did not meet his gaze. "I have done this before, you know, and it is quite easy. One simply says good-bye, and, *voilà!*, no more fool to be had here." She tugged on the door. It stuck. She put her shoulder into it. It did not budge. Leam went forward, reached over her, and bent to her tightly bound hair. He inhaled her fragrance, the dangerous beauty in his senses like nothing he had known in an eon. Very likely, he'd never known it.

He stroked the backs of his fingers along her cheek and neck, and she gasped in air and her body quivered. She ducked her head.

"Please open it." Her voice was tight.

"Kitty—"

She grabbed the edge of the door and pulled hard. Leam shoved it open, his stomach hollow. She marched through.

A crack sounded across the space. She screamed, pivoted about, and tumbled into a snowbank.

Chapter 12

L eam leaped forward, darting his gaze to the surrounding buildings.

"Yale!" he bellowed. "*Yale!*" He dropped to his knees beside her. Snow enveloped her, red speckling the white.

Frantically he searched. *Dear God, please no.* He unfolded the cloak tangled about her. A small circle of blood settled on the wool of her sleeve, spread through the torn fabric of her gown. He yanked his cravat loose, swallowing around the panic.

Where was the shooter?

A flash of dark moved about the edge of the building opposite.

Goddamn it. "Yale!"

The inn door burst open.

"Pistol shot! From the north. Get the dogs."

Yale whistled into the inn, then took off across the street, Hermes and Bella streaking out the door and leaping ahead of him.

Kitty opened her eyes. Her lips and cheeks were pale. It looked a minor wound, but it would pain her greatly when he made her move, which he must do without delay.

"Good heavens." She sounded more surprised than distressed.

"Good God." He had done this to her. The shot must have been meant for him. The man following him must have a nervous trigger finger to have mistaken it. "Kitty, ma girl."

"I believe I have been shot."

"That ye hae. Lie still, lass."

Gently, he lifted her arm. She screamed. He slid the cravat beneath it, looped it quickly again, then pulled it tight.

"*Oh, God*," she groaned weakly. "Will you never cease torturing me?"

Leam tied off the cravat and gathered her in his arms. He carried her through the stable door and into the tack room. Carefully he set her down, propping her elbow upon a bench as she breathed fast and shallow, her eyes and lips clenched. He reached for a blanket, smelling of horse but it would have to do, and wrapped it about her shoulders, then slid an empty bucket to her side.

"An ye need tae be ill, gae at it."

"I am to suppose, then, that you know of what you speak?" she gritted out.

"Aye." He stood. "Stey here."

At the door he scanned the yard. The shooter had run, but he might have a partner, although it seemed unlikely. He hadn't even shot twice.

Lady Emily and Mrs. Milch appeared in the inn's doorway.

"Gae inside," he called over. They retreated and the door closed.

Yale appeared around the building across the way, moving fast, Hermes loping alongside.

"Someone's gone in a boat beyond the beaver dam, but I don't know if it's the shooter," he shouted as he neared. "Bella's tracking the bank. I'll ride."

"Nae." He moved aside for the Welshman and wolfhound to enter and pulled the door closed to a crack. "We dinna ken the land."

"Or if he's alone." He dropped the pistol into his coat pocket. "Blast and damn, Leam."

"Yale." He moved toward Kitty. She sat with her legs curled beneath her as he'd left her. "Pardon ma friend. He's a whelp a'times."

"I have already heard you curse, my lord. He may as well do so too." She regarded him steadily as he crouched down beside her and moved the blanket aside. The cravat had absorbed some of the blood on her gown, but only a tiny fresh dot of red had come through it. The wound was merely a nick. The shooter had not intended to hit her, perhaps had balked at the last moment. But the knot in Leam's belly would not unwind.

"We'll be needing tae properly see tae the scratch, lass. An ye canna stand, A'll—"

"My lord, it has not escaped my notice that you and Mr. Yale seem remarkably unsurprised at the fact that someone shot me just now." Her voice quivered.

"Nae at all."

"Sir, we have already discussed fools. Pay me the compliment of recalling that."

"You two have some interesting conversations."

Leam shot a glare over his shoulder. He looked back at the beautiful noblewoman sitting in a pile of straw because of him.

"Maleddy—"

"You will tell me this moment what is going on here or—"

"Or whit?" His temper flared. "Ye'll go haring aff after the shooter an ask him instead?"

"Some ladies have more hair than brains," Yale murmured.

"A'll thank ye tae keep out o this, ye boor. Miscaw the leddy again an A'll belt ye."

"Twice in one week? You flatter me with your attentions, old chap."

"Whin A'm finished here."

"Oh, I daresay you are finished already." Her tone was curt, but strain played about her generous lips, and her glorious eyes were dull.

"Lass, A'm gang tae carry ye tae the inn. A'll thank ye nae tae protest."

"Would it matter if I did?"

He nodded. "Aye."

She allowed him to lift her again, tucking her against his chest, and she curved her good arm about his neck. But she averted her face. Still he could smell her and feel her and want her, and he cursed himself for a whelp now. Bella came into sight and Yale went swiftly across the yard while the dogs scouted the surrounding buildings. Leam waited in the doorway until the Welshman knocked, hand in his pocket on his firearm. The door opened. Leam headed across.

The others hovered about the foyer.

"Glory be!"

"Kitty, good gracious! Is she all right?"

"Aye, miss. Juist a wee scratch." Leam laid her on the sofa.

"Someone shot me, Marie," Kitty said quietly. "Do take care when strolling in the yard today."

"Shot! Mrs. Milch said it but I did not believe it. Oh, Kitty. Whyever would someone wish to shoot you? And who?"

"I do not know. But it is possible I was not the intended target."

The innkeeper's wife brought a blanket and Lady Emily tucked it about her.

"Milch," Yale said, "His Lordship requires boiled water, sharp shears, bandages, and salve if you've any."

"A've some in ma kit." Leam gestured.

Yale headed toward the stairs.

"Lord Blackwood has wound salve in his traveling kit? Whatever for?"

"His nefarious life leads him into frequent scrapes, I daresay." Kitty's cheeks looked gray now. Milch had presumably gone for supplies. Leam bent to the hearth and piled logs on the grate.

"Milord, the Quality's better not doing such a thing," Mrs. Milch said, but her voice sounded thin. Not many gunshots in this tiny Shropshire village, apparently.

"Ma'am, a pot o tea an a biscuit woud be walcome nou for the leddy."

"Of course, milord."

"Kitty." Lady Emily shook her head. "I don't know anything at all about seeing to injuries, I'm afraid. But I don't know that Mrs. Milch will prove very useful either. She swooned when she saw you in the snow. I was obliged to revive her with smelling salts."

"Very nice sensibilities for the laboring class, hm?" Yale said with a grin, handing over the salve. "But no need for concern. Blackwood is a dab hand at dressing wounds."

"Sir," Cox said stiffly. "I don't believe that would be at all proper. Lady Katherine ought to be moved to her bedchamber and attended by the women."

Yale's grin widened.

"I'm sure I don't know why, Mr. Cox," Lady Emily said. "If Lord Blackwood is the best among us to do the job, petty niceties ought not to allow Lady Katherine to remain in any sort of danger."

Leam crouched down beside Kitty. "She's nae in ony danger, miss." Not with him sitting beside her, she wouldn't be.

"Merely excessive discomfort," the beauty reclining before him said softly. "Will this hurt?"

"Nae mair than a wee pinch."

"Now, why don't I believe you?" Her gaze slipped across his shoulders and down his chest.

"I still say it's not the thing at all," Cox said more stridently now. "Neither for a gentleman to be playing nursemaid, nor for a gently bred female to be subjected to public prodding."

"Sir, have a spot of tea, why don't you?" Mr. Milch gestured toward the dining area.

"Yes, Cox," Yale murmured. "Absent yourself and the prodding will be considerably less public. Lady Marie Antoine, tea?"

"The big dog got into the biscuits and ate them all."

"Then you shall have to turn your talents to baking sweets now, ma'am."

"Sir, you cannot improve my opinion of you with false flattery."

"I am crushed. Truly."

"But it's true, the bread was quite good." They moved toward the table, Lady Emily glancing back with concern.

"A'll hae tae cut aff the sleeve," Leam said quietly.

Kitty's eyes glimmered. "Will you keep the part, then, in lieu of the whole?"

He smiled and set the shears to fabric. "Shuirly."

"You planned this, I daresay." She watched as he cut. "You could not bear relinquishing this gown in the end. But now you will only have a piece. A torn one at that."

Smiling, Leam lifted her arm gently and drew the ruined sleeve off. He tucked the blanket around her hand. She had beautiful skin, pale and soft like a Lothians winter dawn. He wanted to touch every inch of it, to kiss every silken dip and curve.

"Aye, but this scrap o fabric bears the treasure o a lady's blue bluid."

"If you recite poetry to me now, my lord, I shall scream again."

"Ye inspire me tae it, Kitty Savege." And she did. To his very marrow.

"That, I suppose, must be your ill fortune. It seems a rather shallow wound to be so painful." Her lips were taut as she studied the scratch.

"Dinna watch."

"I will not swoon. I am not a Shropshire innkeeper, you know."

He glanced up, his dark eyes catching her, and as usual Kitty could not look away.

"Nae. Yer a lady." With the gentlest touch he applied several drops of salve to the raw flesh. She should not be surprised. He astounded her at every turn.

"Where did you learn to dress wounds, Lord Blackwood?"

"In the East Indies, Lady Kath'rine."

"Remarkable," she said to cover her pleasure at such a small exchange, one that seemed now as natural as breathing. And as unwise as breathing fire. "Hadn't you a valet to do such tasks at the time?"

"The year wis 'eleven, lass. A hadn't onybody."

His brother and wife had both perished in 'ten. But he'd had his son. Some men of course cared little for their children, like Kitty's own father.

He wrapped a clean strip of linen about her arm, his hand brushing her breast as though it were nothing. As though he did not even notice it, while Kitty's entire being awoke.

His hands stilled.

"Are you finished, then?"

"Aye. Ye'll be all right nou." He drew the blanket over her arm, stood, and moved away.

But she would not be all right. Amid the pleasure and frustration, he frightened her.

Kitty did not understand Leam Blackwood. A man had shot her, presumably intending to shoot him. The earl would not tell her the truth about the poetry, the shooter—any of it. On the surface he seemed the simplest of men, easy tempered and somewhat indolent, rather in the fashion of his big dogs. But she feared he hid a great deal behind those hooded dark eyes and rough speech.

She was angry and hurt, and infatuated, and confused. The man who caused it all seemed entirely unrepentant. The remainder of her sojourn in a remote Shropshire inn did not appear in the least bit promising.

Early the following morning, after a restless night during which her arm ached dreadfully and elsewhere inside her more so, the remainder of Kitty's sojourn at the inn abruptly became much shorter.

Madame Roche appeared upon the inn's threshold, snow clinging to her cloak, her full cheeks patches of bright rose, and as stunningly French as ever. Her raven hair streaked with silver was swept up beneath a neat little cap of violet taffeta and dyed ostrich feathers, and her gown was gloriously inappropriate for both traveling and the season, short puffy sleeves and a crinkling mass of tulle all sparkling with tiny purple and black sequins.

She lifted her lorgnette to study the parlor and dining area, and with a little sniff pronounced it "*Bon.*"

"The mail coach came through at dawn this morning," Mr. Yale explained, entering and removing her coat. "Blackwood posted to the farm Cox told us about and found them. And now we are beset by females." He grinned and stepped out of the way to admit two other women.

Kitty went forward and clasped hands with Madame Roche, smiling at her maid and Emily's. "We are so glad you are well."

"*Bon Dieu*, you are peaked, Lady Katrine!" The French-woman grasped Kitty's hand and snapped with her other at the maids. "*Vite, vite*, you lazy *filles*! Brandy there must be for to prepare the water of rose *tout de suite*." She dragged Kitty to the stairs. "And the gown. *Hélas*, the gowns! *Ma petite*, come!" She snapped again at Emily.

"Lady Marie Antoine," Mr. Yale drawled, "you have the most unusual servants."

"Yes. But they are very good to me."

Kitty glanced back. The earl had entered, carrying in a bandbox and another parcel from the second carriage. She turned and hurried up the stair to be un-peaked. It seemed she could not wait another moment to don a fresh gown.

If mortal woman had been created to tempt mortal man, then Leam was the first in the queue to sin.

Appearing at luncheon newly gowned in elegant rose and ivory that caressed her curves, her shimmering hair loosely arranged with sparkling combs he had once removed, Kitty glided like a goddess across the parlor. That he preferred seeing her with nothing on at all and her hair tumbling about her shoulders—and had spent the endless night think-ing along those lines and with great effort holding himself back from knocking on her door despite the certainty that she would repel him—did not help matters any.

He escaped, again flinging himself into the snowy cold but this time with thorough futility of purpose. He pretended he was looking for the shooter. He knew perfectly well the fellow was long gone. Men like that knew better than to linger, and the dogs had searched the place thoroughly the night before and brought up nothing.

Cox had departed before dawn, even before the mail coach came through, claiming he had an appointment he mustn't miss. Pen, standing sentry at the time, said he had departed in an easterly direction. Yale had gone pale hearing the news. He'd been out of the parlor when the shooter attacked, it seemed. Leam plowed through knee-high snowbanks along the river anyway, his feet blocks of ice, his nose and head frosted. At least the dogs were stretching their legs. Cox might well be the fellow trailing him and the one who had tried to shoot him. Or he might not. Leam might have only suspected him because he flirted with Kitty. Because he himself had wanted her entire attention.

By God, it was a good thing he was no longer an agent of the crown. He wasn't thinking straight. Since the moment Kitty Savege had kissed him two days earlier, he hadn't been in his right mind. He did not bed respectable ladies, even those who'd had lovers already. Neither did he haul them up against barn walls and maul them. The mere notion of some scoundrel doing that to his sisters or his cousin Constance had his fingers itching for a pistol.

He had put her in danger. Now he would leave her be, as he had last night with great difficulty. And as soon as he had a particular word with her.

He rounded the smithy's, tracking back to the inn along the rear yard. He found the others in the parlor. Wyn lounged by the hearth, dozing by all appearances. The attitude never fooled Leam. The Welshman was as alert as he with an assassin so close by. Likewise pretending—to read, on her part—Madame Roche flickered Yale quick, interested glances. Lady Emily sat with her nose in a book, oblivious.

Kitty stirred a cup of tea. She lifted her dark lashes, her raincloud eyes as richly expressive as they had been in the intimacy of her bedchamber, then again in the stable when she told him good-bye. Just as she had done before with other men, she'd said.

He cleared his throat. "Lady Kath'rine, might A hae a maument o yer company beneath the eave?" He gestured with her cloak laid over his arm. She stood and came toward him. He draped the cloak about her shoulders. The brush of her fingers as she grasped the collar went directly to his groin.

"Just without?"

He nodded.

The Frenchwoman looked on with undisguised interest. Leam motioned Kitty before him, and outside. He pulled the heavy door shut and followed her into the angle of sunlight cutting across the porch beneath the overhanging roof where a million heartbeats ago he had first held her and discovered her thundercloud eyes. Icicles made a jagged curtain above his head and she raised her face to his.

"Have you decided to tell me the truth after all?" she said without preamble, all soft curves yet sharp mind set on a single course. He scanned her face. Beauty. She was so beautiful the angels might have sculpted her from a fragment of the heavens.

"Nae."

"I believe I made my position perfectly clear yesterday afternoon, my lord. I will have the truth from you about the shooting and poetry and what have you, or you will have nothing more from me."

He could not respond.

"Well, then." Her lips made a firm line. "I cannot imagine what you must say to me that merits this privacy."

Anger prickled in him. She had insisted she was no schoolroom miss. Her touch in the dark of midnight had proven it. But, by God, she must have given herself to some extraordinary cads before him. At least one, Leam already knew.

"Lass." He stepped closer. There was no easy way to say such a thing. "An ye find yerself wi' child, A'll dae the right thing by ye. Ye've anely tae tell me."

By the acute glimmer in her eyes it seemed he had chosen perhaps the wrong difficult way to say it.

"That is gallant of you, my lord, and I daresay I should be comforted. But you have nothing to concern yourself upon that account." She moved to brush past him toward the door. He took gentle hold of her uninjured arm. She halted. Her curvaceous mouth held aloof, yet her eyes could not hide her warmth. Candid need gazed up at him, though she mustn't know it. She would not willingly reveal such a weakness, he now knew. Leam's gut twisted. Perhaps she was no more than the girl he had imagined.

"A didna intend tae insult ye, lass."

"I cannot fathom what gives you the idea that I think you have."

He swallowed thickly. She had no idea how a man could be caught by that glance, vulnerability cloaked in sophisticated lucidity. That he could wish to drop to his knees and do her bidding whatever it be. She believed herself jaded.

He opened his mouth to reply. She spoke first.

"I cannot conceive a child." Her gaze shifted away from his to the white blanket of snow. "I have not, although I have been foolishly careless. Quite foolish, really." She seemed thoughtful on the matter. Leam hadn't felt so ill in five years, lost in Bengal, a lead ball lodged in his shoulder and a fever to match the jungle heat.

"A see," he managed.

"Yes. Now you do. So clearly you have nothing to worry over." She took a step to move away, but he held her firm.

"A wisna worried." Petrified. Sick to his stomach. But now, much more so, because he needn't worry and he found quite abruptly that he rather wished to.

She only looked at him oddly, as though he had spoken out of turn although not grievously so.

This time she pulled her arm free with purpose, with control and poise and supreme nonchalance. Leam's brother,

James, had perfected such firm insouciance, and he'd been no older than this woman.

He watched her go inside. He could not follow. He had won a reprieve he did not deserve.

He scowled. This was the way of callow fools.

But he wanted his hands all over her. He wanted her body, her mouth, and his tongue deep in her making her moan. He hadn't had enough of her. Not nearly enough. He wanted to recite goddamned poetry to her in six languages. He wanted her so badly he could taste the words, taste her replies, taste the rain in her gaze.

She had cast off Poole without a backward glance, it seemed. Perhaps other men as well. She had been careless, she'd said. *Careless.*

A pattering on his shoulder wrested Leam from bemusement. Droplets of water made a puddle on his greatcoat cape with ever increasing speed. The thaw had come. He found his hands curled into fists.

Where was a Welshman's willing jaw when a man needed it?

"I have devised *un plan d'attaque*!" Madame Roche announced in grand tones with a flourish of scented lace kerchief. It suited her dramatic pose on the sofa, all white and black with red lips and cheeks. Not above fifty, she was a handsome woman, already a widow to four husbands.

Lord Blackwood came into the chamber from the rear foyer. Kitty spoke so that she would not be tempted to look at him.

"A plan of attack to have us on the road shortly, Madame?" She did not take up her teacup. She did not trust in the steadiness of her hands, and in any event the tea had turned cold while he offered to marry her if necessary and she spoke aloud her secret for the first time to anyone. The secret only Lambert Poole knew. When she had discovered her barrenness, still so angry and vengeful, she welcomed it; no inconvenient pregnancy would send her into exile from society. She could continue to pursue her course of collecting information from him without anxiety.

At the time it had seemed ideal, because at the time she had ignored the ache inside her telling her it was all horribly wrong. Now she was sick with the woman she had been.

"Oh, no, no, Lady Katrine! The gentlemen will see to those arrangements tomorrow morning, will you not, sirs?"

The earl bowed.

"It will be our greatest pleasure," Mr. Yale concurred.

"So kind, these gentlemen. And so very handsome! Which is how I have invented *mon plan*."

"Clarice"—Emily raised her attention from her book—"what on earth are you talking about?"

"Only this: together we will all go to the Willows Hall where His Lordship and Monsieur Yale will court you assiduously, making love to you openly with the pretty words and gestures until your parents cast off the unconscionable program to wed you to *le gros canard*, Warts More." She crossed her arms over her bosom and appeared all satisfaction.

Mr. Yale's face went blank.

Emily did not bat an eyelash. "Is Mr. Worthmore really a fat duck?"

"*Mais oui!* All men three times your age that wish to wed *ma petite* are *les gros canards*. And he is . . . how does one say? The dandy! The collars up to here." She jerked the edge of her hand against her chin. "But how do you like my plan?"

"It will not go over," Emily said, returning her attention to her book. "Everyone in society knows Lord Blackwood will never marry again on account of the tragic loss of his young wife shortly after the birth of their son, and Mr. Yale does not like me."

"You are too modest, ma'am." To his credit, Mr. Yale sounded sincere.

"And I don't like him."

"Haven't the funds for a wife at present, in any case."

"It wouldn't matter. My dowry is grotesquely enormous. My parents wish to make a statement."

"No no, monsieur! *Ma petite!*" Madame Roche lifted a forefinger and tapped it twice on the table top with a click of her nail. "No one will marry. It will be only for—how do you say?—the display."

"For show, Clarice."

"*Oui.* For the show. Your parents, they will send away *le gros canard*, and you and I, Emilie, we will return to Londre where you may choose from all the gentlemen that admire you."

Emily laid down her book. "My parents are quite vain and admire people who spend a great deal on carriages and clothing and what have you. They will not seriously consider a suitor who is not in possession of a considerable estate or at least an ample income. Lord Blackwood is quite wealthy, but Mr. Yale has no funds."

"I said, at *present.*"

"Well, do you wish to pretend to court me or not?" She frowned at him.

He lifted his brows.

Kitty felt queasy. The earl appeared to be studying the floor planking.

The notion of marriage to him had not repelled her. It made her heady with alarm and—even more alarmingly— pleasure. Had he offered the same to every woman with whom he had made love since his wife's death, despite his vow to remain unwed? Had he recited poetry to those women too?

Kitty's queasiness redoubled, shifting upward beneath her ribs.

"Then it is all settled. Monsieur Yale and Monseigneur Blackwood will be *les galants extraordinaires*." The Frenchwoman clapped her hands. "What fun we shall have!"

Mr. Yale leaned back, closed his eyes, and pinched the bridge of his nose with two fingers.

"If you do it," Emily said to him, "I might begin to think more highly of you. It would be a selfless gesture and prove you are not entirely motivated by vanity ."

He cracked open an eye. "I am all gratitude, my lady."

"You are odiously narcissistic." Her voice lacked its usual conviction. "But I will appreciate your help, nonetheless. And Lord Blackwood's." At that moment, she sounded as young and uncertain as Kitty had ever heard her.

Kitty placed her hand in her friend's. "We will not allow them to force you into an unpalatable marriage, Marie." She squeezed. "We will do all we can, won't we, gentlemen?"

Mr. Yale bowed from his chair. "Your servant, Lady Katherine."

She steeled her courage and looked across at the earl. He leaned against the edge of the mantel, eyes hooded.

A whorl of cold air rushed into the parlor, stirring the hearth flames. Mr. Pen stomped into the chamber, his jowly face ruddy with cold

"Road's passable, miss. A coach and six passed long 'bout a quarter hour ago. Driver said it's fair going all the way to Oswestry."

"Oswestry? So distant." Emily's voice had not yet recovered.

"The melt's happening right quick. We'd be better to set off now before there's floods on the road. I'll go ahead and hitch up the teams and we'll be at the Hall this evening." He tromped back outside.

Madame Roche's face wreathed in smiles. "*Bon*. Then the project of the courtship, it will commence! The handsome gentlemen, they will sweep *ma petite* off her feet before the eyes of her parents, and all shall be well."

"Then I suppose we must pack." Emily released Kitty's hand and headed toward the stair with purpose. Kitty followed, imagining the earl's gaze on her and wishing she were not about to be obliged to watch him flirt with another woman, even her friend, and even in play.

Especially not in play.

Her Christmas idyll was over. Her fantasy of escape had been played out to no one's harm but her own.

Chapter 13

Willows Hall rested on a gentle hill not five miles distant from the town and castle of Shrewsbury and only two from the tiny inn in which Kitty had spent Christmas making love to an exasperating Scot. Built sturdily of gray stone, with a single Tudor-style gable rising above the front portal and a well-proportioned portico of limestone columns and rails, it seemed far too modest a manor for Emily's fashion-conscious parents.

The carriage approached along a circling drive, the park spreading along the slope through copses of oak and willow. Draped in snow, a terraced garden spread off to the manor's south side, evidenced by a fountain and statuary poking out of the drifts. In the distance the wide Severn sparkled as it made its way slowly south and east.

As Pen handed them down from the carriage and the gentlemen dismounted, six girls, all in white frothy skirts and pinafores, and of descending heights and ages, burst from the house and tumbled down the slushy steps with vociferous glee. Each of them but one sported delightfully pale gold locks like Emily's, the sixth and apparently eldest, with hair the color of fire.

"Sister!"

"Emily!"

"You are home!"

"Reesey!"

"Hooray!"

"Oh, Madame!"

They swirled about Emily and her companion, hugging their waist and legs, a jumble of white and gold and arms and smiles.

"The petticoat set," Mr. Yale murmured at Lord Blackwood's shoulder.

"Behave yourself, whelp."

"Especially with the redhead, I daresay."

"Most especially."

Stomach hot, Kitty moved out of range of the earl's undisguised voice. For that it must be; he spoke to his friend as an Englishman. She ought to be furious. But, foolishly, she hurt. Her capacity for hearing what she was not intended to hear was not doing her service now.

Emily's parents appeared at the top of the stair. They were a handsome pair. Lord Vale was perhaps a decade his young wife's senior, at one time probably athletic but now going to seed, and dressed to the nines in collars to his ears and wasp-waist coat with enormous gold buttons. He made a leg and drew his wife forward. Lady Vale extended small hands dripping with Italian lace and encrusted with gems to grasp Kitty's.

"Dearest Lady Katherine, how we have anticipated your visit."

Kitty allowed her hostess to kiss her on the cheek, momentarily sucked into a cloud of pale curls, organza, and lily.

"Your home is quite lovely. How do you like the snow?"

"It is tiresome, to be sure! But Lord Vale sees that I am happy."

Generally, Kitty found Emily's mother to be silly, with little sense and less conversation. Her single accomplishment seemed to be doting upon her doting husband. But they appeared at least as enamored of each other as of their own reflections, so she admired them. They were honest.

Emily came up the step. "Hello, Papa. Mama." She allowed herself to be embraced by her mother.

"My darling Emily! And Madame Roche, of course." Lady Vale bowed her head to the older, striking Frenchwoman, her employee.

Emily went into the house, followed by the little girls and her companion, leaving only the sister with the fiery hair. The girl lingered, casting shy glances toward the gentlemen who followed the footmen bearing their traveling trunks up the steps.

"My lord and lady," Kitty said, "may I present to you the Earl of Blackwood and Mr. Yale? We met them upon the road and they kindly escorted us here."

Lady Vale's lashes flittered. "My lord, do not tell me you must go on any farther today! Lord Vale and I would be so happy for you to remain as our guests."

"Not only for the night, I trust." Lord Vale bowed. "I have been cooped up in this house for far too many days with seven females and now it shall be more—begging your pardon, Lady Katherine." He bowed again, and Kitty heard the distinct crack of stays. "I've only Mr. Worthmore to keep me company. We would be glad for a third and fourth at the table, and, Lord Blackwood, I know you are a fine card player."

"'Twoud be ma pleasure. Thank ye. An maleddy." The earl bowed to Lady Vale. No stays. Nothing but pure muscle and sinew, Kitty knew.

Coats and cloaks shed, they entered an overheated drawing room appointed in the latest stare with white and yellow striped wallpaper and claw-footed chairs and tables trimmed in gilt. Kitty welcomed the chamber's excessive warmth, moving as close to the hearth as possible. Then anyone might attribute her flushed cheeks to the fire, and perhaps she would not even feel the heat jumbled inside her at the memory of his naked body.

Madame Roche and Emily appeared at the door, a gentleman in their wake.

"Ah, Worthmore! Come meet our guests."

"He is only a guest too, Papa." Emily moved swiftly into the chamber. Mr. Worthmore traced her progress across the room with round, protruding eyes. Otherwise his appearance was unremarkable. He was over middle age and not at all handsome like his friends, but just as smartly dressed, with gleaming Hessians capped with white and a gold quizzing glass hanging from his waistcoat pocket, glittering with diamond chips.

"Emily, come make your bow to Mr. Worthmore," her father said pleasantly, but with a firm edge. "You and he must become well acquainted."

She recrossed the chamber to Mr. Worthmore.

Mr. Yale followed her.

Madame Roche grinned like a cat and glanced at Lord Blackwood.

And so it would begin. Kitty wished to flee, but a treacly fascination held her. The earl would join the game and she would have to watch how he would fool them all just as he had fooled her.

"How do you do, sir?" Emily curtsied. Mr. Worthmore took her hand and lifted it to his mouth. Her nostrils flared, her fine-boned jaw tight.

"My dear, your parents have told me so much of your beauty, I am your humble devotee already."

"Worthmore, I'm Yale." Mr. Yale thrust out his hand.

Mr. Worthmore was obliged to leave off making love to Emily's fingers to shake it. Discreetly Emily wiped hers on her skirt.

Mr. Worthmore looked the handsome young Welshman up and down in a leisurely fashion. "How do you do, sir? What brings you to Willows Hall?"

Mr. Yale took a noticeable breath and said rather firmly, "Lady Marie Antoine, if you must have it. She and I have formed something of an attachment and I'm not fond of the notion of you getting in the way of it."

Lady Vale gasped.

Lord Vale choked.

Madame Roche tittered.

Lord Blackwood chuckled.

Mr. Worthmore's round eyes rounded yet further as he looked from one member of the party to another. "Who in Nancy's goat is Lady Marie Antoine?"

"It was priceless. I shall never forget his face." Kitty sat down before the dressing table to plait her hair into a long braid for the night.

"He looks like a fish. And his voice is horrid, squeaky and far too certain of his welcome here." Emily plopped onto her stomach on Kitty's bed, a high four-poster in the style of feminine froth Lady Vale seemed to favor in clothing and everything else. "I cannot understand what my father likes about him. His conversation at dinner proves he is not a clever man. Papa usually likes clever men, as long as they are rich."

Her fingers moved deftly about a tangled mass of ribbons, picking here and unthreading there. It was the most domestic activity Kitty had ever seen her young friend perform, and yet seemed so natural. Beneath the veneer of studious plain speaker, Emily Vale was just a girl. As Kitty had once been. As she had felt for a few precious moments in a Shropshire inn, until the man she was infatuated with told her he would marry her if it became necessary.

In fact she was no longer a girl. Far from it, indeed.

"I was not speaking of Mr. Worthmore. I meant your other suitor's face."

Emily's emerald eyes rolled. "He was odious."

"He was charming. And very kind to do what he did."

"He made a cake of himself, and of me." She sat up, dropping the ribbons into her lap. "I have no doubt, Kitty, that he wishes me to squirm with discomfort through it all."

"It is possible. But he didn't look very happy about any of it either."

"Hm." Emily seemed to seriously consider. "At least Lord Blackwood has more sense than to be that silly."

Kitty could not respond. At the inn, he had not assented to or declined his part in Madame Roche's plan. But Kitty assumed he would agree. Yet tonight he had shown no indication of intending to play along.

A golden-red head peeked through the door. "Lady Katherine, may I enter?"

"Of course."

"Amarantha, you should be in bed by now. Is Nurse not looking for you?"

"I am no longer under Nurse's governance." She jumped up on the bed and curled an arm about her sister's waist. "Mama says I am old enough to have my own room. Yours!"

Emily petted her sister's shining hair. "I rather like town, with all its museums and such, and hope to remain there. You are welcome to my bedchamber here."

"Only to share with you, Emmie." Amarantha popped up on her elbows. "You simply mustn't like Mr. Worthmore. He is nasty." A shy smile crept across her lips. "And Mr. Yale is so agreeable."

Kitty watched a war of thoughts pass behind her friend's spectacles.

"I am glad you admire him," Emily finally said.

"He is very handsome."

"One might think so."

"How old is he?"

"It has not occurred to me to ask."

"Emmie! A lady must always discover her suitor's age and birth date."

Emily's eyes widened. "Whatever for?"

"So that she may send him a note wishing him happy upon the day each year."

"Who told you that?"

"Mama. She does so with Papa. Every year."

Emily seemed to digest that information with some degree of discomfort. Kitty's chest felt warm. To see her friend lying to her family now did not sit well with her, and she knew perfectly well why.

She could not run away forever. That night after Lambert told her he would never marry her, her mother held her while she cried for hours. Kitty had not told her everything that happened, but from the dowager's comforting words it seemed she had understood. Why else would she have allowed her daughter to remain unwed, unless she knew she was in fact unweddable?

But now, for the first time in years, she could no longer bear the silent understanding her mother had given her for so long. She wished she had told her the truth immediately, before she had plunged into revenge and discovered her inability to conceive. Perhaps nothing could have been done then, anyway. Kitty was ruined. What man would have her? But at least she would not have been alone in her grief and anger. Perhaps her mother might have helped her free herself of it, and she would not have had to wait for the glance of a Scottish lord to do it herself.

"Mr. Yale might send you a posy, Emmie, so you must inform him of your birth date as well, but not your age," Amarantha cautioned her sister. "You will not want him to think you are too old to marry."

Too old and misguided and barren. But maudlin musings would not aid her now, and she had Emily's situation to see to.

"Your sister needn't have a care about that, Amarantha." Kitty rose from the table and drew on her dressing gown over shift and stays, a sleeveless covering of sheerest silk. It was the greatest luxury to have all her clothing, save one gown she would never again wear. "Mr. Yale is quite as devoted to her as your parents are to one another."

"And he is *so* handsome."

"You said that already, Amy," Emily muttered.

"And tall. Not as tall as Lord Blackwood, but the earl is an old man, nearly as old as Mama, I daresay! He cannot help that streak of white in his hair, although it is dashing for an elderly gentleman, and I suppose he *is* handsome nevertheless. But Mr. Yale's hair is entirely black, isn't it?"

"I haven't the foggiest."

The fifteen-year-old peered queerly at her sister.

Emily blinked. "Yes. All black. Very nice hair."

Kitty stifled a laugh. Emily slid off the bed and went to the door, casting her a narrow look.

"I am going to sleep. Amy, are you coming?"

Amarantha jumped to the floor. Emily opened the door. Gentlemen's voices sounded in the corridor and then the gentlemen themselves walked past. They paused. Mr. Yale seemed weary; nothing in his erect carriage gave a sign to it, but his silvery eyes looked somewhat sunken.

Lord Blackwood bowed. "Leddies."

Amarantha giggled. Emily pursed her lips. Kitty pulled the wrapper over her breasts and endeavored not to notice his gaze dipping there.

"My lord, Mr. Yale," she said as smoothly as her voice would allow, "thank you for your fine company tonight. Lady Marie Antoine and I are so grateful."

Mr. Yale bowed rather stiffly, then continued along the corridor. The earl met Kitty's gaze and there was nothing of hooded indolence there, only pleasure. She stood in the middle of her bedchamber and wished Emily and her sister away and the earl on her side of the door, with it closed and bolted.

Misguided wishes. She did not need more deception in her life, from herself or anybody else.

"Good night, my lord."

He nodded, gave Emily's sister a lovely smile, and went along. Kitty ushered the girls out, shut the door, and sank against it, praying that Emily and Mr. Yale's courtship would go very swiftly.

"Has it only been one night?" The Welshman tilted his head onto the chair back and tossed down the remainder of his brandy. "Tell me it will end tomorrow."

"You are doing this by choice."

"Hardly."

Leam withheld his thoughts. The Welshman's insouciant manner with females masked a chivalrous nature even stronger than his love of the bottle. Why the mask, Leam had never inquired.

"I believe this is the first time in our acquaintance that I have heard you complain."

"I am not complaining." The lad straightened in his chair. "Merely lamenting lost time." He held out his glass.

Leam tipped the brandy decanter against it and poured,

topping off his own as well. After glimpsing Kitty in her gossamer night rail, her rich hair lying in a plait against her perfect breast, he needed the extra dram or two.

"When shall we head off for Liverpool?"

"Presumably when you have convinced our hosts that you cannot live without their daughter."

Yale set down his glass, stood, and strode toward the door.

"Turning in so early?" Leam murmured.

"Merely leaving you to the company of one much prettier than I. You'd better hurry. She might not wait up for you." He departed.

Leam went to the fire, lit a taper, and moved around the parlor setting candles to blaze. He disliked darkly lit chambers in winter. They reminded him too much of that autumn five years earlier, Alvamoor sunk in darkness and cold, his heart turning to stone within the frozen stone of his house. Before he'd gone down to London again and met up accidentally with Colin Gray.

He could not sleep yet, in any case. He was here for one reason only: to make certain Kitty and Lady Emily were no longer in danger, and that Cox was not hiding somewhere with a pistol waiting for them to emerge. Once all were abed tonight, he would do some prowling about, studying and surveying. His Falcon Club experience would again come in handy.

He settled into a chair, glancing at the journal on the table beside him without interest. He didn't care about the news from London. Or Paris, or Edinburgh, or Calcutta. It was almost a relief to harbor that feeling again—the cool, hard relief of not having a care for anything at all.

Almost.

"Monseigneur, how glad I am to find you!" Madame Roche entered in a swirl of skirts and veils, like a nun crossed with an opera singer.

He stood.

"Oh, *non, non*, sir. You must not! You must treat me as the servant, for that I am in this house."

"Whin a leddy enters a room, ma'am, a gentleman that no stands shoud be nag-whipped."

"And you are the fine gentleman, *n'est-ce pas*, Lord Blackwood?" She tapped him upon the shoulder with her fan and sat in the chair across, fabric flowing over armrests and floor.

He allowed himself a smile. "Woud ye be caring for a bit o spirits, ma'am?" He gestured with his glass.

"No, no. Sit! We must talk."

He obliged. She leaned forward, pursing lips defined by ample rouge.

"You do not still mourn the death of the young wife, *non*?" She peered at him with dark eyes enhanced with kohl. Well accustomed to such prying, Leam did not reply.

"*Bon.*" She patted her palms together. "I thought this. But why will you not play the courtship game?"

He studied her for a moment. Her intent seemed direct, and she clearly doted upon her charge. But women were complicated creatures.

"The lad's taking guid care o it, ma'am."

"*Oui, oui.* Monsieur Yale, he is *extraordinaire.* But I think that is not your reason. Emilie, she is a good girl. And the Lady Katrine, she does not allow *ma petite* to be harmed, *non*? She is like—how do you say?—bloodhound."

He lifted a brow.

"*Non!*" The feathers in her hair jiggled as she shook her head. "*Peut-etre* not the bloodhound. They hunt with the nose on the ground, *n'est-ce pas*?" She pressed a fingertip to her red lips. "The shepherd dog. *Oui.* Have you any?"

Collies and their flocks covered the slopes of Alvamoor.

"Aye."

"Then she is *comme ça*!" She gestured with a nod.

"Ma'am, A wadna be making a leddy evin wi' a wirkin dug."

"Ah, *non*! *Bien sur.* But she is very loyal. She does not wish to see *ma petite* unhappy." Her voice dipped. "For she has suffered so much unhappiness herself, *non*?"

He had no reply. In truth, he knew nothing of the heart of any woman. Nothing he could trust.

"Begging yer pardon, ma'am, but A'm nae a man for blethering." Lies and more lies. He would never be free of them. For over five years he'd made it his particular business to do nothing *but* encourage gossip from women such as this. Now he would be free of it. But the desire to hear about Kitty Savege was too strong, and he remained seated.

Madame Roche leaned in and spoke confidentially as though she had not heard him or understood.

"I do not think she cared for that man." She shook her head. "I do not believe she did. The gossips—the silly friends of my mistress—who tell the Lady Vale that my Emilie must not be in *la belle* Katrine's company, that she is the poor example for a young girl." She waved her hand broadly. "But I say these biddies, they are wrong. *C'est la jalousie!* I tell my mistress. Wicked *jalousie* that drives the heart insane." She peered sharply at him. "Do you know it, the jealousy?"

Leam's palms were cold. "Aye."

"She is very beautiful, the Lady Katrine, *non*?"

More beautiful than he could bear.

"*Oui!* Any gentleman would admire such beauty, as did that *canard* Poole." She made a spitting noise. "Phtt! He is better far and away from *la belle* Katrine, so she must no longer always be running away from him at *les* parties and balls." She shook her head sorrowfully. "So sad always, *la belle*, so beautiful dancing with all the handsome gentlemen. But, *hélas*, they cannot stir her wounded heart." She sighed, her eyelids drifting shut and fingertips moving from side to side.

Her eyes popped open. She stood.

"Ah, *bon*. I am so glad we have had this conversation, monseigneur."

Leam came from his chair and bowed. "Ma'am."

"*Alors*, good night." She traipsed from the chamber, leaving him with a glass full of liquor and fire in his gut.

The temptation to go to Kitty's bedchamber now and make her take him in was great. The desire flickering in her eyes for the briefest moment earlier told him she would accept him, and they would know pleasure again for a night. But one night would not be enough, and he did not trust himself with more.

He left the parlor and turned down the corridor away from the guest chambers. In the dark he would study the manor house. Tomorrow in the light he would spread his research wider. He would discover if any threat had followed him to Willows Hall, if any here were now in danger. When he was satisfied that all was well, he would depart.

Yale and Lady Emily maintained their farce for her parents, who seemed happy with the Welshman's pretty manners and elegant appearance. Having taken the lay of the land, Yale dressed at his smartest, his cravat starched and arranged to a monstrosity, and every sparkling gewgaw he'd brought with him pinned here and there about his person. For her part the girl seemed to be doing her best to put on smiles when he catered to her. It was something of a relief to watch them, a comedy unfolding for her parents' interested appraisal and Worthmore's increasing consternation.

It was not sufficient distraction for Leam. It proved impossible to always be in Kitty's company and not to watch her and want her.

He absented himself from the party. On the first day he took his horse to the nearby villages, trekking across fields sloppy with melting snow. Wearing his shabbiest coat, he made himself comfortable at pubs and fell into conversation with farmers and shopkeepers. He'd learned early in the game to look first to the locals for information. Five years ago he had devised his persona largely because it aided in that task.

He learned nothing of note. No strangers had come through save the members of his own party at Willows Hall. No laborers had been absent from the estate and surrounding areas on Christmas Day. Leam's shooter had not come into or from this neighborhood, it seemed.

On the second day he returned to the inn, Bella and Hermes in tow. Milch welcomed him, and they sat down to a pint and conversation, and Leam learned what he should have days ago if his head had been on straight.

Cox could well have been the shooter. He had indeed gone out for several minutes before the shooting, according to Milch, as Yale had suspected. The Welshman and the dogs had run toward the river when they ought to have been tracking around the rear entrance of the inn. Leam cursed himself for his distraction, for foolishly dismissing his suspicion of Cox because he imagined his jealousy over his attentions to Kitty was clouding his judgment. But his judgment had been fine. His jealousy was damning him yet again.

He continued on to the local magistrate's house, an ancient squire more worried about his lower field flooding with the thaw than the personal squabbles of "trinkery Londoners." He'd been told about the shooting and the ladies and gentlemen all holed up in an inn like loose cards. He glowered at Leam and suggested that he and his friend resolve their differences over their "fancy piece" in private instead of bothering him and everybody else with it. But if they knew what was good for them, henceforth they would keep their "pistols" in their pockets.

Leam returned to Willows Hall late, begged pardon of his hostess for his absence, and went to bed.

He rode out again the third day merely to maintain his distance, eschewing cards and more games within for activity beneath the leaden sky. Upon his return hours later he tended to his horse for as long as he could make that excuse.

In company, Kitty did not address him directly.

That evening after the ladies had gone up, he told Lord Vale that he regretted he must depart so soon. At dawn the following day Leam packed his bag and set off for Liverpool.

Yale caught up with him just before Whitchurch.

"Hell and damnation, Blackwood," he clipped. "If you'd have bothered to divulge your plans I could have told you Jinan sent word to Willows Hall that he's to meet us in Wrexham."

"How did he—"

"How does he discover anything? He has contacts and messengers from Canton to the West Indies that none of us know about."

"He isn't the only one." Leam pulled up on the road overhung with heavy gray clouds. "Why don't you go to work for the Foreign Office now that the Club is finished, Wyn? The Home Office would take you too. You could make yourself useful in France or wherever you choose."

"You've been waiting to ask me that for weeks, haven't you?" The Welshman's eyes showed pure sobriety.

"Not waiting. Simply not interested."

"Then why ask now?"

Leam spurred his horse forward.

"Gray called on me early the morning you and I left town."

Leam snapped his head around. "And you decided not to mention this to me until now?"

"It seems the information concerning Scottish rebels is quite good, from two of the Home Office's best informants. Someone is stirring up seditionist rabble in the Highlands. The Home Office already has a list of possible ringleaders."

"I told the both of you that I don't give a damn about that. I promised to meet Jin and learn the information he has for the director that cannot be conveyed by post. That, after all, is why you are here."

"So that you can then hasten to Alvamoor and send me back as courier to Gray with all the juicy details. Yes. I do recall."

For several minutes only the sloshing of hooves and dripping of tree branches could be heard between them.

"And what of the lovely Lady Katherine?"

Leam reined in, drew the pistol out of his pack, and pointed it across the road. Yale leaned back comfortably in the saddle, his black's delicate hooves splashing in the deep puddles as he passed by.

"You've got to cock it first, old man."

"You'd like it if I shot you, wouldn't you, Wyn? You'd be damned glad of it."

"Speak for yourself."

Leam pocketed the weapon and pressed his mount forward.

"She did not appear crestfallen to learn of your sudden departure," the Welshman commented, "in the event that you were wondering."

"I wasn't."

"Cad."

"You're sounding more like Colin every day, Wyn. Take care."

The Welshman chuckled. "My intended was not sorry to see me go either. Madame Roche, however, made it clear she expected both you and me back within the sennight. Lady Vale added her charming encouragement. Our host even extended a formal invitation. Why, with such a gracious urging, I could not resist. I vowed I would make it so."

Leam peered at his friend.

Yale shrugged. "It seems I have grown accustomed to my fate." He looked at Leam's face and expelled a rare crack of laughter. "My pretended fate! Good Lord, Leam, it would be like marrying my sister."

"You haven't any sisters."

"I do now." He smiled slightly. "I have come to feel somewhat protective of the chit. Like I would of an unprofitable spaniel who is nevertheless too clever to put down."

"And Lady Emily?"

"Informed me yesterday that if I were to kiss her hand one more time she will boil it in oil so that the next time I would be obliged to kiss festering pus."

For the first time in ages, it seemed, Leam grinned.

"Just so," his friend murmured.

"Then on to Wrexham with haste, so that you may return to Willows Hall and pull the remainder of the rug out from under Worthmore's feet."

But their sailor friend was not in Wrexham. Messengers had crossed paths. Jin was on his way to Willows Hall via Oswestry, and Leam and Wyn had missed him on the eastern road.

They spent the night in Wrexham, then as the temperature dropped and snow fell in light gusts once more, made their way south again along byways thick with icy mud. Assisting a pair of carters from a ditch amid the evergreen hills of the Welsh borderlands, Yale's Cambridge drawl slid away, replaced by the rough Celtic lilt of his homeland. Leam barely understood a word the three Welshmen exchanged, but he didn't begrudge it. His friend's secrets were his own, as they had always been.

The snowfall increased, layering the soggy earth afresh. When the rooftop of Willows Hall glimmered on the hill in the distance, Leam's chest tightened.

Lady Vale met them in the foyer as they removed coats and hats.

"Mr. Yale, we are happy you have returned in such short time. And my lord, it is an honor."

Lady Emily appeared at the stair banister above. Her lips pursed. She pivoted about and bumped into Kitty coming onto the landing.

"I beg your pardon, Mar—" Kitty's gaze flickered to the foyer, met his, and a flush rose to her cheeks so swiftly that even her quick palms could not cover it in time for Leam's sake. Air filled his lungs for the first time in days. He bowed. The corner of her mouth tipped up, and Leam knew that returning had been his most foolish decision yet.

He would be a man twice damned, it seemed. He would throw himself beneath the wheels of the carriage and suffer the consequences.

Chapter 14

L ord Blackwood!" The master of Willows Hall came from the corridor, followed by a surly Worthmore, his points drooping. "And Mr. Yale." Lord Vale bowed with pretty grace. "Welcome back. How did you find the road in this dreadful weather?"

"Passable, sir, only in that it brought us quickly here," Yale replied, casting a meaningful look toward the banister where his *fausse amant* hid behind her friend.

Lord Vale was all smiles. "Do go wash that mud from your boots and then join us in the parlor." He gestured toward the stair. "I have had a visit this morning from an acquaintance of yours, it seems. A Mr. Seton of Liverpool. He has been most happy to wait upon your arrival, although we only hoped you would return so soon, and is now in the library."

Leam ascended the steps and found himself facing the woman whose lips tasted like wood smoke and cherries.

"My lord," she said smoothly, only a hint of pink remaining on her porcelain cheeks, "we did not expect to see you again so soon, or indeed at all."

"The whelp needed tending."

Her wood-smoke cherry lips twitched.

"Lady Marie Antoine." Yale bowed deeply, peering around Kitty's shoulder. "You are as lovely as ever."

"Oh, be quiet. My mother and father and that fish-troll man have gone already."

"But I must speak the truth, nonetheless."

"You are abominable."

"Your gratitude touches me deeply, ma'am."

She narrowed her gaze. "You now expect I owe you something in return, don't you? I had that thought while you were gone."

"The lady spares a thought for me. Be still my heart."

Lady Emily whirled about and with quick, firm steps disappeared along the corridor.

Kitty glanced after her. "I believe she is beginning to think you truly intend to offer for her."

"I am all humility," he replied with perfect amiability.

"Yes, I'd thought so. But she is a bit concerned."

The Welshman's mouth curved into a grin. She studied him for a moment.

"Sir, you have broken your promise to me. You said you would not tease her." Her voice had altered, a hitch amid the smoothness. "Honestly, I do not know why I trusted you." She turned her wide gray gaze on Leam. "I don't know you from Adam, after all."

Beneath the scrutiny of the thunderclouds, Leam's throat went dry. She passed him and hurried down the stairs. For once, Yale did not utter a word.

As Leam crossed the library, Jinan stood and came toward him with a handshake.

"It's been too long, Jin."

"I trust you are well, Leam?" Jin settled back in a chair, at ease in the sumptuous apartment yet still slightly alien to it. The foreign, aristocratic cast of his sun-darkened features was at odds with his plain clothing, and his light eyes held sharp intelligence. Several years shy of Leam's age, Jinan Seton had had the rule of himself before Leam had even learned English.

"I am as well as can be expected with Colin still nosing into everybody's business," Leam said, sitting as well.

"Yes. He sent me word shortly before you left London."

"*What?*"

"Rather, about what?" Yale said, entering. Jin stood but the Welshman waved off the formality and headed toward the sideboard.

Leam shook his head. "Goddamn it, Wyn, did you know Colin had been in touch with Jin already?"

"Did I know that our friend the viscount told a little white lie to get you involved in whatever business Jin has come to chat about with us? No. But I'm not surprised. Colin Gray always gets his man."

Leam turned to the privateer. "Colin knew where you've been all along?"

Jin nodded. "Apparently he did not share that information with you. He did, however, send me interesting news and told me you would be coming my way."

"You may as well let Jin tell us, Leam. Colin will find a way to get you involved later if you don't at least appear to be curious now." Yale filled three glasses with claret and carried them over.

Jin set his on the table. "The Home Office has had word from two separate sources that recently a merchant ship intended for Calcutta disappeared after leaving the port at Newcastle Upon Tyne."

"Quite close to the Scottish border." Yale lifted a brow. "Pirates or rebels?"

"As yet the owners of the vessel have not come forward

with an insurance claim, so the cargo has yet to be disclosed. The informants seem to think Scottish rebels took it because they believed it carried cargo of particular value."

"Cargo that could finance an insurrection against the British crown, presumably," Yale supplied. "Those pesky insurgents. What cargo of that value could be on its way to Calcutta? English woolens seem unlikely."

"Rather, intelligence on British tactics in Bengal traveling under cover of commerce to disguise it," Jin replied. "It is sometimes done to protect sensitive information also sent in duplicate on naval ships."

"Aha." Yale leaned back in his chair. "This intelligence is something that the French in the East Indies might be happy to have, I take it? What a pretty little circle of amity. Scottish rebels seeking French assistance and willing to trade English secrets abroad to assure that assistance." The Welshman sipped his drink sparingly now. While working, he rarely indulged.

"Our director asked the Admiralty that I be given permission to board all ships, British and otherwise, in search of information," Jin said.

"Did the Admiralty oblige?"

The sailor nodded. "The *Cavalier* will pull out of Liverpool next week."

"I thought you'd quit too, Jin." Yale eyed him.

"I quit the Falcon Club." Jin finally tipped his glass to his mouth, a thick ring set with a bloodred ruby winking on his hand. "Not my livelihood."

"As though you need any more gold. Rich as Midas."

Jin's lean cheek creased. "Short on funds again, Wyn?"

"Gentlemen." Jaw tight, Leam stood. "As none of this concerns me, I must take leave of you now."

"Leam—"

The door clicked open. Kitty entered and glided across

the room. The others came to their feet. She held out her hands and put them into Jin's.

"Jinan, it is a pleasure to see you." Her smile was genuine. "If I had known you were here earlier, I would have sought you out." She released him.

"Hello, Kitty. How do you come to be in this country?"

"I have come here with my friend, the eldest daughter of Lord and Lady Vale. But tell me, how is your ship?" The thunderclouds sparkled with sunshine in the dim chamber, dancing with affection like Leam had never seen, her complexion high from familiar warmth rather than discomfort. Her elegance was radiant, and it struck him full force in the gut.

It was for another man, and Leam did not like it.

"Very well," Jin said. "And Alex?"

"Likewise. Serena hopes to deliver an heir for him shortly."

"You're acquainted with Lord Savege, then, Seton?" Yale asked.

"Mr. Seton and my brother met years ago in the West Indies. We have known each other an age. But how do you all come to be acquainted? Are you sailors, and all along I have thought you indolent town dandies?" Her words teased, but the shine in her eyes dimmed.

"No, that's Worthmore, of course." Yale chuckled.

"We've a shared acquenntence in Lunnon, maleddy," Leam said, "He's sent us news o common interest."

"Really, my lord? What sort of news?" Nothing changed in her tone, but Leam saw the glint of challenge in her eyes.

"Shipping news," he replied.

"Ah. I see." With a quick glance she took them all in. "Lady Vale bids me alert you that dinner will be served in a quarter hour." She flashed Jin a brief smile, curtsied, and left.

Yale settled into his chair anew and took up his glass.

Jin turned to Leam. "Katherine Savege?"

"Well acquainted with the lady?" Yale murmured. "Spent some time drinking rum with her rogue of a brother in the West Indies before Savage settled down to happily-ever-after, no doubt."

"Something like that." The sailor's light eyes remained pensive. "Leam, she and her mother play cards often with the Earl of Chance, don't they?"

"I believe so."

"He is on our list."

"List?"

"He's a Scot," Yale murmured.

"Whose list?" Leam insisted.

"The director's, with the Admiralty's input," Jin replied. "A list of Scottish lords considered ripe for allying themselves with the French."

Cheroot between thumb and forefinger, Yale lit a taper. "The full truth unfolds. The director wishes Leam to become cozy with these Scottish lords, no doubt."

"Spies and traitors are the business of the Home Office, not the Falcon Club," Leam said, hollowness settling into his gut. "But even if that weren't the case, I no longer work for the crown," he finished slowly, distinctly.

Jin's clear regard never faltered. "Then what are you doing here?"

A younger Leam might have been tempted to say that fate had driven him to the feet of Kitty Savage. But he was no longer that foolish youth, no matter how her presence animated him to jealousy that burned like a branding iron.

Without awaiting a reply, Jin reached into his waistcoat pocket. "I'm off."

Yale slanted him a grin. "Hello and good-bye. Why am I not surprised?"

"I have business to attend to before hauling out." Jin dropped a folded paper onto the table.

"The director's list?"

With only a nod, the shipmaster departed.

Leam drew in a slow breath. He headed for the door.

"Don't you wish to see the other names on that list?" Yale asked.

"I wish to go home. I intend to do so tomorrow." Nothing held him in England. Not a club or Highland rebels or traitorous lords or ships full of secret intelligence. Not even a woman. If an assassin wanted him, he could damned well follow him to Scotland.

In the drawing room after dinner Leam informed his hosts of his departure on the morrow.

"*Si vite!*" Madame Roche tut-tutted. "But you have only now returned."

"Will you be taking Mr. Yale with you?" Worthmore queried dryly.

"I could not leave here in less than a fortnight, sir," the Welshman said. "The company is far too charming to tear oneself away so abruptly." He smiled at his hostess. She tittered, and Leam saw in her a reflection of what Cornelia might have become, still beautiful, entirely obsequious.

"A'm expected at home wi' ma family, maleddy."

"What a fond papa you must be. And how sad that your dear wife could not see her son grow to manhood." She grasped Leam's hands. "We will miss you dreadfully." The light, teasing simper, the sweet, golden sympathy—Cornelia would have been this, indeed. He should have seen it at the time. Instead he had been a naïve, besotted fool. And a jealous one.

But the passion of jealousy was in his nature. He could not change that. He could only avoid situations in which he might become slave to it again.

The party broke up and Leam bid them all adieu. Kitty

did not speak. Her cheeks were again bright, in her eyes hesitancy. Thoroughly unwelcome.

He went to his bedchamber, lifted the stopper from an overwrought crystal decanter, and poured a brandy. An hour later, drink untasted and fire guttering in the grate, he rose from the chair in which he'd sat motionless, drawn to the window. He parted the draperies.

Moonlight glimmered on fresh snow, the clear sky showing black and silvery. On the lawn, moving gracefully through the garden statuary toward a trio of ancient trees at the edge of the hill, cloak billowing behind her, an angel tread. An angel with wide gray eyes and sweet lips, a clever tongue, and a past of careless encounters with gentlemen Leam did not wish to count himself among, damnation.

He watched her lose herself among the boughs of willow and pine, and despite the warning in the pit of his stomach, could not halt himself from going after her.

Kitty's feet sank into the soft snow, cold and wet but welcome. Anything to distract her.

She mustn't allow herself to feel this way because he was departing tomorrow. He had already left Willows Hall once without notice, throwing her into the acutest kind of confusion that he could leave her like that without even saying good-bye. But even before he disappeared so suddenly, he had been playing least in sight at Willows Hall. He seemed to want nothing to do with her now.

That was for the best. She did not trust him. And now she knew, through his association with Jin, that Lord Blackwood was indeed involved in matters far beyond what it appeared.

Jin was no innocent. Not remotely. Handsome, wealthy, and without any morals that she had ever noticed except a fierce loyalty to her eldest brother, Jinan Seton was not a safe man. Alex did not know Jin from the gaming tables; he had not been born into a gentleman's household. Now he sailed his ship at the behest of the crown as a commissioned privateer. But for over a decade on the ocean, he had been a pirate.

An old willow spread out before her, its boughs thickly tangled with the draping pine beside it. A half moon cast all into bluish silvery relief, picking out every shadow with precision. Kitty went beneath the boughs, the snow thinning on the ground and making way for a soft, soundless carpet of dried needles.

If the earl did business with Jin, she should be glad he was leaving. She couldn't be. When he looked at her she saw both the steel and the heat of desire. She wanted to be desired that way. And the things he had said . . .

She removed her glove and pressed her palm into the rough bark, shivering beneath her woolen cloak. She mustn't think it. Shortly she would return to London and take up her old life, too cowardly to alter the manner in which she had lived for years. Or perhaps she could wed an older man like Worthmore, or a man of lesser fortune, one who would take her despite all because of her dowry. Or if her mother married Lord Chamberlayne, she might live the rest of her days in her stepfather's and brothers' homes, moving back and forth between them because she lacked a family of her own. Because she had seen to that herself with such purpose and dedication. With such an angry heart.

But now her heart no longer knew anger, and she wanted another sort of life.

A rustling of branches sounded behind her. She whirled about. He stood just within the fall of green and gray, all black beneath the moon, and white.

He came to her while her legs weakened and her breaths fled, until he stood before her. Without a word he parted her cloak and took her waist into his hands. She caught up her breath, gulping air and feeling his heat through his hands and in the space between them. His eyes were so dark, and as they had been at the inn, full of a longing she feared she had already fallen too far into.

Soundlessly, like a vision from a dream, he went to his knees before her. With his hands around her hips, he pressed his face against her waist and seemed to breathe deeply. Then his thumbs curved down the bones of her hips, and he followed them with his mouth.

She turned her head aside, unable to look. "What are you doing?"

"A hardly know." He spoke low, hushed beneath the winter canopy.

"That is not very encouraging."

"A'm making luve tae a fair lass."

"You should not."

"Aye."

"You don't understand," that something was slipping away from her, the control she had held to so tightly since she vowed to wound a man. Now she knew where she had lied to herself. She had always hoped. Not for Lambert. For something more. Something she should not truly hope for because she had nursed revenge for so long by mimicking attachment, she did not deserve real attachment. She was ruined in her soul.

"Leam." Her voice was a whisper, a plea or a denial, she knew not.

"Kitty, luve?" His hands cupped her buttocks, covering her in warmth amid the cold.

"Why wouldn't you play Madame Roche's game? Why wouldn't you pretend for Emily's sake?"

He lifted his face to her, starkly planed in the moonlight.

"Whit kind of a man ye must think me." His whisper was rough. He slid his hands down the outside of her thighs, possessing with his touch. "How coud A?"

"Do you mean, how could you pretend such a thing with my friend when we had been lovers? But we weren't any longer."

At her back, he gripped the fabric of her gown into fists.

"For a *day*, for God sakes."

"But—"

"Lass, nae all men are scoundrels."

But she did not understand any longer what made a man a scoundrel. Was it a man who offered marriage because he must, or one who offered it as his final cruelty?

"Lord Poole offered for my hand." Her words fell like snowflakes onto the soft, cold ground in the shelter of the boughs. "He had never offered before that night at the masquerade ball when I finally told him to leave me alone. That night three years ago, when you and I met."

He rose to his feet. He touched her face and drew her gaze to his.

"Whit did ye tell him, lass?"

"I told him that if I had wanted marriage I could have had it before many times. That I had not been waiting for him."

"Had ye?"

She couldn't breathe. She wanted him to make this feeling in her breast real. She shook her head. His warm hand curved around her face, beneath the fall of her hair.

"Leam?"

His gaze scanned her face, her cheeks, and brow. "Lass?"

"I think you should go away now, quickly, because if you remain I may cast myself at you again."

He scooped her into his arms like a child, but his kiss was a man's. Kitty surrounded his beautiful face with her hands, warming her chilled blood.

"Where can we go?" she uttered when he kissed her neck and she wrapped her arms about his shoulders, his hold so strong and secure. But he covered her mouth once more, his kiss ravenous now, seeking and making her hot so swiftly. She pressed against him and slipped her tongue into his mouth.

"*Kitty.*"

He went to his knees with her in his arms, cradling her on his lap and kissing her like he would consume her now. She shifted to feel his arousal beneath her behind, he groaned, and his hand sought her bodice. Without warning he shoved his palm beneath her gown and surrounded her breast. She gasped, the cold of his touch shivering through her.

"Forgie me," he rasped, caressing her tight nipple and taking her lips with his, one at a time to tease.

"I will not." She pushed herself into his touch, twisting her knee up, but her skirts impeded her.

"Than forgie me for this?" He pulled her garments down from her breast and set his mouth to the sensitive peak. His tongue stroked, dragging her into pleasure.

"Yes, I will." She moaned, grasping his shoulders and trying to fit her throbbing center to his arousal through their clothing. Frustration drove her hands to his hips, then to her skirts, tugging as he sucked on her and the sweet need built. "But you mus—" She choked upon the pleasure. "You must continue doing that or I shall withdraw my forgiveness."

He lifted his head, a smile of pure delight curving his dampened lips, moonlight glimmering in his eyes.

She shook her head. "Didn't you just hear me?"

"Aye. But yer a beautiful woman, Kitty Savage, wi' a tongue fit for laughter." His voice was deliciously husky, the frigid air coalescing in misty veils between them. "Why dinna ye laugh mair aften?"

"Why don't you mean it when you do?"

They stared at each other for a long moment, the dampness prickling her breast with cold. The boughs of the willow sparkled, moonlight dappling the carpet of soft dried leaves. Everything was soft brown and silver.

He drew her close and his voice came roughly at her ear. " 'I've had a dream, past the wit of man to say what dream it was.' "

"Shakespeare." A smile of pure hopeful happiness crept onto her lips. "In *A Midsummer Night's Dream* he also wrote, 'Out of this wood do not desire to go.' "

"A made a vow tae behave as a gentleman wi' ye, lass," he said with glorious huskiness.

"Don't." She pressed her lips to his and wrapped her arms about his neck. He pulled her to him. Her fingers plucked at his waistcoat and the shirt beneath. "Make love to me right here. Now."

He swept her skirts from her legs and together they managed to get her sitting astride him. She fumbled with his trousers fastenings.

"I don't know what I am doing here," she whimpered, her fingers icy.

"Kitty, ma darling, yer doing everything juist fine." He covered her hand and curved it about his arousal. Through the fabric his stiff heat throbbed. She struggled to breathe. He took her mouth with his and his hand guided hers over his hard shaft, back and forth, as his tongue explored. It made her heady to touch him so, and needy. A sound of pleasure rumbled in his chest. His hand stole beneath her skirts, cold against her skin but she didn't care. She wanted his hands everywhere. He stroked her and she moaned against his mouth.

"Kitty, A want tae taste ye." His voice was so deep, rough and beautiful.

She didn't know what he meant. She would allow him anything.

"Yes."

He swept off his greatcoat, draped it on the ground behind her, and laid her back. But when she thought he would move atop her he pushed her skirts up over her knees and pressed her thigh aside with a firm hand. He bent to her.

"Leam? Wh— *Oh!*"

His tongue was upon her, soft, hot, wet, a fantasy.

"*Yes,*" she whispered.

It must be wrong, so wrong, yet her body opened for him, seeking his kiss. If she had not been made for this, she knew not what purpose her woman's flesh had. It felt right, sublime, a little overwhelming. She thrust to him for more, unable to hold her hips still, her back curving with the pleasure of it. He dipped inside her and she made sounds she had never before made. He caressed, a torment of his mouth on her, and she lost her breath, her will for anything but this, the hot, quick stroking and probing, the fluid rushing of need. She ached and he answered it and she knew there was no mercy on this earth. When she came she cried in silence, throat parched in fulfillment, choked with sobs and laughter.

He released her and she dragged air into her lungs. Her limbs were weak. His hands slid down her thighs, then calves, the cold following, returning her to reality.

"Wickedness," she whispered, a claw of shame scratching at her. "Is that what men do with their mistresses?"

"Nae. That's whit a skellum daes wi' a wumman he canna get out o his blood." His voice was taut, slicing through the chill peace. "Kitty—"

"It's all right." She sat up and pushed her skirts over her legs and her voice quavered. "More than all right. I should thank you."

He grasped her shoulders and pulled her close and spoke over her brow.

"Kitty, A canna make love tae ye as A wish. A dinna ken

why ye believe yer yeld, but A winna take the chance agin. A shoudna the first time."

"I believe that was my choice to make." She should not tremble. She should not despair that his desire to avoid getting her with child and being obliged to marry her was stronger than his desire for her. "But I thank you for the consideration, again." The achy shadow of pleasure in her body tangled with the ache elsewhere. Everywhere.

He wrapped an arm around her waist and tugged her hard against him.

"Dinna thank a man for using ye withoot honor, lass." He spoke harshly, entirely unlike the poetry-reciting lover in the stable. Here was intensity she had only glimpsed before. It thrilled her, and alarmed.

"I probably should not." She searched his glittering eyes, but there was nothing she understood there now. "Still, part of me feels grateful. And since one of us should probably tell the truth, I suppose it will have to be me."

His hand tightened on her. He bent, captured her lips, and kissed her. He kissed her and the world halted except for his mouth on hers that seemed to urge her to give him everything she wanted to give him anyway, this stranger she knew so little of except that he had not ever truly seemed a stranger to her. There was a tension in his body that did not match the sweet lingering pleasure in hers. But she wanted to meet him where he needed her. For the first time in years she wanted to serve a man's desires no matter what it meant to her.

He broke away abruptly and wrapped his hand about the side of her face, forcing her gaze to his.

"Was it anely Poole?" His voice grated. "How many men hae ye been wi'? *Tell* me."

She quailed, melting beneath the heat of his possessive jealousy. Nothing mattered now, nothing of the world in which she had hidden herself. Not even his secrets. On the edge of falling, she cared only for the arms of this most unlikely man that might catch her.

She could not tell him the truth, that it had only been Lambert. She was not such a fool as all that. If he imagined he was unsafe from permanent entanglement with her, she must convince him that he could not get her with child. She wanted him more than she had ever wanted the man to whom she had given her innocence. But she knew how to play games of falsity too.

So it must be. Farewell grace. Farewell hoped-for joy. Grim pretense must suffice once again. Her hungry heart, it seemed, could manage nothing nobler. But at least for a short time, for perhaps only tonight, she might feel an echo of happiness.

"Oh," she forced through her lips, "I daresay at least a dozen."

She laughed, a sad, sweet sound of regret, and Leam was lost. Lost in a place he had vowed never to enter again. He pulled her tight to him, and willingly she gave him her mouth, her hands, and the soft slope of her neck dipping to her breasts. His heart, thick in his chest, pounded as her questing hands sought.

The tip of her tongue slipped along the edge of his ear and she whispered, "Make love to me, Leam. Save me from this need."

Save me.

Save me, Leam.

He dragged her off him, thrusting her away, memories crashing to the fore. Blue eyes pleading, then weeping, tears soaking his skin, jealousy and rage tearing through him. His brother's crumpled body, blood on the earth. Skirts clogged with river filth and a betrothal ring dulled.

He didn't even want me. He didn't want me.

Leam stumbled to his feet, pulling in breaths, and swung around. Five and a half years of impotent fury and grief surged forward.

"No," he choked out, his stomach cramping, head whirling. "No. Kitty, I beg—I beg your pardon for this. For all of it. I cannot."

Without looking back, he fled across the moonlit garden.

Not waiting for dawn, Leam gathered his belongings and escaped Willows Hall, casting off temptation beyond his ability to withstand. Pressing his horse and the hounds, he rode east, then north. North to Alvamoor where his wife and brother awaited him in entombed peace, safely beyond the tumult in his soul they had created. North, where if he was very lucky he would entomb himself as well in a place where that soul could never be tempted again.

Chapter 15

Leam met his sisters on the terrace, the elegant mass of Alvamoor rising up behind him in crenellated red sandstone glory. The park stretched out across slopes to fallow brown fields and misty sheep pastures bordered with serpentine walls of rock. Beyond the stables below, the forest that had given name to his ancestors descended as a great dark shadow down the hill, as though mocking the formal gardens and park close to the house. It was wild Scottish nature and elegant English order combined, and he had missed it.

Wrapped in furs and mufflers, Fiona and Isobel took tea in the brilliant sun. His younger sister leaped up from the table, a graceful sylph of pinstriped muslin, red cloak, and dark curls flying across the terrace. She flung herself upon him and he caught her up.

"You are here!" Her slender arms squeezed. He bent to buss her upon one cheek, then the other. When their mother died in Leam's fifteenth year, Fiona had been a wee one. Now on the verge of eighteen she was a beauty, tall like Isobel yet still slender as a reed. "We thought you would never come!"

He smiled into her laughing eyes. "I began to believe I never would either."

"What delayed you?"

"A snowstorm in Shropshire." He took her hand and led her back to the table. "What are you doing out here? Haven't you a place to enjoy tea within where it is warm?"

"I could not *resist* the sunshine. It is the first in weeks of gray, which makes perfect sense now. Nature knew you were coming home today." Her smile danced.

"What were you doing in Shropshire?" Isobel did not rise or even offer her hand. In five years she had not forgiven him as Fiona and their brother Gavin had. None of them had ever spoken of it, but Leam suspected Gavin understood, and Fiona had never cared much for James. As a child she'd made Leam her favorite, and her character was steeped in loyalty—much as Leam had pretended for years to society concerning his wife. But Fiona's unshakable affection was real.

She squeezed his hand and hung on his arm.

"Yes, do tell us. I wish to know every little bit of everything you have done since we saw you last Christmas. Oh, but it is a terrible shame you missed it this year. Jamie and I made a *croque-en-bouche*."

"Should I know what that is?"

"A French tower of cream puffs, silly!" She pinched his arm. "I read about it in a Parisian fashion magazine and supposed with all your world traveling you *must* have eaten one before. So we made it for you. It remained upright for nearly an hour, until Mary put it too close to the hearth and the sugar melted. The puffs were still quite tasty, though sticky of course."

"Of course."

"We are still waiting to hear what took you to Shropshire, brother." Isobel's skin was pale, her cheeks too hollow, her hair severely dressed. She had done this to herself, and he had not stopped her from it.

"Yale asked me to accompany him to the house party of some acquaintances he preferred not to meet alone."

Fiona's eyes sparkled. "I wish you had brought him here with you instead."

"I have no doubt you wish that." He shook his head. "What will I do with you when I must allow you to enter society this spring?"

"Will you, Leam?" Her eyes brightened for a moment, then her visage fell. "But I will have no one to take me about, for Isa cannot, being unmarried."

"I shall." He took a slow breath. "I intend to remain at Alvamoor permanently."

Her grip on his arm tightened. "Truly?" Hope danced in her eyes.

"You will be eighteen." For all he wished to remain holed up in his house, come the spring it would be his duty to escort her about the countryside around Edinburgh and make her known to the mothers with eligible sons. Their brother Gavin was too young to see to it, only five-and-twenty, the same age as Leam when he had met Miss Cornelia Cobb at the assembly rooms.

"I *will* be eighteen, and you will take me to parties and perhaps even a ball." She hugged him again.

"Not if you don't learn a modicum of comportment by then," Isobel muttered.

Fiona's arms unwrapped from around him and she suppressed her giggles. "I will behave, Leam. I promise." She was all smiles. "Have you seen Jamie yet?"

"I only now arrived."

"He is with his tutor, but I will run and fetch him."

"No. Enjoy your tea while the sunshine remains. I will go, but I fear you will take a chill if you remain here long."

Fiona shook her head with a smile, but Isobel offered him an even stare. "You are so rarely in residence, we suppose you don't care one way or another how we go along in your house."

"It is your house too, Isobel. For as long as you wish."

She narrowed her eyes. Fiona fidgeted. Leam cast his youngest sister a smile, then went inside.

He moved across the entrance hall, and the scent of lilies met him like a punch to his midsection. A bundle of flowers decorated a table. He strode over and snatched the hothouse bouquet from the vase. He turned about and found a footman.

"Dispose of these." He thrust them at a lad he did not recognize. "Who are you?"

"That's the new boy." Leam's housekeeper strode swiftly into the hall, a bustle of efficiency. "Come on this last muin." She shoed away the footman and curtsied to Leam. "Welcome home, malord."

"Hello, Mrs. Phillips. How are you?"

"Well, sir. A thought as ye might be wanting tae clean out milady's personal effects so we can use that bedchamber for guests an the like. Nou that ye'll be staying, that is."

"News travels swiftly, it seems." He nodded. "Yes. I shall see to Lady Blackwood's chambers myself."

He made his way toward the stair, the lingering scent of lilies sickening in his nostrils. The day of James's funeral the church had hung thick with the fragrance. Two months later when Leam buried Cornelia, torn between grief and relief, he'd smelled them again. Within weeks of that second funeral he had joined Colin Gray in his new club, and shortly after that met young Mr. Wyn Yale in Calcutta.

He had run away, changing his life, but *he* had not changed.

Imagining Kitty with other men was enough to drive him mad. Imagining losing his heart entirely to her, only to have her reject it eventually, was even worse. He was the same passionate fool as always, unable to control the depth of his feelings when once he allowed them rein—emotions that would inevitably lead to violence against those he loved, as they had before. The burning within him would never truly be quelled, certainly not when inspired by a woman like Kitty Savege.

Five years of avoiding his own home had not changed him in the least. But at least he had learned how to escape. Recalling Kitty's shocked face beneath the snowy trees, he knew he was a master at that.

He paused on the landing and looked up to meet his wife's smiling gaze. The breath went out of him, as always. Even in oil on canvas her golden beauty dazzled. But that no longer affected him. For the past five years, each time he had come home and seen the portrait, only guilt shook him.

He'd had the likeness painted during their first month of marriage. She sat for Ramsay—the most expensive artist Leam could find—only the best for his perfect bride, the Incomparable nobody from nowhere remarkable whose parents nevertheless disapproved of her wedding a Scot, even a titled man. Only minor gentry, they hadn't even the wherewithal to give their daughter a proper season, but instead had sent her off to visit a Scottish school friend during her first season in Edinburgh. Yet their English snobbery and mistrust of him, a Scot, had run deep.

But Cornelia insisted. She had cried, weeping desperate tears, begging them to allow her to marry him because she simply could not live without him. In the end they had relented.

He stared at the portrait. Posing for Ramsay, she had smiled at Leam just so, with her twinkling blue eyes and dimpled chin. He'd sat watching throughout the long days, glued to his chair every minute, a besotted fool, never knowing his brother's child was growing in her womb. His brother James, who—before Leam even met her—had refused to wed her because of his own broken heart.

"Mother was very beautiful."

The voice at his side was steady and young. He looked down and met his nephew's sober eyes. At nearly six he still looked more like James than Cornelia. And so, Leam mused, he looked like him. Like a Blackwood.

He returned his attention to the portrait.

"She was." Beautiful and selfish and manipulative. But the old anger did not rise as it always had before. Guilt still for what he had done to them after he discovered their secret, but no fury for what they had done to him.

He breathed slowly, testing the sensation. It lasted. When had the anger gone?

"Welcome home, Father." Jamie extended his hand. The boy's bones were sturdy, his grip firm.

"It seems you have grown four inches since last Christmas."

"No, Father. Only two and one quarter inches. Mrs. Phillips measured me last week."

"Did she? Well, Mrs. Phillips must be right. I daresay she's never wrong about anything."

"She was wrong about you coming home for Christmas." He spoke so earnestly, as though he had given it great thought yet accepted this erroneous fact.

Leam crouched down and met the boy's gaze on level.

"I am sorry I did not arrive in time for Christmas. Can you forgive me?"

"Yes, Father." His dark eyes were so steady for one so young. "Did business keep you? Aunt Fiona says you're very occupied with business most of the time, and on account of it you cannot remain here long."

"I intend to remain this time, Jamie. Would you like that?"

The lad's eyes widened and his collar jerked up and down with a thick swallow.

"Yes, sir. I would like that above all things."

Leam nodded, his chest tight with an aching that would not cease. Despite all, he loved this boy, the son of his brother. He had been away far too long. "Good. Then it is settled." He stood. "You must have been on your way somewhere when you encountered me here."

"Mr. Wadsmere says he will read to me about Hercules if I finish my letters before dinner."

"Hercules, hm? Then you must not delay in completing your work." He set his hand on the boy's shoulder. "May I accompany you up and perhaps watch? I was once something of an expert at letters, but I'm afraid I've gotten a bit rusty with that sort of thing. Perhaps you could refresh my memory."

The barest hint of a grin shaped the boy's mouth.

"I don't guess that's true. But Aunt Isobel says gentlemen often tell tales to encourage others to do as they wish. But I don't mind it. You can come along even if you tell the truth." The grin got full rein. He started up the stairs. Throat tight, Leam followed.

Three weeks after returning home, he finally entered Cornelia's chambers to sort through her belongings. No dust clung to surfaces in her bedchamber or dressing room. No spirit-fearing Scottish maidservant would willingly clean a dead woman's effects for five and a half years, but his housekeeper, Mrs. Phillips, was made of stern stuff.

The place still reflected Cornelia's flirtatious femininity, all peach and rose to complement her ivory and golden charms. On her dressing table sat three perfume bottles on a silver tray and a set of silver-backed comb and brush. He touched his fingertips to the brush handle not an inch from where a single shining strand of guinea hair clung to the bristles.

He drew in a breath. For years his heart had no longer raced when he thought of her, only beat dully for what he had done to her. What he had driven her to.

He moved into the dressing chamber. Her garments still hung upon pegs. She'd always dressed in the first stare of fashion, the pale colors and current styles suiting her delicately rounded figure. She was only eighteen when they met, the plumpness of youth dimpling her elbows and cheeks.

At that assembly rooms ball admirers had surrounded her. New to Edinburgh, her perfect English face was animated with giddiness. But after he found an acquaintance to introduce them, all her rosy-lipped smiles were for him. Or so he believed. During the following fortnight he courted her unceasingly. She accepted his suit swiftly, he'd thought, because she was as smitten as he.

Now Leam could admit there had been a great deal of pride laced through his fury. During those three weeks in which the banns were read before the wedding, when either Cornelia or James could have halted it, they let him make a tragic fool of himself instead.

A heavy cedar chest dominated the small chamber. It seemed as good a place as any to begin. He opened the latch and drew forth the contents. They were the stuff of a young lady's life—lacy kerchiefs, ribbons, a dried posy, even a note he had written to her that first week full of poetic declarations of love.

Astoundingly, he cared nothing for it. No pain of betrayal or dashed hopes stirred in him as he sorted his wife's belongings, not even a twinge of resentment. Perhaps he had forgiven her finally. She had been nothing more than an impetuous, selfish girl, not unlike the impetuous, selfish young man she had married to save herself from ruination.

Yet in the end he had brought her to true ruin. He had sent her to her death just as he sent his brother. That pain would live with him like a knife wedged between his ribs forever.

"So you are finally doing it."

Isobel stood in the open doorway. Her once-lovely visage was dour now, a sharp contrast to the feminine charm of Cornelia's chambers.

"It's about time." She gestured to the open trunk.

He nodded. "Perhaps it is."

She stood in silence, staring at him.

"Would you like to assist?" he finally said.

"With that brainless ninny's things? Don't insult me."

"If you are not interested in this project, why are you here?"

She moved forward and extended a slim black volume.

"I found this when I packed away James's belongings after the funeral."

Leam didn't take it. "What is it?"

"He gave it to you for Christmas when you were both at university."

"Why haven't you shown it to me before this?"

"Because you were never in permanent residence until now. And this should remain here. Where he is." She shook the book at him. "Take it."

He stood and accepted the volume.

"I don't suppose you even care to have it," she said tightly, "but it belongs to you and I am no thief."

Without looking up he said, "I loved him too, Isa."

"Then why did you kill him?"

His head came up, his heart thumping hard. She had never said it aloud. In all these years, she had never actually accused him. But they'd both known why she withdrew her affection. After the funeral, he told her about the duel. He'd had to admit it aloud or the secret would have eaten him from within. As it had anyway.

"I—" He struggled for the words buried in his heart. "I never imagined they would go through with it, Isobel. You must know I didn't. I did not wish him dead. I never did. *Never.*"

"Arranging a duel for him was a poor way of assuring that, wasn't it?"

"They were *best friends.*"

"You were his brother!"

"I was—" *a cuckolded husband.* But not truly, because Cornelia and James had been together before the wedding. Not after. James had insisted. Even Cornelia admitted that, miserable in her unrequited love and weak after the birth of their son. Nearly out of her mind, she had confessed everything, to using Leam because she had no recourse in her condition but to marry swiftly. And because married to him in particular she still might be near James. James would not have her, though she had begged, repeating over and over again her heartbreak over his brother's rejection.

So Leam had left her, banishing her to Alvamoor where he vowed never again to live while she still drew breath. Then he had gone to town to find his brother.

But Isobel, not quite out of the schoolroom yet at the time, did not know these things. As everyone else, her memory of James Blackwood was of a laughing, roguish fellow, a sporting, teasing man of open desires and simple amusements. That image must remain. No one would ever know the truth. For James's sake, and for his son's, Leam would never reveal it.

Except one man knew. Felix Vaucoeur. The man who killed him.

"I was angry with him," he said quietly. "I wished to

frighten him. Only that, Isa. And it was a mistake we must now live with."

"You are a cruel, unfeeling man, Leam."

Dear God, he wished he were. He had wished that for five years, to no avail. He still felt far too keenly, far too deeply when his heart was engaged.

He held her gaze, the cold within expanding once more to envelop him like a mantle. He welcomed it.

"You have no idea of the person I am."

"I never wish to." She pivoted and disappeared into the corridor on eerily silent feet, like the ghost she worshiped.

He looked down at the volume and his heedless heart stilled. Carefully he smoothed his fingertips across the leather cover, afraid to open it.

His brother had indeed given it to him while they were both down from Cambridge for the holiday. James had come home weeks before him, dodging his masters before they released him, because he was James Blackwood and he could. Champion cricket player, bruising rider, star sculler, and all-around handsome devil, by the beginning of his second year he had charmed the dean's wives, their daughters, even the deans themselves. He hadn't cared a thing about books, only sport and parties, and he made no secret of it.

No one had chastised him. Everyone loved him. Unfailingly generous and always laughing with good nature at something—whether a bawdy comedy or his elder brother's bookishness—no one had ever blamed him, even for the young ladies' tears that fell on his behalf. His heart was on full view for anybody to see, as it had always been. If a girl believed such a charming, pleasure-seeking rascal loved only her, then she was too silly for her own good.

But that fall, not even two months back at school, James had escaped to Alvamoor. When Leam finally arrived home at the term's break, the youth he met there was nothing like the care-for-nothing young rogue everyone else knew. During Michaelmas term James had met another student, the young French comte, Felix Vaucoeur, and discovered something about himself that he could not bear, and he was suffering. Just as Leam was doing now, he had escaped to Alvamoor in an attempt to escape himself.

Slowly Leam unfolded the cover of the slender volume and scanned the title page.

His brother had not been a scholar, but he'd had the Blackwood brains, and he hadn't spent all his hours at university on the playing field. He had chosen Leam's Christmas gift that year with great care.

It was a book of poetry by a Frenchman. Given James's constant teasing about his love of verse, at first Leam had been astounded. But when he read the poems, he understood. Centuries earlier, the poet Théophile de Viau had written, drunk, and danced his libertine way through the grandest courts of Europe. But in the end his king had betrayed him and he was publicly reviled, left to die in obscurity. Exiled for loving the wrong person.

Leam turned back the title page, and a wash of sheer hopelessness swept through him. Two boldly scrawled lines crossed the paper, just like the confident man James had been. It was the only verse James had ever written, a confession to Leam, the only person with whom he could be honest.

Were I to love freely he whom I chose,
I could love to match the greatest man.

When the tears came, Leam did not halt them. He set the book on the dressing table and pressed his fingers to his eyes, then the heels of his hands, then his sleeve. He had not wept when he watched his brother die, nor when he found his wife in the river two months later, her body swollen and disfigured, recognizable only by her gown and wedding ring. At that time, grief had stunned him into paralysis.

But now the tears fell. Not knowing how he went, Leam found himself in the stable, then his roan beneath him, flying toward the forest. When he reached its dark interior, he lost himself in it, needing the shadows of the ancient trees. He rode, heedless of branches in his face and pulling at his clothing. His horse protested and Leam dismounted and released it. Falling to his knees, alone in the forest with his imperfect soul, he bent his head and wept.

His brother had trusted him with the greatest secret of his life. From that time on, James had struggled daily to defy his own nature, as though someday he might outrun it, outbox it, outshoot it. Outlove it with every woman he could find. In the end, he had not betrayed Leam. Indeed, it was the other way around. He had taken what he'd known of his brother in confidence, and he had turned it against him.

He deserved it that Cornelia would be the only woman he ever loved. He deserved the lifelong punishment of an empty heart. Though she knew only part of the story, Isobel was right. There was no living with what he had done.

By the time Bella found him, the sun was setting behind a wall of gray sky. Returning on foot to the stable with his hound, he found his horse well within, and walked up to the house. He called for tea to be delivered to his study, then went to Cornelia's rooms, where he drew from the trunk his love letter and her diary, then closed the box and locked it.

He gave the key to his housekeeper, instructing her to sort through Lady Blackwood's belongings for personal objects, which she should pack in the attic for Master Jamie to have someday. The gowns and such should be given to charity.

Finished with that, he went to his study and shut himself in. He had been absent for a year and had plenty of work to do, and he could not see his family tonight. Tomorrow he would meet them with a restored countenance. He was no longer a poet. What had seemed in the dark of the cold forest to be immutable truth, before a warm grate in the comfort of his house he recognized as dramatic overindulgence. He had Fiona's future to plan and a son to raise. If he were fortunate, he might even someday convince Isobel to marry and move away from Alvamoor. And he still had a brother. If Gavin needed him, he would be there for him too. *That man to man the world o'er, shall brithers be for a' that.* Life must go on for the living, and he would no longer shirk his responsibilities.

He moved to the hearth and drew forth Cornelia's diary and his note. Carefully he laid them on the grate and stirred the coals until they ignited. Then he poured himself a brandy and sat down to the pile of business his steward had left for him. It was clean work, unencumbered with emotion, and it suited him.

After some time, the new footman entered to light candles, a maid following with more coal. Leam nodded his thanks and waved them out, intent on his documents.

Sometime later he noticed the folded paper on the corner of his desk. He reached for it.

I know you have it. I want it back. No games, and I will leave you alone.

Lady Katherine has returned to London. You would be well advised to do so as well. I will contact you when you arrive. If you do not come, or if you continue to play with me, I will aim for her intentionally this time.

Leam's hands went cold.

He bolted up, pulling the call rope as he raced into the corridor. His butler sprang from a chair.

"Milord?"

"Where is that new boy—the footman? And Jessie, the housemaid, the one who brought in the coal earlier. Fetch them at once."

"A can git ye Jessie, milord. But the new lad asked tae be let tae go down tae the cockfight tae nicht. He ain't had a day aff since afore ye came home a muin ago, so A tald him he coud."

Panic rose in him, but he shoved it back. "How long ago did you give him leave?"

"Juist over an hour, A'd say, sir."

"Send for my horse immediately." There was still time. If the fight lasted long enough, he might find the lad.

In the modest hillside town a mile from Alvamoor, Leam searched, torchlight cutting the cold, misty night enough to see faces in the crowd, all jostling, cursing, laughing drunken men pressed about the animals tearing at one another with beaks and talons. But no footman could be found, as Leam had suspected. And now he had wasted time.

The "it" must refer to the broken gold chain Cox had dropped, or the object that had hung upon it—something of modest weight, according to the village's old jeweler, Freddie Jones. Leam had no idea what games Cox believed he was playing, but the note was a clear threat. Cox wanted the object and imagined Leam possessed it. And he knew he would go to London if Kitty was in danger.

Instructing his manservant to pack his saddlebag, he ran up to the nursery three stairs at a time. Jamie was asleep. Leam watched his breathing, the small replica of his brother's face at perfect peace, and silently vowed to return as soon as he could.

Fiona met him in the corridor.

"Mrs. Phillips told me you ordered Albert to pack a bag." She clutched her dressing gown to her in the cold. "Are you leaving now?"

He touched her chin. "I must. But I will be back."

"In the middle of the night? What is it, Leam? And do not pretend it's nothing. I don't know what you have been doing all these years in London, but it isn't gambling and chasing skirts." She spoke swiftly. "I read the London gossip columns, you know, and the man they describe is not my brother."

"No. It isn't, and you are a very clever minx. But I haven't time to explain now. You must simply trust me."

She screwed up her brow, but she lifted her cheek for him to kiss, then threw her arms about him.

"Don't be gone long. And come back happier than you were today. I do not like to see you sad. It reminds me of James."

"Tell my son I promise to return soon." He turned and made swiftly for his horse.

Chapter 16

Fellow Britons,

I promised I would not relent in my pursuit of information concerning the exclusive gentlemen's club at 14½ Dover Street. I have not. I am now in possession of a curious fact. It is called the Falcon Club. Its members go by the names of birds. I haven't any idea the reason for this, but when I know I will tell you.

It would be wonderful if I discovered them to be a society of bird-watchers. I might even join them if I could spare the time. But I doubt I will find that. Bird watchers are quiet folk, but not to my knowledge particularly secretive.

—Lady Justice

Sir,

Please note the enclosed leaflet. Do you wish me to take any action at this time?

Eagle has returned to town and requested that Mr. Grimm be assigned to watch a house for the safety of its resident. I have allowed it, under the condition that Eagle assent to the other matter on which you are eager for his assistance.

The resident is a party well known to you due to her involvement in the affair concerning L.P. in June. Eagle believes she may be in danger. We have not pinpointed a source, but naturally we shall in short order. In the meantime, Sea Hawk has sent word that the resident may be able to help us in the project he currently pursues. Eagle refuses to divulge more, but I cannot believe this is a coincidence. Do I have your permission to pursue the matter as I see fit?

Peregrine

Chapter 17

She was the only unwed lady present at the political luncheon. She should not be present at all. She never should have. But her mother had always indulged her, pretending not to notice whispered disapproval even at such events where an informed mind counted for more than a lady's stained reputation or unwed status. The Dowager Lady Savege commanded far too much stature to care about what the gossips said, and she was always there to chaperone after all.

But the gossips would talk and Kitty could not avoid hearing some of it. She had never felt the censure quite as acutely as she did now. Perhaps it was because she no longer had a purpose for being in society so constantly. Or perhaps she simply did not care for politics any longer now that she had no desire to expose a rotten politician. Emily should be castigating *her* for shallowness rather than poor Mr. Yale.

"You did not touch the aubergine soufflé, Kitty," her hostess, the Countess of March, said. "I had my chef make it expressly for you."

"Did you? You are too kind, ma'am."

She was predictable. Friends knew what she liked to eat at a party. She could be guaranteed to attend because she hadn't anything else to do. She might as well be eighty, stockings crumpled at her ankles, and telling outrageous stories to anyone who would listen.

But thinking about crumpled stockings made her think of Leam Blackwood. Nearly everything made her think of him. And she did not want to, because every time she did her cheeks burned with shame.

Save me from this need.

Oh, *God.* It made her want to sink into the floor and die to recall it. Could she have been more thoroughly ridiculous? She had begged him to make love to her. *Begged.*

Worse even than the shame, however, was the misery inside her that would not abate. She'd thought returning to town would alleviate that. When Mr. Worthmore, then within the hour Mr. Yale departed Willows Hall and Emily was once again her earnest, distracted self, Kitty had felt free to go home—to leave the place in which he'd made love to her, then abandoned her.

But it had not changed a thing. She still felt like a fool, and miserable.

"You are not yourself since you returned from the countryside, Kitty," Lady March said, shifting closer on the couch. The countess had a quick mind and an air of quiet fashion that Kitty liked. Her crinkled gaze, however, was too knowing.

"Oh, I am as happy as a clam," she replied perhaps too blithely.

The countess lifted a brow. "A clam?"

"Or what have you." Kitty waved her hand about.

Murmured conversation mounted to a cascade of laughter across the drawing room for a moment, then quieted again.

"Tell me, what did you do while in Shropshire?"

She developed a bewilderingly desperate *tendre* for an inappropriate and untrustworthy man.

"I completed a lovely piece of embroidery. My mother has sent it to the cabinetmakers already. You know the one on Cheapside. He will set it into a stool. Roses and cherries on a blush backing, with mahogany stain. I simply adore red."

"Kitty Savege, you sound like a perfect nincompoop."

Kitty's eyes widened.

"What happened to the young lady everyone admired who could converse on politics, books, theater, and the like?" The countess's lips pinched. "Does Chamberlayne's courtship disturb you?"

"Oh, no. I quite like him." Her mother's beau was unfailingly kind to her. He had not entirely fulfilled Kitty's hopes over the holiday, but she had cause to believe an offer forthcoming. She had returned to find her mother in possession of the loveliest necklace of silver and lapis lazuli, a gift from the gentleman. Kitty had clasped the piece about her mother's neck earlier, praising its delicate beauty, and the dowager's cheeks glowed. Kitty's father had never given his wife baubles, reserving them instead for his mistress.

Now Ellen Savege stood beside Lord Chamberlayne across the drawing room, a spark animating her eyes.

"Then what on earth is the matter with you?" Lady March demanded.

"I am no doubt simply bored." Or perhaps something more profound.

Certainly more profound.

"*Bored?*"

"With the season still weeks away, entertainments are so thin and not particularly inspiring." She sounded wretchedly wan. Really not herself at all.

The countess frowned. "Kitty Savege, you have never been rude a day in your life."

"Oh, certainly not." She had been horridly rude to Lord Blackwood. Then she had done to him exactly what he had been doing to her to justify her rudeness: she had held him for too long.

"You have insulted me and you do not even realize it," the countess said without rancor. "I am concerned for your head, my dear."

"What could possibly concern you about such a pretty head, my lady?" Lord Chamberlayne's voice was warm as he stopped before them, her mother on his arm. There wasn't a hint of false flattery about him. Kitty liked that. He seemed so honest, unlike a certain Scot who hid secrets and occasionally spoke to a lady in a rich resonant voice she wanted to eat with a spoon.

"I do feel a bit unstable these days," she admitted.

Lady March peered at her. Lord Chamberlayne furrowed his brow and looked to her mother, who met her gaze evenly, as always.

"Perhaps a quiet evening of play will put you to rights again," her mother suggested.

"Mama." She stood. "I don't wish to play . Cards no longer satisfy me." They never would again after the game she had played Christmas Eve.

"Well, this is sudden, daughter."

Kitty turned from her mother. "My lord, will you sit in for me at tonight's card party?"

"I will be delighted." He turned smiling eyes upon her mother, and her face lightened beneath his appreciative regard. They really were well suited, two people's tastes never more similar. Why hadn't he yet offered for her? Had Kitty thrown herself into a snowstorm and subsequently into the arms of a Scottish rogue *all for nothing*?

She turned to her hostess, despondency the size of a fist balled up in her stomach.

"My lady, I must take leave of your hospitality now. I have had a delightful time."

"Boredom can be so amusing," the countess murmured.

Kitty curtsied. "Good day, my lady. Mama, my lord."

She fled.

Alex's footman let her in through her front door, his black and gold livery neat as a pin. Kitty deposited her cloak, bonnet, and gloves with him, and climbed the elegant stair to the parlor.

The house was nearly empty. Over the holiday Alex and Serena had purchased a larger residence two blocks away, in anticipation of the baby. Kitty and her mother were to remove to the new house within the fortnight. For the time being that left Kitty without any company.

Perhaps she merely needed a good book. Distraction might help, although it had not in a month.

Clearly she needed a change. She could hire a companion and go to France. Everyone said Paris was pleasant in the spring. She could simply run away again, then again and again until old age or some tragic accident took her.

She opened the glass door to the bookcase and ran her fingertips along gilded bindings. Her hand arrested on a volume. She plucked it out. *A History of the Fractious Clans of Scotland* should be interesting reading. She would instruct the footman she was not available to callers and lose herself in the pages.

She set the book on a table, threw herself down into a chair much as Emily might, and draped an arm over her eyes. This simply would not do. She would never be cured of her infatuation if she continually fed it.

She squared her shoulders and grabbed up the book to reshelve. The footman appeared at the door.

"My lady, a gentleman is calling. I invited him to wait in the drawing room."

She pressed the volume into its slot and closed the case, endeavoring not to notice the footman's Meaningful Glance. Over the past few years the servants had all grown wretchedly familiar in the matter of her gentlemen callers. The housekeeper, Mrs. Hopkins, had taken to letting Kitty know of which gentlemen she particularly approved.

"Thank you, John. Please remain on the landing." She smoothed her hands over her hair and down her skirts, then went through the short passageway into the adjoining chamber. The Earl of Blackwood stood in her drawing room.

Quite simply, she lost the ability to speak.

His eyes were not hooded. His hair was a bit long over the collar, but he was clean-shaven. His coat, waistcoat, and breeches were exceedingly elegant, of excellent quality and the finest cut, his boots shining, and his expression perfectly benign. There were no dogs in sight.

"Good afternoon." He bowed, a graceful gesture without a hint of affectation. "I trust I find you well, ma'am."

"You do." She could manage no more. Not a curtsy or another word. She had never imagined he would come to her, and certainly not looking and sounding like this. He held his hat and riding crop in one hand as though he did not intend to remain long.

"May I inquire after your injury?"

Injury?

"The wound on your arm," he provided.

Oh. "It is fine." She could not think. But he allowed only a moment's pause.

"I have come seeking your assistance. I can only hope that despite circumstances you will consider rendering it."

"Circumstances?" The syllables required effort.

"The circumstance of my having withheld from you the truth."

Kitty clasped her hands before her to still their shaking. "What is the truth, my lord?"

"That for several years I have been an agent of the crown in secrecy, playing a role to do my work. I have recently given that up, save for one final loose end that must be knotted now. It is that task for which I seek your aid."

She knew not whether to scream or laugh or cry. Emotions battered.

"You are a *spy*?"

"Were. And no. The organization of which I was a member sought out missing persons of great importance whose retrieval required particular discretion. We gathered information only to find those persons." He spoke as though discussing the time of day, while Kitty's world spun.

"That is nonsensical. How would playing *that* role have assisted you in gaining information?"

He held her gaze steadily. "You trusted me."

She had. With her body.

He was known as a flirt, an affable cretin, but a handsome one. How many women before her had imagined him to be perfectly innocuous? She understood. If he had asked, she might have told him anything.

"No," he said quietly. "In Shropshire I was not seeking information from you, Kitty. I only maintained the pretense to avoid having to tell you the entire truth, which was not mine to share freely."

Her heart thundered. But this did not explain why he had not made love to her at Willows Hall. If only she could still her foolish trembling. The deep, unsullied timbre of his voice sent longing into every crevice of her body. Being near him now . . .

She *had* dreamed it, foolishly, hopefully—that he would come. But not like this. She had not imagined *this*.

"I see," she replied.

"Do you?"

"I suppose I should think it all fantastical. But you haven't wasted any time in coming to the point of your call today, so I must believe you."

He moved toward her.

Nerves racing, she pivoted, went to the door, and shut it on John's curious stare. Leam halted in the middle of the room, his dark eyes darting to the closed panel, then to her face.

She lowered her voice. "I do not understand why for a sennight in Shropshire you did not tell me the truth, but now"—she gestured to the door beyond which the footman sat, then to his elegant clothing—"you seem to be perfectly happy to tell the whole world."

"I am not at all happy about any of it," he countered. "I have come to London for one purpose. When that is settled I intend to return home and none of this"—he lifted his fine silk hat and gestured to the street through the window—"will mean a thing."

She could no longer meet his distant gaze. She dropped hers to the carpet. Oriental design. Tears would not stain it irreparably. She might feel free to fall apart if he weren't standing before her.

"Do you know, Leam, I think I preferred the poetry to this plain speaking."

"It is who I am, Kitty." His voice sounded taut.

"Then I am astounded to find that I liked the false you better."

This time when he came toward her she had nowhere to go. She flattened her back to the door and he halted before her, so close it would only require the slightest movement to touch him. He bent his head and spoke quietly above her brow.

"Allow me to discharge the errand with which I have been

commissioned, and I will leave you in peace." He drew a tight breath, the movement of air in the sliver of space between them stirring the locks of hair on her brow. "I pray you, Kitty."

"All right," she whispered. "Tell me then. With what do you believe I can assist you?"

His hand fisted about the riding crop. She could not tear her gaze away from the sinewy strength that had touched her with such tenderness and possessive passion.

"You and your mother play cards frequently with the Marquess of Drake and the Earl of Chance. Is this true?"

"Yes. But anybody could tell you that."

"Officials in the Home Office are seeking information about Chance. They believe you may have something useful to tell them."

"Lord Chance?" She shot her gaze up. "Whatever about?"

"He is suspected of selling information to the French."

She couldn't help laughing. "Ian *Chance*? That is absurd."

"My associates seem to think otherwise."

"He is an inveterate gambler and something of a libertine, but not a sp—" Her tongue tangled, only partially because of the naïve words she had been about to say. His gaze had fallen to her lips, and quite abruptly she could think of nothing.

"The Home Office," he said, his gaze slowly tracing her mouth and the line of her jaw, "has reason to believe the traitor is a Scot intent on rebellion. Chance's grandfather was a Jacobite."

"But *he* isn't," she said unsteadily. "I don't think he even knows what a Jacobite is."

He said nothing for a moment, then lifted his gaze to hers, and the hunger in it made her weak. Now she might actually cry, from joy and pleasure and some fear. He was too changeable.

"Perhaps not." His voice was rough. "And I think they are fools for suspecting him."

"Then what are you doing here? And *what* are you doing here?" She could reach up and touch his perfect face and be in heaven. She could feel his heat, and pretend it was hers to own. "What do you imagine I can do about Lord Chance's possibly Jacobite leanings?"

"Tell my associate what you know of him."

"That's all?"

He swallowed, his jaw hard. "That is all."

"But you must know at least as much about him as I do. Don't gentlemen do a great deal of gossiping in their clubs? And you play cards as often as my mother."

"His close friend, Drake, talks excessively to ladies. You are likely to know more." His hand moved, Kitty's pulse leaped, and he placed his palm flat against the painted wooden door frame.

She shook her head. "Why are you trusting me with this?"

"The prince regent and the king's cabinet members were grateful for the service you rendered England last summer."

Kitty's heart halted. "Last summer?"

He looked into her eyes. "In the matter of Lord Poole. The prince has great faith in your acuity." He might be speaking of any matter, as though he had not held her tightly and demanded to know if she had given herself to men other than Lambert.

Perhaps she should strike him. Or rant and rail. Or simply dissolve into tears. In a moment of vulnerability she had admitted to him that she had run away from the life she had lived before. Yet here he was forcing it back on her.

She turned her face away.

"That was a particular case." She copied his impersonal tone, while inside she disintegrated as though there were no real Kitty Savege after all.

Silence met her. When she looked up again, she almost expected to see Lambert. But instead it was the dark-eyed Scot she had given herself to during a Shropshire snowstorm and who, it seemed, was using her only now for the first time.

"Was this your idea, to involve me?"

He shook his head. It was a small sort of relief to know.

"Then whose?"

"Jinan Seton did work much like mine. After he encountered you at Willows Hall he suggested to—"

She pushed past him into the center of the chamber, a sob trembling in her throat.

"I will consider it," she said. "Or don't I have a choice?"

"Of course you have a choice." In his gaze she did not know what she saw. Determination. Solemn intensity. Perhaps regret. "Kitty, you can refuse. Please refuse. I will make your excuses and that will be an end to it."

An end, another end with him, this time permanent. He had come to town to do this and when it was finished he would leave. If she declined, she would not see him again.

She knew nothing sinister of Ian Chance, only that he trounced her mother at whist every week and had a different stunning widow on his arm every month.

"If I can provide information that will convince you he is not guilty of treason, I will do what I may."

He seemed to consider that. Finally he nodded. He took his hat into both hands as though in preparation to leave. "Come to the Serpentine at nine o'clock tomorrow morning. Are you able?"

"Am I able? Am I awake, rather." She tried to grin without much success.

"At that hour fewer will see you unattended by a chaperone."

"I will have my maid."

"No. Ride. Accompanied by your groom."

"You sound as though you are giving me an order."

His brow creased. "I am."

Now she could not help smiling. "And yet I did not give you permission to."

"The next time I shall make certain to ask first." The corner of his mouth lifted. The deep familiarity was still there drawing between them, a silent, restless binding.

She tried to fight it with reason. "What am I to expect?"

"I will be there," he only said. And that was all it required for reason to fly and the pleasure of two spirits attuned to each other to overcome her. A breath escaped her that might have been a sigh.

He crossed the space between them, took her hand, and lifted her fingers to his lips.

"Kitty," he said softly, brushing the lightest kiss across her knuckles, sending her last shred of resistance to perdition. "I am terribly sorry. You cannot know how sorry."

She struggled against the heady warmth of his touch, holding back the words she longed to say. That sort of disclosure would not serve anyone well, least of all herself. And he did not want to hear it. He had made that perfectly clear at Willows Hall.

She tugged her hand away.

"Thank you," she managed. "I deserved an apology for your dishonesty."

"I mean that I am sorry you are involved in this now."

"That's all right." She spoke to cover her confusion. "It was only your delivery that lacked finesse. But perhaps if you gave me orders in that horrid accent with your dogs at your heels I might be more inclined to submit to your authority."

"You have already submitted, although I doubt it had anything to do with my authority."

He seemed to realize what he had said at the same moment as she. They stared.

"I am sorry, Kitty," he repeated very low, quite beautifully.

"You said that already. Several times." Their brows nearly touched as he bent his head. Her breaths came short. She could still feel his touch beneath her clothing, on her skin, and inside her body. She wanted him there again more than she could bear.

"I am full of remorse, it seems." His voice was rough.

"And I, it seems—" She struggled for breath. "I must repeat myself as well."

"How so?"

"I must say, 'This is a bad idea.'" She forced the words through her lips because her heart could not bear this teasing. If he would not truly have her, she did not want this. "'You should go now.'"

"I should." But he did not move. "I will leave," he whispered huskily.

"When?" She could lift her face and he would kiss her. So she did.

"Shortly." He did not kiss her. "Now."

"Why? Because you are after all a gentleman and not a barbarian?"

"Because you, Kitty Savege"—his voice was taut—"are a luxury I may not allow myself."

The door creaked open.

They jerked apart. Kitty turned to the window, heartbeat flying.

"O-oh!" the maid stuttered. "Begging your pardon, mum! But your lady mother sent over a note with the request you're to read it right away, so . . . I'll leave it on the table." The door shut.

Kitty peeked over her shoulder.

His knuckles were white around his hat brim. "I will take my leave of you at this time."

She took a series of quick breaths. "All right. But I will not play games like this. If you leave now, you will not be calling on me again. Are we agreed on that?"

The briefest pause. "We are."

She blinked, lost in desire and confusion, her chest aching. Perhaps she should not have offered an ultimatum she was not prepared to live with. He was, she understood now, a man of firm convictions. "Fine."

"Viscount Gray will accompany me to the park in the morning. You are acquainted with him, I believe."

She nodded, not trusting her voice.

"Then, until tomorrow." He bowed, and left.

Kitty sat down, folded her shaky hands between her knees, and rested for several minutes in the company of her triumphant self-respect. Then her heart shoved aside her self-respect, and finally she cried.

Chapter 18

Kitty dressed carefully in a modest habit of burgundy velvet with a high white collar, a simple matching hat with a black crinoline net encircling the crown of her head, and black gloves. She looked a bit like she was in mourning, and rather felt it. Her mother had spent the evening out late with her suitor; she was not yet awake when Kitty stole from the house at the indecent hour of half past eight. The groom met her with her horse and they set off for the park.

Few people of fashion could be seen across the expanse of green—elderly gentlemen taking the air at a slow pace, a barouche landau carrying a pair of ancient ladies in equally ancient lace, and nurses with their young charges, running off the morning's energies in the misty cold.

Kitty rode slowly along the waterside path. When two riders appeared across the green coming toward her at a canter, a pair of big gray shadows loping alongside, she drew in her mount.

The dogs came first, the larger one cavorting about in front of her horse, the other wagging its great shaggy tail from a wiser distance. She forced herself to look at both

gentlemen as they approached, to greet Leam as civilly as
Lord Gray. She wished to be angry with the Earl of Blackwood, to dislike him even, but she could not. She had come
here only because he had asked and so that she could once
again enact the role of a foolish girl devoted to a man who
did not have her best interests at heart. Who had, in fact,
none of her interests at heart.

"My lady." Lord Gray bowed from the saddle. "You are
generous to meet us here this morning." He was an attractive
man, with very dark blue eyes and a commanding air. "May
we walk for a bit?"

She nodded. The gentlemen dismounted and Lord Gray
came to assist her. Leam watched, his expression unremarkable, as when he had first come into her house the previous
day, before he had gazed at her with longing and touched her.

The viscount took her hand on his arm.

"I would not be surprised were you anxious about this
conversation, my lady." He drew her along the path. "You
needn't be. The prince regent and the ministers have great
faith in you."

He must feel the quiver in her hand, which she could not
help, foolish woman that she was in the presence of a taciturn Scot. *Usually* taciturn.

"Lord Blackwood mentioned that yesterday," she replied.
"But, I assure you I am perfectly well. Why don't we simply
get on with it so that I may then enjoy the remainder of my
day as I had planned it? I daresay I have a knothole to be
listening at or some such task awaiting me elsewhere. You
know how it is with lady informants. Never a dull moment."

Lord Gray did not bat an eye. "Of course, my lady. I understand your pique. We shall make this as brief as possible."

She cast a swift glance at Leam. He was looking at the
ground before him as he walked on the other side of the
viscount, but the corner of his mouth tilted up. He had again

donned his loose, unfashionable coat and careless neck cloth, and a shadow darkened his jaw. It seemed he had not given up his false role after all.

"I don't know that anything I can tell you will be of use," she replied. "I haven't any idea of Lord Chance's involvement in politics. Indeed I have always believed him wholly disinterested in such things."

"In point of fact, ma'am, we haven't come here to ask you about Chance."

"Then the Marquess of Drake?"

"No."

Leam's head came up. "Gray." His voice was low on the single syllable. Kitty drew her hand away and halted on the path in the saturating mist.

"My lord, I am not fond of games. Not any longer, at least. You must speak plainly."

"I should like to ask you several questions regarding another gentleman of your acquaintance. Douglas Westcott."

Her gaze shot to Leam. His brow was drawn.

Kitty's eyelids slipped closed, sheer misery sweeping through her. She had not imagined she could ever feel again the height of betrayal Lambert had dealt her. But apparently she had been wrong. Quite naïvely wrong.

"Douglas Westcott, Lord Chamberlayne." She could barely utter the words. "All this time you were seeking information about my mother's beau."

Leam's lips parted, his frown deepening. "Your mother's—"

"Yes," Lord Gray replied. "The Home Office has long held suspicions regarding untoward activities on the part of persons closely associated with Chamberlayne, principally his son, who is still in Scotland. He is known to be interested in fomenting renewed rebellion amongst the clans of the Highlands."

She lifted her eyes to Leam. "How convenient for you that you chanced upon me in Shropshire, Lord Blackwood. Or perhaps it was not chance after all." Her stomach hurt. Everything inside her hurt. "I am sorry I did not voluntarily offer up information concerning the man courting my mother. Perhaps if you had simply asked nicely as Lord Gray is now doing, I might have obliged and we would now be spared this unpleasant little interview."

His jaw was like stone. "I had no knowledge of this."

"Didn't you?"

"My lady, your compliance with our wishes would assist the crown immeasurably."

"Damn you, Gray, this is unconscionable."

"Compliance?" She swung to Leam. "*Did* you know of this?"

The viscount replied first. "Lord Chamberlayne's name was on the list I sent to Mr. Seton some months ago. But earlier this week when Lord Blackwood failed to mention your mother's connection to him, I began to doubt he had seen the list."

"You might have *asked*." Leam's voice grated.

The viscount held Kitty's regard. "I suspected he would be hesitant to arrange this meeting if he knew the whole of it."

"Or even the half." Leam's face was grim in the wintery morning. "Lady Katherine, allow me to escort you home."

She shook her head, her mother's situation coming to her full force. "What untoward activities?"

"I am not at liberty to say," the viscount replied. "But you may assist us by revealing what you know about him."

"I know nothing except that he is a gentleman and very attached to my mother. And I certainly hope there is nothing else to know, for I like him." She knew not what else to say. She turned about and walked swiftly toward her groom holding the horses, a tumble of confusion.

"Lady Katherine"—the viscount's voice carried to her—
"the bullet that caught you in Shropshire was not intended
for you. But the next one may be. Has my friend here yet
told you that?"

She halted and turned. Leam stood very still.

"I don't understand," she managed, but she did.

"There is a slight possibility of revenge," the viscount said
as though reading her thoughts. "But we don't believe that
Lord Poole is now in a position to provoke such an action,
and it would be too easily traceable to him if he did. He is
only in France, and our informants there are impressed with
the rather modest lifestyle he has taken up. They are under
the impression he hopes to someday win a pardon based on
good behavior and to have his estates returned to him."

"But you do not yet know who the shooter is, clearly."
She looked to Leam, and it was nearly painful to do so. "Is
that so?"

His eyes said he did not wish to tell her, but he spoke. "Not
entirely."

"Lord Blackwood received a message from the shooter
less than a fortnight ago in Scotland."

"I don't understand." Her voice quavered. "If someone
wished to harm me, why would he tell you about it?"

A muscle flickered in Leam's jaw.

"My lady." Lord Gray's voice remained firm. "Through
his work for the crown in the past, Lord Blackwood may
have displeased one or two persons intent on Scotland's dis-
union from Britain. We suspect you are being threatened to
control his actions now, to ensure that he does not further
impede these rebels' plans."

Her heart pounded. She could not look away from Leam.
"Is this true?"

"I don't believe it is."

"You also said you aren't a spy."

"I am not. But you are in danger."

"And how shall I wrest myself from that danger?" An unfamiliar, sticky hysteria bubbled up in her with the fear for her mother, and that perhaps he had sought information from her in Shropshire, and that was all she had been to him—the same way Lambert had only used her to dishonor her brothers.

"Shall I admit to you and Lord Gray here everything I know of Lord Chamberlayne?" she continued. "Well then, I have found him partial to claret but truly fond of port. He prefers whist to piquet, and likes his matched grays overly much, although in my opinion they are too showy for a gentleman of his maturity. He recently gave my mother a lovely necklace, quite tasteful really, and I believe he intends to ask her to marry him shortly, although perhaps he already did last night, but I haven't seen her yet today as I was obliged to come out at an early hour to be lied to by a pair of men who insist they are not spies but who behave remarkably like one might imagine spies do."

Lord Gray extended a placating hand. "My lady—"

"What do you wish to know? Ask me and I shall give you my considered responses. Then you can tell me what I must do to protect myself and my mother."

"You needn't protect yourself," Leam said quietly. "We will."

She closed her eyes. Was this reluctant connection all that she was to have of him now? Someone threatened her and so he must remain involved with her?

"My lady," Lord Gray said into the dreary silence. "We do not wish to detain you here longer this morning. Would you consent to writing down what you know of Lord Chamberlayne so that our agents may analyze it?"

These men were not playacting as she had once done in spying on Lambert Poole. This was real, and she should help, especially if it could exonerate her mother's beau. And if it did not ... For her mother's sake, she could not imagine that now. Nearly thirty years with a husband who lived a double life should not be rewarded with another such man. But why would the crown suspect him otherwise?

"How are you protecting me?" she finally asked.

The viscount gestured beyond her shoulder. Fifteen yards distant, a hulking man stood with his back to the trunk of a leafless tree, hands in his trouser pockets.

"That is Mr. Grimm," he said.

"A *bodyguard*?"

"My lady, we must make another request of you."

"No." Leam moved toward her. "Lady Katherine—"

"We wish you to interview your mother about Lord Chamberlayne, and to encourage her to share private information with you, as well as your servants and Chamberlayne's as you are able, then to write that in your report as well."

"Goddamn, Gray." He came very close but did not touch her. "Kitty, you must go now."

Tears pressed at the backs of her eyes, and a horrid thickness in her chest and throat. "Yes." She made herself look up into his face, and what she saw there twisted her insides—steel again, and anger, but also something else, that warmth and intensity that had been there from the first and drew her to him.

"Did you come back to London because of the message that threatened me? Is that the purpose you spoke of that keeps you here when you wish to be in Scotland?"

He took a tight breath and drew her hand to his arm. "Allow me to help you mount."

"You wish me gone so that you can speak with your friend openly. You are very angry, so clearly this interview did not proceed as you expected. What are you going to do, Leam, hit Lord Gray now like you hit Mr. Yale at the inn?"

"It's possible." He drew her toward her horse.

"I saw his bruise on the way to church on Christmas." She spoke whatever words occurred to her because to feel now was too difficult. "I am all curiosity. What was Mr. Yale going to ask me that you found the need to 'send him to the snow,' as he so colorfully put it? Did he want me to put my skills to use interviewing Mr. and Mrs. Milch, or perhaps Emily and Mr. Cox? That would have been wonderful. Just think, I could have learned all their secrets and begun playing them off one another right there trapped in the village. What a drama I might have precipitated." Her voice was brittle, her heart in a welter.

"Yes, that was it," he replied stonily. "You are very clever."

"Mr. Yale does work with you and Lord Gray and Jinan, doesn't he?"

"Yes." He set his hands for her to step into, then tossed her up. She leaned forward on the saddle and he assisted in adjusting her skirts as though he were any gentleman assisting any lady at such a mundanely courteous task. It was all quite normal, as nothing had ever actually been between them and most certainly would never be now.

"I wonder how he felt about being dragged into Emily's petty domestic troubles," she murmured. "A spy pretending to court a girl to save her from a fish man."

"I believe she called him a fish troll. And there is nothing petty about attaching oneself to the wrong person." He finished adjusting her stirrup and his gaze came up to hers. It seemed for a moment that he would speak. Then he stepped away from the horse and smacked it on the flank. It started forward, and Kitty did not look back. At least this time she would not be obliged to watch him leave her.

Leam rounded on Gray.

"Goddamn you for tricking her into this, Colin. And goddamn you for using me to do so. The only reason I arranged this meeting was because of your threat to have me confined to Scotland if I did not." With Cox threatening Kitty, he could not leave London. The blackguard had not yet revealed himself in order to collect the object Leam supposedly possessed. But when he surfaced, Leam would have his neck.

"We need the information." The viscount stood at ease, apparently oblivious to the menacing growl of the wolfhound bitch before him.

"What can she give you that you cannot acquire from another source? From an *actual* trained informant?"

"I know you went to the Secret Office yesterday, Leam. You went there to read the file on Poole."

His hands fisted. "How proud you must be of your network of clerks and footmen, Colin. Admirable."

"You saw the documents. Her letters are detailed, her observations keen. She did all of that for years without the assistance of training, or any other advantage. The director was impressed, and at least two admirals on the board said they hadn't ever seen such careful work from an informant, especially not one thoroughly embedded in society as she. Including Constance."

"Kitty Savage was not an informant. Since you have also read the file you know very well it was a personal matter to her."

"Then it is high time she turn her talents to matters of state."

"Damn you, Colin, I would call you out if I could bear the idea of it. But you know very well I cannot."

"I don't wish to fight you, Leam. I am only here to convince you to come work for us."

He stood stunned for a moment. "*Us?* There isn't an *us* any longer. Or hadn't you noticed that amidst your covert plans? I didn't read the goddamned list of names Jin brought because *I don't give a damn.*"

"I am not speaking of the Falcon Club. They want you in the Home Office. Quite adamantly."

"Tell them to take Yale. He's anxious to be back at it already."

His jaw tightened. "They are suspicious of Yale, though I have assured them they needn't be."

"He is the cleverest one of the lot of you, and they're fools if they cannot accept that." He pivoted about. "Go find yourself a proper candidate, someone in need of work, without a family and estate to see to. Someone who wants your damned secrecy and lies." He strode to his horse. The mist had coalesced into rain and it pattered chill on his hat and shoulders and his roan's glossy coat. Anger roiled in him, hot and desperate. Betrayal had shown in her eyes thicker than the overhanging sky. Perhaps she had trusted him before, but she would not now.

It was for the best.

"They follow you."

He slid the reins into place. "You mean Wyn and Constance. Of course they do. I half raised both of them."

"Even Seton has listened to you on occasion despite his cavalier attitude toward the Club and uncertain loyalty to the crown. Every single one of your quarries has returned home without complaint. People lead where you tell them to go, Leam. The kingdom needs you."

Yes, people did what he wished, like his brother who walked into a duel with his closest friend because Leam arranged it. He set his foot in the stirrup and mounted.

"I'm not interested."

"Would you be interested if I told you Lady Katherine would not be bothered again for information if you agree to their offer?"

Leam's head swung around.

"They want you to resume your previous role and head the unit in France," Gray said.

"You are using her to convince me of this?"

"Not entirely. Her assistance with Chamberlayne would be helpful. Possibly essential. They have no doubt she could continue to be useful after that, with her social connections and natural ability. Unwed she has no husband to hinder her." His brow drew down. "Leam, I am sorry to be the messenger. I truly am. In this case, I am telling you what I have been told to convey. They are willing to give her up for your promise."

Leam fought for breath. How could he have allowed this? He had been blind to everything to which he should have paid the closest attention. Again.

"Colin, I must find David Cox." He had claimed to be with Lloyd's, London's premier insurance company. He'd searched there first, but apparently Cox had not worked for Lloyd's in years. Yet another reason to suspect him—whoever he was.

"When this matter is concluded," Gray said, "we can help with that."

He scowled. "The director and ministers and their network of informants are a pack of idiots and amateurs. Why do they imagine I would wish to ally myself with them?"

"To make certain they never invite Lady Katherine to assist them again."

Leam's chest ached. He shook his head. "I was truly a fool to go to you for help protecting her. You told them precisely how to entrap me."

"I didn't like it any more than you. But I was instructed to do what I must."

"Answer me this: If I agree, how would I be assured of her protection if I am across the Channel or in the north?"

"You would have the director's promise. The prince

regent's if you wish. Say the word and I vow to you the government will forget Katherine Savege ever existed."

Leam gripped the reins with frigid fingers. He had promised his son. He had promised himself.

"I have no heart for it, Colin," he uttered to his old friend. "I would make a poor spy."

"You never had any heart for it, Leam. That is what makes you the perfect spy." The viscount's face wore the same expression of confident sobriety it had five years ago when, over brandy on a chance meeting at their club, he had first spoken to Leam of the Falcon Club. A new secret organization, Gray had said, with a task Leam seemed particularly suited for at the moment. They needed a Scot, and it would allow him to leave England. To leave it all behind.

But now he did not wish to leave. For the first time in years he wished to remain, and in the company of a woman he mustn't have.

So be it.

"I must launch my sister into society this spring." It was the least he could do for her. Married to a suitable man, Fiona might take Jamie into her home when Leam must be away. The boy mustn't remain alone at Alvamoor with Isobel's bitterness to blight his youth.

He lifted his head and met Gray's gaze. "Tell them that I am theirs to do with as they wish. But if anyone importunes Lady Katherine again, I will make you pay for it personally, Colin."

"Of course."

Leam turned his mount's head and rode away.

Kitty waited for her mother to rise. The dowager remained abed. At eleven she went to her mother's room and knocked. A maid answered.

"She hasn't been in today, milady."

Kitty maintained her poise. "Well, that is curious. Perhaps she stayed at my brother's last evening. Lord and Lady Savege hope we will all move into the new house down the street before the baby comes, of course."

"Course, mum." But the maid didn't believe it either.

She would not have even a day, an hour to decide what to tell her mother. Unlike her daughter, the dowager countess would not give herself to a man or risk being discovered consorting with a gentleman without the promise of marriage. Lord Chamberlayne, it seemed, was set to be a member of the family. What would Lord Gray have to say to that? And how could Kitty withhold it from her beloved mother?

She could not.

She went to the parlor and pulled the rope bell, then sat at her writing table and drew out a sheet of paper and ink.

"Milady?" the footman said from the doorway.

"I am not at home to callers this afternoon, John. If my mother should come home, please alert me to it immediately."

He bowed and closed the door.

She wrote, not what Lord Gray wished to read. She could not do what they asked of her. If they sought information about Lord Chamberlayne, they must find it through another source. She would not tell her mother anything, but she would not betray her either. And she was not a spy. She must leave that to others better qualified. If Lord Chamberlayne were guilty of fomenting rebellion among Highlanders, the government would bring him to justice by some other means. She must believe that. But her conscience pricked alongside her anxiety for her mother.

When the ink dried, she sealed the letter and addressed it. She stood, swiping the tears from her cheeks, and went to the door.

"John," she called, and went onto the landing. But the footman was not walking up the steps. Leam was.

Chapter 19

He halted, his hand tight around the banister.

"You have been crying."

"What are you doing here? Go away." She did not plan the words. Apparently they surprised him as much as her; his eyes widened.

"Go back inside the parlor." He advanced up the steps.

"Stop giving me orders. You have no right to."

"I damned well do." He came to her and grasped her arm.

"No you don't. And stop cursing at me too. You are a cretin after all."

"I am not cursing at you. Not precisely." He snatched the missive from her hand. "You should not have written this."

"I did not—"

"Milady?" The footman peered up at her from the foyer below.

"I am fine, John. Who admitted Lord Blackwood?"

"The door was wide open," the earl snapped.

"And you sauntered in uninvited? *Disinvited*, in point of fact. I told you not to come here again."

"Your servants should be horsewhipped for leaving you vulnerable to intruders."

"We are moving the household down the street. There is a great deal of coming and going. Anyway I thought Mr. Grimm was taking care of the intruders."

"Go into the parlor," he ground out.

"John, please see that the front door is properly closed," she called down. "I will not require tea. Lord Blackwood will not be remaining long." She pulled from his hold and went into the parlor and across the chamber, away from him. He shut the door, then moved to the door adjoining the drawing room and closed that as well.

Kitty shook her head. "What are you doing? Don't. Open them up at once." When he came toward her she thrust out her palm. "Stop. Do not come any closer."

But he did, not allowing her the distance she needed from his body, his strength and intensity. He set the letter on the table, his brow severe.

"What did you write?" he demanded.

"You will read it eventually. Why don't you just wait to find out when Lord Gray gives it to you? It will heighten the anticipation to be frustrated now, don't you think? That tactic worked so nicely for us in Shropshire, after all."

He grasped her shoulders, bringing them close, and God help her, she welcomed even so unloverlike a touch.

His gaze scanned her face, his eyes peculiarly bright. "Kitty, this is no game."

"How can you say that to me? To *me*?"

"I cannot allow you to be hurt."

"I understand that. But you must at least be relieved that your enemy chose to threaten me rather than one of your innocent family members. After all, I consorted with a villain for years. I am well able to—"

"You take my breath away," he whispered.

She gaped, and melted. He seemed to drink in her features with his dark eyes. He lifted a hand and curved it around her cheek. Then his other hand. He sank his fingers into her hair and his grip tightened.

"I will not allow him to come close to you again." His voice was hard, hinting at violence.

"Who—who are we talking about? The shooter, Lord Gray, or—"

"You speak and I hear nothing else. You move and I cannot look away," he said roughly. "It seems I cannot resist you." He bent and brushed his lips across the corner of her mouth. She sucked in air, trembling toward him.

"But you are trying to resist?" she barely managed.

"I am failing." His hands holding her were warm, certain.

"Tell me that you did not know of their suspicions of Lord Chamberlayne before, in Shropshire. Tell me so that I can believe you. Please, Leam."

"I knew of your glance and your smile, your words and the touch of your hand, and nothing else. Your very existence mesmerizes me, Kitty Savege. It has since the moment I first saw you three years ago. Is that sufficient to convince you?"

"P-perha—"

He captured her lips, openmouthed. She wound her arms about his neck and let him pull her close, closer until their bodies met everywhere and the relief of touching him again filled her. His palms moved down her back, then over her behind, grabbing her up. She let herself touch him, to revel in the strong planes of his face, his shoulders and hard arms, and the pleasure of it. She could lose herself in his kiss and never wish to be found again. She was on the verge of allowing that to happen.

She already had. She was lost.

He sought her jaw with his mouth, the tender place beneath her ear.

"I have not ceased thinking of you," he uttered. "Not an hour has gone by that I have not recalled the music of your voice, the perfume of your skin, or the pleasure of being inside you."

"You left Willows Hall abruptly. I thought you despised me for wanting you. Yet now you say this. And you kiss me. I cannot think."

"You did not tell me the truth, did you?" His mouth pressed against her hair, his voice low. "It was only Poole, wasn't it? Why did you wish me to believe otherwise?"

She squeezed her eyes shut. "I wanted you to be certain of my inability to conceive. What did it matter if I'd had one or a hundred lovers?"

"What did he do to you, Kitty?"

"What drove me to seek revenge on him? Nothing," she whispered. "He did nothing." She had done it to herself, nursing her hurt into vengeance. She understood that now.

His breathing seemed uneven. "He must have."

"You needn't worry, Leam. I will not come after you when we are through with one another. One man's ruination suffices for me this lifetime."

"Kitty, do not speak such words. Do not." His big hands bracketed her hips and slid up her waist, in command of her body as though it were his to do with as he wished. He spoke against her cheek. "I do not wish to be through with one another."

"Not yet. But—"

His mouth found hers. She twined her fingers in his hair and let him kiss her as though they never would be through with one another.

He drew away, his hand again circling her face, thumb caressing her lips as he had done before.

"I must see to a matter now." His gaze moved across her features, then to her eyes. "Promise me you will not do what Gray has asked of you."

"Why not?"

"Because it does not become your soul to muddle in such pretense. Leave it to those whose souls are already blackened." He touched his lips to hers gently, tenderly, then more fully. "I must go," he whispered against her mouth, then released her and stepped back. He took a deep breath.

"Will you return?" Kitty bit her lip, but the words had already tripped out.

He smiled. "Is the ban on my entrance into this house lifted, then?"

She wanted to ask him if it should be. If he returned, did it mean that he was returning with sincere intentions?

"Perhaps we should leave it open to interpretation," she said instead.

He nodded, bowed, and went out. This time when Kitty sank down upon a chair, jelly-legged and weak, she did not cry. She hoped.

London never quieted, not even in the drenching cold of a February rain. Leam worked his way through carriages and carts and pedestrians, through puddles and across sparkling roads rising with the stench of a city awash in busy commerce, intent upon his destination.

On a neat block he gave his horse into the keeping of a boy. For a moment he stared at the narrow town house before him, nothing of particular note about its plain brown façade and black iron rail. Its resident might not even be at home now. The knocker, however, was up; the man was at least in town.

Leam was as impetuous as ever. His presence here proved it. His brief call on Kitty the day before proved it even more surely. She wanted him and he needed to be with her. If that meant tackling his demons, he would do so.

First he must find David Cox. In the sennight Leam had been back in town, Cox had not contacted him. Leam and his solicitor had both visited Lloyd's, looking for information on the insurance agent, but none knew anything of him after his departure for America five years earlier.

He would not be defeated. He did not pause to regret his haste in paying this particular call. But his gut was tight as he went to the door and knocked. A servant answered, narrow-faced and pale. He assessed Leam's bedraggled appearance before lifting his brows.

"May I help you, monsieur?"

Leam handed him a calling card. "Fesh me yer master."

The manservant's nostrils flared. He nodded, ushered him into the foyer, and took his coat and hat.

"Swith awa, man." Leam gestured impatiently. "A dinna hae aw day." He could gladly wait forever to have this conversation, but the time had come, and he had purpose now he'd never had before.

"*Je vous en prie,* my lord," the manservant said with stiff disapproval. "If you will wait in the parlor."

Leam went into the chamber and to the window, and stared into the gray day at the neat row of elegant buildings across the street. By God, he wanted out of town houses. Out of London. Out of *England.* She would never have him anyway. Not for long, at least. For all the passion and warmth beneath her society hauteur, she had been made for this world. The world he had lied to for years.

A footstep at the threshold turned his head. Nearly as tall as Leam, with a slash of straight black hair falling across his brow, penetrating green eyes, and a Gallic elegance to his clothing and air, Felix Vaucoeur was a handsome man.

"I saw your card," he said without any trace of accent, his English as fluid as Leam's when he wished it, "but did not quite believe it."

"Your manservant is an impertinent snob, Vaucoeur. Do you pay him to frighten away callers?"

The comte moved to the sideboard and took up a carafe of dark liquid.

"Rather late to be paying me a call finally, Blackwood." He poured out two glasses, then turned and came across the chamber. He handed one to Leam and met his gaze. "And hypocritical."

Leam studied the man who had killed his brother. In nearly six years their paths had not crossed. To protect both Leam and James from scandal, their uncle, the Duke of Read, had seen to it that Vaucoeur received a pardon, and the duel was put about as a hunting accident. Vaucoeur had gone into the countryside to avoid gossip, where he remained until the war ended and he returned for a time to his estate on the Continent. But the English half of Vaucoeur's blood had always been stronger, despite his French title.

Leam set his glass on a table. "You haven't any idea why I am here."

"Ah." The comte turned and went back to the sideboard.

"I need your help."

Vaucoeur paused in lifting the carafe.

"I am looking for a man who claims to have served with you and my brother on the Peninsula," Leam said. "David Cox. Fair, good-looking. Says he is in insurance now. Do you remember such a fellow?"

"Why not inquire at the War Office?"

"I've more interest in him than his address."

Vaucoeur's eyes narrowed. "What business is that of mine?"

"I don't know that it's any. Cox has been following me, and he has threatened those close to me. I must make certain it hasn't anything to do with my brother before I pursue other avenues."

"You imagine I might have had something to do with him, this tradesman who claims to have known James. A good-looking fellow, one of our regiment mates." Vaucoeur set down his glass with a quiet click. "What?"

"What do you mean?"

"What business might I have had with this Mr. Cox that could have involved your brother?"

For a long stretch of silence they stared at each other.

"Why did you allow me to goad you into it?" Leam finally uttered. "Even so, I exaggerate. I barely had to nudge you to challenge him."

Vaucoeur spoke slowly. "He violated my sister."

"He violated a great many men's sisters," Leam replied. "But he was in love with you."

"That was his misfortune." The reply came too swiftly, too smoothly, practiced, as though he had been waiting to say the words for almost six years.

It did not suit Leam. Not after so long.

"What happened on the Peninsula, Felix? Two young men thrown together at war, sharing the same battlefield and tent, like Philip Augustus and Richard *Coeur de Lion* marching across the desert against a heathen enemy. Which one were you? Young King Philip, the tease? The opportunist." His mouth tasted metallic. "To my brother's anguished Richard."

"Get out, Blackwood." The words were like ice, but something in his eyes arrested Leam, something keen and deeply scarred even after years. Vaucoeur had not yet made peace with his part in James's death.

"You did care for him. Didn't you?" It had never before occurred to Leam. Not in such a manner.

"Of course I did. He was my best friend."

"But not your lover."

"Never." His gaze bored into Leam's. "I am, you see, quite exclusively fond of women."

Finally Leam understood his brother's torment, and perhaps this man's pain and regret as well. Vaucoeur had never been what James both wanted him to be and feared. For years anger had burned in Leam for how his brother had lied in not telling him about Cornelia's baby. James might have married her; men like him married women they did not want frequently enough. But the desperation that had driven James to bed every female he could had made actual marriage to a woman impossible. His brother had wanted someone he could not have and it had driven him to the edge of insanity. The Blackwood passion had not been reserved to Leam alone.

"Am I to understand then," he said, "that you have nothing to help me in the matter of David Cox?"

The comte turned away, replacing the stopper on the brandy. "I don't remember him."

Leam nodded and went toward the door, an odd emptiness in his chest.

"He hated himself." Vaucoeur's voice came behind him, steady and certain.

"Yes," Leam said quietly. "And he suffered for who he was," in a way Leam had never in his life suffered. While James despised his own nature, Leam hadn't given a damn what his fellow classmates thought of him. Quietly he studied and wrote and took the teasing along with his high marks and masters' praise. But he hadn't cared about any of it, only the poetry, the expression of true emotion he'd believed in so deeply at the time.

But for too long he had watched his brother suffer and felt it in his own heart. After a time, he wanted to suffer as well, to finally share some of that pain. Cornelia Cobb had offered him the perfect opportunity.

Her youthful levity had attracted him. But not for its own sake, he understood now. Falling for her had finally made him feel like he was betraying his nature. Fool that he was, he had reveled in knowing she was not suitable for him with her gay, light smiles and superficial flirtations. After all those years watching his brother and hurting for him, Leam had welcomed the suffering too.

He had not paused a moment to consider what would actually happen if she accepted him.

"You did not kill him." Vaucoeur's voice was hard. "I would like to believe that even I did not. He wanted to die and he used us because he hadn't the courage to pull the trigger himself."

Leam looked into the man's glittering eyes and saw a coldness there he never wished to live again, a cold that Kitty's wide gaze and eager touch had begun to thaw within him.

He bowed. "Vaucoeur."

The comte nodded. "My lord."

Leam departed. The city streets were still crowded with vehicles and people, the sky thick with rainclouds the color of her eyes. He must head for the War Office and the information on Cox that might or might not be there. Still he felt peculiarly adrift, without anchor.

He paused to allow a cart to trundle past on the muddy street, the clatter of wheels and shouts and the smell of rain all about.

Not adrift.

Free. Free of guilt. Free of regret and pain.

His hands tightened on the reins and he sucked in a lungful of damp air, water dripping off his greatcoat capes and the brim of his hat. He pushed his mount forward toward the War Office.

Chapter 20

Kitty did not speak to her mother about Viscount Gray's suspicions of Lord Chamberlayne. She simply did not know where to begin. *Mama, I have had an affair—and it seems that perhaps I still am having it—with Lord Blackwood, whose fellow spies believe your beau is involved with persons planning sedition, and they have asked me to assist them in acquiring information about Lord Chamberlayne's family and possible illegal activities.* No, that would not do. But she could not do what Lord Gray asked and conceal it from her mother either.

Standing by her bedchamber hearth, she drew her letter to him from her pocket and placed it on the grate. She must have time to consider, especially to understand how important Lord Chamberlayne was to her mother in truth.

The following day she joined her mother in paying calls. The day after that passed much the same, including a drive with Lord Chamberlayne in the park. The days crept into a week. Leam did not return.

"Kitty, you are fidgeting," her mother said to her as the

carriage halted at the curb on Berkeley Square to collect Emily and Madame Roche.

"I am not. I never fidget." She untangled her fingers from her reticule strings. "Mama, where were you when you did not come home in the evening a sennight ago?"

The dowager met her placid look with a glimmer in her eye.

"I wondered when you would ask that."

"I was waiting for you to make an announcement. I expected you to. Where were you?"

"There is no announcement to be made. I was at your brother's house. Serena was feeling poorly, and you know I am the only mother she has now. You might have asked me at any time." The dowager folded hands gloved in the finest kid on her lap of striped taffeta.

"I am sorry Serena is unwell. I will call on her tomorrow." She exhaled sharply. "But this is ridiculous. When will Lord Chamberlayne make an offer?"

"He already has."

She stared, a tangled mess of relief and disappointment inside. "You did not accept him?"

Her mother reached across the seat and took her chin into her hand as though she were a child.

"Kitty, I spent nearly thirty years married to a man who ill suited me. I am tempted, but I shan't dive into another marriage quite so swiftly."

Kitty nudged her face away. She *must* make certain.

"But you have had ample time. He has been courting you for months."

"And what of your suitors, daughter? Several have been calling on you for years."

Kitty looked out the carriage window. Emily and her companion were descending the steps of their house. Her mother had never asked her this. Never pressed her. Why now?

"They do it mostly for the novelty of it," she said. "None of them have a sincere attachment. It is the image of cool, reserved inaccessibility in the face of rumor that attracts them, not I."

Her mother's thin brows dipped into a V.

"Katherine, I never wish to hear you say such a thing. You disrespect a gentleman by judging his attentions in such a manner."

Kitty's head snapped around. "Mama, you cannot be serious."

"Your pride has outrun you, daughter. You have become far too comfortable dismissing any man you don't feel lives up to your exalted idea of what a gentleman should be."

Kitty's cheeks flamed. "And what precisely is that?"

"He must be extraordinarily learned, well placed in fashionable circles, an exceptional conversationalist, titled, wealthy, a man of taste and elegance, as loyal as yourself to his loved ones, and I daresay handsome as well."

"I never said such a thing." Her heart beat very swiftly.

"You needn't. You live it. But you will not find such a paragon, daughter. Men like that do not exist. Most of them are rather more like your father." There was no bitterness to her mother's voice, only the clean, uncluttered sense Kitty had always admired. But, even so, this was not honesty.

"Mama, I must know something. Why did you never—"

The carriage door opened.

"*Bonjour*, Katrine! My lady." Madame Roche was all gracious smiles, black and red and white fluttering with frills. Emily tucked her slender frame into the seat beside Kitty and placed a book in her hand.

"Here is the one I promised you. It is not nearly as tumultuous as the Racine play Lord Blackwood lent me, but I think you may like it, and you said you had seen *Phaedra* before, in any case."

"It was such a *plaisir* to encounter His Lordship again so soon. What a kind gentleman!"

"We saw him yesterday at Lady Carmichael's drawing room," Emily supplied.

"*Hélas*, with the large dogs." The elegant widow sniffed.

"I did not know you were acquainted with Lord Blackwood, Kitty." Her mother's gaze sharpened.

"A little."

"Quite a lot, I should say," Emily commented. "But that was to be expected given the circumstances."

Kitty's heart thudded. Her mother studied her. The carriage rumbled into motion.

"I have been thinking about that duel, Kitty, the one in which his brother died." Emily's lips pinched together. "It was insensibly tragic."

"It is men, dear girl," the dowager said.

"I don't think I understand them very well," Emily replied.

Kitty felt her mother's regard on her. She was wrong. She did not hold all gentlemen to impossibly high standards. Perhaps, like Emily, she simply did not understand them.

The exhibition opening spread through three high-ceilinged chambers of the British Museum. It was a spectacular show, a display of oil paintings of the Italian masters of the late Renaissance. Thick-muscled Masaccios competed for position on the wall with delicate Botticellis and dark, brooding Caravaggios.

Kitty had attention for little of it. Once she would have enjoyed such a display. Now her distraction, apparently, knew no bounds.

"Kitty, you are not yourself. Lady March remarked on it recently and I daresay she has the right of it."

She clutched her reticule to hide her distress. "Then, Mama, that simply must be."

"Give me your arm."

"No. I will take Emily's." She searched for her friend in the crowd.

"Do not frown, Katherine. It causes wrinkles."

"I needn't have any concern over wrinkles. As you so kindly pointed out in the carriage, I apparently have no interest in securing a gentleman's notice."

"You are twisting my words." The dowager studied a graceful portrait of the Virgin and child, the chubby babe reaching negligently for his mother's exposed breast, pacific grace etched on both their glowing faces. "You have notice, only little interest."

But she was interested. More than she could bear.

The dowager reached for her arm, but she turned away. If she had told her mother the truth years ago, perhaps she could confide in her now. But it was too late. She must bear this uncertainty and confusion alone.

She searched for Emily again and found her by a portrait of a peasant girl sitting beside a brace of soggy birds tied with twine.

"It is quite lifelike, don't you think?" Emily said pensively.

"Too." Kitty took her arm and drew her away, sucking in steadying breaths. "What have you been doing this past sennight back in town, Marie Antoine?"

"I have finished with that name, Kitty," she replied. "I am resolved to find another."

"I am certain you will come up with something lovely, as always."

Beneath her hand, Emily's body went stiff and she halted. Kitty followed the direction of her attention. Several yards away through a parting in the crowd stood a young, darkly handsome gentleman with a striking beauty on his arm. Mr. Yale with Lady Constance Read, Leam's cousin.

"Why look, Emily. It is Mr. Yale," she said quite unnecessarily, but her thoughts had scrambled. "Have you seen him since Shropshire?"

"No." Emily's lips were tight. Kitty's heart thudded. The gentleman and his companion were looking quite obviously at them. If she spoke with them, she might hear something of Leam. He had made her no promises. She didn't even know if he remained in London. Apparently he had found the ability to resist her after all, but that certainty made no difference to her aching heart and the warmth in her blood each night when she lay awake thinking of him. Thinking of him and wishing she lived another woman's life, a woman who needn't regret and remember and fantasize, yet never truly live.

"He has seen us. We must say hello." Kitty drew her friend forward.

Mr. Yale smiled quite pleasantly. Emily slipped her arm from Kitty's, turned completely about, and disappeared into the crowd.

"Lady Katherine, how do you do?" He bowed. "Allow me to present to you Lady Constance Read."

The sumptuous girl smiled and made a very pretty curtsy. She was taller than Kitty by an inch or two, all golden tresses, fashionable attire, and vibrant blue eyes.

"Lady Katherine, I am delighted to make your acquaintance," she said with a soft northern lilt. "My friend here has told me such diverting stories of your holiday sojourn in Shropshire. My cousin is rather more close-lipped about it, but you know how Scottish men can be rather taciturn."

Kitty's hands were damp. Abruptly she felt . . . *studied*. Both pairs of eyes watched her, it seemed, the sparkling blue and the silver rather too acute for a chance meeting.

"I know very little of Scottish gentlemen, in fact, Lady Constance," she said quite honestly.

"But your mother's beau, Lord Chamberlayne, is my countryman, of course, although from quite farther north than either Read Hall or Alvamoor," she said with a lovely smile that looked perfectly genuine. "You are better acquainted with Scotsmen than you know."

Kitty met Mr. Yale's quick gaze.

"My intended spurns me, it seems," he only said, glancing into the crowd.

"Then I am to understand Lady Constance knows of your charade at Willows Hall?"

"She does."

"It had the desired effect, you know. Her parents have left off with their plans to betroth her to Mr. Worthmore. Did she thank you?"

"A terse word or two." He smiled slightly. "And speaking of charades, my lady, have you come across our other mutual acquaintance recently? This week, perhaps?"

Kitty struggled for words. "I think you must know I have."

"More recently than in the park with our worthy viscount? By the way, neither of them told me of that meeting or I would have been there to throw down my gauntlet on your behalf, before both." He bowed. "I was obliged to learn of it through other channels."

She could barely think. "I don't know what you mean to ask me."

"He means, Lady Katherine— Oh, may I call you Kitty?" Lady Constance said prettily. "I do so dislike excessive formality."

Excessive?

Kitty nodded.

"He means to ask, Kitty, if you have seen Leam in the past several days since he re-donned his farmer's garb and began going about ladies' drawing rooms with his dogs again?"

"Slow down, Con. You are bewildering the lady, I imagine."

"Thank you, sir," Kitty replied with more composure than her racing pulse recommended, "but I am not such a slow top as all that." Lady Constance was involved in the secrets, clearly.

"Of course you aren't. Pray, forgive me, ma'am."

"Do cease all this bowing, sir." The visitors to the exhibition seemed to flow about her like a quick creek, she in the center of it with her feet sunk in icy water. She *was* bewildered, and yet her skin prickled with excitement. They were speaking to her as a confidante, as if they knew she knew everything. But, after all, they were spies. Or not quite, if Leam was to be believed. "If he did not tell you about the meeting with Lord Gray, then does he know you are speaking with me like this now?"

Mr. Yale shook his head slowly.

"Why are you? Isn't this all secret information?"

"In point of fact, we are no longer at it, my lady. We've all quit, except Gray, which makes it all the more worrisome that Blackwood has returned to it. He was the one who most wanted out."

"More to the point, Kitty." Constance laid a gentle hand on Kitty's arm. "My cousin trusted you."

In Shropshire it had all gone too fast, their coming together like a sudden storm. It felt the same now, the rush of the unreal carrying her away. But, just as before, she welcomed it. She *longed* for it.

"He said he intended to abandon that role and return to Scotland. Why is he doing this?"

Lady Constance lifted slender brows. "We thought perhaps you might know."

"Did you come here today to speak with me, then?"

The golden beauty nodded.

"I feel as though I am being watched."

Mr. Yale grinned. "You are."

"But not only by Mr. Grimm," Lady Constance said. "Which is why we are seeking your assistance now. Will you help us? In doing so, you will be helping your mother, of course. You cannot like not knowing the truth of matters."

"What—what do you think I know?"

"Something of what we know." A glimmer lit Mr. Yale's eyes. "That there are those who suspect Chamberlayne of consorting with Scottish rebels, perhaps even instigating rebellion and selling state secrets to the French, and that you were asked to provide information corroborating this. Have you?"

She shook her head.

Lady Constance smiled. "Good, because we have a better plan, one that should end this business once and for all."

"A plan?"

"One that you may not entirely like," Constance added.

Kitty remained silent.

"Not long ago an English ship with a valuable cargo went missing off the east coast of Scotland. We want you to pretend to Lord Chamberlayne that you have had an *affaire* with Leam during which he revealed to you that he was involved in this piracy, and that you are now willing to share this secret with your mother's trusted friend because Leam broke your heart and you wish to get revenge upon him."

The wide chamber seemed to close in on Kitty, centuries of vibrant colors and saints' faces crowding her.

"Perhaps a bit too bluntly put, Con," Mr. Yale murmured, his gaze steady on her.

"Oh, I don't imagine so. Leam would not admire her so much if she weren't capable of a great deal of subtle understanding."

Kitty was obliged to swallow across the dryness of her tongue. "Involved in the piracy exactly how?"

Lady Constance's cerulean eyes sparkled. Mr. Yale grinned.

Constance said softly, "You must tell Lord Chamberlayne that Leam knows where the cargo is located and is working with a confederate to see it delivered to Highland rebels intent on separation from England."

A shiver climbed up Kitty's spine. She looked from one to the other. "Does he?"

"Not that we know," Mr. Yale replied. "But if Chamberlayne is involved with the rebels, he won't want the cargo's location or its new owners bandied about, will he?"

"What would he do to someone who knew?"

The gentleman's gaze remained steady. "Plotting rebellion, my lady, makes men anxious to remove obstacles."

"You believe Lord Chamberlayne is truly consorting with rebels?" She could barely utter the words.

"Frankly we haven't any idea. But informants suggest he is."

"Then why does— Why doesn't *he*? He told me he doesn't believe any of it."

Constance's eyes shaded. Mr. Yale folded his hands behind his back.

Kitty's heart raced. "He doesn't care about it one way or the other, does he?"

"Not in the least."

"Then why doesn't he just go home? Isn't that where he wishes to be anyway?"

Mr. Yale inclined his head, but did not speak. Constance's soft gaze grew very direct. Kitty could not quite breathe.

He could not be doing it all for her. But they seemed to be saying exactly that. And Lord Gray. Even Leam had admitted it, to a point. Somehow her safety had something to do with this.

"Does he know you wish me to do this?"

"Oh, no. In fact he mustn't just yet or he will spoil it all. He won't like to have you involved."

"Not remotely," Mr. Yale murmured.

"Will it put him in danger?"

"Ultimately, if we are right, it will remove him from danger entirely, and you as well."

Her heart pounded. "How do I know to trust you?"

"Because we care for him. Quite a lot." Constance smiled with such genuine warmth it could not be a lie. Mr. Yale lifted a brow and grinned from the side of his mouth, looking uncannily boyish.

Kitty took a deep breath, her heart racing. "Yes."

Her mother could not accuse her of not behaving as herself on the carriage ride, even after they dropped Emily and Madame Roche home. Kitty chatted as though she hadn't a care in the world. She'd never had more. The following night at a ball she was to put the plan in motion. Her nerves jittered and tangled.

"Mama," she said as they entered the foyer, "I am going for a ride." She could not sit still, not to embroider or read or write letters or even to accept callers.

"I won't join you, dear. I must finish my correspondence, and Lord Chamberlayne is to take tea here later." The dowager removed her gloves and set them on the foyer table. "Here is a package for you. Perhaps another token of affection from one of your disinterested suitors."

Kitty shot the footman a glance. John flashed a grin, then pokered up.

She took up the large envelope and went to the stairs. She did not recognize the hand, but it was firm and bold. Her fingers shook a bit as she tore an opening in the top. This spy business was making her edgy. Gathering information to ruin Lambert had been more hobby than anything else, albeit a wretched one. Last summer when she had turned over that information to the authorities, she had done so in panic and only as a last-minute effort to help Alex. Now she had no such excuse except the conviction in her heart, and she was working with real spies. It made her . . . *fidgety*.

Good heavens. Next she would be admitting to pride and disobedience. Then her mother and Leam could have a congratulatory toast over how well they knew her character flaws.

She drew out the contents of the envelope. Halfway up the stair, she paused to grip the rail to steady herself.

It was a crisp, newly printed booklet of sheet music: Racine's play *Phaedra* in the original French, set to music. A calling card was tucked into one of the pages. She opened to it, and the Earl of Blackwood's embossed card dropped into her palm.

Beneath the bars of graceful notes at the top of the page were the lyrics, the playwright's poetry. It was the prince Hippolyte's speech to a friend. In it he spoke of the woman he secretly loved although he knew he should not.

Kitty's hands trembled as she read the line of verse. *Si je la haïssais, je ne la fuirais pas.* "If I hated her," she read in a shaky whisper, "I should not fly."

"How shall we celebrate your birthday tomorrow, Kitty?" Her mother's voice came close behind her.

Kitty slipped Leam's card into her sleeve and continued up the stairs, tucking the music under her arm as though it were nothing. As though it weren't *everything*.

Well, not precisely everything. *Phaedra* was still a tragedy no matter what sort of music one put it to. Kitty recalled bodies strewn about the stage at the end of the last act. But she refused to live a tragedy. Tragedies were for foolish girls. Not for her. Not any longer.

"However you wish, Mama." She willed her voice steady, but her step was light, her breaths short now from something more than nerves, much more than anxiety. She went into the drawing room, set the music on the pianoforte's stand and folded back the instrument's cover. Her hands quivered as she slipped onto the bench and put them to the keys.

She still played regularly, and now the notes came easily, rich and sorrowful beneath her fingertips. But under the bars of music the lyrics were beautiful, full of longing and betrayal, hope and the heartbreak of impossible love, and she could not remain silent. She sang, knowing he meant for her to sing, and she sounded awful. Her throat was unaccustomed to it and in any case clogged with emotion. It made her laugh, but she allowed herself the sweet release. She allowed herself to feel.

It was very frightening, and her fingers tripped on the keys.

"Kitty, whatever are you singing? It sounds perfectly dreadful." Her mother stood at the door.

"Oh, it isn't the music." Her hands moved across the ivory and ebony bars. "It is rather *me*. But I shall get it right eventually. I need practice." Practice allowing life to live inside her again. Practice leaving behind the past.

"I thought you were going riding."

"Perhaps later." She hummed the melancholy melody, her lips irrepressibly curved upward. He was a peculiar man, an impossible man, and she loved him.

Chapter 21

L eam scanned the crowded ballroom, nothing in his hooded gaze to reveal his particular interest in anyone or anything. This time, his façade was more a lie than ever.

He'd found little at the War Office on Cox, only a name in a register and a record of payments, but no address or county of origin. Cox had not lied about sharing James's regiment. Still, he seemed a ghost. A ghost with a pistol pointed at Kitty Savege and who had not yet shown himself to collect his property. Who, it seemed, was now the one playing games.

"I cannot believe I am standing beside you looking like that," Constance murmured, taking a glass of ratafia from a passing footman's tray.

"You've done so plenty of times before, my dear, and you needn't stand beside me a'tall. I am sure there are at least a dozen gentlemen who would be glad of your company." Dancers pirouetted across the boards accompanied by harpsichord, violins, celli, and flute. Two chandeliers suspended from the high ceiling cast the assembly in a heated glow, the chamber stuffy, overly dark, and full to the brim with high society.

"I wouldn't," she said, "but I am afraid you will leave if I step away for a moment." She glanced at his shabby evening finery.

"I have no plans to depart just yet." Before Leam had left his house to pick up Constance, a boy had come bearing a note from Grimm. Kitty was to attend this ball tonight. Leam knew not whether to flee or remain and test his fortitude. He had vowed to himself that he would not demand anything of her until he was perfectly assured of her safety. He owed her that.

So he remained. He ached to simply see her.

"And I am not such a rogue as all that to abandon you to your eager admirers without suitable protection," he muttered to his cousin. "Where is your companion, Mrs. Jacobs?"

"In some corner having a cozy gossip." Constance smiled. "I thought my uncle would attend tonight."

"Papa changed his plans. But perhaps— Oh, there is Wyn. What a pleasant surprise."

But Leam could not follow her attention. A woman had appeared at the ballroom's entrance. A clever-tongued woman. A woman of as much pride and warmth as beauty. Through the shifting dancers he glimpsed her rich tresses arranged loosely atop her head with sparkling combs, the gentle curve of her cheek, her silken shoulders and arms left nearly bare by a shimmering gown of ivory. A man parched with thirst, he drank in the sight of her. She smiled at her companion, an elegant gentleman, and a streak of mingled pleasure and possessive heat worked its way from Leam's chest into his tight throat.

But it lacked the edge of mania he'd felt long ago. Instead, confidence curled around the jealousy. She wanted him, and she did not wish to play games.

Yale strolled to Constance's side.

"Evening, cousins." He bowed, hands folded behind his back. "Haven't seen you in an age, Blackwood. Where have you been this week?"

"None of your business."

"Tracking down Scottish rebels, like you said you wouldn't? Pursuing information on Chamberlayne, I suspect. The director certainly seems to have you in the harness again, doesn't he?"

"I cannot hit you here, Yale, but I'll be happy to do so outside. Join me?"

"Charmed, I'm sure. You look like one of your dogs again, whiskers and all."

Leam turned to his cousin. "Now that you have suitable company, Constance, I will depart. Yale, put yourself to good use and see the lady home when she desires it, why don't you."

Constance rested her fingertips on his arm.

"Leam, we must speak with you now. Privately."

He glanced at the Welshman. The lad lifted a single black brow.

Leam frowned. " 'What a pleasant surprise'? Constance," he said quietly, "your acting abilities impress even me occasionally."

She dimpled. "Thank you."

"And if I refuse?"

"You don't want to refuse." The Welshman's gaze shifted across the crowd. Leam followed it. To Kitty.

Anger rose swiftly. "Am I to assume the two of you are in league with Gray again?" he said with a great deal more control than the hot blood racing in his veins merited.

"Oh, not at all," Constance demurred. "Quite the opposite. But don't scowl. You are in costume. Unfortunately." Gently she tugged on his sleeve, offering a generous chuckle as though she were vastly diverted.

Leam looked back to Kitty. She lifted her gaze to him. Clear across the ballroom, the thunderclouds invited him in, a smile playing about her lips, and nothing seemed to exist between them but perfectly pure desire and that beauty of understanding in which he still could not quite trust. Not entirely. But he would. Now he would go to her, take her from the ball, and make love to her. Then there would be nothing between them but what they both wanted.

Her gaze flickered past his shoulder and her smile faded. She turned away and, slipping through the crowd, disappeared into another room.

"Come, my lord," Yale said at his shoulder. "It is time we apprise you of certain matters."

He went.

Kitty approached Lord Chamberlayne, moving through the crowd from friend to acquaintance as she did at all such events, holding her head high and with serene countenance, ignoring the stares and gossip that floated in her wake, renewed since Lambert was exiled.

"My lord," she said, touching him on the sleeve, like a daughter. "May I have a brief word with you?"

"Of course, Lady Katherine." He bowed to his companions and moved aside with her. About them the music rose and fell, only to rise again. She felt Leam's gaze still in her blood, warm and speaking so many things without a word. As always.

"Is your mother unwell?" Lord Chamberlayne asked. "I'm afraid I have lost her in this crush."

"Oh, no, my lord. I sought you out on my own mission. You see . . ."

It was difficult to mouth the lies. His eyes shone clear gray, much lighter than her father's. In his face was compassion too, she had never noticed in her father's when he still lived. This man was kind at heart. If only there were another way. But nothing could convince her of the necessity of her pantomime if not Leam's bedraggled appearance, his bearded jaw, and, most of all, the look in his eyes before she had caught his gaze. She must do this and discover the truth for her mother's sake. And for Leam's.

Lord Chamberlayne tucked her hand into his elbow.

"Kitty, I hope you will trust me with any concern, large or small. You are like my own daughter, you know, if I'd had one."

"You have only your son, of course."

"Yes. And I see so little of him, as he prefers to remain at home in Scotland."

"Yes." She paused. "You see, I have come seeking advice—rather, assistance regarding a Scottish gentleman."

"Have you an admirer you wish me to speak with? I know I am not your father, but I hope someday to be of such assistance to you."

"Oh, well, yes, in a manner of speaking." She plunged in. "But you see, my lord, he is not an admirer. I fear his attentions went a great deal farther than admiration and now I am in something of a quandary."

His arm went stiff. "Has a gentleman insulted you?"

"Not—not without my consent," she said hastily, the words slippery on her tongue. "You see, well, I am not entirely ashamed to admit that I expected more of him. But he has disappointed me."

His face was stony.

"Do you wish me to call him out on your behalf, Kitty? If so, you may expect it of me. I consider your family my own."

She nearly lost courage. How could a man of such fidelity to her mother be a traitor to his country?

"I believe," she said slowly, "that will not be necessary. I believe, in fact, that he may be made uncomfortable in quite another manner entirely."

His brow creased. "It would be simpler for my understanding if you named the man."

So she did, naming him and pouring out the remainder of her false story, the ship and its stolen cargo and her trust that a friend like Lord Chamberlayne could help her reveal the Earl of Blackwood's villainy to the proper authorities. She included the time and place the following morning at which Leam planned to meet an informant. Wouldn't it be marvelous if government officials were there to apprehend them for their crime?

It astounded her how quickly Lord Chamberlayne's eyes glimmered with interest, and how he asked her for details. Her heart ached. She reminded herself that her mother and Leam's safety were both bound into this pretense.

Lord Chamberlayne patted her hand, his brow taut. "I will see to it that the gentleman is brought to task for his treasonous activities if such they are."

"I will see it as well. I will be there tomorrow morning too."

"I cannot allow that," he said firmly. "These men are not playing games."

"Kitty? Douglas?" Her mother appeared beside her. "The two of you have the appearance of plotters. I hope I am not interrupting."

"Not at all, Mama. We were saying good night. I have danced myself into exhaustion and cannot remain a minute longer. Will you find another way if I take the carriage?"

Her mother regarded her through wise brown eyes and finally said, "Yes, dear. Of course."

Kitty fled from the drawing room into the ballroom. But there she found no respite from her tumult of feelings either. Pressing through the crowd of guests merry now with wine and dance and the wee hours, she made her way to a parlor filled with revelers, then another chamber, and another. She descended the stairs of the mansion into the cool lower story. What had she done? Why had she trusted them? All she had truly wanted was to see him again, be with him, and now this dishonesty, this pretense once more.

She came into a corridor behind the stairwell, empty of all but a maid rushing from one place to the next. The girl passed by with a swift curtsy and Kitty pressed her back against a wall, trapping her unsteady hands behind her, and drew slow breaths.

A door opened at the corridor's opposite end and the Earl of Blackwood came through it. Music trickled down the stairs from above, but the beat of her heart drowned it out. They looked at each other without moving, his eyes darkly shining.

"It—" The words tumbled from her lips. "It is my birthday today."

He smiled, a sort of lopsided smile not entirely in control that turned Kitty's insides out.

"Aye," he replied in a low voice. "That i'tis."

He did not move. She did not.

"They told you about the plan, didn't they?"

"Aye."

On the stair just above, voices sounded and feet descended. She had many questions, and unspoken needs better left unspoken. Tearing her gaze away, she went across the landing to the front of the house, to the foyer and out, to her carriage and home.

The footman greeted her with sleepy eyes. She told him to turn in and went to the parlor to pace. She could not rest, not anticipating the morning's assignation and what it could mean to her mother and to Leam. He would spend the night making a pretense of drinking and playing cards somewhere with Mr. Yale for the benefit of anyone who might be watching. Then in the morning he would go to the rendezvous place to await Lord Chamberlayne.

Stomach tight, she descended to the basement and set a pot of water on the kitchen stove. Better to await her mother's return alone and confront her with the truth without fear of being overheard by curious ears. For she must tell her tonight.

The knocker clanking on the front door made her jump. She set down the teapot and went to the stair, nerves on end. The footman appeared.

"I said you might turn in, John," she murmured as he moved toward the front door.

"Yes, mum." He wore a nightshirt, and a wig dropped over both his hair and nightcap. He threw back the bolts and opened the door. A boy stood on the stoop.

"From milady," he piped cheerily, as though it were broad daylight. John took the missive, dropped a coin into his palm, and bolted the door once more.

"Milady, can I be making you a cuppa?"

"No, thank you." She unfolded the missive. "I can do so my—"

A knock sounded on the tradesman's door at the rear of the house. Kitty and the footman looked at each other, then she shrugged. He passed her on the stairs and moved along the basement corridor lit only by a single candle in a sconce. Peering into the gloom, she read the note. Her shoulders fell. Apparently her mother would not be returning tonight. Mere weeks from her confinement, Serena felt unwell again; the dowager would stay at the other house.

Kitty could not bear it, this waiting *for everything*. She felt as though she had already waited a lifetime.

She put her hand to her face, closed her eyes, and when she opened them again Leam stood in the doorway, the sparkling dark of the rain-speckled night casting him in silhouette.

"Milady?" John asked, presumably surprised to find an earl standing in her basement corridor in the middle of the night. Perhaps not quite as surprised as Kitty; John hadn't any notion why the earl should not be there, after all—except for the most obvious reasons.

"Please close the door, John. Then you may go to bed."

Momentarily they were once again alone at opposite ends of an empty corridor. This time the light was barely sufficient for her to see his handsome face, to discern the glimmer in his eyes, and to imprint the image of him upon her memory before she had to make him go.

"This is not a good idea," she said. "Someone might have seen you come. Everything could be ruined."

"True. But it might well have been ruined if I hadn't come. I couldn't think straight. Nearly ran my horse into a lamp-post. Not the best state in which to work."

"You are not—you are not drunk, are you?"

"Not in the usual manner. Now come here. Or would you be wishing me to come over there?"

She caught her breath. "We could meet halfway?"

He nodded. "Fair enough."

The floor was crossed. She was in his arms. He clamped her tight to his chest. She pressed her face to his lapel, her body to his, spreading her hands on his back and sinking her fingers in.

"Why are you here?" she whispered.

"I came to deliver your birthday gift."

She turned her head up. He loosened her, and when she

looked into his eyes, what she saw there pressed her breath into submission—need, and vulnerability so raw it hollowed her within.

She tried to smile. "Then what was the beautiful music I received only yesterday, if not for my birthday?"

His hand came up around the side of her face, the pad of his thumb passing roughly across her cheek into her hair. "Why are you doing this?"

"Because I am the most suitable person for the job. Really, I could not be more suitable." She ran her palm across his smooth jaw, loving the feeling of him. She could touch him forever. "You shaved before coming here."

"A gentleman canna pay a call on a leddy an he's shaggy as a barbarian."

"Leam—"

"Kitty, I did not come here to talk."

Her throat closed. Still she managed to croak, "Leam, I live with my *mother*."

"She has gone to your brother's house for the night. Your sister-in-law is feeling unwell."

"How do you know that? Mr. Grimm?"

"Little is sacred to the below-stairs set when gossip and guineas are involved."

"Oh, my. I shall have to tell Alex to turn them all off—"

"Actually, I heard it at the ball." The corner of his mouth quirked up.

She laughed.

He covered her mouth with his, and his arms pulled her off her feet. Barely breaching the seam of her lips, he kissed her, satisfying and stoking her hunger for him at once. He tilted her face up and kissed her jaw, his fingertips straying along her throat and neck as he returned to her mouth. Ever so gently the tip of his tongue brushed along the edge of her parted lips. She sighed, clutching his coat in tight fingers. He broke away to draw off his greatcoat, then surrounded her face with his hands and kissed her anew.

"I cannot get enough of your mouth." He stroked her lower lip with his thumb, making her tremble, and followed it with his mouth. His hands, large and strong, surrounded her shoulders and she felt held, treasured.

She wound her arms about his neck, and with his hands he pressed her body to his, from belly to thighs. At the inn he had held her like this, like he must touch all of her at once. Now his tongue swept her lips and she allowed him inside, and sighed at the delectable intimacy. Urgency gathered in her. When his hands slid from her shoulders to her waist, then around the sides of her breasts she welcomed it.

"It seems I cannot get enough of every part of you," he uttered against her mouth, the jagged unevenness of his breathing echoing hers. "The contour of your cheek. The curve of your throat. You are perfection, Kitty Savege." His thumbs stroked across her bodice, and her knees weakened. "Did you sing? Tell me you did."

She clutched his shoulders, aching for his caresses.

"I did. Terribly." She pressed her hips to his. A rumbling pleasure sounded in his chest and he swept his hands to her behind, pulling her against him. There was no mistaking his need, and she could not breathe for wanting him inside her. But he would not give her that again. He had said so at Willows Hall.

"I need you now, Kitty." He gathered her skirts. "Now."

Chill air swirled about her calves. He was undressing her in the corridor. He *wanted* her. She tugged at his coat, pushing it over his shoulders. "The servants," she barely managed.

He tore off his coat and lifted her entirely off the floor, sweeping her into his arms, and went through the nearest open door.

"The kitchen? *Leam*."

He set her on the counter, closed and bolted the door, and went directly to the scullery closet. She watched, bemused, quivering in anticipation. Behind her hung rows of copper pots gleaming immaculately in the red glow of the hearth's remaining embers.

"No maid on a mat within." He came from the closet and moved to her. "I am glad to see you are compassionate employers."

"Yes, she has a bed in the upper st—"

He seized her mouth with his and dragged her against him. She sank her fingers into his hair as he pushed her skirts to her hips and her knees apart. His hand around her thigh was deliciously hot, his other unfastening his trousers as he kissed her again.

"Leam?" Her voice trembled.

His palm surrounded her nape, holding her close, then smoothed down her back swiftly to her behind, pulling her closer, forcing her legs open.

"You mayn't say no." It was a growl. His cock pressed against her aching flesh, hot and rigid, and she was dizzy with it.

She shook her head. "No."

His brow compressed, his eyes squeezed shut. "*Kitty*"—in agony.

"I mean I will not say no! I could not. You— *Ohh, Leam*."

He pulled her onto him, guiding her until he was inside her fully, hot and thick, as she had dreamed. His hands grasped her hips beneath her skirts, and his breathing against her brow was taut like his every muscle, it seemed.

"Dear God." He barely whispered it.

She grabbed his shoulders, quivering, momentary satisfaction growing swiftly to aching need. She shifted on him.

"*No*." His grip tightened, holding her still. "*Don't* move."

"But—"

"Be still."

She obeyed. But her whole body thrummed. After a moment he smoothed his palm to her breasts that pressed tight against her bodice with her quick breaths. Gently he eased her back, and she leaned onto her palms. His thumb stole beneath the fabric and stroked her tight nipple.

"*Oh.*" She felt it everywhere. She throbbed for him. This time he did not bid her remain still when she moved her hips against his, drunk on the friction inside her and wanting more. He let her swivel on him, to feel him fully and remember how he had taken her before and need that now. Then he grasped her hips and thrust into her. Then again so hard her elbow jarred against the cabinet.

"Oh, God. *Again.*" She heard the words in her throat, on her lips, dropped back her head and let him take her. Begged him to do it again and again. His fingers dug into her flesh, tilting her hips. She whimpered her need.

She barely felt her shoulder nudge the pot, then strike it. It dislodged from its hook and crashed to the counter, then the floor, with two mighty clangs.

She gasped. He pulled her up and covered her mouth with his again, dragging her to him harder. She reached back, seeking a purchase, the pleasure inside her aching for completion. Her hand met porcelain, a soup tureen. Leam jerked her hips forward, driving sensation through her. She moaned and grabbed the cupboard. The tureen teetered, smashed to the ground. He did not ease, his thrusts fast. With one hand she grasped his shoulder, the other reaching out, meeting metal as her climax rose swiftly, a spinning spiral of pleasure. She clutched, he drove high into her, her back arched.

"*Oh, God!*"

She swept her arm round his shoulders, knocking copper

against copper. He reached for the wall, pressing his palm into it and hitching up her knee. Pots cascaded.

"*Kitty.*" With deep, powerful thrusts he forced them together. She threw back her head and gasped, crying out sounds until he gripped her tight and suddenly stilled. He filled her. She felt it, and she wanted to weep and laugh at once, breathless and shuddering in his embrace.

She gulped in air, their chests moving hard against each other, his arms around her tight, bodies thoroughly joined. He rested his mouth on her brow. He kissed there, then her temple, beside her eye, the bridge of her nose.

A light flickered at the edge of the broad windows at the street level. Then it bobbed, moving quickly to set the kitchen aglow.

"Good heavens." Her eyes popped wide. "Can it be the Watch?"

He pulled away and they dragged their clothing in order. Trousers fastened, he tugged her skirts around her legs and lifted her off the counter and put her before him through the door just in time for the full lantern light to shine through onto the pots and broken dishes strewn over the floor.

Leam pulled the door shut and Kitty looked around to meet the wide-eyed stares of the footman, the housekeeper, and her mother's prim French chef. John was blushing, the chef glowering. The housekeeper's brows were high, her lips twitching.

Mrs. Hopkins curtsied. "Is everything all right, milady?"

Kitty smoothed her hair. "Of course. I— Oh, good *heavens.*" She rolled her eyes and against her back felt Leam's chuckle. "Mrs. Hopkins, Monsieur Claude, I regret tha—"

The doorknocker echoed in the foyer on the floor above.

For a moment, no one moved. One hand on her waist, Leam turned the knob on the kitchen door and cracked it open. Light from the front stoop shone clear as day through the kitchen windows.

"The Watch, I'm afraid," he murmured, a smile in his voice. She wanted to turn around, take his face into her hands, and kiss him with everything in her.

The doorbell rang like Easter church bells in a full peal. Then a second time.

"What on earth?" she whispered.

"He'll wake the whole neighborhood," the housekeeper warned, glancing back and forth between Kitty and Leam.

"Someone must go," Kitty said. "John."

He bit his lip and headed for the stair. Leam followed to the landing and halted in the shadow. In the pregnant silence they all heard the bolts thrown. Then muffled voices.

Monsieur Claude stepped forward and set his nose in the air. "Madame, may I?" He gestured with a nod to the kitchen.

Kitty moved aside. Gingerly, the cook pressed the panel open and peeked within. He gasped, palm flat on his chest, and his eyes fell back in his head.

"*Sacre bleu.*" With a pointed glare, he passed her by into the chamber.

Laughter welled sweetly in her, then tumbled forth. Leam's dark eyes sparkled.

John appeared on the landing. "He wants to see the gen'leman of the house."

"Hm." Kitty went up the steps. Leam's smile was nothing less than perfect. She felt too full, her nerves singing. He grasped her arm, the gentlest touch, and held her back.

"Allow me." He studied John. "May I borrow your cap and dressing gown?"

The footman promptly removed his night gear and handed them to the nobleman. Leam disappeared up the stairs.

"If you don't mind me saying so, milady," the housekeeper whispered, "that one is a right fine gentleman."

Kitty simply could not reply.

"Weel, whit're ye caterwalling aboot, man?" His rough accents careened down the stairs, louder than all the pots and pans put together. "Ye've gone an woke ma wifie, nou A'll ne're hair the end o it, ye glaik. Och! An thar's the babe ye've gone an woke too, crying. Ye canna hair him? Weel dae ye like tae be chynging hippins nou, man? Acause ma wee one's nurse be abed wi' the croup, an ma wifie ower-worn tae rise in the mids, an A'll nae be chyngng the thang masel!"

A mumbling sound filtered down the stairs for at least a minute. Kitty's ears strained, her nerves a jumble of pleasure and hilarity.

"A dinna ken, lad," he said in much more reasonable tones. "Mebbe the baudrons."

Mumble.

"Cats, man. Cats! An ye dinna ken the odd atween a cat an a brigand, ye best be seeking ither wirk." The door shut with a thud and the bolts slid. A moment later, he appeared on the landing again, dressing gown over his arm, tugging the floppy cap from his head. A smile lurked at one corner of his mouth.

"Apparently the neighbors were concerned over robbers. I do not believe he will be back." He handed the garments to the footman. "Thank you for the loan."

"John," Kitty said, and turned to the housekeeper and cook. "Monsieur Claude, Mrs. Hopkins. Thank you for your assistance. We will see to the kitchen in the morning. You may return to bed now."

With a quick curtsy the housekeeper nodded and passed the earl on the landing and went up, the grinning footman following, and the chef at their heels still holding his palm against his head. When their footsteps and murmurs had faded into the upper story, Kitty finally found the courage to look up. Leaning against the wall, he was smiling ever so beautifully. He had not put his coat back on, and with his arms crossed over his chest she could see his muscles well defined through the damp linen.

"I daresay they will have plenty to tell the others first thing in the morning," she said somewhat quaveringly. "Or perhaps right away."

He came down the steps, curved his hand around her face, and tilted her head up. His gaze scanned her features, resting finally on her mouth.

"No. They haven't enough fodder for gossip quite yet. We must give them more." He bent and nuzzled the corner of her lips, sending tingles of pleasure all the way to her toes. "Where is your bedchamber?"

Kitty trembled. He did not intend to leave.

"I suspect you can guess well enough." She tilted her face so that he could continue kissing her throat, her hands seeking his hard arms.

"In inquiring, I am trying to be civilized," he murmured against her skin. "Belatedly, and relatively speaking."

"But I find I quite like you barbaric. Barbaric in the kitchen just now suited me perfectly well, in case you hadn't noticed."

"I noticed." He lifted his head and looked into her eyes. His were gloriously dark. "Kitty, I want to stay."

She drew out of his arms and moved toward the stair. She glanced over her shoulder.

"Second story, first door, overlooking the street. We can watch the chastened Watch from the window."

Chapter 22

Her thundercloud eyes twinkled as though lined with silvery sun and Leam's heart beat harder than it ever had. He maintained his voice with the greatest effort.

"I have no intention of watching anything but a beautiful woman in the throes of passion."

Marvelously, her cheeks glowed.

"Then what, my lord," she whispered, "are you waiting for?"

She went swiftly up the stairs before him, her hips a sweet enticement draped in the sheerest linen and silk he had shoved aside so he could have her because he could not wait another moment. To slow the heat still pounding in his blood, at her door he slipped his hands around her waist and bent to her ear.

"Kitty." He passed his cheek along the satin of her hair. "You enchant me."

Her fingers gripped the doorknob, her other hand stealing along his thigh boldly. She turned about, pressed her sweet curves to him, and drew him down to kiss her. She gave him her lips as she had given him her body below stairs. He wanted all of her, body and soul. Words rose to his tongue and he kissed her so that he would not speak them aloud. He reached behind her and opened the door.

She went within, taking his hand to draw him into a lady's chamber of elegant simplicity. No gilding decorated the furniture of fine quality yet little ornamentation, no flounces lined the bed draped in plain brocaded silk. It did not surprise him. She needed no contrived embellishments to make her a woman, no feminine arts to render her beautiful. But the colors were all rich and warm, like her soul beneath the cool surface.

"How many guineas will I be obliged to part with to hold the servants' tongues, do you think?" She seemed thoughtful.

"I will see to it that they do not speak of this."

She turned a curious regard on him. "Do you have that sort of power?"

"Influence, perhaps. And associates. And not only in this." He drew her to him. "They wish me to take a position in the Home Office."

"Here in London?"

"Paris."

"I see." Her gaze dipped to his waistcoat. "Your friends gave me to believe that the charade we are all enacting now would allow you to finally quit. Did they lie?"

"I have yet to find the man who shot you, Kitty." He stroked his thumb across her palm and she released a little sigh, her eyelids fluttering.

"You are still involved because I am in danger?" Her voice was thin.

"Do you wish the truth?"

Her eyes widened. "Of course."

"If I refuse they will not leave you alone. They will ask

you to assist them again, and if you refuse they will ask again, until you have agreed like you did this time. After that, you will have no peace."

A flurry of thoughts seemed to pass behind the thunder-clouds. Leam wished he could read them, wished he could have invented a reason that she might believe. But he could not lie to her, not even to spare her pain.

"I—" Her throat seemed to catch. "Why don't *I* go to Paris then?" The corner of her mouth curved up uncertainly. "They cannot very well pester me there." Her brow furrowed. "Or I suspect they could. Instead I will go to Italy. I have always wanted to see Italy. Or Greece. The Parthenon, and most particularly the ruins of the temple to the oracle at Delphi. Perhaps even a few islands. And Egypt, of course. That would be quite distant. Oh, how I would adore seeing Eg—"

He pressed his mouth to her beautiful lips. "You are clever enough," he murmured, "that no doubt they would pursue you even to the tops of the pyramids at Cairo."

She freed herself, laughing.

"The East Indies, then? Emily wishes to visit the East. I could accompany her on her tour. If I ceaselessly moved around they might grow weary of pursuing me." Her brows quirked up. "Are spies truly that persistent?"

"Some."

"Are you?"

"I was never a spy. But, yes, I was that persistent."

"You won't continue with it now, will you?" Her gaze seemed to retreat.

He nodded.

"I see." She placed her palm softly on his chest and her lashes dipped once more. "Touch me, please, Leam. Touch me now."

He stroked the swell of her breast and she sighed, her eyes

closing. She was exquisite, asking him to give her pleasure and nothing else when he would give her everything if she requested it. His fingers sought the sleeves of her shimmering gown and drew the scraps of fabric over her shoulders.

" 'A creature sent from Heaven to stay on earth, and show a miracle made sure.' " He touched his lips to her satin skin, sensing the quiver in her body, his own hands not entirely steady. "That you might have worn this gown for anyone but me fills me with jealousy."

"I wore it for myself." She lifted her lashes, regarding him through curtains over the soft gray. "But if you wish, I will wear it for you the next time. Now remove it, if you please. And—and everything else."

As at the inn, in an instant the confident woman became a girl. He could not bear to hurt her. He could not bear to bring her more unhappiness. So he gave her pleasure while he could.

Doing as she bid, he unfastened the elegant gown and it lay where it fell as he undressed her, discarding the layers of her cloak of sophistication. Only hazy need lit her eyes as he carried her to the bed and there touched her as she desired. He kissed her body, beauty formed of woman made for pleasure, her shoulders and waist, her breasts and the sweet curve of her hip. Easily she rose to his caresses, eagerly her slender hands explored him, driving him mad as they grew more confident. Her lips on him, and tentative tongue, undid him wholly. He could wait no longer.

"Kitty, love, give me yourself."

She did, her hair cascading across the counterpane, eyes half lidded in passion. He entered her and her back arched, her peaked breasts jutting up as her lips parted and she pressed her palms to the mattress. Embedded in her heat, he could not draw breath. His chest seemed compressed, his heart struggling for its every beat.

Her gaze came to his.

"Leam?" she whispered.

"Kitty, I—" He could not speak.

She laid her hand upon his chest, then trailed her fingers down to his waist, then around to the small of his back.

"Do you remember in Shropshire when you promised you would make it last?" The velvet caress of her voice stroked his senses like her hand on his skin. She slid her knee up, the satin of her thigh cradling him. "Make it last now. Please."

She spoke with her body but there was something more in her eyes, something he barely dared hope. Trust.

He made it last. As long as he reasonably could. She was tight and wet, and despite her words, impatient, a woman of passion whose body had barely known pleasure. Leam gave her what she asked for, bringing her to the edge with his mouth and hands, then again, until she whimpered, begging for release. When her shudders caressed his cock, her lips breathing his name, he let himself have her fully, possessing her so that she convulsed again, gasping and clutching at him in surprise.

She clung, trembling, her eyes closed and breathing fast. Catching his own breath he stroked damp tresses from her brow and kissed her parted lips. She opened onto him her rainclouds, and there was no longer any place for Leam's heart but in her.

"Thank you," she whispered.

His chest constricted. He brushed his thumb across her lower lip reddened from his kisses.

"If you continually thank me for making love to you," he managed to utter, "I shall at some point grow too embarrassed to do so effectively."

Her lips curved up. "I do not entirely understand what you mean, but in any case I do not believe that is possible."

"Let us not find out, shall we?" he said tenderly enough,

but his brow seemed taut and he drew away, leaving Kitty suddenly lighter, and cold. He only went far enough to gather the blanket and pull it over her, once again stroking the hair from her face when she turned onto her side. But he did not hold her. Instead he rested on his back and passed his hand across his mouth and jaw.

Kitty drew in steadying breaths, willing her heartbeats to slow. This was what it was to be a man's mistress. To give him her body. To make love to him in her bed—or on a kitchen countertop, apparently—until she knew only him. And to pretend in public that they barely knew each other. And to not really completely understand him. Still, to fear him a little. Mostly to fear the power he had over her.

"Kitty, my son is not my own." His face illuminated in the flickering light from the hearth was drawn, his cheekbones and jaw hard. The blanket came only to his hips, the masculine strength of his arms and chest taut with tension.

"Who is his father?" she finally whispered.

He turned his head and met her gaze. "My brother. And I had him murdered for it."

Kitty's heart turned over, and her stomach. "The duel?"

"I arranged it." He looked again at the canopy above. "I meant only to frighten him. And, I suppose, to threaten him. I was insane with jealousy."

"Then you did not—did not want him to die?" She knew the answer already. She would not love him so if he were capable of that sort of hatred.

"No." He shook his head. "But he deloped. And as his opponent's tricks with a pistol were well known to him, he chose to step into the shot intended to pass him by."

For a long moment the only sound in the chamber was the soft hiss of flames in the grate.

"My wife disappeared shortly after that," he finally said. "I think she feared for my sanity. She told her family she was going on holiday with me. But she was not. She left the baby in Scotland and came here to hide, I think. They found her two months later in the Thames. She had apparently been there for some time."

A soft bluster of warm air rose from the hearth, sending the light dancing along walls and bedding and the man beside her who had told her a horror story.

"Does your son know?"

"No one knows. None among the living."

"Why did you tell me?"

He shifted onto his side and took her hand. "Because," he said roughly, "I would have no secrets between us. And because I am by nature a jealous man."

"How jealous?"

His brow creased. "I should think that is now obvious."

"You did not mind it when you thought I was flirting with Mr. Yale at the inn."

"I did."

"You did not."

"Then he is an exception."

"What about Mr. Cox?"

His face went still. "I was. Very much so."

She wanted to tell him he hadn't anything to concern himself over, that her heart was thoroughly his and no other man would ever touch it. But she kept her counsel. She was at least wise enough to know she must not continue to set herself in comparison to his adored wife.

She drew her hand away and tucked it into the coverlet against her chest.

"Kitty, I read the file on Poole." His voice remained low. "He was a villain."

She hadn't thought she had any breath left to give, but a sound ushered forth, soft and short.

"I hope the man courting your mother is not as well."

She nodded, swallowing past the tears gathering at the back of her throat. "Do you think this trap will work?"

"If he is guilty."

"Must you really go there in the morning yourself?"

He nodded. Then, watching her, his brow furrowed anew. He leaned up on his elbow.

"Kitty, you are not thinking of going. Do not tell me you are."

"Then I will not tell you. But I will be withholding the truth. I told Lord Chamberlayne I would meet him there."

"No."

"Yes. I must be completely convincing. What sort of self-respecting jilted woman would not wish to actually see her lover ruined? I cannot simply leave it to faith. That would be contrary to what Lord Chamberlayne knows of me, after all. What *everyone* knows."

"He agreed to it?"

"I told him he hadn't any choice."

"Kitty, this is foolhardy." His eyes looked intense. "If Gray's suspicions are accurate, Chamberlayne cannot be happy believing I know the location of the ship's cargo."

"But I must know if he is guilty. Do you think this is easy for me, Leam? Betraying my mother so that I do not betray my country?"

"No." He captured her hand and pressed her palm to his lips. "I know it cannot be. But if I believe you to be in danger, I will not be at my best."

She squeezed her eyes shut, his words bittersweet. "It is too . . . *complicated.*"

He did not respond. Instead he cupped his hand around her face and kissed her. She reached for his arms, running her palms along his smooth muscles.

"Kitty." He stroked the side of her breast. "Do you wish me to remain here for a while yet tonight?"

"Yes." She could not lie. "More than I can say." Good riddance, wisdom and circumspection! Her tongue would reveal her, after all, it seemed.

His thumb passed over her hardening nipple, sending a tingling ache into every part of her.

"Then promise me," he whispered, "that you will not go to the meeting tomorrow morning." His hand tortured, his hip shifting against hers.

"Blackmail does not become you, my lord," she uttered, then gasped as he touched her between her legs. She had not known this was possible, to be roused so easily so many times in one night. But she was still hot from their lovemaking and so easily stirred by his touch.

"Promise me." He caressed and she was lost.

"Yes," she breathed. Then again, "Yes," when he came inside her with his finger. And again, "*Yes*," when he made her come with only his hand, slowly and beautifully, his mouth caressing her breasts, the need inside her now perpetually longing for him.

Then he gave her more. And he made it last even longer than before, until she was nothing but liquid pleasure to do with as he willed. Which she had been from the start, in any case, in a tiny inn in Shropshire when she had believed the worst thing in life could be surrendering her reason to a man who went about with great shaggy dogs.

When it was over, he settled her against his chest in the circle of his arm.

"I trust I needn't repeat that you have promised." He spoke against her hair, and it seemed so intimate and familiar.

"You blackmailed. I promised. It seems fairly clear which of us has had practice convincing others to do as we wish."

"Not in precisely that manner." He sounded as though he were falling asleep. But his words pleased her far too much.

It seemed, perhaps, she had something of a jealous nature too, after all.

After a time she felt certain he slept. She stroked two fingertips along the taut sinew of his forearm. He did not stir, his breaths even, the hollow plane of cheek to jaw and the sensuous curve of his mouth holding her rapt. She whispered, "I want to go back to Shropshire," because longing filled her heart with a sorrowful sort of joy and she could not hold it inside any longer. And because she could say foolish things to him now and he would not hear.

But he said, "As do I." He wrapped her hand in his and drew it to his chest. "Now go to sleep."

"Why? You will be leaving soon, won't you?"

"Too soon. And as much as I enjoy your conversation, to-night I wish the pleasure of sleeping beside you, even for a short time."

What could she say to that?

He pressed a kiss onto her brow. "Happy birthday, Kitty." He held her, and remarkably soon she slept.

When she awoke, he was gone.

Chapter 23

When the dowager appeared at the breakfast table, her eyes were lively, her gaze on Kitty keen. Unfortunately Kitty could do nothing to hide the flush on her cheeks or anxious cold of her palms. By now the meeting between Leam and Lord Chamberlayne had taken place. She had only to wait, praying he would send word.

"I did not expect you up for hours yet, Kitty dear." Her mother lifted a cup to her mouth. "Mrs. Hopkins told me of your late visit from the Watch. An incident with dishes in the kitchen, apparently."

Kitty's cheeks flamed. "She told you that?"

The housekeeper came into the chamber with a fresh pot of tea. "Lady Katherine was very kind to pick up those broke dishes before she turned in." She poured tea for Kitty and handed it to her with only a flicker of a winking eye and a lightning-quick smile. "Monsieur Claude was most appreciative. Myself as well, ma'am." She curtsied.

"You are welcome, Mrs. Hopkins. It was my—" Her throat stuck. "Pleasure." Had he cleaned up the dishes before leaving? She wouldn't disbelieve it of the strangest nobleman she'd ever known. She forced her attention to her plate. "How is Serena, Mama? Your note did not say how ill she was feeling."

"I did not stay at the other house last night, Kitty. I told you that so you would not worry." Her mother shuffled through the small pile of the post at her elbow. "Mrs. Hopkins, you may go now, and close the door."

The housekeeper cast Kitty a quick glance and left.

Kitty held her breath. "Where were you, Mama, if not at Alex's?"

"With Douglas." The dowager lifted her regard, her face serene with contentment and sparkling with happiness. "We are to be wed. Will you wish me happy, my dear daughter?"

"Oh, Mama." How could she wish her anything of the sort? "*Mama.*" She stood and wrapped her arms about her mother's shoulders and held on to her. "I thought you indifferent to his offer." Her voice shook.

The dowager drew her away and studied her face.

"Only cautious. Kitty dear, what is amiss?"

Kitty gripped her hands together. "I wish only for your happiness."

"You are not happy with this, then? I had hoped you would be. You and he seem so comfortable with one another."

"Oh, but Mama, you see—" Kitty cast about for words to begin. She should not have waited to tell her. She should have been brave. She could not bear her mother's steady regard and dropped her gaze. On the table beside her cup was a sealed note, her name on it.

Like a schoolgirl with a *tendre*, she had memorized Leam's hand from the envelope in which he had sent the music. Her heart thumped. She grabbed up the note and tore it open.

"Kitty?"

"Mama, I—" A whoosh of air went out of her. Lord Chamberlayne was innocent of wrongdoing. But the note said little more, only that she was to come to the park at eleven.

She glanced at the clock on the sideboard, and leaped up. "Mama." She went to her mother, grasped her hands, and kissed them one after the other. "I am so very happy for you. I like Lord Chamberlayne very much and am thrilled he is to be part of our family."

"Kitty, this is highly unusual."

"Perhaps. But now I must go."

"Katherine."

"Truly, I have an appointment." She went toward the door, flashing John a speaking look as she went. He was doing a poor job of concealing a grin.

Her nerves raced. Why did he wish to meet her at the park? Why not come here to tell her? He had never been shy of calling before. Not exactly.

"Mama." She pivoted around. Her mother stood as though bemused. Kitty returned to her, threw her arms about her, and held her tight. "Mama, I love you dearly. You know that, don't you? Of course you do. And I am so very, *very* happy for you."

She ran to change.

Never had a drive to the park taken so long. Beneath the clearing sky above, Kitty sat huddled into a corner of the carriage and chewed the tips of her gloves. She was fatigued from lack of sleep, sore in places she had never imagined she could be sore, and alarmingly edgy given all.

When they turned through the gates of the park her stomach somersaulted. She had thought of every possibility, even that the note was a forgery and she was walking into a trap. Strangely, she had not imagined Leam astride his muscular roan waiting for her near the entrance. The wolfhounds wandered close by, their heads coming up as the carriage neared.

She nodded. "How do you do, my lord?"

He drew his horse alongside the carriage and bowed from the saddle. "Good morning, my lady. Would you care for a stroll?"

"Thank you, yes."

It was all highly civilized. Her heart hammered. The carriage halted, and by the time the coachman let down the step Leam had dismounted and was there to take her hand and assist her out. He did so with gentlemanly grace, holding her gloved fingers only as long as propriety allowed. Momentarily Kitty felt a pang of disappointment, but he could not very well ravish her in the park, and she had noticed his clothing. Elegant once more, tasteful and fine. She understood, or thought she did, and it excited her.

He offered his arm. She shook her head, too wrought with nerves to touch him now. She started away from the carriage and the curious servants. One of the dogs came alongside her and pushed its muzzle beneath her hand. She stroked it distractedly.

"He is not guilty of any crime?" she asked when they were sufficient paces in front of her maid not to be heard.

"He is not." He walked close beside her, his hands folded behind his back. "He sought me only to beg me not to give over the cargo to the rebels, of which his son is the leader. He was ready to pay me to have it destroyed. He hadn't any idea what it was."

"What was it?"

"It still is not clear. The Home Office wishes proof beyond his word before it is willing to trust him entirely. His son is a known instigator, but I believe in Chamberlayne's innocence."

Kitty drew in breath through her teeth. "I have heard him speak of his son. They are quite close."

"Apparently." Leam's voice was sober. "He fears for him, and hopes to make this rebellion impossible by putting spokes in the way of it. But it was difficult for him to admit to it, although I believe he wished to and was glad for the opportunity. He is a proud man." He turned to her. "Much like a young lady of my acquaintance."

Relief trickled through her. "I am not young. Yesterday I turned six-and—"

"Twenty. Yes. You told me that almost immediately upon speaking to me in Shropshire. I wonder why."

"Because you had called me a lass and I was endeavoring to put you in your place."

His gaze lingered upon her lips. "Peculiarly done."

"Could we return to the subject at hand, sir?"

He stopped and she was obliged to as well.

"Which is?" Beneath the soft blue sky his eyes shone with warmth.

"The innocence of my mother's beau, and, frankly, why you insisted I come here instead of calling on me at home to tell me this news. It gave me a frightful case of nerves and I think you are beastly to have arranged it this way."

"Not mincing words this morning, are we?"

"We never do. Or at least rarely. Now have you anything else to tell me about Lord Chamberlayne? My mother and he have become betrothed—last night, in fact, although he asked her quite a while ago, I understand. So I should like to know if I shall be asked to tell my prospective father-in-law further horrid lies, which I won't in any case, you know."

"It is the very reason we are here." The amusement faded from his eyes. "I asked Gray to meet me."

"You did not tell him I would be here as well?"

"Beautiful and clever," he murmured, scanning her face.

"Why not?"

"He might have avoided it." His gaze flickered over her shoulder. "Will you meet him?"

"I think you are trying to frighten me. You are not sufficiently chastened by my reprimand, it seems." She turned in the direction of his attention. The viscount rode across the green in their direction.

"You have no need to be frightened of me, Kitty." Leam spoke at her shoulder softly. "You never will."

She looked up. A bright intensity lit his eyes. Delicious weakness slipped through her veins.

"Last night, Leam," she said before she could halt her tongue, "when you told me—when you read the documents about Lambert Poole, what did you understand of my part in it?"

"That you had been hurt. That is all."

Everything was forgotten—the park, their purpose. Nothing mattered but what she must finally say aloud for the first time, and to this man. She whispered, "He told me no other man would ever want me. Not for more than dalliance. He told me this when I was barely fifteen. Then he told me again when I was nineteen, many times. I was ruined, and I could not bear children. I was young and believed I was in love with him, and he said a gentleman would only take me for my dowry if he took me at all, and then he would find me disappointing." She did not want to say these things. She wanted to say that the foolishness of her youth no longer commanded her and that she loved him. She wanted to throw herself into his arms because he was looking at her as he had the night before when he had been inside her and unable to speak.

"I want you," he said.

She hadn't thought it possible, not after the night, everything, but she could no longer bear not knowing how greatly he wanted her. To what extent? But she could not find the words.

"Damn Gray and all of this," he uttered low. "Kitty, this afternoon, will you be at home to callers? No, damn it. To *me*?"

"But, of course. Leam—"

"To *only* me. In your drawing room"—his eyes sparked—"with the draperies thrown wide, door open, servants poised upon the threshold?" He smiled.

"You are being very odd." Her heart raced, and now the words she ached to declare came to her tongue swiftly and strongly. "Yes," she whispered instead, because *this* abandonment was new and it deserved what he asked of her, though she would have it all said now; she did not want to wait another moment for it to begin. "Yes."

Hoofbeats sounded on the turf close by. Kitty tore her gaze away and Lord Gray dismounted. As he came forward she felt Leam at her shoulder, his strength and thorough mastery of her heart. Happiness buoyed her curtsy.

"Lady Katherine." The viscount bowed. He turned to Leam. "Yale met me at the Club this morning. He already told me all."

"I asked him to do so."

Kitty darted a glance at Leam. His jaw was taut but his eyes still sparkled.

"I asked you here for another reason," he said. "I require you now to apologize to Lady Katherine for burdening her with your previous demands, and to assure her that you will not in the future make similar demands."

Lord Gray's gaze flickered aside. "You have the dogs with you, I see, yet dressed as you are."

"Indeed."

"So you are finished finally, then?"

Leam nodded.

The viscount seemed to draw a slow breath. He turned to

her. "My lady, on behalf of the king and country I serve, I render thanks to you and assure you we will not be seeking your assistance again. It seems we may have been mistaken in information we had of Lord Chamberlayne. We will, of course, continue to pursue the rebels, including his son, but Lord Chamberlayne will not bear any measure of guilt."

"Now the apology," Leam ground out.

Lord Gray bowed deeply. "I sincerely beg your pardon, ma'am."

"Accepted, my lord."

"Prettily done, Gray." Leam's voice was dry. "Now go to the devil."

The viscount grinned, then nodded. "In the matter of Cox, you will still want Grimm about, I presume."

"For now."

Kitty looked between them. "Mr. Cox, from Shropshire?"

Leam's brow creased.

"I can see my presence has become *de trop*." Lord Gray bowed again. "My lady. Blackwood." He went to his horse, mounted, and spurred away.

She turned to Leam. "What haven't you told me? Is Mr. Cox involved in all of this too?"

He moved close to her. "Not Gray's project." Again his gaze seemed thoroughly hers, his eyes scanning her face. "As soon as I know more, I will tell you all. But now you must go home so that I can call on you properly."

She could sink into that gaze and never leave it. "But I don't know why—"

"Kitty." He smiled. "Not here, where I cannot—" His eyes flickered up. A carriage approached. He stared over her shoulder and his gaze lost its intoxicating intensity, growing momentarily fixed, then . . . haunted.

She pivoted around.

Descending to the path from an elegant black carriage

with the assistance of a footman, a lady lifted her face to them. She wore a glimmering white carriage gown, with frothy silk of pale blue gathered about her shoulders, gloves the color of the winter sky, and a tiny parasol on her arm trimmed in lace. A wide-brimmed hat of eyelet dipped over her brow, tilting jauntily to one side, revealing a fringe of blond ringlets and bow-shaped, petal-pink lips.

Leam's cheeks were gray, his face stark.

"Leam, who is she?" But in the pit of her stomach, and in her heedless heart, Kitty knew. She had never truly deserved happiness.

It was an angel, of course, come to steal heaven away now that she stood upon its threshold.

Chapter 24

W ho is she?" Kitty repeated, in a whisper now.

"She—she is my—" Leam struggled for air, sanity. It could not be. He dragged his gaze away from the ghostly vision to the serene elegance of the woman beside him.

But Kitty's beautiful eyes were fraught. "Your?"

The words rose upon a choke. "My *wife*."

"Did she perhaps have a twin?"

Kitty's mouth tilted up, quivering, and Leam's entire body went numb. She was perfect and he wanted to grab her and crush her to him and never release her. But Cornelia walked toward him, ticking her parasol lightly from side to side in the crook of her elbow. No twin, even identical, could reproduce those twinkling blue eyes, that delicate smile that always seemed a bit uncertain and had never failed to tie him in knots, the dimples in her rounded cheeks, and her dainty stride. Nearly six years older, she was none the worse for it, still stunningly pretty, and moving directly toward him.

He stared.

She halted two yards away, hat brim shading her face from the sun. Her lips curved into a tremulous smile.

"Good day, my lord husband." Her voice was the same, light and demure and like a nightmare. She curtsied, dipping her gold head gracefully.

Kitty pivoted and moved straight for her carriage.

Pulling his gaze from Cornelia, Leam went after her. She tried to avoid his touch, but he made her take his hand to assist her into the carriage. She was shaking, or he. She would not meet his gaze. Shock dizzied him.

"Kitty, say something." His voice was a rasp.

She laced her fingers tightly together in her lap. "Felicitations, my lord."

"*What?*"

He had to move aside for her maid to climb in. Shoulders back and chin high, Kitty directed her attention forward.

"Move on," she said to the coachman, the fellow snapped the traces, and Leam stepped back as the carriage jolted into motion.

He watched her go, the woman he had come to love more than life, unable to turn toward the woman who, almost six years earlier, had changed that life forever. She and James and he together, a wicked, sorry tangle.

He swung around and strode to Cornelia. She backed up a step.

"Leam?" Her blue eyes darted over his face. "You—you are still very handsome. Are these your dogs? Who was that lady and why did she cut me?"

"*Cut* you?" He shook his head. "I." He nearly gagged on his voice. "Thought." He pressed out the words. "You." But they would not come easily. "*Dead.*" He could not breathe. His world had turned upside down. "I *buried* you."

"But I am here. You can see that." Her pink lips trembled

like her tiny hands around her parasol stem. "Leam, you are frightening me."

"Who is that woman lying in the tomb at Alvamoor? Did you kill someone and falsify your death?"

"No! *You* killed someone! James!" Tears sprang to her eyes. She whirled about and hurried toward her carriage. He pursued. The footman handed her up. An elderly lady dressed in black glared at him from within.

"Go, go, Frank," Cornelia called out, waving at the coachman. "Go quickly! I knew I should not do this."

Leam went to the lead horse and grabbed its bridle. The coachman darted looks between them.

"Do not move this carriage, man, or I will take that whip and use it on you."

"He would not, Frank. He is not that sort. Go."

"You haven't known me for five years, Cornelia. You have no idea of what I am now capable."

"Yes, milord." The coachman tugged his cap.

"Leam, you are causing a scene." Cornelia's hunted gaze darted about. Another carriage and a pair of riders had halted, the gentlemen and ladies watching without any show of discretion.

"Inform me of your direction in London, then, and I will join you there momentarily for private conversation." He could not believe his own words. His heart beat so swiftly he could not think.

"Twenty-five Portman Street, number four."

"You will meet me there in half an hour or I will hunt you down this time until I find you, Cornelia."

"Yes. I promise." She squeezed her eyes shut. "Now go, Frank."

Leam released the horse and let the carriage pass him by. He watched blankly as Hermes ran after it for a dozen yards, then in playful bounds returned to his side. He stared at the water in the Serpentine, coolly gray beneath the pale blue sky. Then he went to his horse, gave a coin to the lad who held it, and set off toward his past.

The apartment address Cornelia had given him was modest in appearance, but suitably proper. Leam made a quick perusal of the neat garments of the manservant who admitted him, and the well-appointed parlor into which he was taken to await his wife.

She did not make him wait long. Entering, she glanced at him, then went to the sideboard and poured a glass of sherry. With trembling hands she drank it all.

"Taken to the bottle in your absence?" He studied her. Without gloves, shawl, and hat, she looked much like the girl he had first met, but for the preylike hesitation in her blue eyes now.

"No. It is for my nerves." She turned to him, pressing her hands into the sideboard behind her. "You are overset."

"Come now. You would not have appeared to me like a ghost if you had not wished to make a dramatic effect."

She threw herself toward the window, clutching the draperies and averting her face.

"I didn't know how to— I thought of all the ways I might . . ." She peeked over her shoulder, her golden lashes fluttering. "I was so anxious to see you, I did not know how to do it."

"Where have you been, Cornelia?" He spoke evenly, an odd calm settling over him.

"Here and there."

"Where in particular?"

"It does not matter anymore, does it? I am here now."

"It matters quite a great deal to me. *Where?*"

She turned halfway to him, still gripping the curtains and

her gaze darted to the bottle on the sideboard. "Italy."

"Don't lie to me. You haven't any reason to now."

She whirled about. "I *was* in Italy. For nearly three years."

"And before that?"

"America. I hated it. I was glad to leave."

"Who," he said, "is keeping you?"

Her eyes went wide as saucers. "Keeping me?"

"Your lover, Cornelia. Your protector. Tell me his name."

"Why?" she shot out. "So that you can—" She clamped her rosebud lips shut. "I haven't a lover."

"Then who"—he gestured about him—"is maintaining you here? I do not recall my solicitor requesting that funds be sent to my dead wife lately."

"Don't tease, Leam." Her brow crinkled. "I never wished everybody to believe me dead. I swear I did not."

"*Who*, Cornelia?"

"My parents!" She crumpled onto a chair, casting her face into her hands. "I ran away and they helped me flee."

Leam swallowed back the cold in his throat.

"Your parents attended your funeral. Do your sisters and brothers also know you are still alive?"

She lifted eyes and cheeks glistening prettily with tears. "No. Only Mama and Papa. They were as frightened of what you might do to me as I."

"They knew about your affair with my brother, then."

Her lips trembled. She nodded. "What will you do now, Leam?"

His hands fisted, nails biting into his palms.

"For more than five years, Cornelia, you allowed me to believe you killed yourself. That I drove you to it." He could no longer bear to look at her. He crossed to the sideboard and poured a brandy. Then when he had swallowed that, another.

"Taken to drinking in my absence, husband?"

The back of his neck prickled. The voice was petulant and

harder than he had ever heard it. She was no longer a girl even if she looked like one.

"Who is in the Blackwood mausoleum, Cornelia?" He spoke with his back to her.

A moment's hesitation. "I don't know."

"She wore your gown, the one I bought on our wedding trip. And your betrothal ring." For weeks after they found the body he hadn't allowed his housekeeper to touch the filthy rag and muck-encrusted gold and diamond band. Looking upon them each day had been his penance. His own living hell.

"I had them when I ran away to find my parents. I thought Mama and Papa were here in town, but they were not. I sold the gown and ring to a girl on the street for money so that I could hire a wretched room. It was horrifying, filthy, and there were rats. I didn't sleep. But I was able to send word to Papa and Mama and they came and fetched me. When I heard about the girl and how you and everyone else believed her to be me, I was sorry."

"*Sorry?* Did you pause to consider her family?"

"I don't think she had one. She was a—a—" Her brow grew more fretful. "From the people I saw her with, I've no doubt she met the end she expected to someday."

"That is unforgivably cold, Cornelia."

"I was frightened of you! You had—" Her voice broke off. "James had died and I did not know what you would do next."

He turned. "An affecting story, to be sure."

She stared at him.

"Do you hate me so much still?" she whispered.

"No. I never did." The admission no longer surprised him. "Rather, myself."

Her lower lip quivered.

"Then do you— Can— Leam? Husband, can you *love* me still?"

His stomach turned.

"When, I wonder"—he could barely mouth the words—"will you ask after your son?"

Her eyes widened. She folded her hands in her lap. "How is he?"

"Well."

"Does he . . . ?" She blinked as though deterring tears. "Does he ever speak of me?"

"Rarely, which is to be expected. You know, your maternal devotion intrigues me." He took up his glass and refilled it, the brandy barely touching the icy center of his chest.

"What do you mean? I have missed knowing him dreadfully," she said quickly, a slight whine to her tone now. "I have, Leam. You must believe that."

"I don't, really." He downed the spirit, then lowered the empty glass from his lips and set it on the table. "Especially since you left him in the care of a man you feared would do you serious harm. For years."

Her mouth opened and closed.

Taking up his hat and crop, he moved toward the door. The rustle of her skirts preceded her light footsteps across the floor. She grasped his sleeve.

"Don't go, Leam. Please."

He looked down at her small hand wrapped around his arm like a talon, her knuckles white.

"Do not worry yourself needlessly, my dear," he said, drawing air into his compressed lungs. "I will return. And when I do, I expect you to still be here."

She released him. "I—I will be."

"Cornelia?"

"Yes, Leam?"

He looked into her face, so close now, and saw fear and uncertainty behind her blue eyes. "Why did you reveal yourself now?"

"Mama and Papa said you had thrown off your ungentlemanly ways quite abruptly," she whispered. "As long as you adopted them, I knew you would not remarry." Her pink lips curved into a quivering smile, and for a moment her dimples flickered to life. "My Leam would not court a lady looking like anything but a perfect prince."

She reached to touch him again. He moved away.

Not swiftly enough he was on the street, mounting his horse, and riding—he knew not where, he knew not for how long. Only that he sought motion to give rest to his careening mind. He would move until he could no longer, then he would drink. In the activity or alcohol he might find sanity.

Something in her eyes and tone rang false. Falser than years ago. He would discover it and finally lay his ghosts to rest.

Kitty did not receive callers or pay calls. She kept to her personal chambers, once daily walking to her brother's house. She read to Serena, and brought over interesting books and music. When her sister-in-law wished to rest she went home and locked herself in her rooms once more.

She told her mother she was unwell and disinterested in company, and indeed felt perfectly wretched, inside a welter of unhappiness. At lunch near the end of the week her mother questioned her.

"You look pale, Kitty. This malady is persisting far longer than I like."

"Oh, no doubt I will be well enough shortly." In a hundred years or so. Dear Lord, she hadn't imagined anything could hurt so much. Her heartbreak over Lambert Poole held nothing to the pain inside her over losing Leam *to his dead wife*. She felt faint perpetually, as though living in a terrible dream.

"You are not eating."

"It is a stomach complaint, Mama." Nausea beyond anything she had ever felt, thorough, endless, filling her heart and head. She folded her napkin and placed it on the table. The footman came forward to pull out her chair.

"John, Lady Katherine is not yet ready to retire from the table," the dowager said. "That will be all."

"Yes, mum." He left them alone.

"Mama, truly I feel quite peaked. Allow me to wish you a pleasant afternoon at the salon with Lord Chamberlayne and—"

"Kitty." Her mother's voice was soft and firm. "Lord Blackwood has called on you several times daily for nearly a sennight."

Kitty barely managed to lift her brow in an attitude of curiosity. It was difficult to do so and not succumb to tears.

"Oh, really?" John and Mrs. Hopkins had delivered each of his calling cards to her personally. "How persistent of him." She should speak with him. But once they spoke it would be truly over and she was not yet ready for that. She needed time to accustom herself to losing him before she had ever really had him.

"You have heard, no doubt, the remarkable news?"

"What news is that, Mama?"

"His wife appears to have returned from the dead. Apparently she suffered an accident and amnesia. Her parents have only just discovered her in an Italian convent."

"How nice for them all." She pushed out her chair, holding the tears at bay as she had been doing for days. "Mama, I really feel quite ill. Please excuse me."

She went to her room and, sitting on her bed, she did not

cry. Instead, she grabbed the chamber pot and cast up her accounts.

She cleaned herself up and went to the clothes press for a fresh gown. Misery, it seemed, would not be tidy.

Her new riding habit beckoned to her. Charcoal gray, with black lace about the high neckline and cuffs and a matching pillbox hat, it suited her. But she hadn't any place to wear funereal garb.

Except, perhaps, she did.

She rang for her maid and dressed, calmer than she had been in weeks.

Within a half an hour she was dismounting before a modestly stylish town house on a quiet street. The gated park across the way was charming, the neighborhood of good quality, the homes of genteel ladies and well-to-do merchants and such. A pair of school-aged boys played at spinning wheels on the corner and gave her friendly tugs on their caps before she ascended the steps to the front door.

The drawing room was elegant, devoid of pretension yet fashionable, with silk hangings in the Oriental style and Chinese and East Indian vases and urns all about. A half-dozen ladies sat around the tea table. The butler announced her.

The chamber went silent. A single titter sounded, a lady pressed her kerchief to her lips. Then silence once more.

"Do come in, Lady Katherine. My friends were just leaving." The lady's voice was smooth and perfectly modulated.

Mrs. Cecelia Graves had always, in Kitty's memory, seemed enormously elegant. She still did. Her taffeta gown of mauve was modestly cut and trimmed in black fur and embroidery with tiny black beads sewn in for glimmer. It was a gown much like Kitty might someday choose for herself, suitable to a woman of mature yet not advanced years. Her hair, dark gold with only a hint of gray, curled neatly beneath a cap of the finest Belgian lace, and on her ears and neck shone deep, rich amethysts set in gold.

Kitty's father had given Mrs. Graves those amethysts. She knew this because one day shortly after her return from Barbados, she had stolen into her father's study late at night, searching for some correspondence from Lambert indicating that he sought Kitty's hand.

Instead, on her father's desk, she had noticed a receipt for the amethysts from the jeweler's. But, contrary to her expectations, Kitty had never seen them on her mother. One day she asked her mother about them, and the countess told her all that she had not known before.

The lady had been widowed at a very young age. She lived alone in town and off-season in Derbyshire, with an elderly female relative as a companion. She was something of an heiress and had no need to remarry.

Her mother never told her the lady's name. But eventually, when Kitty made her own bows to society, she heard it from girls who called themselves friends, from girls who pretended to disapprove yet were secretly titillated, Kitty understood now.

One by one the other ladies stood, said their good-byes, and departed, each giving Kitty a curtsy or nod, a few even a smile as they passed her. Finally the room was empty. Kitty could not move, attached to the threshold of the drawing room of the woman she had never once spoken to although she had shared her father's life for decades.

"Come now. You have come here of your own accord, and I shan't bite."

She went forward. Mrs. Graves's expression of benign interest did not change. Without a word, she shifted her cool blue gaze from Kitty's face down her person, then back up again.

"You were a plump little thing back then," she finally said.

"All cheeks and round belly. I never imagined you would become such a beauty."

Kitty's tongue finally loosened. "I suppose I am to take that as a compliment."

The lady studied her thoughtfully. "Why have you come here, child?"

"Could you never have any of your own?" She did not pause for niceties. There were none in her heart. "Is that why you chose a man who already had his own family? Because you could not conceive a child and did not wish to ally yourself with a man who expected children? You were young when your husband died, after all. You could have married again."

Mrs. Graves's lips pursed. "You are impertinent. But you have clearly given this a great deal of thought."

"I have wondered all these years." Kitty clasped her hands over her own useless womb. "I wish to know finally."

The lady regarded her for a long moment, her eyes ever cool.

"He did give me a family. Yours." She assessed Kitty again, this time only her face, but her gaze was penetrating. "I knew you when you were a babe, when you were a girl, and when you grew nearly to womanhood. Then he died and I haven't known a thing about you since, except what I read in the papers and hear through the gossips." She gestured about her drawing room as though indicating the women who had just left. "The same with your brothers, of course." Her lips grew stiff. "Do you think a woman could wish to have a family in that manner?"

"He never cared about us. Or even you, I think," Kitty heard herself say. "He could not have been a caring person and have done what he did to my mother. He was a hard man."

"But a constant one."

"To one too many women."

"I loved him, you know. With my whole heart."

"That," Kitty said through clenched teeth, "does not excuse you."

Mrs. Graves stood, a small woman, compact and exquisitely elegant.

"Spend your life hating me, child, if you wish. You will not be the first." She moved past Kitty and out of the chamber.

Kitty rode home blindly, tears clogging her eyes that she strove to hide from passersby. She hurried up the stairs to her bedchamber, nearly stumbling on the steps. But her mother sat in her room, staring out the window. She looked around and her elegant features fell into sorrow.

"My dearest daughter." She sighed.

"I paid a call on Mrs. Graves."

The dowager's eyes widened. "Whatever for?"

"Whatever for? *Mama*." Moisture trickled down Kitty's cheeks. She tore off her gloves already ruined by tears and swiped them across her eyes. But without the shield of tears through which to see her mother, she found the compassionate, wise brown eyes too much to bear. She turned away, pressing the back of her hand to her mouth. "She told me I could choose to hate her my entire life, if I wished, but that I would not be the first."

"You would not. She is a lady of influence in some circles and has enemies. But none of them is I."

Kitty swung around. "What do you mean, not you?" She shook her head. "You have never spoken with her in society. You have never called on her. You never even spoke of her to me except that once."

"Kitty dear, it would not have mattered if I had. She and I are nothing alike and I daresay would have little to speak about if we did meet in society."

Kitty stared. "Then you did not cut her because of Papa?"

"I never cut her at all."

"You did! We have been at the same balls and parties with her on any number of occasions."

"We avoid one another, it is true."

Kitty sucked in breath. "But why don't you hate her?" she exclaimed, her voice breaking.

"Why should I? I had what I wished from your father, three wonderful children and several comfortable homes. She did not hurt me."

"But—but, Mama." Kitty's insides twisted. "Those months you sent me to Barbados with Alex and Aaron, when Papa rusticated Alex for whatever indiscretion he'd committed that time . . ." After so many years, the words stumbled from her. "Why did you send me there, Mama, all alone, with only my governess, if not because you were fighting to win him back?"

The dowager's face went still, only her eyes alight with feeling now.

"I was fighting then still. You are correct. I still hoped. But not to win his heart, only to win a certain measure of discretion from him." Finally her brow wrinkled. "He was taking her about in society a great deal in those days, and I was to bring you out soon. I did not want your first season colored by gossips' wagging tongues. I fought for months to force him to cease publicly flaunting their alliance, and I won."

"At my expense. You left me alone and Lambert Poole used me."

The dowager's throat worked. "I could not have known that would occur at the time."

"Why," Kitty whispered. "Why did you never speak of it to me?"

"I did not truly realize the extent of the injury until after your first season."

"After I let him finally ruin me."

"You are never *ruined*, Katherine." The dowager's voice was stern, her eyes suddenly flashing. "You have a spirit within you that cannot be cowed by any man, or even a woman. Or all of society. You must always remember that. No matter what another person may do to you or say of you, your heart is your own."

"Do you know, I have sometimes thought—sometimes, that I did that to him because I couldn't do it to Papa. I could not hurt Papa like he hurt you by allowing that woman to come first with him. So I hurt another man instead." Kitty's whole body shook. She knelt at her mother's feet and laid her head upon her lap. "Oh, Mama, I am so unhappy."

She wept. Softly her mother stroked her hair.

"Mama," she finally whispered when the tears had slowed. "I want what you had. I want a family of my own. I do not want to become her."

"You needn't become her. You are still young enough to have a splendid family. You might yet fill a nursery."

She lifted her head and sat back on her heels, wiping her cheeks.

"I cannot conceive a child. There. I have said it to you. It is proven I cannot."

Her mother's face stiffened. "*How* is it proven?"

"I was with Lambert many times, Mama. At first it was because I loved him and believed he would marry me. After it became clear that he wished only for Alex to suffer through my ruination, I devised a plan of revenge. I determined to do whatever I must to learn his secrets so that someday I might publish them to the world and bring him shame. I allowed him to believe I still loved him and I continued to allow him liberties. In this way, on occasion, I gained access to his personal chambers."

Her mother's cheeks were white. "For how long did this

persist, Kitty? Until last summer when he was exposed?"

"No." Until three years ago when a Scottish lord laid his beautiful gaze upon her and she began to imagine a manner of living free of twisted anger and pretense. "But for long enough."

The dowager's voice quieted. "I knew of the first occasion only. That night when you came to me in tears, I realized what you were not able to tell me directly."

"I suspected so. I did not imagine you would allow me to remain unwed unless you understood that I was no longer fit to be a gentleman's bride." She took a trembling breath. "I saw a physician, and Lambert even showed me proof of his own ability to father children. I shan't have a family of my own. But I will be happy to be aunt to Alex and Serena's children."

Her mother studied her for a moment, then touched her fingertip to Kitty's chin and lifted her face to the light.

"You will be a wonderful aunt." She kissed Kitty's brow. "Will you come out with me and Douglas tonight? It may improve your disposition to see friends, to remember that you are admired and appreciated by many."

Kitty shook her head. "I must look frightful and I feel wretched. Perhaps tomorrow, Mama."

She did not attend her mother on any outings for the following several days. Her illness persisted, allowing her an unexceptionable excuse to remain within. But finally she was able to eat some dinner. The following day she walked in the park with Serena and paid a call on Lady March, agreeing with both the countess and her mother that she would attend the season's opening ball that evening. It was sure to be a thorough crush; she would be able to escape it early if she wished without her mother's notice.

When she returned to the house Mrs. Hopkins announced

with a dour look that there were no calling cards from any *earls* on the foyer tray. The day before he had not called either. He had given up, and quite swiftly at that, which was for the best. Kitty wondered how a man could switch his affections from one woman to another with such ease. Certainly if she were a gentleman she would now be at her club, deep in her cups, and likely to remain so for many weeks to come.

But Lambert had taught her that men were a different sort of creature, a sort she would never understand. And anyway if she were a man she would not be where she was now, wishing to be deep in her cups and happy to remain so forever but unfortunately without that recourse to grief.

Chapter 25

Wouldn't you rather leave that bottle to me, old man?"

Leam's boot tips bumped the edge of the sideboard. Hefting the crystal decanter, he set it unsteadily to the rim of his glass, then lifted the glass and took a long swallow before swinging his gaze to the Welshman at the parlor door.

"Welcome tae share it. Plenty more in the cellar." He shuffled back to his chair before the hearth. Through half-lidded eyes he glanced at the page of foolscap on the table beside him.

Yale sauntered over and took up a glass. "I cannot recall the last time I saw you disguised."

"S' time ago." Leam shifted his gaze into the flames, the smoke curling into his senses. Outside it might be daytime, but the curtains were drawn and he was dead drunk. Finally, after ten days. Drunk as an emperor. In the gun, with no intention of ever climbing out again.

Yale took a seat across from him. He sipped. "Fine year."

Leam grunted.

"What's this?" The Welshman picked up the paper. He made a sound under his breath. "Hm. Chamberlayne is freed from all guilt, and his rebel son too. Did you have a hand in it?"

"They needed hard proof. I found it." He'd spent the past sennight in every hellhole in London, not to mention a dozen clubs, hounding down the owners of that ship. Through contacts he and his solicitor had made at Lloyd's while searching for Cox, he met with success. "Cargo wasn't anything of note."

"Not British tactical secrets after all?"

Leam shook his head. "Just contraband. Illegal goods. Home Office's informant at Newcastle Upon Tyne was getting a cut o the profit."

"Ah. And he tried to cover up the operation with alarmist talk of Scottish rebels and French spies? Clever of him. More clever of you to have unearthed it. " Yale paused. "And here I thought you had quit."

He'd quit now. The man soon to be Kitty's stepfather was now fully exonerated.

He tilted a glance at his friend. "Come tae convince me tae stay?"

Yale regarded him steadily. "I have come to help, of course."

"As ye did when ye dragged her into this business?"

"You *are* foxed. Usually I'm the one that must introduce the lady into conversation."

Leam closed his eyes.

"There's no help for it." He sounded exhausted. He hadn't slept in days. For years he'd thought himself a widower. Now he was a husband, he'd made Kitty an adulteress, and she would not see him. Drink seemed the only option. Probably until death.

"There must be something we can do," Yale murmured.

He shook his head, passing his hand across his stubbled jaw and blinking, but his vision would not clear. Good. Let it remain foggy forevermore.

"Parents support her story," he muttered. "Been safe in the companionship of a bloodhound of an Italian duenna. A Catholic no less. Lived in a convent."

"Don't tell me she became a nun!"

Leam swung his gaze to his friend. "If ye find my life's tragedy amusing, Yale, feel free to leave nou. Won't mind a'tall."

"You have entirely lost your sense of humor. In the abysmals, indeed."

He had lost his heart. One in the same.

"I've no grounds for divorcing her, even were I such a man to do so. She's not been unfaithful."

Yale did not reply.

"She wants tae go home."

"To her parents'?"

"Alvamoor."

"To see young Jamie," the Welshman murmured. "Will you allow it?"

Leam ran his hands up his face and sank them into his hair. "I canna bear the thought o it."

"Then we must devise an alternative."

Leam shifted his gaze up. "Frae where comes the optimism?"

Yale stood. "Frankly, *I* cannot bear to see you like this. Neither can Constance."

"Did someone say my name?" His cousin sailed into the chamber, the scent of white roses attending her. Leam had never noticed the scent she wore. Before knowing Kitty, he'd noticed precious little of anything pleasing or colorful. He'd been cold. Asleep. Now he was awake, alive, smelling and hearing and seeing everything, and he wanted it all cold again. All gray. But the grayness was like her eyes, and so even in his fantasies of reclaiming living death she haunted him.

His cousin kissed him on the cheek, then moved away to perch on a chair. "You wish to see Lady Katherine, don't you?"

As he'd never wished for anything else. But she had been wise in refusing his calls. He had nothing to say to her save those declarations that his wedding vows now made dishonorable.

"Aye." He wished to see her and touch her and have her as his own. And now he could not.

But he could still protect her. Tomorrow when he regained his sobriety and wits, he would redouble his efforts to find the fox that hadn't yet come out of his hiding hole. Cox.

"Then listen to this gossip." Constance leaned in. "The dowager Lady Savege and her daughter are expected at Lady Beaufetheringstone's ball tonight. I heard it from the dowager herself, via two other ladies, of course."

Leam's head came up. "A ball?"

"Lord and Lady B. You were invited."

Momentarily his vision became crystal clear. He mustn't go. It would not do either of them any good.

Constance surveyed his appearance. "Lady B is exceptional *ton*. You will have to tidy yourself up. Would you like to escort me?"

"*Aye.*"

As soon as they stepped onto the landing, he scanned the crowded ballroom as he had nearly a fortnight earlier, searching. Constance drew her hand from him and leaned close.

"Good luck," she whispered, and left him on the step.

Despite the crowd, he found Kitty swiftly. Surrounded by

friends, elegant, intelligent people, she appeared perfectly at ease. Her gown shimmered, soft gray and sparkling through some artifice that on her seemed like stardust, revealing her graceful shoulders and beautiful curves. Her hair was dressed simply with diamond-studded combs. She was exquisite, and she deserved everything he could not give her, and more.

He went forward, ignoring the stares and titters. He had not been out in society since Cornelia's return. He did not plan on being so for longer than the moments it would require to speak to Kitty. Not long enough.

She turned and looked directly at him. Her wide, thundercloud eyes were not clear, but tinted with pink, delicate smudges of gray nesting beneath them. She looked thin—too thin—as though she had been ill, yet she held her chin high.

She moved from her cluster of friends straight to him.

"I had hoped you would not seek me out in public," she said quietly as soon as she stood before him. "I thought you had given up and I was glad of it." Her full lips were a line.

His mouth was dry. The orchestra lilted, a waltz, by God. Only one out of ten households allowed the dance, and of all the houses in London this should be one of them. Fate tormented at every turn.

"Dance with me."

"No." Her eyelids flickered. "I mean to say, thank you, my lord, but I do not care to dance."

"Allow me to hold you, Kitty, in the only manner in which I am permitted now." It was wrong. He knew it and she did.

But she allowed it. On the floor he took her into his arms, and her touch, even so slight, bore into him the fire beneath her cool exterior. Her gaze fixed over his shoulder.

"Perhaps if you simply say to me what you wish to say we shall be able to get it out of the way," she murmured. "As long as it is not an apology I will hear it. I do not believe I could bear an apology."

For what could he apologize? For falling in love with her? For not having wed her instantly when he realized he was in love? Then their situation might have been entirely public now.

No. "No apology."

"Well, that is a small relief." For a moment she said nothing. "Will you tell me about Mr. Cox?" She did not allow him the clasp of her fingers, only her gloved palm, her other hand holding the train of her gown. But through his palm upon her back he could feel the rush of her heat and beat of her heart. He would remember her shape and texture and the sweet thrum of life within her forever.

"Cox believes I possess something that belongs to him. I must assume he followed me to Shropshire in order to retrieve it, and he threatened you to ensure that I would return to London and give it to him. But as yet he has not come forward and I have not been able to find him."

A muscle in his jaw contracted and Kitty knew this had been a mistake. She wanted to drink in his face, to touch his skin and feel again his heartbeat next to hers. She was not made for such teasing.

She would go to the country, at least as long as he lived in London. She could not continually meet him in society. But Serena would soon have her baby. She must remain for that. Then she would escape.

"I understand you were instrumental in freeing Lord Chamberlayne from all suspicion," she said, casting her gaze away from the hollow planes and hardness of his face, the dark, feeling eyes she loved. "Thank you for that."

He looked at her in the manner he had beneath the trees at Willows Hall, and her breath thinned.

"In any case," she made herself say, "they are to be wed

shortly, and everybody in my family is quite gay about the prospect. Unfortunately his son is not able to attend, although it is probably for the best that he does not come to London at this time, all things considered. Not knowing the whole story, my mother is somewhat disappointed. It seems that on the request of his father, he sent down from Scotland a beautiful silver necklace that Lord Chamberlayne then gave my mother as a gift at Christmas—" Her voice fumbled. She found her tongue, but Leam's jaw had gone hard. "My mother is determined to thank him for his thoughtfulness in person, and hopes this summer to travel—"

"Kitty, I must ask you to cease this." His voice was rough.

"Don't, Leam. I must talk about inanities. Otherwise I will be obliged to leave you in the middle of the set. I would rather not make a scene, and as everyone is gossiping about you already I prefer not to draw attention to myself. But you asked and—" She dropped her gaze to the ground. "This was a remarkably bad idea."

"Kitty—"

"Lord Chamberlayne gave that necklace to my mother out of affection. My father gave his mistress an amethyst necklace and earrings. She still wears those amethysts. Apparently she keeps them as a token." She spoke swiftly to block the tears rising in her throat. "Because that is what we do. We carry tokens of affection close to us, like your brother carrying your portrait onto the battlefield. Even Mr. Cox said he always kept a cameo of his—"

"Kitty, stop."

"I do not wish to carry around tokens of your affection, Leam. I do not wish anything from you any longer." Except everything. "If you have sought me out in the hope that I might—"

"No. I would never ask that of you."

"I am now going to make a scene." She blinked rapidly,

pulling out of his hold, and pushed her way through the other dancers, then the clusters of people beside the dance floor. She made it to the foyer before the first tears fell, but they would persist in coming against her will, and she hadn't time to wait for her cloak. Into the cold she went, alone, seeking her carriage in the crush of vehicles along the block, the target of stares and muted whispers. But she didn't mind those; they had been her closest companions for years.

Kitty slept, weary in every crevice of her body. But before dawn she awoke, her mind abruptly whirling.

Mr. Cox believed Leam possessed something of his so precious that he was willing to hurt her to retrieve it, but now he was playing hide and seek and refusing to come out into the open. Speaking of him with Leam had jogged her memory of Mr. Cox demanding that Mr. Milch help him find a valuable lost object. It seemed outrageously far-fetched, but Kitty believed she had seen that object. She had complimented young Ned on it.

She lit a candle, went to her escritoire and pulled out two sheets of paper, one blank foolscap, the other her monogrammed stationery. When she had finished both missives, she sealed them and gave them to John with precise instructions.

Emily's reply arrived before Kitty finished breakfast.

Dear Kitty,

To your request—of course! Clarice is honored you asked. She will be ready promptly Thursday at one o'clock. I do wish I could go as well, but Papa is making a terrible stink about a visit I made last week to the London docks without a footman or maid. Mama will not leave my side now, and since she does

*not much like Clarice, this is perhaps the perfect
moment for your journey.*

*You must tell me all the details on your return. Until
then, of course, I shan't breathe a word of it, even
were the entire Roman army to insist.*

Fondly,
Boadicea

Apparently Emily had chosen her new name. A Celtic
princess who rebelled against the Roman Empire was at
least as scandalously impressive as a guillotined French
queen. Kitty smiled, but the sensation felt alien on her lips.

On the following day, the wedding day, Lord Chamberlayne arrived during lunch and met with her mother in
private. When they emerged the dowager's face was paler,
but her hand rested snug in his elbow.

"Kitty," he said, his light eyes softly relieved. "I have told
your mother all."

A breath of relief escaped her. "Mama, I am so sorry I
kept this from you."

The dowager came to her and set her fingertips to Kitty's
cheek.

"My dear, I am grateful you had the courage to see it
through."

She accepted her mother's embrace.

Later she donned a gown of modest blue and attended her
mother at her wedding. It was a small affair, only family
and closest friends. Kitty put on smiles, wished her mother
and stepfather happy, and fell into bed exhausted from her
pretense.

In the morning she saw her mother and stepfather off in
Lord Chamberlayne's carriage to Brighton, where the new-
lyweds were to spend a sennight's wedding holiday while
Kitty finally moved into her brother's house down the street.

She returned to her bedchamber to pack, then wrote a note and instructed John to deliver it to her brother and Serena once she had departed. John frowned in obvious disapproval. But Mrs. Hopkins seemed content with the subterfuge, and Monsieur Claude packed a cold supper to be eaten on the road.

In front of the Vales' Berkeley Square house, Madame Roche climbed into the carriage and fell back onto the facing seat with a grand sigh.

"*L'aventure!* Lady Katrine, I commend you."

"Thank you for coming with me, Madame. You are very kind to do so." She was quite abandoned in terms of body and heart, but at least the Frenchwoman's company would lend some propriety to her journey.

The carriage pulled away from the curb and Madame Roche arranged her filmy garments about her. "As there is no snow, we shall return within the fortnight, *non*?"

"Depending on the state of the roads." She wished she were never returning. She wished, like the last time she had taken to the road, she were running away toward an adventure she had never imagined.

Throat tight, she turned to the window.

"*Mon Dieu*, but you are thin as a straw. You must eat, *belle* Katrine, to support the strength."

"I haven't the stomach for it lately, I'm afraid."

"It is very sad, this news of the wife." The Frenchwoman made a sort of spitting sound, then her red lips pursed, black eyes assessing. "But what does he do about *le bébé*?"

Kitty shook her head, an aching in the pit of her belly now. "What baby?" Was Lady Blackwood increasing? Was it another man's? Was that why she had returned? Or . . . ? *No.* Kitty could not think the other possibility. He could not have pretended his shock at seeing his wife for the first time in the park that day, and otherwise it was too soon for such a thing.

Her stomach churned. Oh, God, she must not dwell on him and his wife together.

"*Ce bébé, la!*" Madame Roche pointed to Kitty's lap. Kitty looked down and saw only her hands resting on her queasy stomach.

In an instant a sickening flush spread from her throat to her entire body. She struggled for breath.

"*This* baby?" she uttered.

Dear God, how naïve she was. How foolish. She had never imagined. Never questioned. She had believed—

"You cannot eat, *ma petite* says to me." Madame Roche shook her head. "But you sleep *tout le temps* of the day, *non?*"

Kitty gaped. She had watched Serena go through this in her early months. Even uninstructed in matronly matters, she ought to have known. Instead she had attributed her illness to misery.

Swift, prickly panic swept through her. Then, twining with the panic, something else. Something warm and rich.

Elation.

She gripped the seat and tried to breathe. To think. But no thoughts would come, only feelings. There were no tears left to cry, and anyway she no longer wished to. She pressed back into the soft squabs and closed her eyes. The carriage's rocking made her ill, but now she did not fight it.

He had been right to mistrust her assurances. And she had never been happier and more terrified in her entire life.

Chapter 26

Fellow Britons,

I recently received the following communication through my publisher:

Dear Lady Justice,

Your impertinence astounds me. But your tenacity must be commended. I fear I have already, in fact, come to admire you for that. But, dear lady, if you wish admittance to the Falcon Club so desperately, you have only to discover the names of its members and apply to join. One, I regret to report, has recently left us. But four of us remain. Among these is myself,

Your servant,
Peregrine
Secretary, The Falcon Club

Impertinence, indeed. This Peregrine seeks to intimidate me with soft words and flatteries, common methods by which the powerful and wealthy cajole and control society. Rest assured, my head will not be turned. I shall continue to seek out wasteful expenditures of funds and lay them open to examination before the entire kingdom.

I am, it seems, beset by correspondents. Another letter came across my desk only two days ago. Its anonymous author (a lady, by the genteel hand) begged me to print it. Her reasons for wishing this were sufficiently intriguing that I do so now:

To the Particular Gentleman it may concern: I am on my way to Shropshire in search of a portrait cameo.

That, my friends, is all it said. I am enormously curious and ask only that upon her return from Shropshire, the lady will inform us as to the success of her quest.

Lady Justice

Leam cast the pamphlet into the grate and watched it float on a swell of hot air to the edge of the ashes, untouched by the flames. He pressed his palm into the mantel.

So, Jin, Yale, and Constance had not finished with the Club after all. And Gray. . . . Leam did not understand his old friend. This seemed foolhardy. Colin was arrogant, but he was also directed and disciplined, and possessed of a single purpose: England's safety.

As Leam's single purpose was Kitty's safety.

Tomorrow he would don his roughest costume and delve into London's seamy underworld once again. He would turn over every stone until he found the one under which David Cox was hiding. Then, when Kitty was free of threats, he would bend his mind finally to deciding what to do with his wife.

Cornelia had not mentioned Jamie again, but Leam had only called on her once since the first occasion. She had fluttered her lashes and begged him not to divorce her. He had told her the truth, that he had no honest grounds for it, and would not perjure himself by claiming her infidelity, the only justifiable basis for divorce. He requested only that she remain at the apartment until he made suitable arrangements for her residence at his own expense. She said she preferred a smaller house so that she could spend her funds on charity rather than unnecessary servants. At the convent in Italy she had become accustomed to giving to the needy poor; she wished to continue that practice now in London.

He did not believe a word of it. But he didn't care.

His vision blurred staring at the pamphlet. So close to the flames, yet not consumed.

It seemed curious that the one place he thought about almost constantly these days should appear in Lady Justice's leaflet. Shropshire was a large enough county, and there were any number of places in it one could find a cameo, none of which was undoubtedly a shabby inn in a tiny riverside village. The corner of his mouth crept up.

But swiftly his smile faded. He bent and snatched the smoking paper from the hearth.

At the ball, Kitty had spoken of a cameo belonging to Cox. The next day Lady Justice received a letter from a lady about a cameo, clearly intended to inspire a gentleman to take the bait. Had Kitty known something he did not? He wouldn't blame her for not telling him. But . . .

This was madness. A sane man would never put the two together. After all, his eyes and mind and heart sought Kitty in everything anyway. He was imagining hints and clues where they did not exist.

Or he was not, and she was the clever beauty he had fallen in love with.

He ran out of his house, grabbing his coat and barely strapping the saddle onto his horse before bolting down the street in the direction of the pamphleteer's publishing house.

The clerk in the publisher's office would not give him Lady Justice's address or name. Leam asked to see the letter from the anonymous lady. The clerk refused. Leam put money on the table. The clerk treated him to a pointed speech on journalistic integrity and the arrogance of the aristocratic class. Leam threatened legal action. The clerk rang a bell on his desk, and a burly fellow who looked like he could load crates onto ships with his bare hands walked into the chamber and gave Leam a dark look.

Leam did not have any particular desire to spend the next fortnight in bed nursing broken bones. He departed, leaving his card and a request that should Lady Justice find it in her heart to pay him a call, he would be much obliged. Perhaps Gray's methods had some merit.

He could not sleep, and the following morning stole himself to pay a call at the house where he was least wanted. He knocked on Kitty's door. The footman opened it, round eyes brightening noticeably.

"Milord!"

"Is Lady Katherine in?"

"No, milord. She's gone."

"Gone?"

The fellow nodded, his wig bobbing up and down.

"Lady Katherine has gone to Shropshire, my lord." The housekeeper stood at the far end of the foyer, a spark in her eye.

"Shropshire." His blood pounded. "Are you certain of this?"

"Quite, sir. My mistress has recently been wed and is on

her wedding trip in Brighton. Lady Katherine set out for Shropshire yesterday."

"Alone?" *God, no.*

"With Madame Roche, my lord."

Leam released a pent-up breath. "Thank you." He cast a nod at the footman and went to his horse.

He must pay a call before he took to the road. He hadn't any idea why Kitty thought Cox had lost his cameo, or why Cox might think Leam had it, or what it had to do with him at all. But she must know something about the man that he did not. She had brought down a lord committing treason against the crown through years of quietly observing others, of listening and paying close attention. Now her cleverness and bravery had dislodged his own brain from bemusement. The parts would not come together, but they were tantalizingly close.

Without waiting for Cornelia to come to him, he went straight along the corridor, the manservant glowering at his shoulder. He found her in a bedchamber strewn with gowns and underclothing. A traveling trunk sat amid it all.

"Leam!" She leaped up from a table at which she was taking tea. "What are you doing here?"

"Where are you going?" He gestured to the scene of packing.

"To Alvamoor, of course. To see my son," she added hastily.

He moved toward her. She cowered. He had never wanted that, but now he had no patience for her histrionics.

"Cornelia, what do you know of a man named David Cox?"

Her cheeks went white. "What should I know?"

Leam's heart raced. "You do know him, then. How? What is your connection with him?"

She slid from behind the table and moved across the chamber. "Whatever are you talking about, Leam?" Her voice trembled. "I told you, since I ran away I have not been with any man, only my parents and my companion, Chiara." She turned wide eyes upon him, gold lashes fanning outward.

"Did you know Cox before our marriage?"

She twisted a napkin between her pale fingers, her eyes abruptly distressed. "What do you wish me to say?"

"The truth, Cornelia. After all these years of lies, I deserve it from you."

"I did." She squeezed her eyes shut, her hands banded about the napkin. "I knew him before."

"When?"

Her eyes opened, full of uncertainty. "Your brother introduced me to him. They were in the same regiment. Is that what you wish to hear?"

"Did you give him a cameo?"

"A—a cameo?"

"Perhaps a portrait of yourself. Or of James."

"Of *James*?"

"*Did* you?"

"Yes!" The word seemed to tear out of her. "Yes. A picture of me. He begged me for it." She pressed the linen against her mouth. "What will you do now, Leam? Will you punish me for it?"

"I never meant to punish you, Cornelia. I hurt, and I did not understand why you and James could not have told me the truth before it was too late." It seemed so simple now. So honest.

"I wish I had." A tear escaped her eye and dripped over her knuckles pressed to her cheek. "Maybe then you would have forgiven me."

"Sooner than I did, probably." But then he might not have known Kitty. He would not have known love.

"*Have* you forgiven me, Leam?"

He nodded.

"Then why won't you take me back?"

"Cornelia." Tension gripped him. He must be off to Shropshire without further delay. But her gaze beckoned and he wanted this finished once and for all. "Why have you come back? I know you don't care about your son. So then, what do you want of me?"

She drew the linen away and her lips quivered, a second tear escaping.

"I do care about Jamie, and I don't want anything from you," she whispered. "*He* does."

Leam's blood stilled. "Tell me now."

Her eyes were round as saucers. "His business went horribly wrong in America. He needs money desperately and says he will hurt Jamie if I don't get the funds from you and give them to him." Her tone had risen.

"Who, Cornelia?"

"David! Don't you see? He was so greedy. I did not understand it at first, but then he wanted so much. More than I could give him even with the generous allowance you provided me. Then the baby came so soon after our wedding and James died and I could not think straight. I was frightened of you *and* David, and so confused."

"Cornelia," Leam broke into her mounting agitation. "Why does David Cox need this cameo?"

"He lost it in Shropshire at that inn. He thought you took it, and he was wild with fear that you were playing him to frighten him. He searched your bedchambers on Christmas night when you were all playing cards, he said, but he could not find it. So he thought that if you were dead he would get the money anyway through me once I returned to society, so he tried to shoot you. But that went awry and he realized he was not a murderer after all, even though he is a horrid thief and extortionist."

"Why would I have been playing him? About what?"

"He thought I had told you everything already and that you didn't care because you were with Lady Katherine now."

"*What?*"

But she seemed not to hear him, her words tumbling forth swiftly. "When I would not go to Alvamoor to show you I was alive and seek money from you, he threatened her so that you would come to London and I would be forced to meet you. I told him I would not, even so, that I would return to Italy and you would never know. But he vowed he would go to Alvamoor and hurt my son. I could not allow that to happen, Leam. I have not seen little Jamie in five years but he is my flesh and blood and I always loved him. I pray you to believe me!"

"I do." It was too fantastical to disbelieve, and her eyes rolled with the same manic distress as on that day she'd told him about her affair with James. "But I still do not understand, Cornelia. What is this cameo to him?"

"His insurance, but only until he needs it. I inscribed it before I gave it to him."

"What is the inscription?"

"It says . . ." She released a whimper like an injured animal. "It says *To my dear husband, David.*"

Chapter 27

L eam's breaths came in uneven chunks.

"Our . . ." An ocean seemed to wash through his head. "Our son is—?"

"*Not* his. For all the lies I have told you, I swear this upon my soul. He is James's."

It must be. The child looked exactly as his brother had at that age.

"But how long before—"

"I married David three weeks before you offered for me." She seemed to shrink back against the wall. "Over the anvil in a village near the border."

He shook his head, shaking space in it for the knowledge. The truth. The miraculous truth.

"Then why did you need *me*? You already had a husband. You would not have been ruined."

"I *told* you. I could not bear being parted from your brother. I still cannot." Her voice quavered. "Sometimes I don't believe he is dead. I dream of him at night and believe when I wake he will be there."

"And Cox?"

She turned her face away. "Before meeting you, I was desperate, afraid to tell my parents I was increasing. Only James knew, and he had abandoned me. David said beautiful things to me, that he would protect me and care for me. I was heartbroken. I went with him, but he insisted we not tell anyone, though I begged. That same week you started courting me, admiring me so greatly. I think he saw opportunity. You had a fortune and are to be a duke—"

"*Cornelia.*"

She fell silent, staring at him with wide eyes. He passed his hand across his face. *It could not be.* But it *was.*

"Have you proof of your wedding other than the inscription on the cameo?"

"I kept the receipt of payment from the blacksmith who performed the ceremony. And it has not been very long since then, after all. I think I would recognize the witnesses if they were before me. David has never had any money, so I don't believe he could have bribed them to maintain their silence, even now. He wanted to blackmail you, but I don't know that he thought he would be able to do so for long. I don't think he thought it out clearly at all. He is very impetuous, and always believing that others seek to harm him."

He crossed the chamber and as gently as his racing pulse allowed, grasped her arms and looked down at her.

"We are not married. *We are not married,*" he repeated for good measure and because his life had abruptly begun again.

She shook her head. "We never were." Then she whispered, "What will you do with Jamie?"

Amid the euphoria expanding in him, regret sliced.

"Keep him, if you will allow me. Even if you will not. He is my blood. It cannot be helped that he must learn of your marriage, but he needn't know he is not mine. And I will treat him as my son, Cornelia. I could not do otherwise."

Her head bobbed. She reached up and set a small hand atop his. "Leam, I beg your forgiveness for what I have done to you. What I did. It is as though an enormous weight has lifted from me now, having told you all."

He released her. "Where is Cox now?"

"I don't know. This morning he came and was very agitated. He said something about returning to Shropshire, but—"

"I am going after him now. He has committed crimes and must be punished for them. The truth will have to be revealed publicly."

She nodded. Then she looked away, pressing the linen to her lips once more.

"Cornelia, do your parents know of your real marriage?"

She shook her head.

"I can help you."

"After all I have done to you? No. I deserve whatever I will suffer now." She lifted her gaze again. "You needn't worry about me. After all, you have another lady to worry about now, I think."

He could only hope. And pray. And wish upon every star in the heavens.

"Good-bye, Cornelia."

"Good-bye, Leam. Write to me of my son, if you will, occasionally. I should like to hear of him."

He departed.

The day had advanced, and his quick breaths turned to smoke in the cold. But the sky without was pale and low, the glow of the lowering sun fighting early spring clouds laden with uncertain rain. Leam mounted his horse and set off. For Shropshire. To chase down a man bent on harm. And to seek out a lady worth more than the stars and sky combined.

* * *

He found Cox just shy of Bridgnorth in the taproom of a farmers' tavern. It had not been difficult tracking him. At each stop for food and bed, Cox had left his bills unpaid.

Leam crossed the room.

Cox caught sight of him, and his face turned ashen.

It was certainly an exaggeration to claim—as some did later to others not present at the event—that just as the late-winter sun was setting on the Severn nearby, a barbarian of a Scot that none in the place could understand stormed in, threw about chairs until at least five were ruined and another three badly splintered, then proceeded to do more or less the same to a smartly dressed gentleman from Londontown who hadn't been bothering a soul.

That the Scotsman, while standing over his bleeding, broken prey, had the effrontery to demand a magistrate be summoned also received poor press from the locals. But, after the magistrate arrived, heard all, and departed with both strangers, then returned alone some hours later to explain that the brute was in fact heir to a duke, and the pretty fellow a low character by any standards, some were willing to reconsider their opinion on the matter. When in due course it became known that the duke's heir was already an earl, and not only paid the tavern keep for the destruction to his property but also left a pile of guineas to be spent on ale for everyone he had bothered in the dust-up, forgiveness flowed like said ale throughout the pub.

What was the good in being a grand lord, after all, if a fellow couldn't have a right rowdy knock-around with a scoundrel every now and again?

"The ass made the noises all the night yesterday. I am— how do you say?—exhausted! *Et toi, belle* Katrine?" The Frenchwoman laid her hand gloved in fingerless black lace on Kitty's knee and tut-tutted. "You must go up to the sleep *tout de suite*."

Kitty flipped a page in her book and tried to focus. "Not yet. I have a bit more to read, then I will turn in." And remain awake staring at the ceiling beneath which she had made love to a barbaric Scot, this time with her nerves strained in fear and anticipation.

She should not have done this. It was unpardonably rash. Either Mr. Cox would never arrive and she would waste away waiting for him in a tiny Shropshire inn with a French widow as her only companion, other than a little boy and a pair of the most solicitous innkeepers she had ever met, due to Madame Roche informing them of Kitty's delicate condition. Or Mr. Cox *would* arrive and she would be in serious danger.

Madame Roche stood. "Good night, then, *ma belle*." Kitty watched her mount the stairs, somewhat bemused as always by the woman. But the widow had begun to call her *ma belle* as she called Emily *ma petite*. During this journey Kitty had apparently become one of her charges. That suited her. She would need friends in the coming months while she determined what to do with her life that was to change rather dramatically.

The front door rattled against its bolts. Kitty's heart leaped. She stood, every nerve stretched. A heavy knock sounded on the panel. Mr. Milch came from the kitchen. He shook his head as he moved toward the foyer.

"Now don't you be worrying yourself over this, my lady. We won't be inviting in anybody we don't know."

She nodded. It was an inn, for pity's sake, yet he had cleared out the whole place for her and her traveling companion so she could wait upon a man who might never show. But she had a cameo portrait of an angelically lovely lady in her pocket to prove that if Mr. Cox had seen the pamphlet he must at least be on his way now.

From where she stood in the center of the sitting room, she heard Mr. Milch snap open the lock on the peek window.

"Well, now, good evening, sir! Welcome back."

The bolts on the door clanked, Kitty's palms went damp, and the door creaked open. It could not be Mr. Cox. A gust of wind smelling of snow caught up the flames in the hearth. Boots sounded in the foyer, then the new arrival's voice, deep and familiar.

"I trust you are well, Milch?"

Her knees turned to porridge. There was nothing for it but to grasp the back of the chair for support and hope she did not collapse.

"I am, my lord. My good wife too. There's to be snow tonight, by the looks of it." The door thumped shut.

"Tell me at once if you will, has Lady Katherine returned here of late?"

"She's just within, sir. I'll take your coat now."

Boot steps, and he came through the door. He halted.

"*Kitty.*" Her name was a mere breath. His shoulders seemed to settle as he scanned her face, then all of her from neck to toe, then her face once more. Mr. Milch crossed the chamber to the kitchen and out, and Kitty drank in the sight of the man she loved.

"Hello, Leam." She folded her hands in a vain attempt to still their mad trembling. "What brings you to Shropshire?"

Remarkably, he laughed. "I suppose I should say the fishing." He smiled, and everything inside her fused together into one messy heap of honey. "But instead I shall tell the truth. You brought me, of course."

"Then did you see Lady Justice's pamphlet, or speak with my servants?"

"Kitty, Cox is apprehended. I left him in a magistrate's jail not thirty miles from here."

She clutched the sofa harder. "Then he was the one? Oh, I am relieved."

His gaze seemed quite warm. "How did you discover the business with the cameo?"

"Ned had it on Christmas Eve. He said he'd found it months earlier on the road."

"And you doubted his word so much that you connected it to Cox, then to me?" His beautiful mouth still hinted at a smile.

"Well, yes. And no. At the time I thought it strange how Mr. Cox had been so friendly with you at first, then decidedly less so later. Also anxious. Then that day at the park—" For the first time in days her throat was thick with tears. Being so near him, alone in this place where she had fallen in love with him, was not conducive to her well-being. "She is very beautiful and I thought I had seen her before. Then I remembered Ned's cameo and realized how I recognized her. When you told me Mr. Cox had lost something valuable and believed you had it, it all seemed to make sense, although I am not certain it should have. But I felt I had to do something and you could not find him, so I sent the letter to Lady Justice hoping that she would print it and he would see it and show himself. Really, I never imagined it would all work out." But it had given her another excuse to flee.

He shook his head slowly, then took a deep breath and opened his mouth. But she could not allow him to speak and say things she would remember forever, such as he thought her wonderfully clever.

"It was to my advantage to rout him out," she said quickly, "but I am glad you did because I honestly don't know what I would have done except try to blackmail him if he had come here. But I am not a blackmailer by nature. A snitch, certainly, but—"

"Kitty, I am not leaving here tonight. You cannot talk me gone from this place no matter how you go on."

"I was merely explaining. And you did ask. Yesterday Ned admitted to me that Hermes found it out by the stable and brought it to him the night of the storm." Beneath his intimate gaze, the familiar ache of longing wound its way around her so tightly it stole her breath, wonderful and awful at once. "What did Mr. Cox want of her cameo?"

"He kept it to ensure he could extort money from me through her. When he lost it, he became somewhat unglued, it seems. Thus the shooting and threats."

"That is nonsensical."

His eyes intensified. "Did you read the inscription on the back?"

"No." She reached into her pocket for the trinket. It felt like tiny knives every time she touched it. She flipped it over.

Her breaths stuttered.

"I—I do not understand. Did—did he divorce her before she married you?"

"He never divorced her. They are still married, as they were when she and I said our vows."

Kitty's heart slammed against her lungs.

"Oh, Leam," she breathed. "I am sorry."

His eyes widened. "You are *sorry*?"

"Yes, *I* am sorry this time. So very sorry for you, and for your son of course." And miserable again in a manner she could never have anticipated. Euphorically miserable. She suspected what was to come next. She wanted it more than life, yet she could not bear it. "Here." She went forward and placed the cameo on the table, then moved away from it. "You must wish at least to have this."

"I've no wish whatsoever to have it."

"But—"

"Kitty, marry me."

For the second time in as many months, her palm met her nose and she could not seem to detach it. "Oh. That was abrupt."

Through her fingers she saw him swallow jerkily.

"That is not precisely how I hoped you would respond." His voice was tight. "Is that a no? Do you wish, after all, to remain unwed?"

Kitty's hand slid from her face to her constricted throat. "No," she whispered. "Not remotely. But—but . . ."

"But perhaps you have another offer, or simply wish to await one from another quarter."

"No. I have no such offers or wishes." She must say it aloud, no matter how painful. "But your feelings for her, Leam—I cannot compete with that. Before, it was imaginable, but now that she is actually still *alive* . . ." Perhaps it was too painful to say after all.

Incomprehension shifted across his features. Then, abruptly, understanding.

"Kitty," he said, his voice quite low, "my feelings for her were shallow and disintegrated swiftly. Half of the guilt I carried these years was because of my sheer relief over having narrowly missed living my entire life with a person so ill-suited to me. I was *relieved* I had driven her to the grave. You may despise me now for it, but it is the truth and I told you I wish no secrets between us."

She gaped. "But all these years, people— Gossips have said—"

"It was all an act. To gain sympathy and trust."

"*All?* Did you never feel for her anything profound?"

"I desired her then, infatuated as only a young man can be, foolish beyond measure and full of my own consequence and vanity." He stepped forward. "But, my sweet girl, I had no idea then—" His voice was rough. "Nothing within me of this longing to give until I am empty, of drowning in the deluge of being filled again with each word, each touch. I had no idea of you." His eyes were so beautiful, full of everything she dreamed.

"Poetry, my lord?" She could barely grasp breath to whisper. "How very fine."

His brow knit. "Don't toy with me, Kitty. With a word you can crush me. If it is to be that word, give it to me now. I am not a patient man and I have already had to wait too long to know if you will ever be mine."

"Oh, Leam." Her voice nearly failed. "How can you be asking me this now? After everything?"

His handsome face washed with despair. "Then I am too late, or perhaps too recklessly honest. I am dismissed."

"You are *not* dismissed. You—" She sucked in breath, flooded with his mistaken anguish, her fear, their love. "*I love you*. I love you so desperately. So—"

He crossed the space and crushed her in his embrace, then her mouth beneath his. Kitty gave herself up to his kiss, to his arms holding her and the fantasy of his love, now real. She wrapped her arms about him and willed it to go on forever.

"Never stop," she whispered, then again, "never stop."

"Never. Especially if you promise to never stop pressing yourself up against me." Laughter rumbled in his voice. He kissed her neck and the tender place at the base of her throat and her mouth and eyes, as though he would not stop indeed.

With effort she drew away from his mouth, her hand stealing up to smooth along his jaw. "I am frightened, Leam." She searched his hungry eyes. "Frightened that you doubted even a little. You must have been certain of my feelings for you."

"A man is certain only about that for which he cares little. And in this, my love, there is no measure for how greatly I care. Never assume my certainty. Tell me every day, I beg of you, my Kitty."

"I daresay I will have difficulty confining it to once a day." She stroked her fingers through the streak in his hair. "I can be tenacious when suitably motivated."

His mouth tipped into a half smile. "Madame Roche said you are like a bloodhound. Or a shepherd dog. I cannot recall which she decided on."

"The impertinence. When did you speak with her about me?"

"At Willows Hall."

"Whatever for? Were you spying on me?"

"I was falling in love with you, and endeavoring with all my might not to write sonnets to the divine gracefulness of your little finger. I had to at least talk about you. She was eager." He smiled unevenly, and in his eyes shone all the emotion of youth and passion, all the hope and drama of the poet she adored.

"Then why did you put me off?" she whispered.

"I feared to hurt you. I feared the violence of my jealous nature."

"But no longer?"

"No." He stroked the backs of his fingers along her cheek tenderly. "I have remembered what love is. It is honesty. It is goodness. It is living for another's heart. I love you, Kitty."

She put her hands on his cheeks, drew his face down, and kissed him warmly. Then more warmly still.

"You may write sonnets to my little finger now, if you wish," she murmured. "Are you still inspired to?"

"More than ever," he said against her neck. "I shall write them to your little toe, as well, not to mention my other favorite parts of you. But not until I have put those parts to more pleasing uses first."

"Does that mean you are going to show me more wicked things men do with their mistresses?"

He chuckled. "If you wish."

"I wish." She trailed her fingers to his cravat and began loosening it. "But first, I have something of great importance to tell you."

"More important than that you love me?"

"Very important."

He drew away to look into her face, his sober once more. Kitty's palm slipped to her belly, then over her abdomen. His gaze followed, then lifted to hers, his lips parting.

"I had always believed . . ." She could only whisper.

His chest rose in heavy breaths. "Kitty?"

"I was wrong. You were right. It is very difficult for a woman of such enormous pride to admit—"

He dragged her into his arms again. This time his kiss did not simply please, it consumed, and she gave him her hunger and wonder and happiness in return.

"I have undressed you in this chamber before," he said huskily, his wandering hands making her heady. "But I should like to do so tonight in greater privacy." He laced their fingers together and drew her toward the stair.

She held back, quirking a grin. "Ask me like a barbarian." She went onto her tiptoes and kissed his jaw. "When you talk like that, you see, I want to cast myself at you quite urgently."

He curved his warm, strong palms around her face, then lowered his mouth to hers and possessed her with such gentle, thorough, intoxicating care she was obliged to cling to his arms to remain standing.

"Come lie wi' me, lass," he murmured, his eyes bright with all the spoken desires that were no longer secret. "Make me the happiest man the nicht."

She sighed. "You will make it last forever?"

He kissed her again. "An foriver."

"That, my lord," she whispered against his lips, "is the best idea I have ever heard."

Author's Note

A Regency gentleman's classical education introduced him to not only the great prose authors of the ancient past, but also to quite a lot of poetry. At the forefront of the European Enlightenment, Scotland boasted a university in Edinburgh that produced engineers and physicians who went forth to labor throughout the vast British colonial world. But, as Leam tells Kitty, Edinburgh was also lauded for its philosophers, churchmen, and poets. You can find more on the love poetry Leam recites to Kitty on my Web site, www.katharineashe.com.

In the mid-eighteenth century, Scotland's long struggle to remain free of English domination came to a head. The outcome (among other influences) was to prove England's making as an empire, securely investing Britain with the fruits of Scottish talent and labor, both at home in government, and abroad throughout Britain's ever-expanding colonial territories. In the north, however, not all Scots were entirely content to be subjects of a conqueror's crown. My Highland rebels are, nevertheless, fictitious.

My profound thanks go to Jackie Skinner of the Assembly Rooms in Edinburgh, and to the wonderful people of the British Red Cross who were using the Assembly Rooms for a blood drive when I visited and who welcomed me so kindly (and with such tasty treats!). Thanks also to Amy Drysdale and the fabulous volunteers of Georgian House, who were fonts of marvelous information. While the story in this book did not make it to Edinburgh, the people of that beautiful city gifted me with their generosity and a flavor of sincere and whimsical kindness, laughter, and intelligence that now means Scotland to me. Gwen and Jake Scott of The Glebe House in North Berwick offered me residence in their beautiful Georgian manse filled with period antiques, a home from which I happily—joyfully!—explored the breathtaking Lothians. This author is a convert to lowland Scotland for life.

Warm thanks go to Sandy Blair, who delightfully introduced me to the wonders of writing Scots, to Marie-Claude Dubois for her invaluable assistance with French, and to Miranda Neville for sharing with me her expertise in piquet (and wine and general hilarity) and for editing what we fondly refer to as "the strip piquet scene." Thanks also to Melissa Ford Lucken for helping me see who Kitty and Leam really wanted to be, for her precious friendship in tears and laughter, and for agreeing with me that loyal readers are quite wonderfully like champagne.

I am especially indebted to two people whose work on Leam and Kitty's story truly brought it forth: my mother, Georgann Brophy, and my husband, Laurent Dubois. They make my books possible, they make my books better, and they do so with endless patience, grace, and love.

Turn the page for
an excerpt from
Katharine Ashe's next book,

HOW TO BE A PROPER LADY

**Coming in 2012
from Avon Books**

Prologue

Devonshire, 1803

The girls played as though nothing could harm them. For nothing could on the crest of the scrubby green Devonshire hill overlooking the ocean where they had played their whole lives. Their father was a baron, and they wore white quilted muslin to their calves and pinafores embroidered with silk.

The wind was mild, blowing their skirts about slender legs and whipping up their hair, dislodging bonnets again and again. The elder, twelve, tall and long-limbed like a boy, picked the most delicate bluebells, fashioning them into a bouquet. The younger, petite and laughing, swung her arms wide, scattering wild violets in a circle about her. She ran, dark ringlets streaming behind, toward the edge of the cliff. Her sister followed, a dreaming glimmer in her eyes, golden locks swishing about her shoulders.

A sail appeared upon the horizon leagues away where azure sky met glittering ocean.

"If I were a sailor, Ser," the younger sister called across

the hillock, "I would become captain of a great tall ship and sail to the ends of the earth and back again simply to say that I had."

Serena shook her head fondly. "They do not allow girls to become sailors, Vi."

"Who gives a rotten fig for what they allow?" Viola's laughter caught in the breeze curling about her.

"If any girl could be a sea captain, it would be you." Serena's eyes shone warm with affection.

Viola rushed to swing her arms about her sister's waist. "You are a princess, Serena."

"And you are an imp, for which I admire you greatly."

"Mama admires sailors." Viola skipped along the edge of the sheer drop. "I saw her speaking with one when we were in Clovelly for the ribbons."

"Mama is kind to everyone." Serena smiled. "She must have been giving the man an alms."

But it had not looked like Mama was giving him alms. She had spoken with the sailor for many minutes, and when she returned to Viola, tears teetered in her eyes.

"Perhaps he wished for more alms than Mama could give him."

The ship came closer and lowered a longboat, twelve men at oars. The sisters watched. They were accustomed enough to the sight, living so close to a harbor as they did, yet ever curious as the young are.

"Do you think they are smugglers, Ser?"

"I suppose they could be. Cook said smugglers were about when she went to market Wednesday. Papa says smugglers are to be welcomed because of the war now."

"I don't recognize the ship."

"How would you know to recognize any ship?"

Viola rolled her dark eyes. "Its banner, silly."

The boat came toward the beach fifty feet below, knocking against the surf, its bow jutting up and down like a butter churn. Men jumped out, soaking their trousers in the waves. They pulled the craft onto the pebbly sand. Four of them moved toward the narrow path that wound its way up the cliff side.

"It looks as though they mean to climb straight up," Serena said, taking her lower lip between her teeth. "Onto Papa's land?"

Viola grasped her sister's fingers. To be so close to real smugglers was something she had only dreamed. She might ask them about their travels. Or their cargo. They could have something truly precious aboard, priceless treasure from afar. They would surely have stories to tell of those far-off places.

"Hold my hand, Ser," she said on an excited quaver. "We shall greet them and ask their business."

The sailor in the lead was a stocky man and well-looking in a dark fashion, not in the least scabrous or filthy as one might expect. He and his companions came along the crest of their father's land directly toward Viola and Serena.

"Why," Viola exclaimed, "that is the same sailor Mama gave alms to the other day." But nothing concerned the girls in this, or in the sailor's greeting, broad and smiling as he glanced at their locked hands. For they had the love of sisters, fierce and tender, and nothing could harm them.

Chapter 1

London, 1818

Fellow Britons,

The people of our great kingdom must not see another farthing of their livelihoods squandered on the idle rich. Thus, my quest continues! In rooting out information concerning that mysterious gentleman's establishment at 14½ Dover Street, the so-called Falcon Club, I have learned an intriguing morsel of information. One of its members is a sailor and they call him Sea Hawk.

Birds, birds, and more birds! Who will it be next, Mother Goose?

Unfortunately I have not learned the name of his vessel. But would it not be unsurprising to discover him to be a member of our navy or a commissioned privateer? Yet another expenditure of public funds on the personal interests of those whose privilege is already mammoth.

I will not rest until all members of the Falcon Club are revealed or, due to my investigating, the club itself disbands in fear of thorough detection.

—Lady Justice

Lady Justice
In Care of Brittle & Sons, Printers
London

Madam,

Your persistence in seeking the identities of the members of our humble club cannot but gratify. How splendid for us to claim the marked attentions of a lady of such enterprise.

You have hit the mark. One of us is indeed a sailor. I wish you the best of good fortune in determining which of the legion of Englishmen upon the seas at this time he is. But, wait! May I assist? I am in possession of a modest skiff. If you wish, I shall happily lend it to you so that you may put to sea in search of your quarry. Better yet, I shall work the oars. Perhaps sitting opposite as you peer over the foamy swells I will find myself as enamored of your beauty as I am of your tenacious intelligence—for only a beauty would hide her sharp wit behind such a daunting name and project.

I confess myself curious beyond endurance, on the verge of seeking your identity as assiduously as you seek ours. Say the word, madam, and I shall have my boat at your dock this instant.

Yours,
Peregrine
Secretary, The Falcon Club

Dear Sir,

I planted the missive bearing the code name so that L.J. might find it and busy herself chasing shadows. The old girl's pockets are no doubt as empty as her boasts, and she must keep her publishers happy.

In fact, the code name Sea Hawk may well be defunct. I have had no direct communication from him in fifteen months. The Admiralty reports that he yet holds a privateer's commission, but has had no news from him since the conclusion of the Scottish business more than a year ago. Even in his work for the Club he has rarely followed any lead but his own. I suspect he has resigned as we previously imagined. We must count England fortunate that he is now at least nominally loyal to the crown, rather than its enemy.

In service,
Peregrine

Chapter 2

Jinan Seton stared at his true love and the blood ran cold in his veins. Rain-splattered wind whipped about him as he watched her, beauty incarnate, sink in a mass of flames and black smoke into the Atlantic Ocean.

The most graceful little schooner ever upon the seas. Gone.

His chest heaved in a silent groan as the final remnants of burning wood, canvas, and hemp disappeared beneath foamy green swells. A scattering of parts bobbed to the surface, slices of planking, snapped spars, empty barrels, shreds of sail. Her lovely corpse rent asunder.

The American brig's deck rocked beneath his braced feet, rain slashing thicker now, obscuring the wreckage of his ship fifty yards away. He clamped his eyes shut against the pain.

"She was a good 'un, Master Jin." The hulking beast standing beside him shook his chestnut head mournfully. "Weren't your fault she's gone into the drink."

Jin scowled. *Not his fault*. Damn and blast American privateers shooting at anything with a sail.

"They acted like pirates," he said through gritted teeth, his voice rough. "They lowered a longboat. They shot without warning."

"Snuck up on us right good." The massive head bobbed.

Jin sucked a breath through quivering nostrils and clenched his jaw, arms straining against the ropes trapping him to the brig's mast. Someone would pay for this. In the most uncomfortable manner possible.

"Treated her likes a queen, you did," Mattie mumbled above the increasing roar of anger in Jin's ears that obscured the shouts around him and moans of wounded men. Jin swung his head about, craning to see past his helmsman's bulk, searching, counting. There was Matouba strapped to a rail, Juan tied to rigging, Little Billy struggling in the hands of a sailor twice his breadth. Big Mattie blocked his view of the rest of the deck, but thirty more—

"Th'others scrambled for the boats when she caught afire." Mattie grunted. "Boys are well enough, seeing as these fellas ain't pirates after all. Nothing to worry about."

"Nothing to worry about." Jin cracked a hard laugh. "I am trussed like a roast pig and the *Cavalier* is hundreds of feet below. No, I haven't a care in the world."

"Don't you try fooling me. I knows you care more about our boys than your lady, no matter how much you doted on her."

"Wrong, as usual, Matt." He glanced up and saw clearly now the flag of the state of Massachusetts hanging limp in the rain that pattered his face. He'd lost his hat. No doubt it happened at some point during the scuffle from longboat to enemy deck when he'd abruptly realized he had ordered his men to board an American privateer, *not* a pirate vessel. Rain dripped from the tip of his nose into his mouth. He spit it out and slewed his gaze around.

Shrouded in silvery gray, the deck of the brig was littered

with human and nautical debris. Men from both crews lay
prone, sailors seeing to wounds with hasty triage. Square
sails hung loose from masts, several torn, a yardarm broken,
sections of rail splintered and cut through with cannon shot,
black powder marks everywhere. Even taken unaware, the
Cavalier had given good fight. But the Yank vessel was still
afloat. While Jin's ship was at the bottom of the sea.

He closed his eyes again. His men were alive, and he
could afford another ship. He could afford a dozen more.
Of course, he had promised the *Cavalier*'s former owner he
would take care of her. But he had promised himself even
more. This setback would not cow him.

"We seen worse." Mattie lifted bushy brows.

Jin cut him a sharp look.

"What I means to say is, you seen worse," his helmsman
amended.

Considerably worse. But nothing quite so painfully hu-
miliating. No one bested him. *No one.*

"Who did this?" he growled, narrowing his eyes into the
rain. "Who in hell could have crept up on us like that so
swiftly?"

"That'd be Her Highness, sir." The piping voice came
from about waist-high. The lad, skinny and freckled, with
a shock of carrot hair, stretched a gap-toothed grin, swept a
hand to his waist, and bowed. "Welcomes aboard the *April
Storm*, Master Pharaoh."

Every muscle in Jin's body stilled.

April Storm.

"Who is the master of this vessel, boy?"

The lad flinched at his hard tone. He flashed a glance at
the ropes binding Jin and his helmsman about waists, chests,
and hands to the mizzenmast, and the scrawny shoulders
relaxed.

"Violet Laveel, sir," he chirped.

"Quit smirking, you whelp, and call your mistress over," Mattie barked.

The boy's eyes widened and he scampered off.

"Violet *la Vile*?" Mattie mumbled, then pursed his thick lips. "Hnh."

Jin drew in a slow, steadying breath, but his heart hammered unaccustomedly quick. "The boys are prepared?"

"Been pr'pared for months. Won't do a lick o' good now they're all tied up."

"I will do the talking."

Mattie screwed up his cauliflower nose.

"Keep your mouth shut with her, Mattie, or so help me I will find a way to keep it shut despite these ropes."

"Yessir, Cap'n, sir."

"Damn it, Mattie, if after all this time you so much as think of throwing a wrench in—"

"Well, well, well. What do we have here, boys?" The voice came before the woman, smooth, rich, and sweet, like the caress of brushed silk against skin. Unlike any female sailor Jin had ever heard.

But as she sauntered into view from around the other side of Jin's helmsman, she looked common enough. Through the thinning rain, he had his first view of the notoriously successful Massachusetts female privateer, Violet the Vile.

The woman he had been searching out for two years.

Sailors flanked her protectively, casting dog-eyed glances at her and scowls at Jin and his mate. She stood a head shorter than her guard, coming to about Jin's chin. Garbed in loose trousers and a long, shapeless coat of worn leather, a thick bundle of black neck cloth stuffed beneath her chin, a sash with no fewer than three mismatched pistols hanging from it, and a wide-brimmed hat obscuring her face, she didn't particularly resemble her sister. But Jin had spent countless nights in ports from Boston to Vera Cruz drinking sailors and merchants under the table and bribing men with everything he had at hand in search of information about the girl who had gone missing a decade and a half ago. That she looked less like a fine English lady than any woman he'd ever seen did not mean a damned thing.

Violet la Vile was Viola Carlyle, the girl he had set out from Devonshire twenty-two months earlier to find. The girl who, at the age of ten, had been abducted from a gentleman's home by an American smuggler. The girl all except her sister believed dead.

The brim of her hat rose slowly through the rain. A narrow chin came into view, then a scowling mouth, a slight, suntouched nose, and finally a pair of squinting eyes, crinkled at the corners. They assessed Jin from toe to crown. A single brow lifted and her lips curved up at one side in a mocking salute.

"So this is the famed Jinan Seton I've heard so many stories of? The Pharaoh." Her voice drawled like a sheet sliding through a well-oiled block. Thick lashes fanned down, then back up again, taking him in this time with a swift perusal. She wagged her head back and forth and her lower lip protruded. "Disappointing."

Mattie made a choking sound.

Jin's eyes narrowed. "How do you know who I am?"

"Your crewmen. Boasting of you even as they were losing the fight." A full-throated chortle came forth and she plunked her fists onto her hips and pivoted around to the sailors gathering about. "Lookee here, boys! The British navy sent its dirtiest pirate scum to haul me in."

A cheer went up, huzzahs and whistles across deck. Seamen crowded closer with toothless grins and crackling guffaws, brandishing muskets and cutlasses high. She raised her hand and silence descended but for the whoosh of waves against the brig's hull and the patter of rain on canvas and wood. Her gaze slewed back to Jin, sharp as a tack.

"Guess I should be flattered, shouldn't I?" Her voice was like velvet. For a moment—a wholly unprecedented moment—Jin's throat thickened. No woman should have a voice like that. Except in bed.

"Why did you sink my ship?" The steely edge he had learned as a lad came to his own voice without effort. "She was the fastest vessel on the Atlantic. What kind of privateer are you, putting a prize like that under water? She would have taken a fine price."

She screwed up her brows.

"It's true, I could've kept her, Master Brit. Or sold her. But it was such fun seeing the mighty *Cavalier* go down, I couldn't resist."

Red washed across Jin's vision. He tried to blink it away. His gut hurt. Damn and blast, he wanted a cutlass and pistol more than life at this moment. Or perhaps just a bottle of rum.

She smirked.

Two bottles.

They said she was a fine sailor for a woman, but no one had ever said she was mad.